TESSA HARRIS, born in Lincolnshire, holds a history degree from Oxford University. After four years of working on local newspapers, she moved to national women's magazines. She is regularly heard on BBC local radio and, over the years, has written for many national and international publications. Her first novel, *The Anatomist's Apprentice*, won the *Romantic Times* Best First Mystery Reviewers' Award 2012 in the United States. She lives in Berkshire with her husband and their two children.

Also by Tessa Harris

The Anatomist's Apprentice
The Dead Shall Not Rest
The Devil's Breath
The Lazarus Curse

SHADOW OF THE RAVEN

A DR. THOMAS SILKSTONE MYSTERY

TESSA HARRIS

Constable • London

CONSTABLE

First published by Kensington Books, a division
of Kensington Publishing Corp., New York, 2015

This paperback edition published in Great Britain in 2016 by Constable

1 3 5 7 9 8 6 4 2

A CIP catalogue record for this book is available from the British Library.

ISBN 978-1-47211-824-0 (B-format paperback)
ISBN 978-1-47211-825-7 (ebook)

Printed and bound in Great Britain by CPI (UK) Ltd, Croydon CR0 4YY

Papers used by Constable are from well-managed forests and
other responsible sources

MIX
Paper from
responsible sources
FSC® C104740

Constable
is an imprint of
Little, Brown Book Group
Carmelite House
50 Victoria Embankment
London EC4Y 0DZ

An Hachette UK Company
www.hachette.co.uk

www.littlebrown.co.uk

To Katie and Gabriella, with love

Author's Notes and Acknowledgments

Picture a typical English landscape and it will probably look something like this: gently rolling green hills divided into neat fields, lined with high hedgerows and dotted with deciduous woodland.

But this "green and pleasant land," as the poet William Blake so famously called it, is not natural. It is the product of man, and more precisely of landowners. Over the centuries the English countryside has been both hunted and fought over, foraged and farmed, burned and felled, divided and developed, to produce the landscape we know today: a crowded network of cities, towns, and villages with patches of agricultural land in between. And in a very few places, tracts of land are allowed to be natural, even though they still need managing. These are England's commons and common woodlands, where the public is free to roam. Some of these areas fall within the boundaries of national parks or are owned by the National Trust, a conservation charity. Others give access and rights of way, and they form the backdrop to this, the fifth novel in the Dr. Thomas Silkstone Mystery series.

As usual I have taken my inspiration from a true story. Between 1604 and 1905 almost eleven thousand square miles of land were "enclosed" by Acts of Parliament in the United Kingdom. These acts became more numerous as the effects of the Industrial Revolution of the late eighteenth and early nineteenth centuries began to take hold. Land once farmed and enjoyed by the community was fenced off to produce higher yields, and rents were increased. As a result, many peasants were forced away from their homes to seek work in towns and cities, causing huge disruption, dispossession, and discontent, which, in turn, culminated in major riots in the 1830s.

Otmoor is an area of land that lies to the north of Oxford, and my inspiration came from the resistance of its inhabitants to enclose it. Although the moorland was eventually enclosed, it took almost forty-five years, several attempts at sabotage, and many violent protests before the estate's owner, the Duke of Marlborough, could achieve his goal. The people of Otmoor put up a courageous fight, often landing in jail and even risking execution, to preserve their rights, which, they seemed to have believed in all sincerity, were given to them by a mythical lady. Some even said the Virgin Mary had originally bestowed the land upon them. In their struggle they had much sympathy. The extraordinary account of their release from custody by an Oxford mob is well documented, as are numerous gatherings around the area that saw the deliberate destruction of scores of miles of fencing. In a handful of cases the military was called upon to restore order. A permanent police presence had to be maintained to keep the peace. The unrest continued intermittently for many years, eventually leading to the riots of 1829–1830. Finally, two years later, opposition to enclosure seemed to have melted away and the landowners in the area had their way.

In my research I have been helped and encouraged by the following people: historic firearms expert Geoff Walker, Ian Macintosh with his knowledge of fulling mills, and woodsman Jon Roberts of the Weald and Downland Open Air Museum. As ever, my thanks go to my editor, John Scognamiglio; my agent, Melissa Jeglinski; John and Alicia Makin, Dr. Kate Dyerson, Katy Eachus, John and Mary Washington-Smith, and Liz Fisher. Finally, I wish to acknowledge the love and support of my husband, Simon, my children, Charlie and Sophie, and my parents, Patsy and Geoffrey.

Thus, with the poor, scared freedom bade goodbye
And much they feel it in the smothered sigh
And birds and trees and flowers without a name
All sighed when lawless law's enclosure came
And dreams of plunder in such rebel schemes
Have found too truly that they were but dreams.

—"The Mores," John Clare (1793–1864)

Chapter 1

Oxfordshire, England
April in the Year of Our Lord 1784

Was that blood on his stockings? For the second time, or maybe the third, the gentleman had stumbled on the steep slope. Catching his buckled shoe on a slippery shard of flint, he had lurched forward.

His young assistant's head darted 'round in shock as his master clipped his shoulder. "S-s-sir!" he stammered.

Cursing under his breath, the older man righted himself, tugging at his fustian coat. As he did so there was a clatter. An object fell from his pocket onto the stony ground below. Having a good idea what it might be, he peered down. And now, as he did so, he noticed that his worsted stockings, although thankfully not torn, were spattered dark red. A closer inspection, however, confirmed the substance was only loamy mud. What concerned him more was the fact that a few inches from his feet he spied the pistol. Mercifully, although fully cocked, it had not fired. Bending low to retrieve it, he secreted the weapon in his pocket once more and allowed a shallow sigh of relief to escape his lips. He felt safer with it about his person. It would be a deterrent, if one were needed, against any undesirables they might encounter. A quick glance up ahead reassured him that his assistant had not seen.

"Infernal stones," cursed the gentleman out loud, making sure his complaint was heard by Charlton, his chainman. The freckle-faced young man turned 'round and nodded his red head in agreement.

Jeffrey Turgoose, master surveyor and cartographer, a man held in high regard by the rest of his profession, should have worn stout boots more suited to a woodland trail, although, admittedly, he had not anticipated having to make his way through the forest on foot. A series of unfortunate events had, however, necessitated it.

First and foremost, his employment, thus far spent in the service of Sir Montagu Malthus, the new caretaker of the Boughton Estate and lawyer and guardian to the late sixth Earl Crick, had been fraught with difficulties. Every time he had set up his theodolite in the estate village of Brandwick, he had been taunted by barefoot urchins or impudent fellows intent on disrupting his mission. There had been threats, too. In his pocket he carried the note that had been slipped under his door the other night. *Beware of Raven's Wood,* it warned him. Heaven forbid that Charlton should see that! The boy would run all the way back to Oxford. Turgoose harrumphed at the very thought of it. No, it would take more than ignorant peasants and a badly scrawled warning from a lower sort to deter him. Nonetheless, such unpleasantness did, of course, rankle. He could not pretend otherwise, and it added to a certain miasma that seemed to hang low over Brandwick and its surrounds.

From what he had gleaned, there seemed to have been great ructions on the estate. Apparently, the death of Lord Edward Crick, swiftly followed by that of his brother-in-law, Captain Michael Farrell, had been most inopportune. They meant that the latter's widow, Lady Lydia Farrell, had inherited Boughton. It was thought she was childless, but the reemergence of her long-lost young son and heir, thanks in no small part to an American anatomist by the name of Dr. Thomas Silkstone, had put a fly in the proverbial ointment. What's more, it appeared that such upheavals had taken their toll on the poor woman and sent her quite insane. She was now safely ensconced in a madhouse, and Sir Montagu had installed a steward to take charge of the quotidian running of the estate.

If that were not enough, Jeffrey Turgoose was encountering his own problems. First the cart that carried himself and his equipment became bogged down and stuck fast in the yielding ground leading up to the wood. For the past few months now man and beast had left their imprint on the sodden earth. Now the cartway was so beaten down by wheels and hooves it had become impassable. Not wishing to abandon his plans, the surveyor had continued with just one blasted mount that went by the name of a horse, although in reality it was just as stubborn as a mule. His assistant, Mr. James Charlton, had been forced to dismount and walk in order to lay the burden of all the paraphernalia of their profession on his own horse. Peeping out of one pannier were bundles of markers and a circumferentor, while the other was packed with measuring chains. A tripod was strapped to the saddle, along with some measuring poles, making the poor horse appear as if she had been run through with a picador's lances.

Such unforeseen irritations had put the surveyor in a very sour humor. Was his mission not onerous enough? He was not accustomed to exercising his profession under threat from local ruffians, but such had been the villagers' reaction to their presence, he had been compelled to take precautionary measures. The ignorant peasants were harboring the notion that the common land had been bestowed upon them by some mythical woman. "The Lady of Brandwick" they called her, and they all knew the legend. While still at the breast they were taught how, in the days before Bastard William invaded, a lady had ridden a circuit of the area from the edge of the woods to where the oxen could ford the river. In her hand she held a flaming brand and by her favor she gave the land to the villagers. That was how the parish came to be known as Brandwick, and that was how they came by their ancient rights. Or so they thought.

In fact, Boughton's steward, the Right Honorable Nicholas

Lupton, appointed by Sir Montagu as the new custodian of the estate, had indicated that he felt his own position was being compromised by such innate insubordination. The Chiltern charcoal burners, turners, and pit sawyers who labored in the forest all day were not known to be militant men, Lupton had told him, but since their livelihoods were under threat, since their cherished rights were in peril, there was no telling what they might do. Pointing out that there had been riots in other parts of the country where landowners had endeavored to enact similar measures, the steward had persuaded Turgoose to have a greater care for his own safety and that of his assistant. He had been persuaded by Lupton's recommendation of a guard and guide, Seth Talland, an occasional prizefighter and an uncouth sort. The man seemed competent enough, and, as it turned out, he was most thankful for his presence. Apart from the threat of lurking highwaymen and footpads, there were gin traps, too, set about the woodland floor to deter poachers. There were still a few men in Brandwick who'd suffered a leg snapped in two by the iron jaws of such a brutal device. They never poached, or walked without a limp, again.

Lupton had told him there were upward of three hundred acres of woodland, and measuring the boundaries alone would take three days at a conservative estimate. He'd heard that in America they'd surveyed seventeen thousand acres in just over a sennight in Virginia. But they had not measured angles to the nearest degree, and their distances were to the nearest pole. Such slipshod work would not pass muster with Jeffrey Turgoose.

"W-would you r-rest, s-sir?" Charlton's speech was always labored, and often the most frequently used words seemed to cause him anguish, yet he looked even more concerned than usual.

"A moment," Turgoose replied, turning his back to the slope and looking down into the valley at Brandwick. A fading sun hung in a patchy sky, offering a less-than-perfect light. He was glad of his decision to bring his trusty old circumferentor instead of his usual theodolite. Akin to a large compass, it worked on the principle of measuring bearings. It would be particularly advantageous, he felt, in such a heavily forested area, where a direct line of sight could not be maintained between two survey stations, even though he could see the tower of St. Swithin's Church clearly enough. He shook his head as he took in the view. He'd even heard of some of his colleagues having to survey land under cover of darkness, like fly-by-night poachers, such was the strength of feeling against enclosure.

Of course, Turgoose, too, had expected some suspicion and resentment. He was accustomed to that from those who had most to fear from enclosure, cottagers, mainly, and those who faced losing their livelihoods. A free rabbit for the pot or kindling for the fire had been the mainstay of many a paltry existence over the centuries. But times were changing. Land was a precious commodity, best managed by those who knew how to make it pay. So he and his assistant had been commissioned to plant themselves on Brandwick Common like unwelcome thistles, to record the mills and monuments, the wetlands and ponds, and the bridleways and tracks and paths made by feet that had trodden them freely since time immemorial.

To those ignorant peasants, he and his assistant may as well have been alchemists, with their strange equipment in tow. There was, of course, an analogy. Alchemists turned metal into gold, while he and his cohort were turning land into potential profit. That is what his client, Sir Montagu, wanted to do on behalf of Lord Richard Crick, Boughton's six-year-old master.

Despite the hostility from the villagers, the surveyors had managed to do a good job thus far. The weather, although on the chilly side, had been fair, the sky clear, and their observations and measurements easily recorded. After the common land, they had turned their attention to the village dwellings, the market cross, and the church, all lying within the boundaries of the Boughton Estate. Precision and order could be imposed on this chaotic fretwork of man's own making using that most noble of shapes, the triangle. Trigonometry was the answer to all humankind's conundrums; at least that is what Jeffrey Turgoose had told Charlton and anyone else who would listen. After all, was it not Euclid, the father of geometry, who said that the laws of nature were but the mathematical thoughts of God? To that end, he had convinced himself that he was doing the Almighty's work, and this confounded wood was his final task.

Up ahead, Talland, his scalp as bald as a bone, looked 'round to see what had happened to his charges. Set square as a thick-necked dog, he carried a club for protection, and a small sickle hung from his waist.

"All well, sirs?" he called back in a coarse whisper. Thankfully he was a man of few words, thought the surveyor.

"Well enough," replied Turgoose. He gave Charlton a knowing look and proceeded to delve into his frock coat pocket. He checked that the pistol was still there. The youth did not suspect. Such knowledge would send him into paroxysms of fear. Instead Turgoose brought out a hip flask and took a swig.

Talland emerged from the lengthening shadows a moment later.

"I'll make safe our way, sirs," he told them. "I 'eard sounds from up yonder."

Turgoose nodded, then turned his back and gave a derisory snort. "I'll wager you have heard sounds, man," he said to himself as much as to Charlton. "We are on the edge of a wood. There are foxes, squirrels, and all manner of creatures, not to mention the wretched charcoal burners and sawyers." He shrugged, took another swig, then plugged the flask once more.

The old mare shifted as she stood and began to fidget under the weight of her burden. Charlton frowned at his master.

"Wh-what if there's s-someone up there, s-sir?" he asked. Turgoose noted that when his assistant was anxious, the register of his voice went even higher than usual. Dropping the flask into his pocket, the surveyor shook his head.

"Then Talland will deal with them," he reassured the chainman, even though he did not feel entirely secure himself. This was no way to carry on: three men, and a mare that should've been boiled down for glue a long time ago. His was a most burdensome and precise task, so why had he been made to feel like a cutpurse or a scoundrel going about his business?

As they breasted a small ridge, Talland, who had momentarily been lost from sight behind a screen of spiky gorse, came into view once more. The prizefighter had made it to the trees and was entering the wood through an avenue of tight-packed hawthorns. If need be, he would clear a path for them to follow a few paces behind.

The beeches were still naked after one of the longest winters in memory. Crows' nests clotted their bare branches and russet leaves still patterned the woodland carpet. Crunching over cast-off acorn caps and husks of beech mast, the small party proceeded at a tolerable rate. They wove through green-slimed trunks and past thickets as tangled as an old man's beard. By now they had left behind the birdsong and the caw of the crows, although the odd pheasant would let loose a throaty call. All the while they were heading deeper and deeper into the woods.

Turgoose's plan was to determine the apex of the hill in the wood and then take measurements using the church tower as a fixed point. The task would have presented its own challenges had he been operating in clear conditions, but with the fading light the execution of such an undertaking would rightly be considered sheer folly by many of his fellow surveyors.

Moments later the party found themselves progressing along the narrow avenue of hawthorns. Underfoot it remained muddy, but Talland had found a serviceable path that, judging by the lack of vegetation, seemed to be in regular use. They were forced to travel in single file, with Charlton leading the horse first. They had journeyed perhaps a mile into the woods when the mare's ears pricked and she came to a sudden halt. The young man tugged at her leading rein.

"Come on, old girl," he said firmly. Instead of obeying the command, however, she began to backstep, forcing Turgoose to retreat.

"What goes on?" he called from the rear.

"She's afraid, sir. . . . S-something tr-troubles her."

Turgoose tutted and, seeing a row of dried-out stalks at his side, he broke one off near its root and thwacked the mare's hindquarters.

"Get on with you," he cried.

The shock had the desired effect and the horse moved at once. It was Charlton who was now reluctant to budge.

"Well, man?" asked Turgoose impatiently. "What is it now?" Passing the horse, he drew up alongside his nervous assistant to find him squinting into the distance.

" 'Tis T-Talland, s-sir. I've lost s-sight of him."

Turgoose strained his eyes in the woodland gloom.

"Talland," he called. "Talland."

They waited in silence for a reply. None came. Charlton's expression grew even more fearful. He started to say something. His mouth opened and he tried to form a word. His tongue jutted out and he grunted, but his master cut him off.

"We'd best catch up," said Turgoose in his no-nonsense fashion. He did not want to betray his own unease at the prospect of losing their guard. If they were waylaid by an unruly mob here, they would have little chance of assistance from any quarter. He barged forward, past Charlton, intent on finding Talland, only as he did so he heard something crunch beneath the thin sole of his shoe. It was definitely not a twig. He glanced down. The carcass of a dead raven, or rather part of a carcass, lay under his foot. Its head was the only recognizable feature that remained intact. The rest of its body, save for a few feathers, was nowhere to be seen. The surveyor's nostrils flared in disgust as he scraped the sole of his shoe on nearby leaves.

"What time is it?" he barked, looking up to see the young man's anxious face.

Retrieving his watch on a chain from his pocket, Charlton flipped open the cover.

"Almost f-five of the clock, sir."

"We must press on." There was an urgency in the surveyor's voice. "Talland! Talland!" he called.

They quickened their pace in the direction where they had last seen their guide. Without him they were lost. They were too far into the woods now to retrace their steps. The old mare was happy to oblige at first and hurried her pace, too, but then slowed again, becoming agitated after only a few yards. The trees were pressing in around them, their branches twisted into grotesque shapes against the sulfur yellow of a dusky sky. A mist was rising from the woodland floor, making it harder to find their footing as the gradient began to climb again.

"Talland. Talland," Turgoose called. Still no reply, but a noise.

"Wh-what . . . ?"

They stopped in their tracks to listen. They heard footsteps heading toward them through the undergrowth. Talland reappeared.

"All clear up ahead, sir," the guard shouted to Turgoose.

Charlton edged forward, tugging at the mare's leading rein, but she refused to budge. Seeing that the young surveyor was having difficulty with the horse, Talland offered to lead her.

"Let me, sir," he said, walking over to the mare and taking her by the rein. He began to walk on ahead once more.

Despite the fact that Talland had endeavored to clear it, the path grew narrower and the trees' gnarled fingers still reached across it. To make matters worse, the mist was thickening and made visibility poor. In his mind Turgoose determined that they should abandon this foray altogether. He would inform Talland of his decision. Before he could do so, however, he felt the whip of a twig lash his cheek, and the stinging sensation momentarily robbed him of his breath. He gasped and let out a sharp cry.

"S-sir!" came Charlton's plaintive voice from behind him.

"A scratch! Nothing to worry about." Turgoose rubbed his cheek and felt the syrup of warm blood on his fingers. Talland, a few paces up ahead with the horse, did not even bother to look 'round. They set off once more. They had gone only another few paces, however, when, from somewhere nearby—it was hard to tell where—there came a shuffling and the sound of cracking twigs.

"S-sir, d-did . . . ?"

"Yes, I heard it, Charlton," snapped Turgoose. Suddenly he found himself feeling very slightly afraid. Perhaps they were being watched by the villagers, mocked silently as they braved the woods. Or worse still, a highwayman. He would give the villain anything he wanted: his pocket compass, his silver flask, even all his equipment. But he digressed. He gathered his courage and tried to dismiss his fears. He looked up ahead. The horse's rump appeared now and again through the trees, but Talland seemed to be powering on regardless of his charges' much slower pace.

"S-sir. We must g-go back," Charlton whined again.

"You're probably right," conceded Turgoose. "We shall try again tomorrow."

"Y-yes, s-sir," answered the youth, his shoulders heaving in a sigh of relief.

No sooner had Turgoose decided to call to Talland, however, than up ahead he heard the horse let out a loud whinny.

"What the . . . ? Talland?" the surveyor called. There was no reply.

Charlton stayed rooted to the spot, his legs planted by fear. His body, however, began to shake violently. Turgoose shot the sniveling wreck of a youth an irritated look. He may have been his master, but he was not a soothsayer. How was he to know what had happened to Talland up ahead, any more than the chainman? Naturally the surveyor feared he had been ambushed, waylaid by the mob, but he must not show his own trepidation to Charlton. He appeared circumspect.

"Wait here," he said.

"S-sir?" His assistant looked at him with baleful eyes, as if pleading not to be left alone. His master, however, was adamant. Charlton was more of a hindrance than a help. Nevertheless, as he started to walk toward where he had last seen Talland, he remembered the pistol. He patted his pocket. It was still there. He turned.

"If it makes you feel any safer, take this," he said, plunging his hand into his coat and placing the firearm in the youth's palm. He closed Charlton's fingers 'round the walnut grip.

The chainman's eyes bulged as if he had just been handed a poisoned chalice or dubbed with a mariner's black spot.

"You'll not need to discharge it, I'm sure," his master reassured him, "but if you are threatened, just point it at anyone who challenges you. They will take fright and run."

Charlton, looking down at his hand, his mouth wide open, swallowed hard.

"Y-yes, sir," he said.

Satisfied he had gone some way to relieving his assistant's anxiety, Turgoose turned and resumed his quest to find the guard. "Talland!" he called.

Within seconds Turgoose had disappeared from Charlton's sight and had located the prizefighter a few yards ahead. He was struggling with the mare. The old horse had stumbled into what seemed like a deep ditch and appeared unable to extricate herself. Talland was tugging at her rein, trying to coax her out, but she was reluctant to oblige.

"A sawpit, sir," he explained, pulling at the horse. "Woods are full of 'em."

Although he appreciated the difficulty that the situation presented, Turgoose found himself smiling. It was a minor inconvenience compared with the ambush he had envisaged.

"I must fetch Charlton. He will help you," he told the guide. He turned back to retrace his steps. How relieved his chainman would be, he told himself, rustling back through the bushes once more. He could see him now, still visibly shaking, his back to him, but only a few feet away. His gangling body was framed by thick foliage. The surveyor opened his mouth to call to him, but before he could make a sound, the youth twisted 'round violently, his eyes wide in terror. Suddenly a high note split the air, a semiquaver of a shout, a warning perhaps. It was followed a heartbeat later by a shot, a single report that sent a murder of crows scattering above the trees. There was an odd gurgling sound, as if a new spring had bubbled its way above ground, a rustling of leaves, and a dull thud as Jeffrey Turgoose hit the strew of the woodland floor. Then silence. This time the dark stains that spattered his worsted stockings were not just mud. They were most definitely blood.

Chapter 2

Had he not known what horrors lay within its walls, Dr. Thomas Silkstone would have surmised this magnificent building was a bishop's palace or the Lord Mayor of London's residence. The fine, towering façade of Bethlem Hospital was surrounded by pleasant avenues of trees and shrubs that afforded a place of recreation for those of its patients well enough to enjoy them. Yet, despite its pleasing aspect, the edifice before which he now stood held only trepidation for him. Somewhere inside those thick walls with their grand pediments and colonnades, Lady Lydia Farrell was held captive. Taken against her will and certified insane by a corrupt physician on the orders of her late brother's guardian, Sir Montagu Malthus, she was a prisoner. Thomas had not set eyes on her for almost two months. Despite repeated requests and letters to the hospital's principal physician, Angus Cameron, his efforts had drawn a blank.

Once more Thomas found himself proceeding toward the grandiose entrance. He had lost count of the number of visits he had made. Glancing up he saw the familiar elaborate carvings depicting melancholy and raving madness on either side of the door. At this point he always found himself seized by the same sense of deep unease that he had experienced when poised on the threshold of Newgate Jail. This institution may have called itself a hospital, but care and compassion were seldom prescribed.

Proceeding through a grand central door and down a hall

that opened out onto a great central staircase at its end, Thomas was directed into a reception office. There, behind a high desk, sat an officious clerk with bulging eyes. Thomas noted that they were probably a symptom of goiter, but the man's brusque manner did nothing to solicit empathy. Thomas had encountered him on several previous occasions, but the man had never endeared himself to him. Yet again the doctor felt himself tense. His efforts to see Lydia had never taken him beyond this point. He had always been refused admission. Judging by the clerk's familiar expression of contempt, today would be no different.

"Yes?"

"I am come to see Lady Lydia Farrell," Thomas heard himself say for the umpteenth time, knowing the fellow was fully aware of his intentions. His voice sounded thin and hollow, as if it belonged to someone else, and the words scratched in his mouth.

With the supercilious air bestowed on him by his modicum of authority, the clerk looked down a list in a ledger before him. He cleared his throat but said finally, "I regret, sir, her ladyship remains indisposed."

These regular encounters had degenerated into a type of pantomime farce, with each man having his set lines and gestures. After the first shake of the head, Thomas would move forward and repeat his request. The clerk would lean backward, blink—slowly because of the size of his eyes—and look vaguely indignant; then the doctor would sigh heavily and retreat, admitting defeat once more. Only on this occasion it was different. On this particular morning the clerk conveyed a further message to Thomas. "Her ladyship is indisposed, and furthermore I am to tell you, Dr. Silkstone, that you will no longer be allowed within the hospital grounds until further notice." His words were haughty and deliberate. He was clearly a willing messenger.

Thomas dipped his brows. Unprepared for such a rebuke, he felt his normal self-control tested to its limits. "I demand to see Dr. Cameron!" he said firmly. "Fetch him, if you please." He slapped the desk. The clerk's bulging eyes registered an affront, but he withdrew, leaving the doctor to pace the room. Suddenly, from a low door at the side, two men in hospital livery marched in. Approaching the doctor, but without warning, they grabbed him by both arms.

"What is the meaning of this?" Thomas asked indignantly.

The clerk reappeared, his eyes seeming to protrude even further from their sockets. "Orders, Dr. Silkstone," he said, barely able to hide his satisfaction. "You must be escorted from the premises."

Dr. William Carruthers had never known his protégé so dispirited. Despite the fact that he could not see the frustration on Thomas's face, the scowl on his lips, or the furrow on his brow, the old anatomist could hear the drawers being rifled and the cupboard doors being slammed in wrath.

"You were refused entry again?"

He knew there could be no other reason for Thomas to exhibit such uncustomary ire. He had tapped his way to the laboratory with his stick to investigate the noise and found the young doctor gathering his equipment with undue haste. Thomas paused as he packed his medical case.

"Worse, sir," he replied, pausing to look up. "This time I was thrown out of the hospital like a common criminal." His voice trembled slightly as he spoke, not with weakness but with rage.

Carruthers shook his head sympathetically. "So what will you do now, dear boy?"

Not usually one to abandon any goal, Thomas took a deep breath. "It is useless trying to gain access to Lydia by conventional means," he said enigmatically. He reached for a reference book from the shelf, sending dust motes dancing about the room, and dropped it into the case.

"Ah!" Dr. Carruthers raised a finger, certain that his protégé had formulated another plan. "So you will approach the conundrum by an unconventional route. What other means do you propose?"

Thomas shrugged his shoulders and continued packing his case. There was nothing scientific in his methods of dealing with

Lupton or Sir Montagu Malthus. He only wished there could have been. Had they been tumors, he would have cut them out long ago and been rid of them both. As it was, there seemed no logical way of dealing with these Machiavellian charlatans who had so blighted his beloved Lydia's life and, therefore, his own.

"I shall simply go to Boughton and see if I can persuade Nicholas Lupton of the error of his ways before I confront Sir Montagu," he told his mentor, securing the stopper on a bottle of iodine.

"So you believe Lupton is Malthus's weak spot, as it were?"

Thomas detected a note of skepticism in the old anatomist's voice. He nodded to himself and paused in thought for a moment. "I do. I refuse to believe that there is not a shred of humanity within him. He befriended her ladyship and her son, and the young earl's affection for him was clear to see. Call me naïve, but that surely counts for something."

Dr. Carruthers nodded. "It is good to know that even after all the betrayal you've suffered, you can still see goodness in everyone."

Thomas looked up suddenly, slightly taken aback by the observation. "It is the only way forward," he replied.

The old anatomist clicked his tongue. "This is such a ghastly business, dear boy," he said. "So removed from the tenets of our vocation."

Carruthers's words pulled Thomas up short. His mentor was right, of course. He had not traveled more than three thousand miles, leaving his family home in Philadelphia, to endure the hostility and suspicion of an enemy nation, only to throw away all the vast knowledge he had gleaned on some vengeful quest. How different, how ordered and logical his life had been up until the day Lydia had walked into his laboratory. She had pleaded for his help to uncover how her brother, Edward, the sixth Earl Crick, had died, and he had found himself incapable of resisting her entreaties. She had turned his methodical, organized world upside down. It had been a world of clear delineation. There had been boundaries: sickness and health, life and death. If a tooth was decayed, it was removed. If a foot was gangrenous, it was amputated. But in this new and unexplored realm, nothing was so straightforward. Contagion spread, arteries leaked, infection set in, and prognoses were harder to give, let alone remedies. But of one thing he remained sure. He would not allow the corruption of others around him to infect his own beliefs and principles.

He walked over to Carruthers and laid a hand on his shoulder. "*Primum non nocerum,*" he declared.

The words of affirmation from the Hippocratic Corpus brought a smile to the old man's lips.

"Quite right." Carruthers nodded and clapped his hands as if spontaneously applauding Hippocrates himself. "Never forget you must first do no harm, dear boy."

"I shall not, sir," Thomas assured him.

Returning to his case, the young doctor was about to resume his preparations for travel when Mistress Finesilver, the anatomists' peevish housekeeper and cook, arrived at the open laboratory door. She sucked in her cheeks and took a deep breath as she handed a missive to Thomas on a salver.

"A message came for you not two minutes ago, sir," she told him with an unthinking curtsy.

Opening the seal, Thomas read the letter. It was from Sir Theodisius Pettigrew, the Oxford coroner and his most powerful ally in his battle against Sir Montagu.

"Well, young fellow?" Carruthers tapped his stick impatiently.

Thomas looked up. "It seems, sir, that I will need to break my journey in Oxford before I reach Boughton."

"Oh? And why might that be?" asked a baffled Dr. Carruthers.

"Sir Theodisius wishes to see me urgently," he replied. "There's been a murder on the Boughton Estate."

Chapter 3

There had been a hanging at Oxford. Or, more precisely, three. After breaking his journey in Amersham, Thomas arrived in the city shortly after eight o'clock in the morning, to see a stream of people flowing from the gates of the castle. Some women seemed most distressed and in need of comfort. He shot a look into the courtyard as his carriage passed and saw that the gallows had recently taken the weight of three men. They still hung from the crossbeam like limp rag poppets. Yet the mood among the spectators was not one of raucous celebration, as he had so often witnessed at Tyburn. Those who came away from watching the gruesome spectacle seemed more solemn and reflective. There were those who seemed even angry, the scowls on their faces speaking of some great injustice. A few hapless souls clustered 'round the dead men's feet with cups to catch any sweat that might drip from their corpses. Thomas knew they believed the secretions contained healing properties. He turned his head away with a mixture of despair and disgust.

The carriage set him down in the High and he ordered his baggage to be taken to the Jolly Trooper, where Sir Theodisius had booked him a room. From there he made his way to the coroner's office. It was only a short walk, and after the rigors of the journey he felt as stiff as a wrung-out rag and was glad to stretch his aching limbs.

Ushered into his office by the coroner's familiar sneezing clerk,

Thomas found his old friend chomping his way through a pear, the juice squelching down his chin.

"Silkstone, my dear fellow! How good to see you," Sir Theodisius called through his mouthful, then in a more measured mood, added, "But at such a testing time." He gestured to the chair in front of his desk. "You have heard no word of her ladyship?" The coroner frowned as he spoke and cocked his head. He and his wife, Lady Harriet, had remained childless and regarded Lydia with an affection that would have been shown to their own daughter. He had already gleaned from the aggrieved expression on the young doctor's face that she was not faring well in Bethlem.

"It seems I am forbidden to see her ladyship," Thomas replied, seating himself on the edge of the chair.

"Malthus?" asked the coroner, wiping his juice-spattered chin with a napkin.

"I can think of no other reason, sir," conceded Thomas.

Sir Theodisius nodded. "He is tightening his grip," he muttered cryptically, eyeing the bowl of fruit that sat on his desk.

"Your note spoke of a murder," said Thomas, still unaware of the circumstances of his summons. His own eyes settled on the fruit. He noted that one of the pears was overripe and a dark brown stain of mold was blooming on its skin.

Sir Theodisius paused to frame his reply, fingering a goblet of claret on his desk with his sticky fingers. "Yes. Murder. A most distressing affair," he said. "An old friend of mine, as a matter of fact."

Thomas showed his concern. "What happened, sir?"

The coroner relaxed into his chair and sighed deeply. "'Tis a long story, Silkstone."

"I shall not leave until I hear it," replied the doctor, dipping his brows.

"Then you'll be needing one of these," the coroner said, reaching forward and pouring out another glass of claret. He pushed it across the desk to Thomas, then took another gulp of his own, as if he needed the strength it gave him to continue. "Great changes are afoot at Boughton," he began.

"Changes?" Thomas leaned forward in his seat.

Sir Theodisius heaved his frame closer to Thomas, his elbows on the desk. He lowered his voice. "An Act of Enclosure was lodged at the quarter sessions last month."

"Enclosure?" Thomas repeated. The implications of such an act were not entirely familiar to him. Even so, he knew it would involve the fencing off of much of the Boughton Estate. His mind flashed to the common land, with its vast acreage that was home to cattle, geese, and pigs; the wetlands, too, around Plover's Lake. He thought of the beech forests that skirted the village of Brandwick and covered the surrounding hills, and he thought of the people who relied upon them. Such land, held as it was by the community, bestowed its bounty without charge, or stint as it was known. He knew it to support many a man and his family. At this time of year, the woods would be singing to the sound of saws as the beeches were pollarded, their branches cut for firewood and their canopies thinned so that animals could graze on the growth below.

"This will have a most detrimental effect on all those who live on the estate and in Brandwick," Thomas ventured.

The coroner's shoulders suddenly shook in a mocking laugh.

"My dear boy, 'twill change everything. It means that Sir Montagu is applying to take control of the whole area, to use the land for his own profit."

Thomas paused for a moment, digesting the unwelcome news.

"And he can do this with the sanction of the law?"

Sir Theodisius nodded. "Young Richard is his ward. Malthus argues that he is acting in his best interests and that enclosure is necessary for economic improvement. Remember he is a lawyer, too. His case will be watertight."

The coroner's logic made perfect sense to Thomas. Sir Montagu's estate near Banbury bordered Boughton at its northernmost reach. It was as if a fog had suddenly lifted to reveal the lawyer's real intentions. The man's machinations were even more far-reaching than Thomas had ever envisaged. He had always believed that the enmity Sir Montagu had shown him was purely personal, that it was entirely due to his American citizenship. He had never imagined that there was some greater plan for the control of the Boughton Estate. Yet here it was, evidence that his adversary had set his sights on a bigger prize.

Thomas looked at the coroner incredulously. "So this is why he wanted Lydia put away, to add Boughton to his own lands and profit from their annexation."

"Exactly so," said Sir Theodisius, nodding. He took another gulp of claret.

"And he would make the young earl his puppet while . . ."

". . . while the Right Honorable Nicholas Lupton holds sway on his behalf."

Thomas shifted uncomfortably in his seat. "And this act will give him even more power."

"Indeed," said the coroner with a nod. "The common land and the woodlands where parishioners are allowed to roam freely will be fenced off and become exclusively part of the Boughton Estate. The villagers will lose their rights to graze their cattle, to gather firewood, to catch rabbits—" He broke off, shaking his head in tacit disagreement with the policy.

Thomas was aware of the new thinking in agriculture. He had seen for himself the puny cattle and the bare-worn grass of the commons. He knew from inspecting Boughton's own ledgers that the common harvest never yielded as much as those crops planted on estate land. He'd heard landowners argue that the soil possessed by many in common was neglected by all and that greater efficiency and productivity could be achieved only by taking complete control of it. And yet he was also aware that such progress came at a price and the poor would have to pay for it.

"Will there be no compensation?"

Sir Theodisius heaved his great shoulders. "Some landowners are fair. Tenants are granted allotments in return for giving up their parcels of land, but you know as well as I, Silkstone, that fairness and decency are not words in Montagu Malthus's vocabulary."

Thomas thought of Brandwick's poor cottagers, the people whose meager homes he had entered on so many occasions to treat their various ills. Their misfortunes were often brought on by their wretched living conditions. Lydia had made it her goal to improve the lot of her tenants, but now Malthus, it seemed, wished to reverse their fortunes. He appeared intent not on mending their roofs and repairing their windows, but on driving these people out altogether.

"But surely the villagers will protest?"

Sir Theodisius raised a brow. "If they do they'll end up dangling at the end of a rope like the peasants this morning."

The image of the three lifeless bodies strung up from the gallows resurfaced in Thomas's mind. "They were hanged for protesting?"

"Arson. They set fire to a hayrick, and I doubt if they'll be the last to resort to such violence."

"And you fear the same will happen at Boughton?"

"I fear it has already started."

"Your friend's murder?" asked Thomas.

Sir Theodisius raised his hands and rolled his eyes in a gesture of despair. "Jeffrey Turgoose was his name. Known him since Eton. Fine surveyor with a practice here in Oxford. I saw him last month. Told me he had been commissioned to work at Boughton, asked to make a preliminary map of the whole estate before the posting of the Act of Enclosure."

"So that Sir Montagu knows just how much land he would control?" interrupted Thomas.

"Exactly so, but Turgoose was having trouble—I knew that much."

"Trouble?"

"The villagers resented his work. Jeered and taunted him and his chainman as they went about measuring. I dined with him one evening. Told me his surveying chains had been sabotaged."

The coroner paused to slurp more claret. "He was mapping the woodland when he was shot."

"Shot?" echoed Thomas. The word rang out across the room. "And you think one or more of the villagers killed him?"

"Malthus thinks so. He looks on each and every man, woman, and child as guilty. He's enforcing a curfew, and until the murderer is caught, the entire village will suffer." The coroner's eyes had settled once more on the bowl of fruit.

"And you, sir? Who do you think is responsible?"

Sir Theodisius shrugged and reached for the moldy pear.

"A vengeful villager, a highwayman—I believe the woods are plagued by them. . . ." The coroner's voice trailed off as he considered the options.

"I see," said Thomas. He knew that Sir Theodisius was looking to him to uncover the perpetrator of this heinous act. Moreover, until the surveyor's murderer was apprehended, the people of Brandwick would continue to endure their new master's wrath. The killing offered Sir Montagu the perfect excuse to run roughshod over the whole community. "And you wish me to conduct a postmortem on Mr. Turgoose?"

The coroner was studying the moldy pear as it lay in the palm of his hand; then, without warning, he closed his fist 'round it and squeezed. It squelched in his hand, so that the juice oozed through his fingers, leaving behind a mushy pulp. He looked up at Thomas, who had been observing him with a strange fascination.

"His body arrived this morning," he said.

Chapter 4

Sir Montagu Malthus received Gilbert Fothergill in his study at Draycott House, near Banbury. His clerk's arrival from London just as the light was fading could not have been more fortuitous, coming as it did at the end of a meeting with the neighboring landowners. Of course there had been some expectation that the good news would arrive that day, but the way in which the little man entered the room, flourishing this most important scroll, proved, in the lawyer's opinion, rather a coup de théâtre.

Nor did Fothergill arrive a moment too soon. Talk had inevitably turned to the murder of the Boughton surveyor three days before. Sir Montagu had shaken his head and said he was doing all in his power to apprehend the vile peasants who had carried out such a villainous crime. It was an unwelcome diversion from the matter in hand, so when the clerk arrived from London, his mood lightened.

Present that afternoon was the elderly and ailing Sir John Thorndike, whose estate bordered Boughton, along with Lord William Fitzwarren, the owner of three thousand acres in Northamptonshire, and the Earl of Rainton, whose lands also fell within the proposed, but as yet most secret, scheme. Another landowner, Sir Arthur Warbeck, who happened to be Brandwick's magistrate, was also present. Nicholas Lupton had ridden up from Boughton Hall that morning.

Fothergill had clearly not expected such a reception. Never a man given to showing his emotions, he nevertheless managed a gracious, if slightly awkward, nod of his gray goat-wigged head as the gentlemen rose and applauded his entrance.

"Bravo!" guffawed Lord Fitzwarren, a ruddy-faced man and the loudest of them all.

"Hear, hear!" echoed Rainton and Lupton in unison.

Sir John Thorndike, however, remained seated. His heart condition was growing steadily worse. Nevertheless, he still managed to raise his glass of sack to Fothergill.

Sir Montagu stood to pat the bemused clerk on the back. It was the first time he had shown such a gesture of appreciation to Fothergill in more than thirty years' service.

"So, gentlemen," he began, "we have successfully reached the first milestone in our exciting journey." He was beaming as he scanned the assembled faces for shows of appreciation.

"But there are many more hurdles to jump," butted in Lupton, continuing the traveling analogy.

Sir Montagu threw him a disapproving look. There was no love lost between the two men. It suited the lawyer's purpose to have Lupton in place at Boughton as his temporary steward, but he was not showing himself to be the man of vision Sir Montagu had originally thought. Rather too egotistical, he felt, although time would tell.

"But we shall overcome them!" exclaimed Fitzwarren, as bullish as ever.

From his seat, Sir John nodded. "Indeed we shall, but it will take time."

Rainton concurred. "'Twill be another year until the act is passed, at the earliest."

Sir Montagu was clearly irked by his companions' wavering. "But it will be passed. Of that there can be no doubt, and in the meantime, we can enlist the support of more backers, gentlemen. Do you not see? We cannot fail in our endeavors."

Rainton, however, seemed unconvinced. "And what of the objectors?"

Lupton shot an anxious look at Sir Montagu, who parried the question. "A minor setback." He nodded dismissively.

Rainton snorted. "You call the murder of your surveyor a minor setback?" he retorted, casting around for support from his fellow landowners.

Sir John nodded and looked pointedly at Sir Montagu. "The villagers obviously hold you responsible for depriving them of their beloved Lady Lydia and stepping too hastily into her shoes," he said plainly, adding: "There is a general ill feeling at Boughton and in Brandwick."

"'Twas ever thus among the proletariat," sneered Fitzwarren, coming to the lawyer's rescue.

Sir Montagu's nostrils flared as he shot a look of disdain at the ailing old knight.

"Those responsible will be made an example of; I can assure you of that, gentlemen," he said, adding: "And, of course, Lupton, as my steward, will see that order is kept on the estate and in the village."

"So you are the proverbial whipping boy?" said Rainton, fixing a look of cynical amusement on Lupton. The steward's expression remained neutral, even though inwardly he acknowledged he would be the one to bear the brunt of the villagers' wrath.

Before he could answer, Sir John piped up. "Speaking of boys, where is young Crick?" he croaked. "Where are you hiding him, Malthus?"

Sir Montagu straightened his back and sniffed. "Not hiding him; merely shielding him from harmful outside influences, sir."

"Does that include us?" Fitzwarren quipped before bursting, once more, into a fit of laughter.

"May we see him?" asked Rainton, ignoring his colleague. "After all, it is he who will ultimately benefit from our scheme."

The lawyer thought for a moment. Lydia's son had been made a ward of the court of Chancery, and he was his guardian. "Very well," he said, pulling the bell cord. A few seconds later his butler was taking instructions to bring in Richard Crick. Before the young earl arrived, however, Sir Montagu had a word of warning for those assembled.

"This matter must be treated with the utmost discretion, gentlemen. If word gets out, I needn't remind you that all hell will break loose."

Lupton raised a brow. "'Tis bad enough now. There is general disquiet among the villagers about us raising rents."

Rainton concurred. "The lower sort could prove a great thorn in our sides. There have been riots at Fritwick."

Sir Montagu smirked. "As I said, I am fully aware of the antipathy of the common horde, dear Rainton, but it is up to us to remove that thorn by fair means or foul."

For a moment there was silence as the gentlemen contemplated the implications of Sir Montagu's words. Then their host lightened the mood as the young earl was announced. The boy, dressed finely and his unruly curls now tamed by a ribbon, stood at the doorway flanked by his nursemaid. The kindly looking matron, Nurse Pring, who had previously been in Lydia's service, gently pushed her charge forward into the room. He turned back to look at her, but she flapped her hand at him and he took a few paces forward.

"Your lordship, I would like to introduce you to some friends of mine," Sir Montagu told the boy, softening his tone.

The child pursed his lips and a look of apprehension settled on his face.

"They would like to be your friends, too," Sir Montagu told him, holding out his hand.

Sir John's eyes widened. "How like his mother he is!" he exclaimed, staring at the young earl's chestnut hair and large eyes.

Sir Montagu chose to ignore the remark. "We have been discussing business," he told his bewildered charge, hooking him close to him.

The boy's expression remained unsettled, his gaze darting from one man to another until he finally settled on Nicholas Lupton's familiar face. He let Sir Montagu's hand drop and hurried over to him.

"Mr. Lupton!" he cried, tugging at the steward's sleeve. But Lupton looked slightly abashed and fended him off in a jovial, but firm, manner.

"No, sir. You are a young man now. Gentlemen do not behave in such a way."

Fitzwarren laughed loudly at this remark, the others sniggered, but the collective smile was soon wiped off their faces by the child's next remark.

"Where is my mamma?" he asked, looking up at Sir Montagu.

The lawyer shifted uneasily. "Why, sir, you know your mamma is unwell and in a hospital."

"But when will I see her again?"

There was an awkward silence. "When she is fully restored."

"But when will that be?" The boy stamped his foot as he spoke.

Offended by such behavior, Sir Montagu nodded to the nursemaid.

"Your lordship," she called harshly. "That is quite enough. Come here now." She slapped her skirts.

The child looked at Lupton, who stared back icily, giving him not a crumb of comfort. It was then that the young earl's eyes filled with tears and his face reddened.

"Now!" repeated the nursemaid, ignoring her charge's sobs.

With heaving shoulders the child dragged his feet over to the door.

"Send him to bed," instructed Sir Montagu. The woman curtsied and was walking out of the door when the lawyer called her back once more. "And no supper!" he barked. She acknowledged his order with a nod, took the boy's hand, and pulled him from the room.

The men listened in an uneasy silence to the child's pleas as he was dragged upstairs once more. It was Sir John who spoke first: "He has his mother's good looks," he said.

"But no manners," ventured Fitzwarren with a snort.

"'Tis hard for him," said Lupton, sympathy softening his tone. "He found his mother after all those years and now she has been taken from him again."

Sir Montagu frowned and upbraided his steward. "Tush, tush, Lupton! Do I detect sentimentality?" He was aware that Lupton had become fond of the boy, and, he dared say, of Lydia, before the steward's treachery had been revealed and he had slipped so effortlessly into the role of estate manager.

Lupton cocked his head. "No, sir, but—"

"Good." Sir Montagu cut him off abruptly. "After all, the boy will benefit from this scheme in the long run," he pointed out. He was ringing the servants' bell once more.

"And what will become of Lady Lydia?" chimed in Sir John.

Sir Montagu's lips twitched. "You always did have a soft spot for her, didn't you, John?" He recalled the time that he had offered his old friend Lydia's hand in marriage if he were to assist him in his plans to fend off Thomas Silkstone.

"You say she has gone quite mad?" asked Rainton.

Sir Montagu twisted his head and nodded warily. It was clear he suddenly felt that his authority was being challenged.

"Quite," he replied firmly.

"So there is no possibility of her recovery?" pressed Sir John. Sir Montagu knew exactly what he was driving at.

"Even if she does recover, she no longer has any say in matters concerning the estate," he said emphatically. He turned to address everyone else in the room. "Your investment will be perfectly sound, I can assure you, gentlemen."

When the butler appeared at the door, Sir Montagu called for glasses to be recharged, endeavoring to lift spirits. The sack poured, he proposed a toast.

"Gentlemen, to our future success," he cried.

Each one eyed the others, drawing on their mutual strengths, and in that moment their confidence seemed to return. They were entrepreneurs, pioneers, men of vision at the dawn of a new age of industry and invention. The power lay in their hands to use as they saw fit. And, as with all worthwhile endeavors, there would be those who would fall by the wayside and be trampled underfoot. The way ahead would be strewn with difficulties, but their power weighted the odds very much in their favor. The men raised their glasses high.

"Our future success," they echoed.

Chapter 5

Great Tom was tolling ten as Thomas walked under Wren's pepper-pot dome and up to the doors of the Christ Church Anatomy School, Oxford. Within moments the familiar shock of hoarfrost hair that belonged to Professor Hans Hascher appeared to greet him. The professor, a native of Saxony, had been most helpful in his dealings with Lydia's late husband, Captain Michael Farrell. He had put his own laboratory at Thomas's disposal as the young anatomist had tried to prove Farrell's innocence.

"It's good to see you again," said the Saxon, lunging forward and kissing Thomas enthusiastically on both cheeks in the continental manner. His English, although understandable, was heavily accented.

"And you, Professor," said the doctor, taken slightly aback by the effusive welcome. "Although I am sorry it is a postmortem that reunites us," he added.

Hascher tilted his snowy white head. "And not a pretty sight, I fear," he groaned.

Without ceremony he led Thomas into a small room with high windows at the back of the school. While the light might have been adequate, the ventilation was not, and the stench so familiar to Thomas, though not yet nauseating, indicated that the unfortunate victim had already made his presence felt. The covered corpse lay on the dissecting table in the middle of the room. The two men approached it, and with a silent nod Thomas indicated he was prepared. The professor then pulled back the cloth to reveal the face of Jeffrey Turgoose, staring blankly up at the ceiling. His eyes were wide open and his features frozen in shock. Apart from a long, thin scratch on the man's cheek, which seemed to have been recently inflicted, there were no other outward signs of violence on his face.

Thomas glanced 'round at his colleague. "So, Professor, we have work to do," he said, divesting himself of his coat.

He donned his leather apron and laid out his instruments. The saw, the curved knives, the trocar were always arranged in the same order so that he could reach for them blindly, without having to turn away from the corpse. The professor, meanwhile, silently lit lanterns and fetched clean water in a sort of well-rehearsed priestly ritual that always preceded an autopsy examination. All was set.

Knowing the story of a dead man in life, when his heart still beat and the blood still coursed through his veins, did not make the anatomist's task any easier. Quite the opposite. Each organ held within it an imprint of his history, each slice of brain tissue a fragment of a memory. Thomas always had to remind himself to put up his emotional shield and render himself detached as long as he was in the presence of a cadaver. A murder, however, threw up its own conundrums. For the task in hand, it was the immediate past of the victim that interested him. Where had Mr. Turgoose been found? By whom? Where was the weapon that had discharged the shot?

Sir Theodisius had been able to answer some of his questions, but not all. The coroner had been given a thirdhand account of events by Nicholas Lupton. The source could therefore not be relied upon for accuracy or impartiality. It was nevertheless all that Thomas had to work on for the time being. The report ran thus:

> *Mr. Turgoose and his assistant, a young man by the name of James Charlton, entered Raven's Wood, with a guide, in order to conduct a preliminary*

survey. Abandoning their conveyance because of the muddy conditions, they continued through the wood on foot. The horse that was carrying their equipment was being led ahead of them by the guide and apparently stumbled into a sawpit. Whether or not this was a diversionary tactic on behalf of the party's attackers is not known, but what reportedly happened next appears straightforward enough, albeit resulting in tragic consequences. Hearing the obvious distress of the horse being led by the guide, a man whose name is Seth Talland, Jeffrey Turgoose went ahead to ascertain the source of the commotion, leaving his assistant alone. According to both Charlton and Talland, it was then that the brigands, their faces blackened with soot, struck. Emerging silently from the cover of the trees, they first ambushed Charlton, threatening him with a gun if he raised the alarm, then robbed him of his pocket watch. The young man, seeing his master approach, let out a scream, but, in response, a varlet discharged his weapon, shooting Jeffrey Turgoose as he returned. When he fell, mortally wounded, the bandits set about Charlton, who feared for his own life, punching him in the face. Hearing the shot, however, Talland came running and frightened off the raiders. They left with only a few trinkets. Finding Charlton injured and his master shot, Talland did what he could. He tended to the surveyor but soon realized it was too late. Jeffrey Turgoose had clearly breathed his last. Shocked and in great distress, the guide and the surveyor's man managed to make their way back toward Boughton Hall, where, as soon as they reached the main gates, the alarm was raised. Both men were traumatized and exhausted, although Charlton's injuries, it is believed, are only minor.

Thomas paused briefly out of a sense of reverence before he began the grisly task in hand. Professor Hascher, at his side, also took a moment to compose himself. At least he could be grateful that this corpse was relatively fresh. Mr. Turgoose had been felled only three days ago, and the cool weather meant that putrefaction had not yet begun in earnest. At the young doctor's signal, Hascher took a deep breath and drew back the rest of the covering to reveal the corpse in its entirety.

Forcing himself to focus, Thomas leaned over the cadaver. Mr. Turgoose had been divested of his clothes and shoes, something of which Thomas did not approve. He felt it vital to view the body as near as possible to how it was at the moment of death. Irritated, he glanced at a pile of garments on a nearby table. There were buckled shoes, too, still caked in mud.

Starting at the feet, his magnifying glass in hand, Thomas detected nothing untoward, save a small bruise on the right foot. The lower torso, too, was devoid of injury on first inspection, so it was to the chest that Thomas devoted most of his attention. Leaning over the thoracic cavity, he examined the mortal wound. There was little doubt in either man's mind that a gunshot was the cause of death. It was also clear from the amount of blood loss that the missile had punctured a main artery.

"The extractor, if you please, Professor," said Thomas, peering into the wound. The shot had entered the victim's body on the right lateral chest, shattering a rib. It had gone on to pierce the right lung and caused damage to the right atrium of the heart and the pulmonary artery before lodging itself between the second rib and the flesh. Death would have been instantaneous.

Taking the instrument, Thomas inserted the shaft deep into the wound; then, turning the handle to lengthen the screw, he could feel it latch onto the lead ball. It was a procedure he had undertaken only once on a living patient, and that was when the shot had pierced the bone and the shards threatened to infect the wound. Too many a man had died of sepsis rather than by the ball, in his experience. There were those who still believed that the shot itself was poisonous. Up until relatively recently, such wounds had been scalded with a red-hot iron or oil. At least Mr. Turgoose had been spared the lingering death accorded to so many soldiers who fell afoul of such ignorant practices in field hospitals. Thomas nearly always preferred to leave the shot in situ, knowing removal would most likely lead to infection and inevitable death. In this case, of course, the threat of corruption was not an issue, and he carefully excised the missile. The mortified flesh made a strange sucking sound but yielded up its unwelcome visitor without too much resistance. Walking over to the window, where the light was much brighter, he inspected the shot. Professor Hascher joined him.

"Vhat make you of zis?" asked the Saxon.

Thomas was silent for a moment as he studied the lead ball under his magnifying glass. "I am puzzled," he said at last.

"Puzzled?" repeated the professor. "How so?"

Thomas walked back to the corpse and dropped the shot into a kidney dish on the adjacent table. "'Tis so small. No bigger than a pea."

Professor Hascher, peering over the dish, had to agree. "But big enough to kill poor Mr. Turgoose," he ventured, shaking his head.

Thomas eyed him intently. "Of that there is no doubt," he replied. "But for highwaymen and footpads the blunderbuss is the usual weapon of choice."

Hascher pictured the large, cumbersome gun with its splayed muzzle, and nodded. "Boom!" His hands jerked upward and he spread out his fingers to signify an explosion before returning to glare at the wound.

"This wound is clean," said Thomas. "This is the only shot and it is small in caliber." He squinted at the lead in the kidney dish.

"So if not a blunderbuss, zen . . ."

"I'd say Mr. Turgoose was shot with a pistol, and a small one at that," said Thomas. He flung a look over at the clothes, crumpled and bloodied, on the nearby table.

Without a word, both men advanced to inspect the disheveled pile. There was something discomforting to Thomas about going through a dead man's clothes, like checking his bills or reading letters from his wife. He picked up the pair of worsted stockings. Both were splashed with blood mingled with spots of mud. The breeches, too, were spattered, but it was the fustian coat that had borne the brunt of the terrible affair. The professor held it aloft so that Thomas could inspect it more easily. The right breast was drenched in dried blood and at the center of the large, dark red stain was a hole. The Saxon was about to fold it and return it to the bundle, when Thomas stopped him. Experience had taught him always to look in a dead man's pockets. He delved in, first to the left, which he noted was torn, then the right.

"What have we here?" he asked, pulling out a crumpled scrap of paper.

The professor leaned in, frowning and hooking his spectacles onto his nose.

"Well, well," muttered Thomas as he scanned the note. Written in an ill-educated hand were scrawled the words: *Beware of Raven's Wood.*

Chapter 6

Up in the woods that spilled onto the Boughton Estate, the men were hard at work coppicing in the coupe. The longer spring days saw them rising with the birds and taking up their tools, not downing them again, save for the odd break, until dusk. The woodland floor should have been bursting into life by now. But where clusters of cowslips and celandine would normally peep their yellow heads above the leaf carpet, the beech mast still lingered underfoot. Spring was late.

The trees in this coupe were hazel, beech, and a few sweet chestnut. They were particularly good for fencing. They stood with their branches thin and straight and pointing upward, like hairs on the heads of frightened men. Because their arms had been lopped before their prime, their branches neither thickened nor spread. They could not reach out and entwine in a thick canopy as they did deeper inside the forest, so that grass and moss grew at their feet, enabling cattle and pigs to graze and forage freely in the mire.

On this particular morning, two men and a boy were working the stools to the northeastern corner of Raven's Wood, cutting mainly hazel, but a few ash and sweet chestnut standards, too, that were allowed to grow bigger for sturdier roof timbers. Although it was mid-April, the leaves of all but the oak had still not been persuaded to unfold themselves. The men did not complain. It made their task much easier. It was seven years since the older ones had last worked the area. The poles on most of the trees had grown high, upward of four feet from the crown, and straight, too. There was good timber to be had for fencing and roofs; firewood, as well. It was Chilterns wood that kept London fires aglow day and night, and the coppicers could barely keep up with the demand. Nearby an old mare grazed contentedly. She'd been unhitched from the wagon and hobbled. By the end of the day, she'd be pulling it down the hill into Brandwick piled high with timber.

Abraham Diggott—or Abe, as he was known—had the most years under his belt. He'd been born in the forest and had worked the trees for near on half a century, and now his face and hands were as gnarled as the broadest oak. It was often said by those who knew him that when he cut himself, it was sap, not blood, that ran from his veins. The dull thud of the ax, followed by the rasp of the saw, were sounds as melodious to him as the call of any nightingale. And seeing the bodies of his son and grandson move in and out of the dappled shade of the coppice as they cut through wood gladdened his heart. This joy, this sense of being alive, was what the forest gave him. These days, however, he knew his body was failing him. It no longer obeyed his commands. Like a blunt ax, it was not fit to work; only unlike an ax, it could not be peened and sharpened. His time was quickly passing, and he knew his son, Adam, tall and broad, would soon have to take charge.

He'd taught him well, showing his heir by example that the quality of the cut was more important than the tool used and that not all species of tree reacted the same. The common alder was best left untouched, and if an ash was coppiced in winter, the stool might not throw out shoots for fifteen months or more.

Adam's son, Jake, was also learning. Just thirteen years of age, he already knew how to slice a clean pole. But his grandfather feared the days of the younger ones could be numbered. Rumors had been blowing around like fallen leaves for days, and when the mapmakers came, the woodsmen knew them to be true. The place his family had called home for generations would soon be subject to an Act of Enclosure. The very trees they were felling would be used by the Boughton Estate to fence off not just the commons, but the forest, too. Their livelihood could be cut away anytime soon, just as surely as their saws could sever a branch from its trunk.

When they stopped to sup their small beer close to midday, it was clear the same thoughts were troubling Adam.

"We're building our own coffins," he told his father. They had become just three in an army of men Nicholas Lupton had engaged to fell trees for the very posts and fences intended to bar them from their livings.

Young Jake was at the whetstone that had been nailed to a stump nearby, sharpening the billhooks. Adam did not want him to hear what he had to say. The older men sat on mossy trunks and ate hunks of bread. A weak sun trickled through the trees. The air smelled sweet with sap and was full of birdsong.

"There'll always be need for us coppicers," replied his father through a half-chewed mouthful of crust.

"Aye, but we won't be our own men. We'll be under Boughton's yoke," countered Adam. He'd heard the stories from Northampton and from south of High Wycombe. Families were being driven out of woodlands and off commons. Forced to pack up their belongings and leave their messuages, they had no other choice but to head for the towns and cities to find work. A few had not gone quietly. They had gathered in the village square and broken windows. They'd even fired a hayrick in Fritwick, but in the end those who weren't jailed still had to pack up what few belongings they had and depart.

"If this petition goes through, we'll be turned out of the forest." Adam clapped his hands on his broad thighs. "Mark my words."

Abe, his gray hair flecked with bark and twigs, shook his head. "We've been through hard times before, son, and we will again."

Adam was not so sure. His father was of the forest, a man of the trees and of the seasons. To him everything had its turn and its place, a natural order and rhythm. But life was not so simple. One family's winter did not always give way to spring, and the promise of a good harvest was so often dashed by violent storms.

"I'll not stand by and do naught as they close the wood to us." The younger man jerked his head in Jake's direction as the boy sat peening an ax. "I owe it to myself and I owe it to him."

His father shrugged his withering shoulders. "You'll do what you must do," he said. "Like you did the other day."

Adam shot him a nervous look. "What do you mean?"

Abe gave a wily nod as he recalled seeing sooty smears on his son's forehead and neck. "I know you'll put up a fight and I know you won't be the only one."

Adam sighed deeply. "We stand to lose everything, Pa," he said.

The old woodsman nodded and was silent for a moment before he raised his gaze toward the crowns of the trees in the coupe, as if he half expected to take some inspiration from them. He chewed his scabby lip until finally he said, "You've a future ahead of you, son. You must do what you think fit. Only have a care for Jake. He needs you, and so do I."

Chapter 7

By the time the postmortem on Jeffrey Turgoose was complete and notes had been made, the light had begun to dwindle. After washing the blood away from his hands and scrubbing his fingernails, Thomas politely declined the offer of a schnapps with Professor Hascher so that he might go and report directly to Sir Theodisius, who was anxiously awaiting news.

A good fire blazed in the grate in the study of the coroner's town house. Thomas found Sir Theodisius seated in a winged chair, staring morosely into the hearth. The voluminous bags under his eyes suggested to the doctor that sleep had evaded his old ally. Indeed, his whole visage seemed to have drooped, as if being pulled downward by the burden of both worry for Lydia and grief for his dead friend. It was clear to Thomas that he was in need of company. A decanter of brandy and a glass sat on a small table at his side. Acknowledging his visitor with a nod, the coroner lifted his tumbler into the air.

"Get yourself one of these, will you, Silkstone," he mumbled, pointing to a cabinet on the other side of the room. Thomas obeyed, poured himself a drink, and joined the older man by the hearth.

Cradling his brandy in his chubby hand, Sir Theodisius gawked blankly as the flames danced in the grate. Sensing his mood, Thomas settled himself opposite and prepared to lend a sympathetic ear. There seemed to be a tacit understanding that as the coroner talked, the anatomist would listen.

"We were friends at Eton, you know," Sir Theodisius began, his eyes remaining fixed on the blaze. "Grew up together, then went our separate ways, yet still remained in touch. Had a practice in the High." His delivery grew more maudlin with every gulp of brandy, until by the time he had told Thomas of his friend's life history, of his wife, three sons, and twelve grandchildren, his eyes were brimming with tears. Not wishing to embarrass the coroner, Thomas also directed his own gaze toward the fire. He had been attentive. As was so often the case with his patients, his presence and the ability to listen were all that had been required.

The fire had begun to die down when, after a reflective pause, Sir Theodisius asked, "What did you find?"

The sudden question, delivered with such surprising bluntness, pulled Thomas back into the moment. There was no delicate answer. "A shot to the heart." He paused to gauge the reaction; then, when none was forthcoming, and to soften the harshness of his words, he added: "It severed a main artery, sir. Death would have been swift." Yet his answer was met by the coroner with an unforeseen show of indignation.

"Damn it, Silkstone. I know how the man died. What I need to know is what varlet discharged the gun so that I may personally see him choke at the end of a rope!"

Thomas nodded. "Of course, sir," he replied, sensing that despite unburdening himself, the coroner remained in a state of deep distress. It was as if he was carrying some of the blame for his friend's death. It seemed to weigh so heavily on his broad shoulders. Here is a man, thought Thomas, who deals daily with mortality and the fragility of human existence, yet he clearly finds it difficult to cope with the passing of an associate.

Sensing more was expected of him, Thomas continued. "The ball was a small caliber. Not a blunderbuss, as one might expect in such a case, but quite possibly a pistol."

At these words, the coroner's bulky frame suddenly gave an odd jerk, as if he was tensing. His hands gripped the arms of his chair.

"A pistol?" he repeated.

"Yes, sir, a flintlock, most probably, a—"

But Sir Theodisius's hand flew up, stopping the anatomist in mid-sentence.

"Not a blunderbuss? You are sure?"

"Quite sure, sir."

Sir Theodisius dipped his brows. A look of unease settled on his face. "I feared as much," he muttered.

"Sir?" Thomas watched as, despite the warmth from the fire, the coroner seemed to grow pale before his very eyes. "There is something—?"

"Yes, Silkstone." The coroner cut him short. "There is something, something most troubling to me, and I must tell you now." His eyes cut to a key that sat on the small round table, next to his brandy glass. Thomas watched in silence as the coroner struggled to pick it up in his plump fingers, then unlocked a concealed drawer in the table. Pulling it open, he brought out a brass-bound mahogany box. He opened the lid.

"You see, I gave him one of these," he said, sliding the box toward Thomas.

The anatomist's eyes widened and his head suddenly shot up when he looked inside at the contents. The open box revealed a red velvet lining upon which lay one flintlock pistol. Its grip was plain walnut and its frame was silver and engraved with an acanthus leaf pattern. Underneath it was an indentation where another pistol—Thomas presumed it was one of a matching pair—usually rested.

"You gave Mr. Turgoose your firearm?" he asked, fixing Sir Theodisius with an incredulous stare.

"God help me, Silkstone, I did," he replied with a nod.

The coroner flattened his lips as if to stop them from trembling. The prospect that had occurred to both men hovered in the air until the coroner summoned up the courage to ask the question outright.

"Could it be he was shot with my pistol?" His eyes were glistening as he spoke. He was looking directly at the anatomist.

Thomas returned his forlorn gaze, but knew he could not deny the possibility. "There is a chance, sir. Yes," he conceded.

"But I cannot say for sure until I have conducted further tests." He shook his head. "Either way, you must not blame yourself, sir."

Suddenly Thomas understood why the coroner might feel weighed down by guilt. He held himself partly responsible for his friend's death.

"I gave it to him purely as a deterrent," explained Sir Theodisius, trying to justify his action. He shook his head. "I never thought . . ."

"I know." Thomas was sympathetic. Even so, he could not let the matter lie. "I will need to examine the other pistol, sir."

The coroner jerked his head backward so that the rolls of flesh beneath his chin came to the fore. "Of course," he replied, closing the lid of the gun box and pushing it away from him, as if it were an evil talisman. "Take it out of my sight."

"Thank you, sir," said Thomas. "I know this is not easy for you."

Chapter 8

Thomas had set off from Oxford for Boughton at first light. Leaving Sir Theodisius's pistol in the care of Professor Hascher, he had asked him to take the weapon, along with the shot retrieved from Mr. Turgoose's body, to a renowned gunmaker in the city. He was to ascertain whether or not the missile removed from the dead man's chest could have been fired from the other pistol in the pair. Until his suspicions were proved, Thomas needed little excuse to concentrate on his original mission: to, at the very least, gain access to Lydia. The delivery of the preliminary postmortem report into the death of the surveyor, who had been in Nicholas Lupton's employ, gave him the perfect excuse.

It was with mixed emotions that he finally turned his horse into Boughton's familiar driveway. He had ridden this way so many times, urging his mount to go faster so that he could see Lydia a few minutes sooner. He pictured how she would stand on the steps to greet him and he would kiss her hand. He would let his lips linger a little longer than was seemly and she would blush. And now she was not here. Nor was young Richard. His heart felt heavy. Everything had changed and nothing had changed. Boughton Hall's façade remained unflinching and sturdy. Its barley-twist chimneys still smoked, but the shutters at most of the windows were closed, and no one was there to greet him. He dismounted, climbed the front steps, and rang the bell.

He was gladdened when Lydia's butler answered the door.

"Dr. Silkstone!" he said, his voice rising in a rare show of emotion. Thomas was not sure if his unannounced visit was welcome or not.

"Howard," Thomas greeted him. "I know my arrival is unexpected, but I was hoping Mr. Lupton would receive me," he said.

The butler bowed and took the visitor's hat and gloves. "I shall inquire, sir," he told him formally, even though the look in his eye told Thomas that his arrival would not be greeted favorably by the new steward. Just as Howard headed off, however, the study door was suddenly flung open and raised voices could be heard. A young man whom Thomas did not recognize stomped out. His hair was flame red and his face freckled. His head was swathed in a bandage that covered his right eye, and he seemed in a most wretched state, snorting back tears. He stormed down the hallway toward the servants' quarters, barging in front of Thomas without bothering to acknowledge his presence. The obvious altercation made even the unflappable Howard arch a brow. He knocked at the open door and entered, reappearing a moment later.

"Mr. Lupton will see you now, sir."

Relieved at being granted an audience, Thomas nevertheless tensed as he was led into the study. He found Nicholas Lupton pacing up and down in a most choleric manner, his hands clasped behind his back. Seeing Thomas, the steward greeted him curtly with a nod of his head, which sat deeply in his broad shoulders, then made his way back to the desk. It was piled high with rolls of parchment.

"So, Silkstone," he sneered, easing himself into his chair, "wherever death is, you seem to follow, like a scavenger crow that picks over carrion." The comparison seemed to amuse him, and he let out an odd sound by way of self-congratulation.

True, Thomas had anticipated a frosty welcome from Lupton, but he was not prepared for such utter derision. The easy and affable manner the steward had displayed in front of Lydia had completely disappeared. Gone was the bluff simplicity of a country estate manager. His sun-bleached hair was now covered in a gray wig that aged him by at least ten years. It was clear he carried a weight of authority on his stocky frame that he had not previously displayed. Nevertheless, the excuse fitted Thomas's plans perfectly.

"I have conducted a postmortem on Jeffrey Turgoose, if that is what you mean," replied the anatomist coolly.

"You have the report?" The steward held out his hand.

"I do." Thomas tapped the document he carried under his arm. "But it is not complete."

"Why not? You have examined the body, have you not?" came the short riposte.

Thomas took a deep breath. "I cannot be sure of the type of weapon used."

Lupton showed his frustration with a grunt, then spoke through clenched teeth, as if trying to check his own irritation. "It was plain for any fool to see that the man died from a gunshot wound. But who pulled the trigger?" He lurched forward, making a grab for the report, but Thomas sidestepped.

"Before I can answer that question, I need to carry out further investigations," he replied. Reining in any temptation to lash back, he kept his voice measured.

"Investigations!" Lupton spat the word out as if it were poison. "It is most obvious to Sir Montagu and me who killed the surveyor."

Thomas's face registered surprise. "Who, pray tell?"

Lupton snorted, as if the question was below contempt. "The benighted villagers, of course! The ones who plagued the man while he was about his work."

Thomas recalled Sir Theodisius's account of his dead friend's travails, but shook his head. "You are jumping to conclusions, and until—"

"Give it here and be damned!" cried Lupton, suddenly lunging at Thomas once more. The doctor, however, stepped backward, hugging his report to his breast. Realizing the encounter was turning into a pantomime charade, Lupton relented, slapping his palm on the desk.

"If you can bring us any further toward finding which of

those village heathens murdered the surveyor, then you must do what is necessary," he conceded, with the grace of a pouting child.

Thomas inclined his head in acknowledgment. "I am most grateful," he replied, his voice tinged with sarcasm. But his reply was followed by another question that took Lupton completely by surprise. "The gentleman who was with you, just now?"

Lupton's head jerked up. "Turgoose's man, Charlton?" he barked. "What of him?"

"He seemed in a most agitated state," observed Thomas.

"He saw his master shot before him and feared for his own life. Of course the man was agitated," Lupton snapped, his thick neck straightening itself indignantly.

The reply, however, did not satisfy Thomas. He persisted. "And his injury?"

The steward did little to hide his growing exasperation. "He was hit about the face and head, Dr. Silkstone."

Thomas nodded but would not be put off. "Then perhaps you would permit me to examine him?"

"Certainly not," came the terse retort. "Dr. Fairweather has already administered to Mr. Charlton."

Hearing this, Thomas realized any further discourse was futile. He would have to pursue another tack if he were to reach the bottom of this mystery. As if Lupton read his thoughts, he added: "Do not waste your time on the murder, Silkstone. We shall want to see your full autopsy report in due course, but my men will apprehend the killer. They are working on it as we speak."

He began rearranging papers on the desk, obviously anxious to rid himself of his uninvited guest. Thomas, however, remained planted to the spot until Lupton raised his gaze, aware that his visitor had not yet moved. "And if that is all . . . ," he said flatly.

Now was Thomas's chance. "It is not all," he retorted, standing his ground. His voice was resolute. "Lady Lydia—"

Lupton's head shot up and he cut in. He threw down the papers he had only just picked up, sending them skidding across the polished surface of the desk. "Of course, you have come to plead her ladyship's cause," he said with a sour smile. "You know she is locked up for her own good."

Thomas felt his nerves tighten. "She is locked up for no one's good apart from Sir Montagu's and your own," he replied, trying to curb his mounting frustration. "I know of your plans to enclose the estate. I also know that her ladyship would never have agreed to them." He heard his own voice rising in anger as he spoke.

Lupton's reaction was, however, surprisingly cool. He slumped back in his chair and eyed Thomas. "What is it that you want, Silkstone? Money? A better position at one of the London hospitals? I am sure it can be arranged."

The volley of insults, coming thick and fast as they did, momentarily disarmed Thomas. He had not anticipated such slanderous suggestions. Nor had he been prepared to be bribed. Such a change of strategy unnerved him, but he nevertheless took advantage.

"I wish to see her ladyship," he said. He knew if he asked for her freedom, he would have even more scorn heaped upon him.

Lupton's head seemed to sink back into his shoulders for a moment. He tented his fingers and sucked in his cheeks in thought. "You wish to see her ladyship?" he repeated. "I am in the midst of seeing through an Act of Parliament for the benefit of this great estate, and you wish to see her ladyship?" He was shaking his head in disbelief, trying to belittle Thomas.

"I am aware you have weighty matters to consider," replied the doctor. He resolved to keep calm. "The villagers' reaction to enclosure and the surveyor's murder must make your task all the harder."

The steward eyed Thomas again and huffed. "You should not get involved in matters that do not concern you!" he snapped. "I really do not have the time—" He slapped the desk with his palm once more.

"Her ladyship's welfare is my concern," replied Thomas, countering Lupton's anger with a coolness that he found very difficult to muster.

"Oh!" Lupton grunted in a show of exasperation. "Very well." Taking a sheet of paper from the desk drawer, he scrawled a few words hastily and blotted the missive.

"Take this and give it to the superintendent at Bethlem," he said, holding a lighted candle to his melting sealing wax. "It will give you access to her."

The red wax dripped like drops of blood onto the paper, pooling into a congealed mass. Lupton then stamped it with his ring. "Here," he said, holding out the letter. He deliberately looked away, as if the very sight of the doctor irked him.

Thomas felt as though he was being summarily dismissed. It was clear his presence was not welcome at Boughton. Nevertheless, he knew he could endure any number of insults just as long as it furthered his purpose. To his great surprise, he had achieved his goal. After all these weeks, he would finally be able to see Lydia.

Chapter 9

As luck would have it, Joseph Makepeace, Brandwick's bury man, as haggard and world-weary as most of the corpses he lowered into their graves, had spotted the party from Boughton as it neared the churchyard toward midday. He had alerted one of Will Ketch's lads, who ran to tell Old Brindle, the bellman. In less than ten minutes he was ringing his bell, broadcasting to the entire High Street what was about to happen, and the villagers began heading toward St. Swithin's.

Moments later Gilbert Fothergill made his appearance. Sir Montagu's envoy was escorted by two of Boughton's newest recruits, burly thugs with permanent scowls on their faces who were paid to enforce Lupton's commands. The fussy little clerk had arrived to read out the Act of Enclosure on the steps of St. Swithin's, as required by law. Soon it seemed that the whole of the village had gathered outside the church to hear what this unimpressive emissary from the estate had to say.

Dressed from head to foot in black and crowned with a wide-brimmed hat, Fothergill looked more like a parson than one of Sir Montagu's men. He cleared his throat and stared with unseeing eyes at his audience. He knew full well that what he had to say would not go down at all favorably among his listeners. The chatter of the crowd faded in anticipation.

"*Notice is hereby given . . .*" Fothergill's voice sounded croaky. He cleared his throat and began again. "*Notice is hereby given that the commissioners named and passed by an Act of Parlia-*

ment, made and passed in the tenth year of His (present) Majesty, intituled an Act for dividing and enclosing the open common, fields, meadows, pastures and woodlands and other commonable lands in the lordship of Brandwick in the County of Oxfordshire."

The clerk looked up. His throat was already dry and he had finished only the first sentence. A crowd of at least three dozen had gathered and was growing at every turn. The noise began to swell again until one of the sidemen called for order. Fothergill resumed reading.

"A meeting is to be held on the thirtieth day of April at ten o'clock in the forenoon at the inn of Mr. Peter Geech in Brandwick for further proceeding in the execution of said Act."

Despite the call to order, Fothergill's voice did not carry well and his words were audible to only a few. It was clear that the clerk was decidedly uncomfortable. His spectacles kept slipping from the bridge of his nose, such was the effect of his perspiration, and his elbow was constantly nudged by the crowd that pressed around him, so that he kept losing his place on the scroll. Nevertheless, he struggled on to deliver his message. Anyone, he declared, interested in undertaking the cutting and making of drains, banks, and sluices for the drainage of the wetlands to be enclosed should contact the commissioners.

"In the meantime," Mr. Fothergill concluded, looking up from his script, "the plans may be inspected at the offices of Turgoose & Mather, surveyors, Oxford."

His mission now complete, the clerk rolled up the scroll, patted the crown of his hat as if securing it for the foray, and made a hasty retreat down the church steps. At first some of the village men tried to prevent him from returning to his conveyance. Obviously they did not care for him, nor, more importantly, for his message. He was gently jostled and his glasses were knocked off his nose—not deliberately, although the incident heightened the tension. The sidemen who accompanied him brandished their coshes and lashed out randomly, keeping the malcontents at bay. Josh Thornley, a sawyer, sustained one of the blows and fell to the ground. Will Ketch, the cowman—all act first, think later—sprang to his defense but soon joined his friend as a blow rained down on him, too. Within a few moments, all opposition and ill temper, such as it was, seemed to dissipate into a subdued sense of fear.

After what seemed an age to him, but which was in reality only a few seconds, Gilbert Fothergill managed to remount the chaise. Flanked by the thugs, he took a certain satisfaction in his performance and gave a self-congratulatory nod as he seated himself. The wheels of enclosure had been set in motion. He had played a vital part, and he was driven back to Boughton Hall secure in the knowledge that his legal duties had been successfully discharged.

It was too late in the day to start back to London, so Thomas rode from Boughton to Brandwick, intending to stay the night at the Three Tuns. As he glanced about him, the countryside seemed strangely dormant. The bitter winter had taken its toll on the land. In the fields the ploughed furrows, normally swollen and pregnant with shoots, remained regimented. No birds pecked for juicy worms among the rows of still-cold clods, as if they knew their foraging would be fruitless. Even the hedgerows, usually hazed with green at this time of year, were bare. There were fewer lambs, too. He could see only a dozen dams at most tending to their sickly offspring. What was more, the weather was still inclement. Eastertide had been and gone, and yet few signs of spring were evident. For the people of Brandwick, he knew it would mean only one thing—continued hardship. With an undoubtedly late harvest, the price of food would be forced up, heaping more suffering onto an already hard-pressed population.

It was midafternoon by the time Thomas reached the outskirts of Brandwick. Passing St. Swithin's, he noticed a sizable huddle of villagers on the church steps. He urged his horse nearer. He could glean that the few men who knew their letters were reading excerpts of some bill or notice out loud. He dismounted and walked up the church path to see what was going on. After a moment or two he understood. The Act of Enclosure, the infamous measure allowing landowners to enclose land and charge rents for what used to be free to all men, had been posted on the church door. It also quickly became clear to him that not everyone understood what they were reading.

"Dr. Silkstone, sir!" came an anxious voice. He turned to see Susannah Kidd, the young widow of Boughton's former head gardener. Grief had furrowed her brow and dulled her complexion.

"What does it mean?" She pointed to the notice. "There's talk of a hanging."

The huddle suddenly parted to allow Thomas up the steps so he could read the document for himself. A quick glance told him that phrases like "the execution of such act" were to blame for causing consternation among some of the womenfolk. He turned to Mistress Kidd. "No hanging," he reassured her, "but changes to how the land is used. The Boughton Estate wishes to fence off the common and woods."

Thomas observed the reaction of those around him to the news. Some of those he knew to be cottagers and commoners muttered among themselves and shook their heads. Thomas knew they were the ones who would lose out to Boughton's grand scheme, but he was confident they were fighters, too. They all knew their rights—handed down by the famous lady who entrusted them with her flaming brand—and those rights over the land were in perpetuity.

As he watched the stragglers disperse down the church steps, Thomas remembered Nicholas Lupton's diatribe. He would have it that these villagers, these downtrodden men and women, were so angry and vicious that they had already killed a man to protect these land rights. Yet all Thomas could see that afternoon was the quiet despair and the dignified anxiety that was etched on their faces as they drifted away from St. Swithin's. He read the act once more, this time for his own interest.

He studied the details, written large in black and white, and as he read, it occurred to him that this piece of parchment bore all the heinous marks of Sir Montagu Malthus himself. Everything had fitted so neatly into place. Gabriel Lawson's death had been most fortuitous in enabling Nicholas Lupton to slide effortlessly into the steward's shoes. While learning the intimate workings of the Boughton Estate and pretending to labor for the benefits of its tenants, as well as Lydia, the snake in the grass had, all the while, been plotting and scheming. And now Sir Montagu's intentions had been made public, exposing him for the tyrant he was.

With a heavy heart Thomas turned and headed toward the Three Tuns. Before he returned to London on the morrow, he still needed to investigate further into Jeffrey Turgoose's murder. He suspected there was much more to it than Lupton would have him believe. With or without the steward's cooperation, he planned to pursue his inquiries.

Thomas rode through the narrow arch and into the courtyard of the inn. Hearing the clatter of hooves on cobbles, the stable lad, his hair greasy and limp, loped forward with an odd gait to greet him. The anatomist quickly noted that he had an artificial leg, a shaft fashioned, it seemed, from metal, and held fast below the knee. It did not appear to hamper the youth, however, and he swiftly took Thomas's mount and unloaded his saddlebags, which contained a change of clothes.

Ducking through the low back entrance, Thomas found himself in the inn's familiar hallway. The flags were sticky with ale, and stale smoke hung in the gloomy air. Since there was no one at the reception desk, he ventured into the bar, where he spied the landlord. Wiry, thin-lipped Peter Geech, his eyes close set and beady, was deep in conversation with a heavily built man Thomas did not recognize. Dapperly dressed for Brandwick in a brocade coat and riding boots, and wearing a black wig, the stranger leaned nonchalantly against the counter. Pulling at his earlobe with his forefinger and thumb, he kept his head low and his face turned from sight. An open bottle of fine French wine was at his side.

Seeing the doctor approach from the corner of his eye, Geech broke off from his patron immediately, as if he were a hot coal. He greeted Thomas cordially enough, although his welcome was not entirely convincing. Peter Geech was a businessman before he was a host. The smartly dressed man demurred. It seemed he took no offense and left.

Forming his features into a shallow smile, Geech greeted his new arrival. "Dr. Silkstone, sir." He beamed with false enthusiasm, adding, "What an unexpected pleasure."

Thomas nodded, brushing aside the remark. "I would stay in one of your rooms for the night, if you please," he said.

He was painfully aware that all of Brandwick knew his business and of the terrible goings-on at Boughton. They would have expected him to stay away, not dare show his face again until Lady Lydia Farrell was returned to her rightful place at the hall. He did not belong in Brandwick, they said. Never had. What did he know of English ways? Granted he had pulled his weight during the Great Fogg, helping the sick and dying. He was savvy enough in his ways with corpses, too, telling how a man died from the contents of his gut, or a murder weapon from the marks it left, but that did not make him one of them. Brandwick mud may have been on his riding boots, but Brandwick blood did not run in his veins.

"I will give you our finest room, sir," said the landlord, his voice thick with false bonhomie. He lifted a key from the board in front of him.

"That is most kind," replied Thomas, recalling a previous stay's damp bedding, chair with uneven legs, and ill-fitting windowpane that allowed the rain in. "But first I must ask for some assistance."

"Oh?" The landlord cocked his head.

"I know that a man, a surveyor, was shot recently in Raven's Wood," Thomas began.

Geech nodded his sleek black head. "Terrible do, sir," he replied. "The curfew's not good for business, neither."

"I'm sure not," said Thomas quickly. "But I've been asked by the Oxford coroner to report on the matter and I need to visit the scene of the incident."

Geech's small eyes narrowed further. "And . . . ?"

"And I wondered if you knew of anyone who might be able to show me."

For a moment, the landlord regarded his patron, as if trying to gauge just how much he wanted to see where the surveyor had been shot.

"I will pay," added Thomas hopefully.

Yet it was clear that even this most wily of landlords did not believe that in such dealings, the law of supply and demand should apply. He shook his head and pursed his lips, making an odd sucking sound as he did so. "You'll not get no one 'round these parts to take you up to Raven's Wood, Doctor," he said finally, "no matter how much money you offer."

Chapter 10

It did not take Thomas long to realize that any investigation he undertook into the surveyor's murder would be conducted on his own. Such was the antipathy toward Sir Montagu and the prospect of enclosure among the villagers that no one would volunteer any assistance. He would have to act alone. So, less than an hour after his arrival at the Three Tuns, Thomas's fresh mount was being saddled to transport him up to Raven's Wood.

The stable lad with the false leg bobbed up and down with remarkable dexterity as he readied the horse. "She's a good girl. Not like the one that kicked me in the shin," he volunteered, patting the mare.

"Is that how you lost your leg?" asked Thomas.

"Aye," came the reply. "But this one's not easily spooked."

Thomas picked up on his words. "Spooked? Is that likely?"

The lad looked away. "You be going into Raven's Wood, ain't ya, sir?"

"Aye."

The youth shook his head. "No one goes there 'less they have to," he said.

"Like Mr. Turgoose and his assistant?" Thomas suggested, poised on the mounting block.

The stable lad nodded warily. "I warned him, sir," he replied, watching Thomas settle himself on the saddle.

"You warned Mr. Turgoose? Of what, pray?"

The boy stood back from the horse, looking up at Thomas,

but his furtive expression gave him away. He knew he had said too much and backtracked. "I told 'em not to go into the woods. 'Tis not a place for gentlemen. 'Tis the Raven, see."

"The Raven?" queried Thomas.

The lad squinted in the bright light. "Him and his gang, sir—" He broke off to allow Thomas to imagine for himself the horrors the eponymous highwayman might wreak. "And you, sir. You take care, too," he said.

"I intend to," replied Thomas with a smile as he tugged the rein. The goings-on in the wood seemed to have cast some sort of ghastly spell on the villagers. Whether local superstition was to blame or other, more earthly, reasons he could not be sure, but if no one in Brandwick would tell him precisely where the murder had taken place, he would try to find someone who would. In all probability that would mean asking a sawyer or a charcoal burner or someone of that ilk who worked in the forest.

He rode up the incline past the fulling mill. On the nearby tenter frames, the woolen cloth flapped in the wind. The noise of the stocks as they pounded the fabric echoed around the narrow valley. There had been rain the previous day, and the river, while not in flood, was flowing well, turning the waterwheel at a goodly pace.

At the foot of the slope Thomas dismounted and led his horse up the steep incline that led to Raven's Wood. It was dotted with shards of flint, and the overnight rain had turned the cart track into a greasy mire. When the hill leveled out at the top of the incline, he remounted his horse and turned left onto a well-trodden path. The trees were not yet in leaf; nevertheless, as Thomas rode on, the branches overhead seemed to thicken and entwine into a single canopy, blocking out much of the light. The birdsong that had been so lively at the beginning of his journey had all but disappeared, save for the shriek of a pheasant or the call of a red kite up above. Rainwater from the earlier downpour hung in droplets from twigs, dripping constantly onto his hat, and wet branches whipped his coat. He carried on deeper into the wood until, at a point where the track narrowed and dipped into a hollow, his horse suddenly jerked its head and pricked up its ears. Patting its neck, Thomas tried to reassure the animal.

"Nothing amiss," he soothed, his own eyes darting from left to right, scanning the wooded terrain. It was then that he spotted what had distracted his horse. A wooden cross, girded with red rowanberries, was dangling from a branch up ahead, directly in the horse's eyeline. He had seen such crosses before, when the Great Fogg, which local people called the Devil's Breath, had covered the countryside and many thought the world was about to end. Such talismans were believed to ward off evil spirits. Thomas gently pulled on the rein so that the animal skirted the disturbing object, then guided her back on the track.

A few yards on, he suddenly spotted great clouds of bluish gray smoke, billowing through the trees. At first he thought he had come across a smoldering forest fire, even though the ground was damp. Quickly he dismounted and, shielding his nose and mouth from the clinging smoke, he approached on foot. It did not take him long to realize his mistake. In the clearing he could see through the gritty haze a huge round mound raised on an earth platform. From it rose plumes that swirled around it and filled the air with the tang of burning wood. Covering the mound were clods of clay and slabs of turf, and at its center stood an odd-looking chimney out of which most of the smoke was escaping. A lone man with a shovel seemed to be tending what appeared to be some sort of kiln, lifting sods of moss and patting them down over vents, choking off the smoke, trapping it inside.

Thomas took the man to be one of the charcoal burners who lived and worked in the wood. He was small but solid in build, and on his head he wore a strange kind of leather bonnet with flaps that covered his ears. It was tied by laces under his chin. His face and hands were so deeply ingrained with soot that he looked as though he had been dipped in tar.

The workman did not notice his visitor at first, or if he did, he did not acknowledge him. He seemed too busy with his shovel, firming down the clods, until after a few moments he stood back to take stock of his work. He coughed and spat forth sooty spew.

It was then that he caught sight of Thomas out of the corner of his eye.

He looked at him warily. "Yes?" he grunted.

Thomas urged his horse forward. "Good day," he said, doffing his tricorn.

The man's eyes looked bright white set in his blackened face, but they narrowed as he studied his visitor. "You come about the mapmaker?" he asked. He had obviously heard of the murder. "I don't want no trouble."

Thomas shook his head. "No, sir, I am not," he replied politely, aware that he needed to tread carefully. "I am a surgeon and physician."

The charcoal burner straightened his grimy neck. "I may have a cough, but I'm not sick," he replied.

Thomas smiled. "I can see that," he conceded, but he refused to be put off. He went straight to the point. "I understand you know these woods."

The charcoal burner shrugged. "As well as any man."

Thomas pried a little deeper. "Did the mapmakers come this way?"

"What's it to you?" came the crabby reply.

"I am sent by the coroner. I need to find out more about how the man died." Thomas did not mean to be officious, but he feared he might have sounded that way. "Do you know the place where he was shot?"

The charcoal burner shuffled his feet and let his shovel take some of his weight. "What if I do?" There was a defiance in his manner that Thomas had not anticipated.

"Then I would ask you to take me to that place," Thomas persisted.

The charcoal burner paused for a moment and eyed the doctor with a simmering resentment. It was plain he did not trust this stranger.

"I will make it worth your while," said the doctor, delving into his pocket and bringing out his purse. "A crown for your pains," he offered, tossing a silver coin into the air. It landed on the carpet of dead leaves by the man's boots. He picked it up and bit into it as if it were an oatcake, before tossing his shovel to the ground, like a surly child.

"I'll take ye," he conceded, but still under sufferance. "'Tis a good walk from here."

The man led the way north through the forest, tramping along leaf-strewn paths and through muddy ruts. Thomas followed on horseback, dipping low under overhanging branches, until eventually they left behind them the coupe full of squat, coppiced hazel and entered the thicker forest. Walking over to a deep depression in the ground, scantily lined with leaves, the workman pointed to the steep-sided pit.

"Here."

Thomas dismounted and skirted the hole. He recalled that Sir Theodisius had told him that the horse had stumbled into a pit before the murder. It was not much deeper than a man's waist, but judging by the fresh spade marks at its sides, it had been quite recently dug out.

"And where did the surveyor fall?" he asked. He glanced at the man, but seeing his reaction, it was obviously a question too far. The charcoal burner shook his head vigorously.

"I dunno," came the quick reply. "Near," was all he would say.

"Yes," said Thomas with a knowing nod. For the woodsman to pinpoint the exact spot would be to incriminate himself. "Thank you. You have been most helpful, Mr. . . ."

"Godson. Zeb Godson," came the reply. "But folk call me Black Zeb."

Again Thomas smiled. "Thank you, Mr. Godson," he said. "I shall find my own way back."

The charcoal burner needed no further encouragement to leave. He disappeared into the trees within seconds, leaving Thomas alone, deep in the woods. He knew the exact site of the murder would be within a radius of a few yards, so he tethered his horse and began pacing along the track that led away from the deep pit. All the while he kept his eyes trained on the ground, following a set of recent hoofprints.

Within seconds, he arrived at what he knew must be the place. Several flies had discovered a cache of blood on top of the leaves, a thick dried pool of dark red, barely discernible among the russets and gold. Thomas crouched down. A small fragment of brown material fluttered among the rest of the leaves, its edges jagged and ripped. Thomas picked it up. It was fustian. His mind flashed to poor Mr. Turgoose's frock coat, torn at the pocket. It was easy to see where he had fallen and lain for a moment or two in this woodland grave. There were gouge marks in the mud where the leaves had been disturbed and the deadweight of his body must have been dragged out and heaved onto the horse.

Thomas looked about him. The clearing was small and surrounded by thick bushes, many of them evergreen. It would be easy for men to lie in wait here, unseen and ready to pounce. He pushed his way into the thick undergrowth, looking for signs, footprints in the mud, scraps of clothing, any clues left behind by Mr. Turgoose's attacker, or attackers. Despite his best efforts, he found nothing and decided to return to his horse. It was just as he put his foot in the stirrup and grabbed hold of the saddle to heave himself up that he noticed his right sleeve. It was covered in what appeared to be black dust. He inspected it more closely but did not brush it off. He dismounted and returned to the bushes from whence he had just come. Peering at the waxy leaves of a large holly bush, his eyes scanned the foliage, looking for something out of the ordinary. It was then he spotted it: some type of blight, he thought at first. When he touched what appeared to be the black mold and rubbed it between his forefinger and thumb, however, he was not so sure. He needed to take a sample.

Meanwhile, less than half a mile away, Maggie Cuthbert, or Mad Maggie as most people called her, sat in her tumbledown cottage nestled among the beeches. Although she was a cunning woman, gifted with certain powers, or so she said, she had not needed any shew stones to tell her that something was wrong in the woods the afternoon the surveyor was killed.

For as long as anyone could remember, she'd hawked her herbal remedies and her hag stones in Brandwick. For the soothing of stomachache, Brandwick belly as it was known, her lavender water was proving particularly popular these days. And for the few who'd cross her palm with silver, for amusement or mere curiosity, she'd read her shew stones. Rolling them on the flat ground with a shake and a flick of her scrawny wrist, she'd study them carefully. Sucking at her gums, she'd either shake her head solemnly or twitch her lips into a smile and nod, depending on what she said she saw. A few people believed her. Many did not, but on this particular afternoon she hadn't needed her powers to know something was amiss. Her fowl had told her, her chickens and turkeys. They'd clucked and squawked and gobbled, and above their din she had heard a horse whinnying. She'd been sitting by a hissing fire at the time. The logs were damp and the room was smoky. Using the last remnants of daylight, she'd been threading a chicken feather through the memory cord that hung by the door; each one marked a week since her husband passed. She'd not wanted to lose track of time, so every seven days she looped another feather into the yarn, just to remind her of her old Jack. She counted the quills. It had been thirty-six weeks since he'd died, choked by the Devil's Breath, like so many others. The monstrous fog had scoured his lungs and caused him to cough blood. Soon she'd have to start a new cord.

At the sound of her hens' clamor, she'd craned her scraggy neck to look out of her window. It was then she heard the noise that caused her most alarm. It had split the peaceful air with a mighty crack, like lightning cleaves a sturdy oak. It was the blast of gunshot; of that she was certain. Her first thought was that the Raven and his men were abroad, out to prey on innocent travelers. She'd drawn her bolts, blown out her candle, and kept low. It was then, from her window, that she saw the bushes shake and the dark shapes of men race away from the thicket. There were three, or maybe four of them. She watched them charging down the track as if the very devil himself were in hot pursuit. She had a good idea who they were, so she was more curious than afraid.

The next time she opened her door was on the following day. Three sidemen in Boughton livery dismounted on the dead leaves outside her cottage. They knocked and called her name. A gentleman had been murdered, they said. Had she seen or heard anything? they asked. She shook her head. She did not like this new breed at Boughton. They would have to break her old bones on a rack wheel before she'd tell their sort anything.

"An old woman like me lives in fear," she cried, spittle flying from her gums. "There's always footpads and highwaymen abroad." She pulled her shawl over her baggy breasts as she spoke. "And there's my hens. Not laid today, they haven't," she told them, even though, in truth, she hadn't ventured out to look.

One of the men, their leader, she guessed, built like a brick barn with not a hair on his head, barged past her and cast an eye around her room: the dried herbs hanging from the rafters, the kettle by the hearth, the filthy rags on the bed, the dark corners festooned with webs. "You heard no men? No gunshot?"

Maggie shook her frizzy gray head. "I heard nothing," she replied. She knew if she told them she'd seen a huddle of woodsmen up ahead fighting their way out of the thicket like things possessed, no matter what their purpose, they'd be hauled over the coals.

Chapter 11

Returning to Brandwick later in the afternoon, Thomas intended to go straight to the Three Tuns. He did not wish to be interrogated by Geech, or anyone else for that matter, on what he had found in Raven's Wood. Circumstances, however, conspired against him. As he rode into town at the top of the High Street, he could see that a crowd of people had gathered 'round the square. He urged on his horse.

"What goes on?" called Thomas to a man on his way to join the throng.

"Commoners' meeting," he yelled over the din.

The commoners—there were one hundred and three of them—were congregating. Their rights were ancient, set in the stones of the common, stored in the sap of the woodland trees, and cut into the boggy turf of the marshes. Had not the Lady of Brandwick herself bestowed the gift upon them? And now they were being challenged. Covering an area two miles to the north of the market cross and three to the east, Brandwick Common spanned grassland and scrubland, a river and several ponds, hillocks and downs, hollows and ridges. An elected council met every year to distribute plots of land and set the stint for pasturing animals to prevent overgrazing. Since time immemorial, each allotment had consisted of long strips of land, often separated from one another so that no one received more than their fair share of the best parcels. And when the harvest was gathered in, the poorer families could glean the grain that remained on the ground. It was then the turn of the horses, cows, and sheep to move in and graze, depositing manure to nourish the earth for the next year's crops. Where the soil was too poor to support such workings, then flocks of turkeys and geese would be set loose to peck and roam as they pleased, while the pigs were put to pannage in the woods. Thus it had always been and thus it would always be, if the commoners had their say. But now that way of life was being challenged, and where better to meet and discuss the matter than on the common itself?

Thomas looked around him at the growing crowd. They were mainly men, although a handful of women, a few with babes in their arms, had come to offer support. Some of them he recognized from his ministrations during the Great Fogg: Maggie Cuthbert, the cunning woman; Will Ketch, the cowherd; Abel Smith, the fowler; and Joseph Makepeace, the bury man. Together they would march toward their meeting place at Arthur's Hollow on the common.

Despite being an outsider, Thomas knew he had a duty to attend this villagers' gathering, for Lydia's sake, if not his own. If the Boughton Estate was to be enclosed by Sir Montagu, then Lydia, as its rightful custodian, must be informed. As the ragtag band started to move off, he decided to leave his horse at the Three Tuns and follow them at a respectable distance on foot.

Arthur's Hollow lay on the southern edge of Brandwick Common. The short walk passed peaceably, but Thomas noted that most of the people wore a slightly bewildered look on their faces, like passengers about to embark on a voyage to they knew not where. Their clothes and general demeanor marked them out as the poorer sort. There were plenty of men in ragged coats with frayed cuffs, their hats dusty and moldy, and women in soiled bonnets. Those from the woods gathered, too, men like the coppicers—the Diggotts, all three of them—and Josh Thornley and his moribund son, Hal.

A stink of sweat and dirt and toil hung about them all, so that those of middling rank who came to see what all the fuss was about held their scented kerchiefs to their noses and stood slightly back from the general melee. But among the poor it was their faces that spoke loudest. Hunger and cold had ploughed deep furrows on foreheads and under eyes. They had little in life, and they feared what little they had might soon be taken away from them. Nevertheless, the atmosphere was fearful rather than angry, curious rather than belligerent. Walter Harker, the watchman, was there to keep order, his cudgel in his hand, but it would be used only to tap unruly apprentice boys rather than to bludgeon honest men.

The rumors they'd heard about the Act of Enclosure were true, and now the proclamation was nailed on the church door for all to see. If their rights and liberties were to be upheld, then they would need to put up a united front against the Boughton Estate.

Will Ketch spoke first. He heaved himself up onto an old tree trunk so he could see above the crowd. His herding dog, a shaggy-coated bitch who'd been with him since she was a pup, sat by his side. He lifted his arms, and, after a moment the crowd fell silent. He was a commoner. He, his wife, and their six children lived in a messuage about a mile away from the village. He'd dwelt there these past ten years and eked out a living with a cow, two pigs, and half an acre of land. He was just thirty years of age, but his hunched shoulders, stooped back, and craggy face, weathered by the bite of so many cold winters, made him look more like a man of fifty.

"Good people of Brandwick," he began. He had heard them addressed as such before by the vicar, or some such dignitary. "We are here today because our livelihoods are threatened." There were grunts of approval from the crowd. "The very land that our fathers and their fathers and their fathers before them lived off may be taken away from us."

A shout went up. "We won't let them!"

Heads were shaken, voices raised.

Buoyed by the response, Will Ketch continued. "Boughton's new masters would turn us out and fence off the land that is our birthright. We must not let them."

"We'll fight!" came a voice from the crowd. This time fists

were lifted. "Tear down the fences," someone called, and another took up the chant. "Tear 'em down. Tear 'em down."

Another shout went up. "We want compensation!" But Jed Lively's was a lone voice. He was a tenant farmer who worked ten acres. No doubt Boughton would negotiate with him, apportion him a good-sized allotment, but most of those gathered stood to lose everything. Lively was shouted down and the atmosphere was turning ugly.

Adam Diggott wanted his voice to be heard, too. He'd been readying himself for this moment. His blood was stirred, so, elbowing his way through the gathering, he made his way to the front and stood on the tree trunk to address the crowd.

"I have lived in the forest all my life, and I'll die there," he began. "And I swear on the life of my son, Jake, that I'll not be turned out of my home."

A chorus of approval followed. He scanned the sea of expectant faces, but just as he was about to rouse them even further, a great rumble sounded from somewhere behind him. Turning 'round, he saw horsemen galloping over the ridge from the direction of Boughton Hall. There were four of them, and they pulled up just short of the crowd, sending men and women scattering to the left and right. One of the riders was recognized by some as the bailiff, Marcus Jupp, a gruff, unforgiving man, who would countenance no challenge to his authority. In his hand he held a scroll. Another of the horsemen shouted for silence, and the gathering suddenly fell still.

In a loud, clear voice, the bailiff began: "*Our Sovereign Lord the King chargeth and commandeth all persons, being assembled, immediately to disperse themselves, and peaceably to depart to their habitations, or to their lawful business, upon the pains contained in the Act made in the first year of King George, for preventing tumults and riotous assemblies. God Save the King!*"

The crowd remained silent, stunned by the reading of the Riot Act. They knew what it meant. They needed to be gone within the hour or face the death penalty. With these words the official folded up the scroll and surveyed his audience, watching for their reaction.

"You heard what the bailiff said!" shouted one of the horsemen. "Go to your homes!"

Only Will Ketch was foolish enough to try to lunge in anger at the bailiff, but his fellows wrenched him back just in time and his folly went unremarked.

The women made the first move to leave. The men, forced by their pride to wait just a little longer, followed shortly afterward. The horsemen watched them disperse slowly but peaceably, until just ten minutes later only the commoners' scrawny cattle remained on Brandwick Common.

Thomas, watching the proceedings from a few yards away, waited until almost everyone had gone before he, too, moved off the common. As he did so, one of the horsemen, his bald head glistening with sweat, called him out.

"Oi! You!" he shouted.

Lowering his head, Thomas quickened his pace. He did not wish to become embroiled with Lupton's thugs. As he kept walking, however, the sound of horses' hooves rumbled in his ears and he saw a shadow loom up behind him. Quickly he turned just as the horseman raised his cudgel. The blow struck hard on his shoulder and he staggered.

"Get you gone! You hear me!" cried the ruffian.

Still reeling, Thomas looked up. He was about to protest, but the man had already ridden off in pursuit of more straggling quarry. Clutching his throbbing shoulder, he made his way back to the Three Tuns.

Upstairs in his room, he managed to ease off his coat, waistcoat, and shirt and inspect his damaged shoulder in the mirror. The fire in his grate was not lit and he shivered as the cold pricked his naked skin. Inspecting himself in the cheval glass, he could see that a sizable bruise was blooming on his left blade. Gently he ran his right hand along the shaft of his clavicle, then back over his scapula. He satisfied himself that no bones had been broken, even though he found himself already debilitated.

He winced with pain as he opened his medical case and retrieved a bottle of trusted arnica oil together with a pad of gauze. With difficulty he managed to dab his purpled skin. The arnica would soothe his throbbing muscles.

Easing on his shirt, he walked to the window and scanned the now deserted High Street. It was barely dark and yet the village was already under curfew. Even the piss-cart men, who collected urine for use in the fulling mill, had to put off their unsavory work until the morning these days. It was only a few weeks since Thomas had last been in Brandwick, and yet so much had changed. Boughton Hall was being inhabited by a usurper, an impostor. Nicholas Lupton was an occupying force. He had no right to be there, and the people of the village were living under siege. Their woes had increased since Lydia's enforced departure and were about to multiply even further if Sir Montagu had his way on enclosure.

Above the rooftops the soft curves of the hills rose gently beyond the town. Thomas lifted his gaze, and as he did so, something caught his eye. He glanced up to his right. The dark stain of Raven's Wood was silhouetted against the fading sky, but somewhere within the forest, he saw two pinpricks of light dancing in its midst. Lydia always teased him that it was a place of nymphs and sprites, of elves and hobgoblins. She'd spoken of the woods with a childish glee that conveyed a mixture of excitement and fear. Thomas watched the lights for a moment. They disappeared, only to reappear a few seconds later. Lydia's fantastic hobgoblins were poachers, he assumed, or worse still highwaymen. He remembered the stable lad's warning about the Raven, preying on unsuspecting travelers who were brave—or foolish—enough to venture through his domain. He had just begun to close the shutters on the night when his eye was snagged by a movement below his window. A cart was rumbling past, its cargo covered with a canvas sheet, and on the driver's bench sat Peter Geech accompanied by the young stable lad. What delivery could be so important that they risked arrest for breaking the curfew? thought Thomas. They trundled unchecked up the High Street in the direction of the fulling mill and the woods. He watched them until they disappeared into the darkness, then let the latch fall on the shutters. Such nighttime pranks were not his concern. He must try to rest before his journey back to London. Tomorrow was an important day. Tomorrow, if all went to plan, he would take another step closer to Lydia.

Chapter 12

The moment the Bethlem clerk lifted his familiar bulging eyes and saw Thomas, he immediately reached for the bell to summon the guards. As soon as he did so, however, the doctor whipped Lupton's letter from his pocket.

"Before I am forcibly ejected, I would ask you to read this," he said, flourishing the missive.

The clerk arched his brow and looked at the anatomist skeptically. He snatched the paper and unfolded it as if it were a foul-smelling rag. Reading the contents quickly, he cleared his throat and looked up to meet Thomas's gaze. His usual scowl suddenly dissipated as he rearranged his features into a less threatening expression.

"Dr. Silkstone. Of course," he said grudgingly. "You wish to see Lady Lydia Farrell."

Thomas resisted the temptation to reply that of course he wished to see Lady Lydia and had been trying to do so, as the clerk knew only too well, for the past eight weeks or so. Instead he simply nodded emphatically to signify what seemed a small, but significant, victory. Yet he remained anxious, even when the clerk issued him a ticket that granted him access. He stared at the small piece of paper. It was as if he were going to see a matinee in Drury Lane. At least Bethlem's patients were now shielded from public view. Up until a few years ago, they were regarded as peep-show freaks. Now, thanks to a decision by the court of governors, they could at least be accorded a little dignity in their various states of madness. Scrutinizing the scrap of paper, he realized it granted him access not to a female ward, but to the principal's office. He was glad of it. Now he would be able to demand answers directly. He could insist on Lydia's release in front of the man who had the power to grant it.

Up ahead lay a great staircase. On either side were large iron grilles, one on the left that opened onto the men's gallery and the other to the women's. Thomas stood in front of the grille and took a deep breath. As he walked through this last door he sensed that his own descent into hell was about to begin; a hell peopled by harpies and viragos who looked at him quizzically, or hissed and spat at him, a place inhabited by scorned mistresses, betrayed wives, ranting priestesses, and malevolent witches. His guide on this disturbing journey was a female warder with a round, benign face and a large bosom. She smiled as she jangled her keys and opened the grille. Waiting ahead, she led Thomas into a long gallery that was as busy as the Bath Assembly Rooms.

"Don't be alarmed, sir," she assured him, seeing Thomas's apprehension. "They mean no harm, and those that do are locked safe in their cells."

Thomas followed the warder, taking in every detail of the scene as if it were one of Mr. Hogarth's paintings. Some of the women merely promenaded, talking among themselves, or to themselves in a few cases, while others lolled about on benches, their expressions dazed and unseeing. As he passed one, he heard snatches of gibberish, as if she were playing the Fool in *King Lear*. There were some who were addressing blank walls or doors they regarded as real people, while one or two sat on the floor, rocking to and fro, mumbling. A toothless crone chewed her words like victuals.

Despite an underlying babel and the odd slamming of doors, the atmosphere was much calmer than he had anticipated. The noise, although constant, was not discordant, and although there was a whiff of urine on the air, he found the general state of cleanliness to be acceptable.

To the female warder, this was a most natural state of affairs. The bunch of keys at her waist rattled with each step she took, but she seemed completely inured to the harmless chaos that surrounded her.

"God put lunatics on this earth to remind us that we are mere mortals," she told Thomas as she led him along the gallery. She did not even bother to look 'round when a patient tapped him on the back. He turned to see a young, elfin-featured woman, pale and drawn, with dark hair and large eyes. For a moment he was transfixed. His chest was robbed of breath. His tongue was hobbled in his mouth.

"Lydia?"

The young woman cocked her head like an inquisitive bird and smiled a knowing smile. The warder, conscious that she was no longer being followed, finally glanced back to see the inmate hold Thomas's hand to her cheek.

"Anna!" scolded the warder. Her tone was that of a governess reprimanding a child, rather than a jailer chastising an inmate. "Leave the gentleman alone." She shook her head. "You must forgive Miss Kent," she told Thomas, her double chin wobbling as she spoke. "Her fiancé's death made her so." Then, as she turned to continue along the corridor, she said something that took Thomas quite by surprise. "She has a look of Lady Lydia, does she not?"

The doctor had to agree. "Yes. Yes, she does," he replied.

"I be convinced that is why Miss Kent is drawn to her," she added.

"Drawn to her?" queried Thomas.

The warder nodded. "She won't leave her ladyship alone," she said. They walked on. Although he was well accustomed to the corridors of St. George's, this hospital set Thomas's nerves on edge. It was as if he had been asked to suspend all reality and rationality. After only a few hours in this madhouse, he could imagine even the sanest person might lose their grip on the everyday and commonplace. Routine and order seemed to have been left behind at the iron gate. His fears for Lydia and her condition grew with each step he took nearer the principal's office.

A set of double doors lay at the end of the gallery. The warder knocked and a man's voice called from inside.

"Come."

The warder flung open the doors and Thomas proceeded to enter a spacious room with a lofty ceiling and walls that were lined with portraits of eminent physicians. An elderly gentleman stood from behind a long table to receive him, nodding graciously as he did so. His flat nose was purplish in color and his cheeks veiny. Thomas noted him for a heavy imbiber.

"Dr. Silkstone." He shook Thomas's hand. "Dr. Angus Cameron, at your service. Welcome to Bethlem. Please." He gestured to a chair opposite him.

As he seated himself, Thomas watched Cameron settle into his chair once more, then proceed to reach for a snuffbox from his desk. In silence he took a pinch, then inserted it into first his left, then his right nostril.

"Snuff, Dr. Silkstone?" He thrust the box in front of Thomas. The doctor declined politely.

The name Cameron was familiar to him. He recalled the physician's treatise on mental illness, published only the previous year. A Scotsman by birth, he had come south as a youth and quickly established a reputation in his chosen field of disorders of the mind. Despite his affable manner, Thomas knew him to be an advocate of radical treatments for those afflicted by insanity.

"So you are come to see your erstwhile patient?" Cameron said, snapping shut the lid of his snuffbox.

Thomas was quick to correct him. "Lady Lydia will continue to be my patient just as soon as you release her, sir." He refused to be disarmed by the physician's easy mien. Caution would be his watchword.

Cameron sniffed and leaned back in his chair. "And what makes you think that her ladyship will ever be released?" The question, so sudden and brutal, took Thomas off guard.

The young doctor edged forward. "It must be clear to you, sir, that Lady Lydia is not mad, but a victim of circumstance." He almost said "a cruel plot" but checked himself. He knew that Cameron might well be in Sir Montagu's pay, or at the very least in his confidence.

The elderly physician began to finger some sort of journal that lay open before him. He scanned its tightly written lines. Without bothering to look up, he said, "Her ladyship is no longer confined to her cell. She may walk unfettered along the galleries now." His voice adopted a cheerful note.

Thomas looked at him askance. "Unfettered?" he repeated. "What have you done to her?"

Cameron's head jerked up. "Och! Calm yourself, sir!" He seemed indignant rather than frightened by the doctor's sudden outburst. Thomas, taking a deep breath, tried to compose himself. "'Twas for her own good. Her ladyship was most distressed on admission, but now she is settling in well," added Cameron. Yet his effort to placate his volatile visitor had little effect.

Thomas leaned over the desk. "I would see her as soon as possible, sir," he told him, his ragged voice unable to disguise his agitation.

Cameron nodded. "You will, sir. You will, but know this . . ." He shut the ledger with a deliberate thud and lifted his index finger threateningly in the air. "Madness depends as much on management as it does on medicine. It responds to coercion, restraints, and physical treatments."

Thomas felt the bile rise in his throat at the inhumanity of this statement. He feared even more for Lydia's physical wellbeing. "There are those who disagree most strongly with you, sir, on that point."

Cameron waved his hand dismissively. "Och! You are not here to talk polemics or discuss the latest treatises on mental health, Dr. Silkstone. You are here because I have consented for you to see your former patient." He put an odd emphasis on the word "former." His tone had switched from its initial civility to one of arrogance. He took another pinch of snuff and snapped shut the lid of his box with a deliberateness that reflected his changed manner.

"I'll be plain with you, Silkstone," he said, also leaning forward over his desk. "I am allowing this visit purely because of this letter from Lupton." He tapped the paper that lay beside him. "Her ladyship's mental state is delicate, and any sudden upsets might cause her to relapse." He reached for a small bell on the table and rang it. "Lady Lydia will be with us shortly," he said with a nod, as the plump warder appeared at the door.

An awkward silence swelled between the two men, and Thomas felt his stomach knot once more. The principal eased himself back in his chair for the wait, intent on making his visitor feel as uncomfortable as possible. Finally he could contain his ire no longer, and he broke the uneasy stillness. "Her ladyship is not mad. You know that, don't you, Cameron?"

The Scotsman's brow furrowed, and a look of puzzlement altered his features. Shaking his head he said, "I am afraid I am at a loss to understand your outrage, Dr. Silkstone. After all, it was you who signed her ladyship's committal papers."

The principal's words stunned Thomas. Momentarily he froze. His tongue cleaved to the roof of his mouth, as his brain tried to process what he had just heard.

"I signed the committal papers? What are you talking about?" His voice registered anger tinged with utter dismay.

Cameron fumbled with a leather wallet on his desk. "I believe I have them here," he said. "Ah, yes." He handed the doctor a sheet of paper. Thomas scanned the document. At the bottom were two signatures: One was Dr. Fairweather's; the other appeared to be his own. He threw it back down on the desk in disgust and leapt up, pushing his chair back so that it scraped loudly on the wooden floor.

"A forgery!" he cried. "I would sooner cut off my right hand than condemn Lady Lydia to stay here any longer." He raked his fingers through his hair and turned in thought. Sir Montagu Malthus and Lupton must have gained access to his letters to Lydia in order to fake his signature. He felt his mouth grow dry and his heart pound. Seconds later he switched back. "Has her ladyship seen this?" He picked up the signed sheet once more and brandished it in the air.

Cameron, clearly bemused by Thomas's display of furious indignation, nodded. "She is aware that you are one of the signatories, yes."

Thomas's shoulders drooped almost instantaneously, as if the whole world had suddenly fallen upon them. "She thinks I sent her here?" His incredulous voice was a loud whisper, addressed to no one in particular. He fixed Cameron with a glare. As he did so, there came a knock, and both heads turned.

"Come," called the principal.

Thomas watched as, at the far end of the room, he saw a small, slight figure take faltering steps through the open door. He could not be sure it was Lydia. The warder was at the woman's arm, supporting her. Forcing himself to check a great urge to run up to the woman, if indeed it was Lydia, and hold her, he watched every achingly slow step with growing alarm.

"What have you done to her?" He shot a look of incomprehension at Cameron, but the principal remained unrepentant. He, too, was watching the woman's deliberate and clearly bewildered progress toward them.

"Nothing more than a purge and a good bleeding. Both requisite to the cure of madness, Dr. Silkstone," came the glib reply.

As the woman drew to within a few feet of him, Thomas felt the blood drain from his own face as surely as if it had been drawn from his body. It was Lydia. Of that he was certain, but her cheeks and forehead were white and papery, and under her eyes were dark shadows. Of her lustrous chestnut hair there was no sign. She had been severely shorn, and what remained barely covered her scalp. What was more, her painfully thin frame was encased in a stiff white jacket with long sleeves. Thomas looked for her hands. He could not see them. Suddenly he realized with dismay that her arms had been crossed in front of her body and tethered by ties on the sleeves at the back. He flashed a look of horror at her and saw her brown eyes suddenly latch onto his. They stayed there for just a moment, but it was a moment in which hope flickered before her gaze swam away from him once more.

Terrified that Lydia might be lost to him, Thomas shot an angry glare at Cameron. "Why is she wearing this vile jacket?"

He heard the fury in his own voice, even though he had tried to suppress it.

The principal simply lifted his marbled features into the sly smile of a man who knew he had the upper hand. "For her own protection, Dr. Silkstone. 'Tis more humane than the usual shackles," he replied.

"Shackles!" Thomas repeated.

But Cameron refused to be riled. "May I remind you that her ladyship tried to take her own life once, Dr. Silkstone. She may attempt to do so again."

Thomas's silence acknowledged the truth of the principal's statement. Lydia's attempt to poison herself during her deep depression the previous year had only compounded her problems and reinforced Sir Montagu's case against her.

Cameron motioned the warden to seat his patient on a chair next to the anatomist, and she helped Lydia lower herself. Her movements reminded Thomas of an arthritic old woman whose joints pained her. He drew closer, his heart sinking with every beat.

"What have you done to her?" he asked incredulously. He jerked his head 'round, only to see the principal nodding knowledgably.

"Acceptance is one of the first stages of recovery, Dr. Silkstone," he said smugly.

"Acceptance?" replied Thomas. "It is clear to me that you, sir, have tortured her ladyship into submission."

Cameron feigned hurt. "Torture, sir, is a very strong word."

Thomas turned to Lydia once more. "You have chained her, bled her, locked her in a cell. If that is not torture, I don't know what is!"

Cameron shook his head. "On the contrary, sir. Everything we have done here for Lady Lydia has been for her own welfare."

Lydia, whose eyes had been moving slowly from Cameron to Thomas, cocked her head at an angle. Her reactions seemed slow and fogged, but Cameron's assertion appeared to jerk her into life. She fixed her gaze on Thomas as if he were a stranger to her; then, with rising alarm, as if her memory was returning in a rush, she reined herself back. Her breathing became labored and she tried to rise. Seeing her sudden apprehension, Thomas moved to calm her, stretching out his hand toward her, but she turned her shoulder toward him and shook her head.

"Lydia, it is I," he said. At first he did not want to sound too intimate in front of Cameron, but when she shook her head, he abandoned all protocol. "It is Thomas," he told her softly.

Yet instead of allaying her fears, his presence seemed only to inflame her. She switched 'round, her lips trembling. "Was it Lupton?" she asked, her voice as brittle as glass.

Thomas jerked back, shocked at her manner, but she continued in the same vein. "Were you jealous of him? Did you think he had taken your place in my affections and this is your revenge?" she asked him. Her voice quavered and her eyes were brimming with tears. "Is that why you put me in here?" She turned her head away, as if the very sight of him sickened her.

Unable to endure the onslaught any longer, Thomas rushed over to her, settling his hands on her shoulders. "I had nothing to do with this. It is not true, my lady. Whatever you have been told, it is a lie."

Lydia raised her reddened eyes to meet his. "Would my own father lie to me?" she asked.

Thomas frowned and lowered his voice, hoping Cameron would not hear. "What did you say?"

Lydia's shoulders heaved in a great sob. "Sir Montagu is my real father. That is what I wanted to tell you before, but—" She broke off.

Thomas suddenly remembered. It was true. She had been about to impart some news to him at Boughton after the lawyer's operation. Taking him by the hand, she had led him over to the window seat in the drawing room, but Howard had called him away. He frowned. "He is your father? He told you himself?" Thomas's words were barely audible, but Lydia kept her gaze on him and nodded. The scenario flashed through the doctor's mind. Thinking he was about to die, Sir Montagu must have confided the truth to her; then, when the procedure was successful, he had been filled with regret, fearing the implications of his admission. The secret was out, only now Malthus wanted it suppressed.

Thomas pulled back from her and straightened himself. "You have been cruelly treated, but believe me I will do everything in my power to see you are released as soon as possible." His glare snagged Cameron's. "Can you not see that her ladyship is a victim in all of this, here at the whim of Sir Montagu Malthus, and that your so-called treatment is a travesty, sir?"

Cameron remained calm. "The ability to manipulate can also be a symptom of madness, Silkstone," he said dryly. "I know of your feelings toward her ladyship, and she is able to abuse your"—he searched for the right word—"affection toward her."

Thomas strode toward the Scotsman. "Lady Lydia Farrell is my patient." He flung a finger behind him in Lydia's direction. "What you are doing is not only unwarranted, 'tis inhumane, and as her ladyship's physician, I must ask you to discharge her immediately!"

Still Cameron refused to be moved. Such scenarios were commonplace to him. How many husbands had come to him, asking him to declare wives insane, because they were either errant or barren, or both? Granted, this case had been slightly more complex—there was no cuckolded husband, no jealous lover—nonetheless, Sir Montagu Malthus's motives for wanting Lady Lydia Farrell put out of harm's way had been sufficient for him to pay ten crowns a month for her incarceration. The principal returned with a valid riposte.

"And what of her unprovoked attack on Mr. Lupton? I am told she flew into an hysterical rage and brought blows down on him." Cameron was staring at Lydia as he delivered his question with a chilling assuredness.

Lydia dropped her gaze and her lip trembled. "I must confess to that most shameful outburst," she said, "but it was not unprovoked. I—"

Cameron's hand flew up to signify he had heard enough. He turned to Thomas. "So, Dr. Silkstone," he said smugly, tenting his fingers. "By her own admission it is right that her ladyship is confined here. Can ye see that? Aye?"

Thomas shot Cameron another incredulous look. He felt wounded but not defeated. "This is not a hospital, but a prison, and you have convicted my patient without a trial," he protested.

The principal sucked in his cheeks and refused to be moved. "As I said, Dr. Silkstone, her ladyship is here for her own protection, as well as that of others, and you sanctioned it. She will remain as long as that is the case."

Thomas rose, grabbed his case and hat, and paused before the principal. "I shall not rest until her ladyship is free," he warned. He turned to look at Lydia.

Seeing all hope of her immediate release fade, Lydia wept, the tears cascading down her face. On his way to the door, Thomas bent over her and began to wipe her cheeks with his thumb, but she quivered and withdrew from his touch.

"No!" she snapped. "How can I trust you? You are like all the rest!"

Withdrawing his hand quickly, Thomas looked at her, horrified. Her harsh words sliced through him like a knife. For a moment it felt as if his world had imploded. He took a breath and tried to compose himself.

"I will have you out just as soon as I can," he told her. But his feigned words of comfort fell on stony ground and were lost amid Lydia's sobs.

Feeling both angry and humiliated, Thomas was escorted out of the hospital. His own soul was in as much turmoil as any Bethlem inmate's. As he strode out from the great portico, he reached into his pocket for his kerchief to dab his own eyes, which had, to his embarrassment, suddenly moistened. As he did so, he felt the cold silver of the locket that Lydia had given him as a keepsake after her mother's death. Retrieving it, he stood still, gazing at it in his palm, in the middle of the busy thoroughfare. People and carts pushed past, but for him, time stood still. Sir Montagu Malthus was Lydia's father. This was the reason he had seen fit to confine her, his illegitimate daughter, to a madhouse. Her son, Richard, was his rightful heir. Through the young earl, Sir Montagu could control not only his own estate, but Boughton, too. He would make the child his puppet. Suddenly it all fell into place: the dogged determination to keep him and Lydia apart at all costs, the hatred that Malthus had displayed toward him. This was the reason why the lawyer had put every obstacle in the way of their union. Now his darkest secret was exposed, it was clear that the lawyer would go to any lengths to suppress it. That was the reason it suited his purpose to lay the blame for Lydia's confinement at Thomas's feet. He sought to drive a wedge between them. If they were divided, Malthus could rule, and although the doctor was utterly loath to admit it, this despicable strategy, for the moment at least, seemed to have succeeded.

Chapter 13

Thomas knew there was no time to waste. He planned to hire a horse and head for Oxford that very morning. He needed to inform Sir Theodisius of Lydia's dire condition and of her extraordinary revelation that Sir Montagu Malthus was her real father. To his relief, however, he found there was no need to travel. Returning to his Hollen Street town house, on the outskirts of London, he found he had a visitor. As he entered the hallway he heard a familiar voice in the study and opened the door to find Sir Theodisius Pettigrew in conversation with Dr. Carruthers.

"Ah, Silkstone, dear fellow," the portly gentleman greeted him. "You have seen Lady Lydia! What news, pray tell!" From the half-filled glass by his side, Thomas could tell he had already been imbibing and that his spirits belied a mixture of anxiety and hope. Thomas knew that what he was about to tell Sir Theodisius would deflate any optimism. He knew, too, that he would be poor company until he could unburden himself. He was also aware that his findings at Bethlem would be better told sooner rather than later.

"I fear it is bad, sirs. There is something I must tell you," he said suddenly, entering the room. He wondered himself where the words had sprung from.

"Oh?" The coroner's forehead was already furrowed with a frown.

Thomas, choosing to remain standing, took a deep breath. "Before she was—" He broke off, searching for the right word. He wanted to say "kidnapped," or "captured," but in the end he simply said, ". . . taken away, Lady Lydia tried to tell me something that I think you both should know."

Sir Theodisius arched a wary brow. "Pray tell."

"What is it, young fellow?" urged Carruthers, leaning forward in his chair.

Thomas eyed both men intently, recalling the moment Lydia must have intended to divulge the shocking news to him in the drawing room at Boughton. "It was when Sir Montagu was so ill, before I operated on him last year."

"Yes," said Dr. Carruthers. "The aneurism."

Thomas continued hesitantly. "Her ladyship told me that he believed he was about to die. It was then that he confided in her."

"Confided what?" pressed the coroner.

"Sir Montagu told her that he is her real father." The words gushed from Thomas's mouth, like blood from a cut vein. "She tried to tell me before, but I had to attend an urgent meeting and remained ignorant until today. Malthus is Lydia's father." He repeated the statement again, as if to convince himself, as much as his stunned audience, that what he was saying was real. "Malthus is her ladyship's father."

The reaction from both men was slow to come, as if it needed to percolate up through their bodies before their mouths were spurred into action. Nevertheless, when their responses were forthcoming, they were decisive.

"By God's wounds!" thundered the coroner. He banged his fist on the table, sending his claret spilling.

Dr. Carruthers was more circumspect. "Well, well. I never!"

Thomas could see the news was having a devastating effect on the coroner in particular.

"It cannot be," said Sir Theodisius.

"I fear it is, sir," Thomas countered, "because when he recovered his health, he realized he had revealed too much."

The coroner slowly nodded. "And that is why he wanted

Lady Lydia locked away and silenced?" He spoke deliberately, as if he were putting together the pieces of a puzzle.

"Precisely," replied Thomas. "Sir Montagu and Lady Felicity had been lovers for years before she married Lord Crick, and they saw no reason to stop their liaison even after the nuptials."

Dr. Carruthers breathed deeply and clicked his tongue. "So that explains why he had always taken such a keen interest in Boughton's affairs."

"And why he does not want Lydia and me to marry. He intends to make young Richard his puppet and control the estate through him," said Thomas gravely. "Ever since Edward Crick's death, he has been scheming toward this end. This enclosure about which you speak would seem the next stage of his plan."

Sir Theodisius, his wine-flushed face now drained of its color, nodded. "Enclosure, yes," he said, as if forcing himself to return to the moment. "It makes more sense now." Then, shaking his head, he added: "My dear Lydia would be distraught if she knew what is happening." He fixed Thomas with a look of such great sorrow that the young doctor found himself forced to turn away for fear he might succumb to emotion.

"There is one more thing I must tell you, sir," said Thomas, steeling himself to deliver another unwelcome blow.

Dr. Carruthers quailed. "Surely not more bad news?"

The doctor felt his stomach churn as he turned once more to face the older men.

"I fear her ladyship has been told I signed her committal papers," he said. As he spoke, he felt an icy cold spread from the center of his chest.

The coroner's eyes flew wide open. "What? But that is preposterous!" His gaze latched onto Thomas's face. "Malthus again?" he asked, not expecting an answer.

"She no longer trusts me." There was a note of defeat in Thomas's voice.

Sensing him to be nearby, Carruthers reached out his arthritic old hand and patted his protégé on the arm. He knew that such a revelation would have come to Thomas as the deepest cut of them all. The room fell silent.

Chapter 14

Despite the curfew and the reading of the Riot Act on the common, the men of Brandwick still talked, only now they spoke in whispers. But more than that, some of them plotted. They huddled in doorways or in the porch of St. Swithin's, but on market days, when the village attracted farmers and traders from miles around, and their gatherings aroused no suspicion, they needed little excuse to congregate in the Three Tuns.

In the snug room, around the fire, before the murder, they had put the world to rights. Cradling pints of cheap gin, they would mull over the price of grain and the recent weather, and they gossiped about King George and about his wayward son and heir apparent. They spoke of horses and of women, usually in that order. But on this occasion, as over the past few days, the talk was of the killing and of enclosure.

Joseph Makepeace, filling his pipe as he spoke, peered up at Adam Diggott from under drooping lids.

"You 'ad a visit from the Boughton men 'bout the map-maker?" he asked, the leathery skin on his face as slack as an empty sack.

The brawny coppicer sat staring into the hearth, seemingly entranced by the dancing flames. He had taken his boots off to warm his chilled feet. Young Jake, forever fidgeting, sat at his side. Now Adam turned and nodded distrustfully.

"Aye," he replied.

"And?"

"What d'ya think?" He scowled. "I told 'em 'owt."

Will Ketch, his dog, Bess, curled up by the hearth, shook his head. "I 'eard that American doctor was up in Raven's Wood yesterday, sniffing around, 'e was. Zeb Godson took 'im to where it 'appened."

Diggott whipped 'round. "What?"

Ketch shrugged. "Offered 'im a guinea, 'e did."

There was a general consensus that any one of them would have done the same for that money, but Adam Diggott remained unsettled.

"That doctor knows what 'e's about," he warned. He'd heard reports after the Great Fogg that this American was a pushy one, always sticking his nose in where it didn't belong. "There could be trouble."

For a moment it seemed that those present caught their breaths, waiting for Adam Diggott's unease to explode into a rage, but his obvious anger was left to simmer, and Abel Smith, the bearded fowler, moved the conversation on.

"I see they've started felling for the fencing," he remarked, stroking his spiky stubble.

"'Alf the woodland'll be gone soon," lamented Josh Thornley. His tawny hair grew in odd tufts, like patches of twitch grass on poor soil, leaving some of his scalp almost bald. He sat with his son, Hal, who constantly wrung his hands, either because he was nervous or because he was cold. No one bothered to ask which.

"We'll not be able to gather the wool clumps no more for our bedding, nor find firewood," growled Ketch. He reached down to stroke his sleeping dog.

"I see'd some posts already stacked up over by Raven's Wood," added Smith.

"Putting the cart before the 'orse, isn't 'e, this new Boughton man?" jibed Makepeace, drawing on his pipe. But his pun did not even raise a smile. This was far too serious a matter.

"'E'll 'ave the commons fenced off before you can say Jack Robinson, and there ain't nothing we can do about it!" said

Smith. He emptied his tankard and plonked it on the table in front of him in an act of resignation.

"There's the meeting next week," Thornley said, his tone more positive than the rest.

"You think they'll listen to us?" sneered Ketch.

Adam Diggott remained fiery. "But what are we going to do about it?"

"Surely they'll give us something in return, like allotments?" chimed in Thornley. "They did that in Solwell."

Abel Smith's ale spurted from his mouth onto his beard as he let out a sudden laugh. "Believe that, you'll believe anything!" he exclaimed.

"Maybe as 'ow we need to show Boughton we mean business, so that they do right by us common folk," suggested Ketch.

"How d'ya mean?" asked Thornley, scratching one of his bald patches.

"We could show 'em we've got the upper 'and and that they can't mess with us," replied Diggott. He shot a glance at his bright-eyed son and nodded to him, as if to solicit his approval.

"Aye, but 'ow?" asked Makepeace, puffing thoughtfully on his pipe.

Diggott leaned forward. "We need a plan," he said conspiratorially.

The other men drew in, too, all except Abel Smith. He flattened his grimy palm in front of Diggott's face. "I want no part of it," he hissed, his words whistling through the gaps between his stained teeth.

But the coppicer's expression told him he had little choice. "Whether you like it or not, Abel Smith, you are in this up to your neck." He scowled, drawing his hands up under his chin. His words were delivered in a harsh, rasping whisper, so as not to arouse the attention of the other drinkers, but their meaning was plain. Whatever happened, they knew they must remain united in the face of their new enemy. Their livelihoods, and indeed their lives, depended on it.

Chapter 15

It was the night watchman, Walter Harker, who spotted them first. The curfew bell had sounded not an hour before, and he was patrolling the northern edge of the common later that same evening, when he saw something scurry toward the path. Guided by the light of his lantern, he was squinting into the darkness when he saw another shape darting across his view.

"Who goes there?" he called.

Before he received an answer, however, his eyes were drawn to a sudden flare of light, a bright cone aglow in the blackness. He was not sure how distant. All he knew was there was something ablaze.

Cupping his hands around his mouth, he began to yell. "Fire! Fire!"

Hearing Harker's cry, Adam Diggott emerged from his cottage nearby, buckling his belt. "What goes on?" he called.

The night watchman twisted 'round. "Fire!" he replied, pointing to the flare. "Call for buckets and pails!" He switched back and saw two silhouettes running away from him. "You there! Stop!" he yelled. He gave chase, heading toward the fulling mill. "Stop!" he called again.

The commotion had woken the fuller, Bart Bailey, who now appeared at the upstairs window of his cottage. He saw the old man lumbering up the slope chasing two sprightly silhouettes. Barging outside in his nightshirt, he also gave chase. He was much faster than Harker and had almost caught up with the two runaways when they split, one veering off into the woods and the other disappearing down toward the river. He chose to pursue the latter and, in the darkness, heard his quarry slipping down the bank. A clatter of stones followed. There was a faint cry. Edging his way carefully along the gulley, his way lit by the full moon on the river, Bailey spotted movement up ahead.

Suddenly a noise came from behind. He turned to see his son, Charles. "There!" cried the youth, pointing, and bounding off down the riverbank. In a moment there was another cry and the sound of a scuffle. The fuller arrived just in time to see his son deliver a blow to the fugitive's jaw.

"Hal Thornley!" cried Bailey in amazement. He rushed forward and helped heave the wretched youth up the bank. Bloodied and bowed, he had given up his fight.

Meanwhile, Walter Harker had been joined, then overtaken, by two men, leaner and fitter than he, who had entered the woods in pursuit of the second runaway. They brought with them dogs that quickly caught the scent and bounded over the bracken. Their prey was now in their sights. The men could see the branches snagging at the youth's shirt as he zigzagged from tree to tree seeking cover. He jinked and tacked for a few minutes more, but he was no match for the hounds or their masters, who had gained much ground. Each second brought them closer, until moments later, there was a terrible wail and they saw their target drop like a stone to the ground. The dogs pounced and set about their quarry until their masters called them off.

"What've we 'ere?" asked the first man, lifting his lantern.

The light illuminated the crumpled face of a whimpering youth.

"Well, if it isn't Jake Diggott," he said above the noise of the barking hounds.

The boy was clasping his leg and rocking to and fro in pain. "For pity's sake . . ." He pointed to his foot.

Peering down, the men could see that the boy's boot was held in the grip of a gin trap, its iron jaws clamped around the toe cap.

"You're lucky, boy," said the first man, bending down. "Could've taken your foot off." He sprung the trap's mechanism open with the blade of his knife and pulled out Jake's leg.

By this time Walter Harker had caught up. "You needs come with me, you young hooligan," he panted.

Meanwhile at the foot of the slope leading up to Raven's Wood, the fire still blazed. It was soon evident to anyone who bothered to investigate that it was the stack of fence posts that was alight. The flames leapt upward to the height of the weavers' cottages. The timber made a fine bonfire and lit up the night sky, so that the inferno could also be seen from Boughton Hall. A party of riders was hastily dispatched. When they arrived, they expected to find the villagers in a human chain, passing pails of water down the line from the nearby river. They were, however, sorely disappointed. No one had lifted a finger to put out the conflagration. Besides, the fire had consumed almost all the stakes and posts by the time the Boughton men got to it, so they let the flames finish their feast undisturbed.

Both boys were consigned to the village lockup that night. Their action was sheer folly, most would agree, but they were not without their sympathizers. Some even brought them drink and crusts of bread to ease their discomfort. Passing them through the narrow grille in the door, they offered words of comfort, sometimes even praise. "You did good, lads," some said. "Brave coves!" lauded others. Someone even gave up a blanket for the delinquents to share.

Jake's mother, Rachel, brought his coat. Pressing it through the bars, she peered at her son with tears running down her cheeks. She was a woman who wore her worries on her face. Her forehead was creased by a frown line, and crow's-feet fanned out from her eyes.

"Why?" she asked him, shaking her head. "You know you'll be punished for this. There'll be no getting off this time. Why?" Her voice dissolved into sobs.

Of course she needed no answer. She knew why. Every commoner understood the boys' motives and admired them, either overtly or secretly. While each youth blamed the other for their capture, both also took pride in the outcome of their escapade. A day in the pillory would be worth it, they told themselves.

Chapter 16

Thomas was in turmoil. Safely back in his laboratory, he did not know where next to turn. He thought about engaging a specialist in the new field of mental health, Dr. William Battie or John Monro, to prove that Lydia was completely sane. Yet, even if King George himself ruled that she should be released, he was sure Sir Montagu would find some way of circumventing a royal command. He thought, too, about organizing her escape. He could disguise her, smuggle her out in a laundry basket, employ any number of ludicrous ruses. And until he could marshal his thoughts coherently, they would remain just that, preposterous flights of fancy that had no hope of success.

For the moment, he would turn his attention to Mr. Turgoose's murder. Sir Theodisius was relying on him to solve the ghastly crime. At least ensconced in his own laboratory, he felt partly cushioned against the rigors of the outside world. Here were logic and order, reason and science. Here it was possible to reduce things to their component parts, to analyze, to dissect, to strip down compounds to their basic elements, to distill the essence of liquids, to deconstruct nature in all its forms.

Opening his case, Thomas took out the notes he had dictated to Professor Hascher during the postmortem on Jeffrey Turgoose and the ones he had made immediately afterward. As he did so, he noticed the glass phial containing the sample from the murder scene. Walking to the window, he held it up to the remaining light. Inside there was less than a salt spoon of gritty black powder. He had a good idea what it might be, but until he conducted tests on the substance, his mind would remain open. Nor did he know just what significance, if any, it bore to his investigation. He was certain, however, that it might be evidence. He set to work.

Unplugging the phial, he sniffed its contents. The tang of carbon stung his nostrils. He suspected that his initial thoughts, that this was some woodland fungus, were misplaced. This strange substance smelled and looked like soot. But if that were the case, how did it come to be in the middle of the wood, and so far from any charcoal kiln? He would test for it.

First he heated a small quantity of potassium nitrate in a flask on the trivet in the fireplace; then he added the grains of black powder. Sure enough they instantly began to dance inside the flask as the carbon reacted with the oxygen liberated by the chemical addition. The grains were most certainly charcoal, but how did they come to be sprinkled on a holly bush in the middle of a wood? Moreover, was this soot in some way connected to Turgoose's murder? There was no escaping it. The deeper he pried, the more unexpected his findings. His heart sank with the realization that in order to solve the murder, he would have to return to the scene of the crime. He needed to go back to Brandwick and to Raven's Wood.

Unfortunately for Jake Diggott and Hal Thornley, the Brandwick parish magistrate, Sir Arthur Warbeck, did not share the view of the commoners that the boys' act of arson was foolhardy rather than criminal. Nor did he regard setting fire to Boughton's fence posts as a childish prank. It was, in his judgment, a willful act of vandalism against the property of the Boughton Estate. At the assizes he sentenced Thornley to twenty-four hours in the pillory, but Diggott, whom he considered the mastermind behind the blaze, he ordered to be publicly whipped through the streets of Brandwick.

There were gasps in the gallery at the pronouncement. Rachel Diggott nearly fainted and had to be eased to her seat. Other women screamed that the boy was but thirteen years old. Adam Diggott swayed and grasped the wooden rail in front of him. But sentence had been passed. The following day it was carried out.

The pillory stood near the market cross in the center of Brandwick. In the past few months, it had been the preserve of the usual drunkards and ne'er-do-wells. The nature of their sojourn, although never enjoyable, depended largely on the villagers' generosity. Abe Diggott had spent the odd day clapped in the pillory for making a nuisance of himself when drunk on his usual tipple, and barely anyone bothered to toss a rotten tomato at him. When Josh Thornley broke his wife's jaw, however, it was a different matter. The women of Brandwick showed solidarity with their injured sister and pelted the culprit with rotten eggs and the refuse from the local slaughterhouse. The reek stayed around the village for the next few days.

Now it was Hal Thornley's turn to be cuffed and collared and to feel the yoke of the heavy beam bear down on his young neck. His wrists were secured and he was forced to stand, back bent, beside the market cross for all to see. Over the next day and night he would endure not just what the weather decided to throw at him, but what the villagers chose to hurl at him, too. He was not well liked in Brandwick, but even his worst enemies had to admire him for his plucky spirit. They did not, however, like the fact that he had played the innocent. He had been, he told the magistrate, encouraged by Jake Diggott—dragooned, coerced, and bullied by the coppicer's son into setting light to the woodpile. So as he stood in the pillory, oaths and curses were shouted at him, followed by the odd worm-eaten apple or pail of slops. But this humiliating consequence seemed as a carnival compared with Jake Diggott's fate.

At a few minutes before midday, the tramp of feet marching in time could be heard at the top end of Brandwick's High Street. A small platoon of militiamen had gathered to escort a cart, flanked by several outriders, toward the market cross. Bringing up the rear of the procession was the magistrate's carriage. Sir Arthur Warbeck, bedizened in all his judicial finery, was accompanied by Sir Montagu Malthus, glowering at the crowd from beneath hooded eyes. They had come to see the deed done. They did not have to wait long.

In the cart sat young Diggott, caged like an animal. The conveyance drew up at the market cross amid jeers and angry jibes from the crowd, directed at the militiamen. As they let the side down, the boy was pulled to his feet. His lips quivered at the command to step down, and the rope that bound his hands was jerked sharply, so that he fell forward and stumbled onto the cobbles. The executioner, come all the way from Oxford to perform the task, now leered over him and stripped him of his shirt. Without any covering, his ribs showing through his pale skin, the boy looked even more vulnerable. The executioner shoved him forward and tied his hands to the cart's tail. Through stinging tears, Jake searched in the crowd for his mother and father, and when he found them, he called to them. When they surged forward, however, the militiamen pushed them back roughly, leaving Rachel Diggott distraught. Adam Diggott, on the other hand, became violent. He started to thrash around, so that Zeb Godson and Will Ketch had to press upon him hard and tell him not to be foolish, unless he, too, wanted a good lashing.

The whole village had turned out to watch, not to rejoice in the grisly spectacle, not to take their macabre delight in the sight, but to support the boy as he began the ascent to his very own Calvary. He was to be whipped all along the High Street and out toward Raven's Wood, where the charred remains of the timbers he had burned served as a blackened reminder of his crime.

Silence fell upon the crowd as the executioner swung back his arm for the first strike. The whip sliced through the still air and seared the youth's skin with a long laceration. He let out a cry, followed by another and another each time the cowhide carved through his young flesh. No count was kept of the number of times the whip lashed, but the boy's anguish lasted a full two hundred yards. The loud lamentations of some of the women, his mother's included, only added to the agonizing chant.

When at last they released Jake Diggott from the cart tail, he fell to the ground like a heap of bloodied meat, his back cut to shreds. Some of the womenfolk hurried forward. Released by his anxious friends, Adam Diggott rushed toward the boy, too. Bending low, he looked in horror for a moment at the crimson fretwork of vicious cuts that crisscrossed his son's back. Then he lifted Jake's puckered face to his. Wiping away the boy's tears with his thumb, his father vowed there and then to avenge his suffering.

"They'll pay for what they've done to you, son," he growled. "By God, they will."

Chapter 17

Thomas did not return to Brandwick village straightaway. Leaving London the previous day, he had stayed once more in Amersham. On the last leg of his journey he had turned off the Oxford road and headed up to Raven's Wood. He wanted to investigate not only the scene of the murder but the old ruins, too. He had been musing on the lights he had seen the other night from his window in the Three Tuns and wished to pursue a new line of inquiry. Perhaps, he told himself, there was a connection between illicit activities in the wood and the surveyor's murder. Until and unless he was able to speak with the surveyor's assistant, James Charlton, and he very much doubted he ever would, he would have to rely on his own intuition.

The steep slope was laced with a fretwork of pathways, well used by men, horses, and carts. During the day parts of the woodland were busy with the sound of industry—the crackle of wood burning in the charcoal kilns or the rasping of the sawyers' saws. In his native homeland of Pennsylvania, man held the vast expanses of forest that covered the landscape in awe. Here, however, it seemed that Englishmen had the desire to tame nature and make it their own. Its riches were commodities to be traded. In their eyes every oak was a ship's timber, every elm a dining table, every walnut tree a chest of drawers.

As he pressed on, he suddenly became aware of a low droning sound and realized it was the rush of fast-flowing water that filled his ears. He could not see the river. It was still obscured by the trees, but he could hear it. It drew him toward it. Making his way nearer the gushing rumble, he soon came to the edge of a steep cliff. It gave him a magnificent view: He could see the river as it tumbled down from the highest point in the forest, cutting its way through a shallow gorge. Pulling up his horse, Thomas peered down. The water was still high after the winter snow-melt. It powered the fulling mill at the head of the valley. The sight lifted his spirits a little, until he remembered that when the woods were fenced off it would no longer be available to all. He turned his horse.

Along the forest path he went, his mind still mired down in the resentment he felt toward Lupton. The beauty of the wood-land seemed to be fading the deeper he went. Oaks and beeches and poplars gave way to more firs, their dark, brooding towers masking the sun. Suddenly he became aware of a change in the dappling of the light to his right. Looking 'round he saw the ruins of an old manor house. He recalled that Lydia had spoken of it, telling him that it once acted as a garrison for Oliver Cromwell's troops in the civil war more than one hundred and fifty years before. She said it had suffered severe damage at the time and had fallen into disrepair. The villagers had helped themselves to most of the stone and wood, crawling over it like busy ants, to build their own homes. Now all that remained was a ghostly footprint on the landscape. Here and there a jagged column might remain, like a stubborn tooth rooted so deep that it refused to budge. A mullioned casement was draped with swathes of ivy and framed a view of coppiced trees. There was a melancholy grace and beauty about it. He suddenly thought of Boughton Hall. Without Lydia, he only hoped it would not suf-fer the same fate.

He rode up to the ruin and tethered his horse to a young tree that had grown at an angle through a broken window. He had little idea of his bearings and he wondered how far from the murder scene he might be. Nevertheless, for now, he felt it of lit-tle consequence. This had to be one of the highest points in the wood, and if lights had been lit here, he may well have seen them from his room at the inn. He began to scrutinize the area for signs of recent human activity. Working methodically, he decided to examine within a twenty-yard radius of the ruin. With his eyes fixed firmly to the ground, he started to pace the circumference. In less than half an hour he had moved to within a yard of the curtilage of the old manor, and it was there, on the mossy earth, that he spotted the odd flakes, spilled near the outer wall. He bent down and picked up some of the strange brown fragments. They appeared to be shredded leaves, but it was only when he smelled them that he realized what they were.

"Tobacco," he said out loud. The sound of his voice prompted a rustle of leaves, and for a moment, his heart missed a beat, until he saw a squirrel suddenly scurry along a branch and run off. This was an eerie place. He could understand why the landlord had told him no one would accompany him into the wood, yet the forest gave work to so many. He resumed his own travail, his eyes latching onto every blade of grass, every leaf in the immediate vicinity, to see if he could find any more shreds of tobacco. Sure enough, he soon found more, much more; a small, thin trail of it led up toward the wall and continued on the other side.

Taking a cotton bag from his pocket, Thomas began to gather up the flakes. In places there was but a sprinkling; in others it had fallen in small heaps. As he collected the shreds, it suddenly occurred to him that a sack must have burst to leave such an amount. He kept his eyes on the trail of flakes until he came to what seemed to be a dead end: a broken-off column of stone, no more than a foot high, where the trace stopped suddenly. Around it tufts of grass grew, but on closer inspection he saw that there was a patch that had been recently flattened. Bending low, he grasped the column with both hands and slowly but surely tried to pull it toward him. It resisted at first but then yielded, causing Thomas to fall back with the effort.

When he picked himself up, however, he was rewarded with an intriguing sight—what appeared to be a trapdoor. Taking a deep breath, Thomas tugged at the large metal handle in the center. To his relief, although the door protested loudly, it opened easily enough. Peering into the gloom below, he could make out a ladder that led into what seemed to be an old cellar. He lowered his head into the mouth of the opening and blinked away the darkness. It took only a few seconds for his eyes to adjust to the light, and even then he could not see much, but he could certainly see enough.

Ranged along the nearest wall were wooden casks and barrels, piled high beside large wooden chests and bulging sacks. He craned his neck and strained his eyes. Could it be that he saw the word "Tea" printed on one of the crates? Here was his proof. The tobacco he had collected was not destined for the pipe of a passing traveler who had fumbled with his pouch and dropped a few flakes. This tobacco was contraband, smuggled before it was smoked. Tea, too, carried a hefty excise tax, as well as gin and brandy. There was much profit to be gleaned from the illegal sale of all these goods. Could it be that Mr. Turgoose and his party had inadvertently stumbled across this illicit stash and the surveyor had paid for the discovery with his life? The theory sounded plausible, but the only people who could verify it—Charlton and the guide—remained at Boughton Hall. It suited Malthus to keep the villagers under suspicion, and from what he had witnessed, there was no way of telling whether this smuggling racket was the work of locals or outsiders.

Suddenly there was a flapping overhead. Thomas looked up to see a large black bird settle on a branch nearby and remembered the words of the stable lad. He had warned of the Raven. Mayhap this was the scoundrel's hideout. Questions whirled around in his head like an eddy of leaves, but very few answers presented themselves to him. Nevertheless, he had evidence to prove that criminal activity occurred in the ruins. Armed with his samples of tobacco, he decided to make for Brandwick before the rest of the day's light was lost to him. His return to the scene of Mr. Turgoose's murder would have to wait.

Once more, to Mr. Geech's great surprise, Thomas found himself back at the Three Tuns, being shown into his usual room.

No sooner had he climbed the stairs, however, than the lank-haired stable lad bounded up behind him and appeared at his door.

"Dr. Silkstone, sir," he began breathlessly. "There's Mistress Diggott downstairs for you. She says she needs you."

Thomas nodded thoughtfully. From the boy's tone, the matter seemed urgent.

Picking up the medical case he had only just laid on the table, Thomas followed the youth immediately as he hopped down the stairs. A woman was waiting for him. Her dark hair peeped from her cap to frame a face that bore the familiar lines of want and worry.

"Oh, Doctor, will you come?" she pleaded. "'Tis my son, Jake."

Young Jake Diggott had lain on his belly for the past two days, barely able to move, as the fever raged. They had carried him home after the whipping and rubbed his wounds with salt to stop corruption, but still the ague came, and his mother was beginning to fear for his life. She had bathed the cuts with cold water, but they still wept as much as she did every time her son cried out in pain.

Old Abe Diggott had taken his grandson's punishment hard, too. He'd been so stricken with grief that he'd been unable to join Adam in the coupe since the whipping. He simply sat in his bentwood chair by the hearth. Gin was his only solace. He kept it by him in a large brown earthenware flagon and drank it as if it were springwater.

"'Tis the only thing that eases my pain," he would moan to anyone who would listen.

That evening Rachel had been standing over the stewpot when Adam returned home from the wood.

"The boy any better?" he asked as soon as he stepped over the threshold.

His wife wiped her hands on her apron and shook her head. Adam walked over to the cot where Jake lay. Gently he lifted the covering over the wounds. A crust had not yet formed and his savaged skin still oozed like a swamp. Every time Adam looked at his son he felt the rage well up inside him. He turned away and kicked the wall. A clump of plaster fell away and crumbled on the ground like stale cake.

It was then Rachel knew she had to act. She had seen the American doctor pass their cottage as he rode down the track from Raven's Wood not an hour before. She understood that her husband remained wary of the colonist, even though she knew him to be a good man, so she slipped out of the house as he dozed with his father by the fire, to ask the doctor to ease her son's pain. He had consented and now stood with her in the cottage.

"Dr. Silkstone is here to help us," announced Rachel. She spoke as if to reassure her menfolk.

Adam Diggott leapt up from his chair and stood to attention, although the angry look he flung his wife did not escape Thomas's notice. Such behavior made him aware that while he might have been a physician, he was first a stranger, and a foreigner to boot.

"I understand your son has been flogged, Mr. Diggott. May I see his wounds?" he asked. "There will be no charge," he added. For a moment there was a stunned silence, until the coppicer bowed his head in a show of both gratitude and acquiescence.

"Thank you, Doctor," he replied.

Relieved at her husband's assent, Rachel guided Thomas toward the cot where the boy lay prone. Damp cloths covered his flayed skin, but they did little to mask the smell of putrescent flesh.

Husband and wife exchanged glances across the room as Thomas gently peeled back the makeshift dressing. Adam clenched his jaw and moved toward the bedside.

"He were whipped through the street for firing a stack of fence posts, Doctor," he said, staring at his son.

Thomas frowned and shook his head. So Malthus's barbarity extended to children now, he told himself. Crouching low, he examined the suppurating wounds. The lacerations were deep, administered with a great force, he surmised. Clearly no allowance was made for his age or strength. The young skin was gouged and puckered into great welts from the neck down to the coccyx. A foul-smelling, watery ooze seeped from the lesions.

Opening his case, Thomas took out a jar of aloe vera unguent. He had come to swear by it since he first used it in the treatment of infected wounds in London.

"Now, Jake, I am going to smear some ointment on your back," he said softly. The boy grunted in reply and shuddered as Thomas began applying the cooling syrup, but he soon quietened as the soothing balm began to take effect. Thomas then covered the wounds in gauze. Next the doctor brought out a jar of willow bark. Knowing it to contain healing properties, he sprinkled the dried flakes into a flask of boiled water and urged the boy to drink it.

"The fever should be gone in the next few hours," Thomas said, finally rising from the bedside.

He had repacked his medical case and begun to walk to the door when he caught sight of old Abe Diggott, sprawled in his bentwood chair. He threw a questioning look at Rachel.

"He is unwell?" asked Thomas.

Rachel regarded her father-in-law, a despairing look in her eyes.

"He's sharing the boy's punishment," she said plainly. "All he's done since the whipping is drink gin to ease his own pain." Her eyes wandered to the earthenware flagon at his side.

Thomas followed her gaze, then looked at the old man, half-awake, half-asleep, a string of saliva spooling from the corner of his mouth.

"Drinks the stuff like mother's milk, 'e does," chimed in Adam, joining them.

All eyes had turned to the stupefied old man, as if he were some curiosity to be pitied.

It was Rachel who changed the subject. "We cannot thank you enough, Doctor," she said, as if wishing to draw Thomas's visit to a close. She gestured him to the door.

Adam, standing at her side, managed a flicker of a smile. "We are grateful to you, sir," he said.

Thomas nodded in reply and turned to go. Just as he did so, however, Adam called him back. "Is there any news of 'er ladyship, Doctor?" he asked.

Taken aback by such a question, Thomas stopped in his tracks. It was a mark of the affection the villagers felt for Lydia that her well-being should concern them even when their own futures were in jeopardy. He thought of her pained expression, her body sheathed in the restraint. The inquiry only served to strengthen his resolve. As he turned to face the coppicer, he felt a sudden surge of energy.

"I intend to bring her back here to Boughton, Mr. Diggott," he replied, adding: "She will be home soon."

Before returning to the Three Tuns down along Brandwick High Street, Thomas made his way to the apothecary's shop. As well as replenishing his supply of gauze, exhausted in the treatment of young Diggott, he wished to pay his respects to Mr. Peabody. The little man, who seemed to be in a continual state of anxiety, had been most helpful to him during the Great Fogg. He found him behind the counter, as active as a weevil in a sack of flour.

"Dr. Silkstone," Peabody greeted the doctor as he walked in the door. The familiar film of perspiration that always added a sheen to his face was still evident.

"Mr. Peabody," said Thomas with a smile. The apothecary was occupied labeling various jars. "I see you are busy, as usual."

Peabody paused for breath in an exaggerated gesture, his shoulders slumping. "If there is a complaint, Doctor, then the people of Brandwick will suffer from it."

Thomas understood his meaning. There were many, especially those better off in the village, who worried themselves unduly over their bowel movements or their occasional aches and pains.

"At least the noxious fog has lifted," said Thomas.

The apothecary nodded. "Now 'tis bellyaches and gripes that ail them," he mumbled, resuming his labeling.

"Bellyaches and gripes?" repeated Thomas.

"Yes," nodded the little man. "And nausea, among the men in particular." He took his kerchief from his pocket and mopped his brow.

"And you know of no especial cause of these symptoms?" pressed Thomas.

The apothecary paused, then shook his head. "I can't say I do, Doctor. But 'tis a sickness that grows daily." He palmed his hands onto the counter as if to draw an end to that line of conversation. "Now, sir, how may I serve you today?" he asked.

Chapter 18

It was Mistress Geech, the landlady of the Three Tuns, who saw to Thomas's needs that evening. She was a cheerful, bawdy sort of woman, popular with the locals. A strand of auburn hair had worked its way loose and hung down from beneath her white cap, giving her a slightly wanton look as she stood behind the bar. Thomas did not know whether that was intentional or not. All he cared about was being left alone in his room to read and to think. He hoped sleep would follow. He ordered a plate of cold cuts and a tankard of ale.

"Early to bed, eh, Doctor?" asked the landlady cheekily.

Ignoring the obvious innuendo, Thomas nodded. "It has been a challenging day," he replied with a tired smile.

"Been up to Raven's Wood again, have we?"

Thomas shot her a curious look. "How . . . ?"

She gave a throaty giggle. "Get to know all sorts here, Doctor," she told him with a wink, adding enigmatically: "The woods have eyes and ears."

Thomas found this last remark somewhat unnerving, although he hoped he did not show it in his face. He took the opportunity to pry deeper. "Yes, I came across an old ruin, quite by chance," he said, watching for any reaction. "Most enchanting," he added. He noted that her eyes slid away for a fraction of a second, before returning to meet his gaze.

"Well, I hope you'll be comfortable here," she told him cheerily, bobbing a curtsy behind the desk. Thomas felt her eyes follow him as he began to ascend, and he even heard what he thought was a heavy sigh, as if she were relieved that he was out of the way for the rest of the evening. He suspected he knew the reason.

In a small outhouse just off the inn's courtyard, Peter Geech was holding up a flask to the lamplight. He'd had great hopes of the new still. He had bought it last year, but the liquid it produced was on the cloudy side. Flattening his thin lips, he clucked like a hen; then after a moment, he shrugged. The murkiness would be an issue for the more genteel sort. They liked their gin, if indeed they liked it at all, to be clear. But he'd mixed his with a measure or two of powdered chalk to lessen the effects of the turpentine. The last thing he wanted was a death on his hands. His gin was a slow pickler, not a poison, as such, although many a regular with a sore head would dispute it. But this latest batch would be passable. He'd just make sure he brought it out late into the evening when most of the punters were well into their cups anyhow and too far gone to notice.

He and his stable lad, Aaron Coutt, would be working well into the early hours. The copper had only just got up to heat and they'd fallen behind. He had left it to his wife and Molly, the serving maid, to round up the last stragglers in the taproom. Mistress Geech had a fine left foot and had been known to kick a man ten paces down the street when minded to. She would clear up the tankards and lock the doors, then join him as soon as she was able in the outhouse to lend a helping hand. This was where he concocted what he called his special mix. His wife and most others called it mother's ruin or mother's milk, depending on their taste. Everyone else called it fire water.

The room was steamy and the windows were misted, which suited his purpose. Working by the light of a couple of lamps, Coutt was pounding the mash for a second batch. Geech watched him run the back of his hand across his forehead to wipe away the sweat. It was tough work, pulping the barley malt. He, meanwhile, prized open the lid of a small cask and peered inside. The vapor wafted up and hit him full in the face, instantly making him splutter and gasp for breath. His eyes began to water and he flapped the fumes away with his hand. Such discomfort, nevertheless, brought a smile to his lips. He knew this would be a good batch.

Careful not to spill a drop, he poured the contents of the flask into the still's condenser and opened the valve. On a square of muslin before him sat a mixture of leaves and seeds: an unappealing pile of detritus from the woodland floor, beechnuts and acorns. He'd long ago given up on using the magic ingredients that transformed the base liquid into a worthy liquor: cardamom, coriander, orrisroot, and lemon peel. Such luxuries were far too expensive and were never appreciated by his clientele. So now he simply mixed beech mast with a dash of powdered chalk and no one was the wiser. The quality of the flavor seemed the last thing to bother his customers. All that interested them was the speed with which oblivion settled upon them, dulling their brains to the cold or hunger or scurvy, or whatever other ill pained them.

He poured in the token crushed juniper berries and the rest of the ingredients and looked at the mixture longingly. He could do with a good tipple himself right now, if he didn't value his guts so much. Business was brisk and he was tired. Ever since the new steward had been installed at Boughton and the rents had gone up, the villagers seemed to look to their bumpers for comfort. How did the saying go? One man's meat is another man's poison. How true, he mused. He was chuckling to himself when he heard footsteps. They were light on the cobbles, but hurried. The latch lifted quickly and in came his wife. He could see that her pretty plump face was sullied by a scowl.

"What is it, my precious?" He put down his flask and walked over to her, his arms outstretched.

Remaining flattened against the door, she regained her breath. "You was right," she panted.

Coutt stopped mashing and looked toward his mistress.

Geech's brow creased. "And?"

"He were up in Raven's Wood. I'm sure he knows something."

Geech, however, seemed not in the least bit concerned. He turned and pulled the stopper from a bottle that rested on his table. This was from a quality batch, the sort he reserved for himself and his friends. Pouring the relatively clear liquid into two pots, he handed his wife one, but she remained on edge.

"What if he finds out? What if he calls the customs men?" Her imagination was running away with her.

"Now, now, my lovely," soothed her husband. "Have no fear. We are beyond the reach of the law, remember?" He drew his wife close to him and hugged her just a little tighter than she found comfortable.

Chapter 19

As the coach bounced and lurched its way back to London, Thomas stared down at the palm of his hand. In it he held the silver locket that Lydia had given him all those months ago. He remembered how he had been riding down Boughton's drive with a heavy heart. He had not known when, or even if, he would see her again, when Will Lovelock, the carrot-haired groom, had come running after him. Gasping for breath, he had panted out his message. Her ladyship wanted Thomas to have the locket as a keepsake. He had slipped it into his pocket and carried it with him ever since. Now, however, he knew she would take it back if she could. She felt he had betrayed her, and knowing that she thought him so utterly dishonorable hurt more than any scalpel ever could. That was why he could stay in Brandwick not a day longer. Adam Diggott's inquiry about Lydia kept repeating itself in his head. It had jolted him back to his own pain. He needed to return to London. His investigation into the surveyor's murder would have to wait. So, early the very next morning, after a near sleepless night, he had ridden to Oxford and from there had taken the next available coach for the capital.

Only four days had passed since Thomas's last visit to Bethlem Hospital, yet, once again, the bulging-eyed receptionist was being exceptionally abstruse.

"Lady Lydia Farrell?" The clerk looked down the list in a ledger, as he had so many times before, and as on previous occasions he cleared his throat. Thomas was preparing himself for another rejection, so the response that came this time was wholly unexpected.

"She is not here, sir."

The words had barely left the man's lips before Thomas felt the room spin. "What do you mean she is not here?"

The clerk looked up imperiously. "Precisely what I say, Dr. Silkstone. Her ladyship left us two days ago."

"But this cannot be." His initial bewilderment started to give way to anger. He felt it rising in him. He clenched his fists in an effort to remain calm. "Let me see."

The clerk obligingly slid the ledger across the desk toward Thomas and pointed at an entry next to Lydia's name. It read: *Transferred.*

"*Transferred,*" Thomas read aloud. "What does this mean? Where has she been taken?"

With a tilt of his head and a smug smile, the clerk replied, "I am not at liberty to say, sir." There was a certain swagger in his manner as he retrieved the ledger with a flamboyant gesture. He had the upper hand, and his arrogance unleashed Thomas's fury.

"Where is Dr. Cameron?" His balled fist thudded on the desk, causing the clerk to shudder. "I would speak with him. Now!" He banged the desk again.

The clerk rose warily, backing away from Thomas. "I am to tell you that Dr. Cameron is away. You are to leave now, Dr. Silkstone," he said, tugging at a cord.

Within seconds the same thugs who had forcibly ejected him before appeared once more and went through their ruffians' routine. Yet again Thomas found himself being marched through the gardens toward the main gate. A few of the patients were being escorted 'round the grounds. Some sat on benches. These were the inmates regarded as posing no threat either to themselves or to others. Perhaps they had endured some mental breakdown and their faculties had temporarily deserted them. Perhaps they had acted rashly out of a moment of passion and lived to regret it. There were so many ways to madness, thought Thomas as the main gates loomed up ahead. And for a moment, his outrage was so great that he felt himself poised on the brink of it himself, when suddenly a vision broke into his thoughts. To his left he fancied he could see the elfin-featured woman who had so reminded him of Lydia. She was out walking with an attendant. He recalled her name.

"Anna!" he cried.

Clearly riled by such impertinence, the guards jostled Thomas on, yet, ignoring his vulgar escorts, the young woman broke away from her nurse and approached him.

"Sir! Sir!" she called to him. She seemed agitated and, despite the presence of the guards, snatched at his hand.

"Where is she, Anna? What have they done with Lydia?" he yelled as she ran alongside him like a faithful dog.

"Shut it, will ya?" one of the guards warned him.

Undeterred, Anna looked up at Thomas with large, dark eyes. "She's gone," she said breathlessly.

"Where did they take her, Anna?" He dragged his feet so that the guards were forced to take all his weight. "I can find her if you tell me."

Suddenly her eyes widened at the prospect of seeing her friend again. For a split second she gave Thomas hope that she knew where Lydia had been taken. He held his breath. But then her expression changed to one of bewilderment.

"Where did she go? I must look for her!" she pined.

She broke away, shaking her head, and began ambling off down the path, calling Lydia's name.

Chapter 20

The bell of St. Swithin's tolled the curfew. It was seven o'clock and the sun had set only minutes before. Doors were bolted and windows shut. The streets of Brandwick were deserted, save for the odd stray dog or contemptuous cat that flaunted the magistrate's edict. Nobody was allowed out in the evening until the surveyor's murderer had been caught. Nicholas Lupton had made the order and the local magistrate had sanctioned it. Until the perpetrators of the most heinous crime against the commissioner were apprehended, all villagers would be confined to their homes after dark. No man, woman, or child was granted leave without express permission and only then in the case of life or death. Evil was abroad in Brandwick once more, and suspicion festered like untreated sores among the villagers. Neighbors gave one another sly glances and women doubted their husbands, but they all harbored the guilty feeling that the surveyor and his man only got what they deserved. They'd no right to measure and map and apportion land as they saw fit; land that had belonged to the village since before the days of French William.

Nevertheless, the general feeling was fearful rather than angry, curious rather than belligerent. What they'd heard were rumors, gossip, tittle-tattle. But there was no smoke without fire—any charcoal burner would tell you that—and if the worst came to pass and an Act of Enclosure was sanctioned by Parliament, then there was nothing to be done.

The watchman, Walter Harker, was charged with enforcing the curfew. He had allowed Widow Treacher to deliver Susan Thornley of her fourth child when she went into labor past midnight, and he had sanctioned the Reverend Unsworth's presence when old Clem Widginton began to fade rapidly in the early hours of a Tuesday morning and wanted to prepare to meet his maker. Other than for those most pressing circumstances, no one had been allowed to leave their dwellings after nightfall. Or so it was said.

Just why Abe Diggott chose to break the curfew that evening was not immediately apparent. It was generally thought that he must have been in his cups, that the gin must have got the better of him yet again. Ever since his grandson had received the lash, he had been acting in a peculiar manner, raucous and confused by turns. His dull pallor was most evident and his weight loss was clear for all to see.

"Who's there?" asked Walter Harker, making his way up the High Street, his lantern in his hand. He saw a shadow moving from cottage to cottage and heard a footfall. His cudgel drawn, he ventured closer, only to find Abe Diggott cowering near a wall.

"What you doin'?" queried Harker, grabbing the old man by the shirt and hoisting him up. It was then that he saw the earthenware flagon in his hand.

"'Twas empty," said the coppicer hoarsely, pointing to the flagon.

"And you went to the Three Tuns to get it filled again?" said Walter Harker, nodding. He leaned closer and sniffed at the old man's breath. "You've had enough already this evening," he told him stiffly, relieving him of the flagon. Taking him by the arm, the constable shook his head. "Don't you know there's a curfew? If Lupton's men find you, there'll be hell to pay, you old fool," he chided.

Abe Diggott came quietly. He seemed not to understand, but obeyed meekly as Walter Harker led him up the High Street, back toward his cottage at the foot of the slope that led to

Raven's Wood. His steps were faltering and once he staggered and had to right himself against a post, but they made steady progress. The fulling mill and the nearby cluster of cottages had just come into view when the sound of horses' hooves splashing through muddy puddles could be heard. Walter Harker turned to see two men on horseback approaching through the gloom. As they drew close, he recognized them as Lupton's sidemen, all brute force and brawn.

"What you got here, then?" called one of them, pulling up his mount beside the constable.

Harker sketched a smile. He identified the man by his flattened nose. He knew him to be the prizefighter, Seth Talland. He also knew he had to make light of old Diggott's transgression.

"A straggler. The old fool's pissed as a newt. Couldn't find his way home." He slapped Abe Diggott playfully on the back and the old man lurched forward, nearly falling. "Look at him, see? I be taking him to his bed," he said laughingly.

Talland, however, did not see the humor in the incident.

"Not so fast," he called as Harker turned to resume his journey. "'E's broken the curfew." The constable stopped in his tracks. "There's a price to pay for that."

Harker wheeled 'round. "The man's done no harm," he complained.

"How can you be sure?" came Talland's riposte. His companion nudged his horse forward now, so that the two of them towered over the constable and his charge.

"I've known Abe Diggott for a good forty years and I know he's no murderer, if that's your meaning," replied Harker.

"You think so, do you?" growled the prizefighter. "Let's see about that, shall we?"

The constable frowned. "What do you mean?"

At that point, Diggott staggered once more and perched himself on a nearby tree stump. "Home," he moaned.

"Yes, old man," said the other sideman gleefully. "Show us where you live, eh?!"

"There's no need—" interjected the constable.

"Show us!" barked Talland, pointing to the cosh that hung from his belt to show he meant business. "Hurry!" he cried.

So with renewed vigor, Walter Harker crooked his arm through Abe Diggott's and half dragged him the fifty yards or so up the track to his cottage. Talland rode at their side, the other sideman behind, corralling both men like sheep, and it was the clatter of hooves that alerted Adam Diggott. He had only just realized that his father was missing and was about to break the curfew himself to search for him when he heard the approaching horses. Opening the shutters he looked out just in time to see the men dismounting. Seconds later one of them was shouldering the door and bursting into the cottage.

Rachel, wiping supper dishes, screamed. Jake, still lying in his cot, moaned.

"What the . . . ?" cried Adam, standing stunned by the door.

Talland and the other thug hustled the old man into the cottage, where he crumpled like a sack of old rags against the wall. Walter Harker stayed close by him, his face like thunder.

"We have authority to search this dwelling," said Talland, hands on hips, the cosh clearly visible as it dangled from his belt.

"What for?" protested Adam. He cast a look at Harker, but it was all the constable could do to shake his head helplessly and shrug.

Without a word, both sidemen marched into the room and began to overturn the few sticks of furniture there were; three chairs and two stools were sent skittering across the earth floor. Talland pulled out drawers in the dresser, emptying the contents where he stood. The other man, thickset and swarthy, went over to the cot at the far side of the room.

"What are you doing?" shouted Adam, remonstrating with the men. "What are you looking for?" He followed them toward where Jake lay.

The swarthy man, rifling through bedcovers and causing the

boy to cry out, turned at Adam's question. "This," he said. In his hand he held up a flintlock pistol like a trophy.

"And this," announced Talland, emerging from the door of a second room, brandishing a large gold pocket watch.

Adam Diggott's jaw dropped open and his eyes bulged at the sight. "No. No, it cannot be!"

Talland moved forward and stood looking down on Abe Diggott as he mumbled and shook in the corner. Bending low, he and the other sideman heaved the old man up; then he clamped his hand on his bony shoulder. "Abe Diggott, I arrest you for the murder of Jeffrey Turgoose," he declared.

The old drunk shook his head. A pewter plate Rachel had been holding fell from her hands and clattered on the floor. And, as if the noise helped him gain a little clarity, Abe began to protest his innocence.

"No. I didn't kill no one! Tell them, Adam!" he shrieked. He tried to stagger over to his son, but the sideman held him fast. Adam moved closer to his father and grabbed the old man by the arm, but the swarthy brute struck him in the face, sending him hurtling to the floor. They pulled the old man's arms behind his back, and he cried out in pain as they tied his hands securely.

Tightening the knots, the other sideman lowered his lips to his prisoner's ear. "Sir Montagu will be pleased to see you," he growled.

By this time Adam was on his feet once more. The sidemen swapped glances.

"Why don't we take the other one, too?" suggested the swarthy one.

Suddenly Abe Diggott was shoved to one side like a discarded sack, and the two sidemen lunged toward Adam.

"No!" screamed Rachel. Running in front of her husband, she tried to bar the men's way, clawing at their faces with her nails. She succeeded for a moment, drawing blood on Talland's cheek with her scratches. Adam seized the opportunity and dashed out of the open door, before his wife was grabbed and thrown to the floor. The ruffians followed outside, but they were too late. Adam Diggott had already jumped on one of their horses and a second later was galloping off up the slope toward Raven's Wood.

Talland mounted his horse, too, and rode off in pursuit, while the other man remained to guard his prisoner.

"He'll get 'im," he snarled, walking back into the cottage. He headed toward the old man, bound and bewildered on the floor. Once again Rachel headed to protect her father-in-law.

"Leave him," she cried, planting her hands against the sideman's chest and trying to push him away. Walter Harker, bewildered and angry by turn, came to her. Putting his arms around her shoulders, he looked deep into her frightened eyes.

"You'll have to let the law take its course, my dear," he told her, as the sideman heaved Abe Diggott toward the door.

They both knew what that meant.

Thomas sat staring at the open volume that lay on the desk in his laboratory. Three days had passed since his last visit to Bedlam; three days spent in anguish. He had no idea where Lydia had been taken, so on Dr. Carruthers's suggestion he had consulted a list of private madhouses within a seven-mile radius of London and Westminster. Such premises were, in theory, licensed by the Royal College of Physicians. He knew, however, that so many of these mansions of misery were simply dumping grounds for discarded wives—women of breeding consigned to the madhouse to enable their husbands to install new mistresses. If they were not mad when they entered such institutions, they were soon turned so by the barbarous treatment they were forced to endure. A pencil tick by a name denoted that Thomas had paid the establishment a visit. There were six ticks, but none of the calls had yielded any useful information, except to confirm what he already knew: that these hospitals were little more than prisons for inconvenient wives, places where well-born women became nameless and faceless and deprived of their children for no crime other than marrying a brute.

Thomas had been working by candlelight, hunched over small print. He rubbed his tired eyes and eased himself back in his chair. The hour was approaching six and he knew that Dr. Carruthers would soon be trying to persuade him to break for supper. Stretching his aching arms wide, he looked up and saw his pet white rat scuttling about the workbench.

"Where is she, Franklin, eh?" he said out loud, sighing deeply. "Where is she?"

"You are talking to that rat again?" came a familiar voice around the door. It was Dr. Carruthers. Thomas had not heard the usual tap of his stick and jumped up from his seat out of habit.

"I am afraid so, sir," he replied, smiling. As he did so, he watched Franklin, frightened by the sudden noise, bolt across the workbench and through the door of his open cage, sending papers flurrying in his wake. "You made us both jump!" he added.

The old anatomist smiled. "I like to keep you on your toes, young fellow," he replied; then, on a more serious note he inquired: "I take it you have made no progress?"

"I regret to say no, sir," Thomas replied, walking over to Franklin's cage to secure the door. The rat had retreated to his normal place of safety, and as he fastened the lock behind the creature, a thought suddenly occurred to Thomas. "Or perhaps I have," he said suddenly.

"Oh?"

"Where is the last place that anyone would expect Lydia to be held captive?"

Dr. Carruthers felt his way farther into the laboratory and leaned against the workbench. "I suppose I would have to say in Sir Montagu's home," he mused.

"Precisely," replied Thomas. "I vouch that he has taken her back to Draycott House, where he can personally see to it that she is denied her liberty."

The old anatomist nodded. "I see your logic," he said slowly. "So next you will be paying Malthus a visit?"

"I am sure my journey will not be wasted."

Buoyed by his latest theory, Thomas joined Carruthers for supper; then both men retired to the study for a nightcap and their usual read of the newssheet.

"You will leave tomorrow?" inquired the old anatomist as Thomas poured him his customary brandy.

"I will, sir," he replied, handing his mentor his drink, then seating himself by the fire.

Picking up the copy of *The London Chronicle* that Mistress Finesilver had laid on the arm of the chair, Thomas scanned the front page. There was news from Parliament and gossip from Bath, alongside sundry other tidbits. As usual he turned to the obituaries next. There would almost invariably be a tribute to someone Dr. Carruthers had treated during his long and illustrious career.

Thomas cleared his throat and began to read out loud. "Let's see who we have today, sir," he began. "The Earl of Harlow, aged ninety-two."

Carruthers's lips lifted at the corners. "I attended him once at Ascot. Kicked by a horse at the races, he was!" he recalled cheerfully.

Thomas continued. "Sir Robert Knox, eighty, Whig politician."

The old anatomist heaved his shoulders and snorted. "'Twas a wonder he lived so long. There were plenty who would have got rid of him sooner, including myself."

Expecting Thomas to continue reading, Carruthers inclined his head to listen once more. When his companion remained silent, however, the old anatomist tapped his white stick on the floor.

"So who's next, young fellow? Tell me another knave or varlet who has shuffled off this mortal coil."

Thomas lifted his head from the newssheet. His face was as

white as the paper on which the words were printed. Looking down once more, he saw the notice swim in front of his eyes. He opened his mouth, but the name snagged in his throat.

"Well?" Carruthers snapped impatiently.

Thomas swallowed and forced himself to push the words onto his tongue.

"Lady Lydia Farrell," he said. "Lydia is dead."

Chapter 21

There was still a chill on the spring breeze, but the sun shone and it called the winter-weary parishioners of Brandwick to market like a peal of bells to church. There was hardly any fresh produce to be had. The harsh frosts had taken their toll on the winter wheat, and the dried legumes were in short supply, but there was enough milk, butter, and cheese to satisfy the demand. And for those whose tastes stretched beyond the dairy parlor, there was tea, too, if you knew whom to ask. Few of the villagers could afford the proper leaves, of course, so they were happy to flout the law and settle for the next best thing. Until recently one of the servants at Boughton Hall had supplemented his living by collecting, drying, and rolling discarded leaves and reselling them for a pretty penny to those whose palates were more discerning than their pockets would allow. Now, however, the village had a new, more plentiful source of tea that bypassed the traditional market. Even the new vicar, the Reverend Unsworth, had been known to imbibe on such ill-gotten leaves. He was riding past the stalls in the High Street on his way to Boughton Hall. The village was in the grip of a general malaise.

News that the traditional annual ceremony of the beating of the bounds was threatened with cancelation only added to the melancholic mood. The day was usually one of mirth and merriment, when villagers walked the boundaries of the parish. Maidens carried nosegays and apprentices were given the day off. There was, however, one bright spot on the Brandwick horizon. Now that at least one of the surveyor's murderers had been apprehended, and the other would be caught soon enough, the vicar hoped for a return to some semblance of normality. Good cheer in the face of adversity was to be encouraged, he told himself. He doffed his hat to anyone who would look his way.

Early that morning he had received a message that bid him pay an urgent visit to Mr. Lupton. He assumed it was in relation to his recent inquiry about the establishment of a workhouse in the village for those who were dispossessed. A letter, written on behalf of the parish board, had been dispatched a few days ago. In it the members of the board informed Mr. Lupton that a vacant property in the village, belonging to the Boughton Estate, had been identified as a possible venue. It would take a little work to convert it into suitable premises for the anticipated dozen or so occupants, but it could be done. He felt encouraged by such a swift response.

The reverend found Mr. Lupton seated at his desk in the study at Boughton. Although he rose to greet him as he entered the room, the steward's expression was so grave it seemed that he was burdened by a huge weight.

"Please be seated," he said. The vicar did as he was bid, while Lupton remained standing, his features set hard. Any feelings of optimism that the reverend had felt on his journey to the hall were now dashed, only to be replaced by a sense of dread.

"I fear I have been in receipt of some tragic news, Reverend Unsworth," Lupton began.

The vicar's thoughts immediately turned to Sir Montagu Malthus. He recalled his surgery a few weeks before and hoped the wound had not become infected and led to his demise.

"Sir Montagu?" he ventured.

The steward frowned and shook his head. "No, I am pleased to say he is in rude health," he said.

"Praise be," said the reverend, lifting his eyes heavenward. He shifted in his seat. "Then . . . ?"

Lupton's body shuddered as he sighed deeply. "I fear it is Lady Lydia."

The vicar leaned forward, his eyes wide and staring. Like

every soul in the parish and its surrounds, he was aware of her hospitalization. "Her ladyship?"

Lupton nodded and pushed the latest copy of the *Oxford Journal* across the desk. "The announcement," he muttered. "You can read it for yourself."

The vicar looked down at the print, which seemed to blur before his very eyes. Trying hard to focus, he pored over the text. An insertion at the bottom of the death notices confirmed the shocking news. *On Friday last Lady Lydia Sarah Farrell, of Boughton Hall, in the parish of Brandwick, following a short illness.* He lifted his gaze.

"But this is most tragic," bleated the vicar. "Most tragic, indeed. Please accept my sincere condolences."

Lupton's brows knitted. "Terrible news, yes, Vicar. A seizure, I believe." He turned his back on the shocked clergyman, as if to hide his own grief. After a moment, he seemed to have composed himself and turned once more. "We will need to make arrangements."

The reverend nodded. "Of course. Her ladyship will be buried in the family vault?"

"Naturally."

"Lady Lydia was well loved. There will be many mourners, no doubt." The vicar was nodding to himself as he spoke, but Lupton was quick to upbraid him.

"No. No mourners, save for her immediate family. This will be a private affair," he snapped.

Taken aback, the vicar twitched his lips into a nervous smile and blinked. "As you wish, sir."

"It is the wish of Sir Montagu, Vicar, who is"—he stopped short and corrected himself—"who was her ladyship's legal representative."

"Very well, sir." The clergyman felt like a small child who was being scolded for speaking out of turn.

Lupton had walked behind him and now stood leering over him. Again Unsworth felt unduly pressured. He hoped for at least three days in which to prepare for the service. Once again he was thwarted.

"The interment needs to take place as soon as possible," Lupton informed him.

"There will be hymns to choose, an order of service—" protested the reverend.

"I am afraid not." The steward shook his head as Unsworth looked at him askance.

"I do not follow, sir." The cleric's expression had changed from one of sympathy to one of deep concern.

Lupton returned to his desk and sat down. "Her ladyship died in London and her remains have been transported here. The journey was delayed, so she needs to be interred as soon as possible." He added by way of clarification, if any were needed, "For delicacy's sake."

The vicar nodded. He understood. He had heard about the unfortunate business of Lord Edward, how his remains were allowed to decay before burial in a most unseemly manner.

"Would Thursday be convenient? That would give me time to—"

Again Lupton broke in. "This afternoon, Vicar, if you please."

The reverend's eyes opened wide once more. "This afternoon?" he repeated.

Lupton nodded. "Her ladyship has been prepared. Her coffin lies in the chapel as we speak."

Reverend Unsworth let out a resigned sigh. He could not think of any further objections he might raise. "Very well. This afternoon it shall be, sir," he said, rising. "I must prepare my vestments."

Lupton pulled the bell cord and Howard soon appeared at the threshold to usher the vicar out. Before he did so, however, another thought occurred to Unsworth. He turned.

"And who will give the eulogy, sir?" he asked with a frown.

Lupton smiled. "Sir Montagu told me he wished to speak," he replied. "This tragedy has hit him harder than anyone."

Thomas was numb to the usual discomfiture experienced on his regular journeys to Oxford. Despite the fact that his shoulder was still not completely healed, the lurching and bounding no longer troubled him. He sat silent and impassive in his shock. Nothing seemed real to him since he had read the news that Lydia was dead. Time was standing still. The world had stopped. His very soul felt bandaged, distanced from reality and emotion. He arrived in the great city, unable to recall much of his journey, despite the fact that he had not slept during the ten hours he had been on the road. He had not even been able to shed a tear. And yet his demeanor was such that it alarmed Sir Theodisius Pettigrew the moment he set eyes on his visitor.

"Good God, Silkstone! But you look like death, man. What has befallen you?" he inquired when Thomas shambled into his office.

Lifting his head, the doctor fixed the coroner with his bloodshot eyes.

At the sight of his visitor's anguished demeanor, Sir Theodisius's forehead crumpled instantly into a frown. "You are the bearer of bad news." It was a statement, not a question.

Thomas nodded. "Oh, sir, I fear so," he replied, dropping into a chair. His expression was so pained and his anguish so plain that the coroner immediately feared the worst.

"Not Lydia?" He did not wait for a reply. It was enough to witness the young anatomist's dire condition. The coroner's own features twisted into a grimace.

"Oh no!" he gasped. "No!" Grasping his desk with both hands, as if to anchor himself in the moment, his eyes suddenly flooded. "'Tis not true! Tell me 'tis not true!" He searched Thomas's face frantically for some reassurance, but, finding none, he brought out his kerchief and held it to his face. The sight was too much for Thomas to bear, and he, too, for the first time, felt himself giving way to tears. Brushing them away with trembling hands, he roused himself from his torpor and made his way 'round the desk to put a comforting arm on Sir Theodisius's shoulders. He knew the coroner regarded Lydia as a daughter.

Lifting his brimming eyes to meet Thomas's, the coroner asked, "How? How did it happen?"

"According to the announcement in the newssheet, it was a 'short illness'." His voice shook as he spoke.

"What sort of illness?" The coroner groaned.

"The last time I saw her, she was in a terrible state. I fear her treatment may have taken its toll, sir." Thomas fought back tears as he thought of Lydia's fragile body swathed in that despicable jacket. "If only I had taken her with me. I should have helped her escape." Suddenly angry, he banged his fist on the desk.

"You must not blame yourself. You could have done no more." Sir Theodisius shook his head as he dabbed his eyes, but the floodgates of Thomas's fury had been opened.

"But I do blame myself!" he cried, suddenly pacing the room. "I was playing by the rules and I should have learned by now that I cannot change anything by complying."

The coroner's jowls quivered in protest. "But the hospital had certain procedures that had to be followed."

Thomas, still pacing the room, shot back, "Don't you see? I let them put me in a straightjacket, too. I was weak. I should have acted!" He strode over to the window and gazed out, as if cursing the rest of humanity for going about its business while his own world seemed at an end. "I should have acted and now it's too late."

Sir Theodisius could see there was no point in arguing with Thomas until the maelstrom in his mind had subsided. He had dealt with too many bereaved loved ones to know that anger and self-recrimination often followed a sudden death. His own experience in the aftermath of Jeffrey Turgoose's demise bore testament to that.

Both men remained silent for a few seconds, lost in their own personal agonies, until the coroner's mind suddenly turned to more practical matters that needed addressing.

"Do you know when the funeral will be?" he asked, his voice quavering.

Thomas, turning back from the window, faced Sir Theodisius, whose cheeks were reddened and his eyes still moist.

"No, sir, but I assume the burial will be in the family vault."

"Of course." The coroner paused for a moment, waiting for Thomas to say what needed to be said. He did not have to wait long. Walking toward the desk in a more measured manner, the doctor nodded, filled his lungs, and sighed deeply. Looking at Sir Theodisius squarely yet purposefully, he said, "We must leave for Boughton without delay."

Chapter 22

Preparations for the formal public meeting at the Three Tuns that morning were well under way. Peter Geech was expecting most of the village to flood into his hostelry, and he knew space would be limited, like pouring a quart into a pint pot, but he could accommodate the gentlemen and more important tenants of the village in the upper room. The rest of the rabble would have to spill into the stableyard. The landlord had been running around like a headless cockerel, wishing he could have been in at least two places at once, so behind was he in his plans. There were seating arrangements to be organized and refreshments of ale, porter, and of course gin for his regulars, or sack for the gentlemen, to be made ready. Sir Montagu Malthus himself was to chair the meeting.

It was midmorning when the coach from Oxford to Brandwick pulled up in the High Street. Thomas had anticipated finding the village in mourning: the bells of St. Swithin's tolling, shops shut, the streets deserted as a mark of respect for Lydia, their mistress. But no, the place was much busier than usual. A regular flow of carriages and other vehicles seemed to be depositing passengers outside the Three Tuns.

Thomas frowned as his conveyance came to a halt opposite the inn. People were gathered on the street outside, seemingly anxious to be granted entry into the courtyard.

"What goes on?" asked the coroner.

Thomas thought for a moment. "What date is it?"

"The thirtieth, I believe," replied Sir Theodisius, looking perplexed.

Thomas nodded. "Then this must be the public meeting called to discuss the Act of Enclosure."

"But surely the meeting should have been postponed!" said the coroner crossly.

"Only if her ladyship's death had been publicly announced," said Thomas, a look of resignation creeping across his face.

"You mean . . . ?"

"The villagers do not know," he said, his voice tinged with disbelief.

Sir Theodisius slapped his huge thighs. "But you must attend the meeting in all haste and tell them," he urged. Then, looking Thomas squarely in the eye, he added: "In her absence, you must be Lydia's mouthpiece. You must speak for her and Boughton." His voice trembled as he spoke these last words.

Thomas knew what the coroner said was right. An image of Lydia flashed across his vision once more. She had never envisaged enclosing the estate, fencing it off and depriving the very poorest of their rights to collect fuel and forage in the woods and on the common.

"I shall. And you, sir; perhaps you could call at Boughton first? Lupton will be occupied at the meeting and the staff at the hall will be more than eager, I am sure, to tell you what they know," he suggested.

The coroner nodded. "They will have been hit hard by the news," he agreed.

Accordingly, Thomas alighted by the Three Tuns and his baggage was flung down to the ground. The coach, with Sir Theodisius still aboard, was soon on its way to Boughton. There was no time to lose. Hurriedly the doctor picked up his valise and headed through the archway of the Three Tuns. He found the courtyard packed with villagers. Men with tankards in their hands were leaning against posts or sitting on casks and hogsheads. Women were in small clusters, their arms crossed over their bosoms in fighting mode. The low drone of anxious chatter filled the air, but it stopped as soon as Thomas was spotted worming his way through the crowd. Heads turned and tongues wagged as the villagers eyed him climbing the staircase that led to the upper meeting room.

They do not know. No one has told them, he thought. Despite being surrounded by so many people, Thomas felt totally isolated. A bitter tang, like ashes, filled his mouth. He knew it to be the taste of sorrow.

Standing at the doorway, but out of view of those gathered, he surveyed the room. He counted sixteen men, seated on three rows of chairs in front of a long table at the top end of the room. Sir Montagu sat haughtily at its center, flanked by Nicholas Lupton and, to Thomas's surprise, the ailing Sir John Thorndike. There were other familiar faces: Bartholomew Bailey, the owner of the fulling mill, and two yeomen whose children he had treated for bronchitis. The other attendees, he assumed by their dress, were reasonably well-off tenants who farmed larger acreages. They were certainly not peasants. Heads to the fore, they were listening intently to a plump man whose shoulders bore a light dusting of wig powder. In his hand he held a short cane, which he used to point out various features on a map affixed to a board on an easel.

"In conclusion, gentlemen, we invite you to lodge your claims within the next two months. As the appointed commissioner"—he turned to defer to Sir Montagu—"I shall endeavor to ensure that all are dealt with fairly and that compensation is awarded where I see fit."

So this must be Jeffrey Turgoose's replacement, thought Thomas. He recalled from the public notice that he had a business partner, a Mr. Mather, if he remembered correctly. He was no doubt a most competent individual, but Thomas also detected a definite whiff of pomposity about him, which seemed so endemic in English professionals. Behind him sat the younger man with the flame-red hair and the bandaged eye whom Thomas had encountered before at Boughton, when he seemed so distressed. He was, he surmised, the late Turgoose's assistant and chainman, James Charlton.

There were nods of approval from among the assembled tenants. Most could see the logic in what the commissioner had to say. It made no sense to farm in narrow bands and let the land lie fallow throughout the winter. Where was the merit in walking furlongs between their various strips when they could have their own neat parcels? As long as they were granted allotments in exchange for the land they held, then they would raise no objections. Polite applause rippled around the chamber.

Just when Thomas thought the meeting was about to end, however, he heard a rumpus from somewhere in the far corner. He craned his neck. A laboring man was elbowing his way to the front.

"I would speak!" cried the workman hoarsely. "I would speak for the commoners!" Thomas recognized him immediately as Will Ketch, who'd lost a daughter to the Great Fogg.

Nicholas Lupton shot Sir Montagu a look, then nodded to a bald-headed man who had been standing at his side throughout the proceedings.

"Commoners have no right to speak!" the steward called loudly over the din, in an effort to restore calm. As Ketch approached, the bald guard grabbed him by his arm and forced it behind his back. Another burly man assisted him and together they dispatched the cowman, cussing and shouting, from the room.

Sir Montagu, whose mask of complete decorum had slipped only a little during the incident, fingered the gavel on the table. He slid a sideways look of disdain at Lupton before moving to establish his authority once more.

"My apologies for that unfortunate interruption, gentlemen." A wry smile played on his lips; then, turning to the surveyor, he said: "Thank you, Mr. Mather, for that most comprehensive review of the proposals, and now, if there is no other business . . ." He lifted the gavel and was just about to bring it down when Thomas knew it was his turn to interrupt the proceedings. Side-stepping into the room he called out, "But there *is* other business, Sir Montagu."

All heads turned to see Thomas standing at the back of the chamber. Lupton leapt to his feet. "Remove this man!" he shouted, and one of the guards pushed his way toward Thomas. Clamping rough hands on his arm, he tried to pull him to the door.

Sir Montagu, however, had other ideas. "Wait," he called, flapping his arm. "Dr. Silkstone is not a resident of this parish, but I am sure these gentlemen are curious to hear what he has to say." He stretched his lips into a smile, but his hooded eyes gave nothing away. He rose in an unhurried manner and addressed Thomas directly. "Pray tell us what other business you would like us to discuss, Doctor," he urged, his voice dripping with sarcasm.

Pulling his arm away from the ruffian, Thomas tugged at his coat.

"I believe you should be making another announcement, sir."

Sir Montagu arched a brow. "Another announcement? Really?"

The anger that his shock had suppressed for so long was now welling up inside Thomas. "An announcement, not just to this room, but to the people of Brandwick."

The lawyer threw his head back in a scornful laugh. "And what might that be, Dr. Silkstone?"

Thomas felt his heart beat faster as he struggled to contain his rage, but the words came tumbling out in a great torrent. "Is it not your duty to announce that Lady Lydia Farrell, the mistress of Boughton and the woman whom the villagers held in the greatest regard and affection"—he was suddenly choked—"is dead?"

A collective gasp rippled 'round the room. The audience was stunned, as if everyone suddenly held their breath. All eyes fastened on the young doctor, who seemed most distressed.

"And that she died at your hand!" Thomas pointed at Sir Montagu.

The mark had been overstepped. At a signal from the lawyer, the guard grabbed hold of Thomas once more and began jostling him back through the door. This time he did not resist. He had said what he had come to say. The pent-up words had flooded from his mouth with such force that he felt drained, but relieved. Now the world knew. The people of Brandwick could join in his mourning and unite against the machinations of the man who was ultimately responsible for Lydia's tragic death. Dazed, he made his way downstairs and out into the courtyard, where the news was seeping out like blood from a severed vein.

A servant must have heard his rant in the upper room and rushed to impart news of it to the waiting crowd. In an instant the commoners who had gathered to hear their own fate no longer cared about themselves. One by one the men took off their hats and bowed their heads as a mark of respect. The women, too, lowered their gazes. Some did not try to staunch their tears.

Thomas stood among them, his chest still heaving with anger. Looking up, he could see that all eyes were on him, willing him to speak. He took a deep breath, trying to still his shaking body. Standing on a low wall, he addressed the crowd.

"I fear that what you have just heard is true," he began. He drew another deep breath, as if to steady his anxiety. "Lady Lydia Farrell is dead."

From the throng, a mournful wail rose into the air. Sobs were heard. Men shook their heads.

"How? How did she die?" came a shout.

"'Tis said she had a short illness," replied Thomas. "I know no more than that, save to say her death was wholly preventable." He surveyed the anxious faces and knew he needed to throw them a crumb of comfort. "But it is my intention to discover the whole truth, and when I do, I shall share it with you." His voice cracked as he uttered these last words, and he bowed his head and stepped down from the wall. He felt the sturdy pats of men's hands on his shoulders. It seemed that finally they were acknowledging him as one of their own, no longer a foreigner. Their sympathy offered him some solace, but no hope. The truth was that after his outburst at the public meeting, he had even dashed any chance he might have had of attending Lydia's funeral. Now he would never be allowed back on Boughton soil, never see his beloved lying at rest in the family vault, never be able to say his final good-bye. As he made his way into the inn, he silently cursed himself for a display of impetuosity that was so at odds with his usual measured character. He felt lost and alone.

Chapter 23

Sir Theodisius Pettigrew lugged his weary hulk to the front steps of Boughton Hall. Glancing up at the mansion's façade, he could see all the drapes were drawn, the house dogs were nowhere in view, and the whole place was seemingly enveloped by a quiet despair, as if the hall had closed in on itself. He supposed it would have been Howard's difficult duty to inform the staff of their mistress's death. The butler, he imagined, would have gathered them downstairs, fighting back his own sadness as he imparted his grim news. And with the news, all hope of ever returning to the way of life that had been before had ebbed away, and now this terrible melancholy had descended upon the residence.

The coroner, his face careworn and deathly pale, was relieved to be greeted by Howard. He had feared that so stalwart a member of the staff might have been dispatched, such had been his loyalty to Lydia. But no, the old butler was still there.

"Sir Theodisius." He bowed stiffly. "You visit us at a terrible time, sir," he ventured.

Sir Theodisius, taken aback by the butler's forthright manner, paused for a moment, considering his words. "A terrible time, indeed," he acknowledged. "Yes, Howard. Her ladyship was loved by all who knew her." He handed a waiting maid his hat and coat.

"I am afraid Sir Montagu is in the village, sir. A meeting—" Howard began.

"Yes, yes," snapped the coroner with a knowing nod. "I am glad of it. It means I can speak freely with you."

The bemused butler made a stiff, jerking motion, then looked about him, hoping that Sir Theodisius's remark had not been overheard by the maid.

"Please, sir, the drawing room," he said, gesturing ahead.

The coroner followed, lumbering through the open door into the room, which was so familiar to him yet seemed oddly empty. He recalled his last visit to this very place at Christmas, only a few weeks before. Young Richard had joined them and they had played games of hunt the slipper and blindman's buff. There had been so much joy and laughter, and he had rarely seen Lydia so happy. The recollection of it sent such an ache through his chest that he thought his heart would break.

"She is gone," he said, shaking his head, as the butler shut the door behind them.

Howard, normally so cool and reserved, found it hard to hold himself in check. "Oh, sir, we are all so deeply sorry for your loss. On behalf of all the staff, may I offer my sincere sympathies."

Sir Theodisius shook his head. "'Tis not just my loss, Howard. A loss to Boughton and to Brandwick and, indeed, to her beloved son." He frowned. "The young earl, has he been informed?"

Howard cleared his throat. "His lordship remains at Sir Montagu's residence, I believe, sir."

The coroner sighed deeply. "No doubt he will travel here to attend the funeral." He threw the remark out as if it were a given or an aside, but Howard seized on it.

"But the funeral has already taken place, sir," he blurted.

Sir Theodisius froze. "What?"

"Yesterday, sir. They buried her ladyship in the family vault yesterday afternoon."

The coroner's expression turned from one of resigned sadness to one of consternation. "But that cannot be!" he boomed. His pale face suddenly reddened, and he plodded angrily across the room to stare out the window.

Howard, struggling to compose himself, gave a flustered shrug. "The staff were not even allowed to attend the service, sir."

The coroner shook his head in disbelief and remained silent for a moment, until he asked, "What has become of the world?" As if in answer to his rhetorical question, at that very moment Sir Montagu Malthus's carriage swept up Boughton's drive. Within seconds it had clattered to a halt by the front steps.

At the sight, Sir Theodisius turned. "You had better leave me now, Howard," he instructed the butler. He hoped at least some of his many questions were about to be answered by the very orchestrator of these calamitous events. The urgent need to confront the situation was obviously mutual. As soon as he was over the threshold, Sir Montagu wasted no time in challenging his visitor.

"How bad news travels fast," he cried, powering into the drawing room in a flurry of self-importance. He slapped his gloves into the palm of his hand.

Sir Theodisius, waiting by the mantelpiece, was in an equally confrontational mood. "When did you intend to tell me, Malthus?" he bellowed.

The lawyer shrugged off his cloak into Howard's waiting hands. "Leave us," he told the butler, then, pointing at the settee, invited Sir Theodisius to sit.

"I prefer to stand," he replied, even though his legs ached under his own weight.

Sir Montagu was indifferent. "As you wish."

He seated himself on the opposite settee and leaned back, as if wishing to make the point that he was the master of Boughton now and at ease in these surroundings.

The coroner took a deep breath. "She was as a daughter to me." His lips trembled as he spoke; then, suddenly remembering he was addressing Lydia's real father, he held his tongue. He did not wish Malthus to glean that he knew his secret.

Sir Montagu nodded but showed no emotion. "I know how much Lydia meant to you, Pettigrew."

The coroner lumbered forward, shaking his head. "Then why did you bury her without letting me say good-bye?" His eyes were welling up with tears again, but the lawyer appeared unmoved.

"The madness," he began. "It had ravaged her beauty." He was looking into the distance, as if picturing Lydia in his mind's eye. "You would not have recognized her."

His pious response only provoked the coroner. "Madness! You know as well as I do Lydia was mad only on your say-so, Malthus."

Sir Montagu shook his head. "Not so, Pettigrew," he countered. "It was your friend Dr. Silkstone who sanctioned her committal to Bedlam." His voice was soured with contempt.

The color now flooded into Sir Theodisius's cheeks as his ire rose. "You forged his name. You had access to all of Lydia's papers. 'Twould not have been hard to find one of his letters to her and to copy his signature. No, you are the one to blame for her death!" His plump finger jabbed at the air and a fleck of spittle from his mouth arced through the space between the two men and landed on the lawyer's cheek.

For a moment Sir Montagu remained silent; then, in a pointed gesture, he took his kerchief from his pocket, flicked it out, and wiped the saliva from his face. "I can see you are not your usual, rational self, old friend," he said in a manner so relaxed that it inflamed Sir Theodisius even more.

Charging toward the window, the coroner gazed out over the front driveway again, toying with the idea of bringing the whole sorry meeting to an unsatisfactory end and storming out. He was therefore taken off guard by Sir Montagu's offer.

"I am, however, prepared to grant you entry into the vault."

The coroner switched 'round as fast as his great frame would allow.

"You would let me see her?"

The lawyer drummed his fingers on the top of the settee. "Not exactly."

Sir Theodisius scowled. "Do not play games with me, Malthus!" he warned.

Sir Montagu's hooded eyes fixed downward for a moment as he gave the matter some thought. "The coffin is sealed, but you could say a few words. Lay flowers, perhaps." It was as if he were negotiating land rights with a tenant.

Sir Theodisius shot him a scornful look. "That is the very least you can allow me, sir," he replied.

The lawyer snorted. "And what else am I expected to offer, pray?"

Sir Theodisius lifted his head quickly so that his jowls flapped. He looked Malthus in the eye. "You must allow Dr. Silkstone to accompany me."

Sir Montagu let out a derisory laugh. "The American parvenu? He is the last person I would allow into the vault!"

Not for the first time in the heated altercation the coroner raised his voice. "May I remind you, sir, that that American parvenu is the man who saved your life, although I am sure he very much regrets it now!" His outburst shocked even him. He held the lawyer's gaze, desperately wanting to swallow the saliva that had pooled in his mouth, but not wishing to do so for fear he would look weak.

Sir Montagu, too, remained staring at his adversary, as if waiting for him to blink first. When his response came, it was as cold and unyielding as granite.

"Over my dead body," he said.

Chapter 24

"I am so truly sorry, dear fellow." Sir Theodisius sat with Thomas at a table set for dinner in the private dining room at the Three Tuns. Both had already confessed to each other that neither had the stomach for a meal. Between them on the table lay an indifferent bottle of claret. It was almost empty, but not even alcohol could help numb their mutual pain, it seemed.

"You must not blame yourself. You did your best," continued the coroner.

Thomas fingered the stem of his glass, contemplating the events of the afternoon. Sir Theodisius had related to him how he had entered the gloomy sepulchre and placed a posy of spring flowers, primroses and celandines, onto Lydia's sarcophagus. Under the hawklike gaze of Sir Montagu, he had said a silent prayer and had bidden her farewell.

"I wish I could have seen her sweet face again," said Sir Theodisius, exhaling a deep sigh. "Just one last time."

The thought snagged in Thomas's mind, like silk on a thorn. He pictured Lydia lying peacefully in her coffin, all the pain gone from her face.

"You asked to see her but were denied?"

Sir Theodisius frowned. "I was told in no uncertain terms that I could not." The coroner's voice was most indignant as he relived the slight. "Malthus told me that her ladyship could not be viewed."

"Can you remember his exact words?"

Sir Theodisius's neck stiffened, lifting the folds of his chin away from his stock pin. "To my dying day, sir," he replied, looking into the distance, preparing to recite verbatim. "He said, 'The madness has ravaged her features so much that you will be hard-pressed to recognize her.' "

Thomas's eyes widened.

"I am so sorry. I did not want you to hear . . ." The coroner was shaking his head, thinking he had grievously offended the young doctor's sensibilities, but he soon realized he was mistaken.

Thomas shifted in his seat and grabbed the edge of the table eagerly with both hands, pulling himself forward toward his friend. "So we only have Sir Montagu's word for it that Lydia is dead!" It was as if a candle had suddenly been lit in his darkness.

The coroner looked flummoxed, then, after a moment's reflection, shook his head. "There was no postmortem," he said slowly.

"Not at Bethlem, and as Oxford coroner, this area falls under your jurisdiction," Thomas pointed out.

Sir Theodisius's brow furrowed. "Surely not even Malthus would stoop that low?"

"I do not believe we can underestimate Sir Montagu," replied Thomas, his face suddenly glowing, not with the wine but with renewed hope.

Sir Theodisius remained puzzled. "So you are saying that perhaps Lydia was not in the coffin I put flowers on?"

"Perhaps not!"

"But then, who?"

"Who knows if it is occupied?" suggested Thomas. "It may be empty."

"You think Sir Montagu is playing games?"

" 'Twould not be the first time." Thomas recalled the lawyer's secret, how he had told Lydia that he was her father, although Sir Theodisius had no notion of the claim at the time.

The coroner cocked his head and gazed at Thomas with glistening eyes. "Are you sure you are not clinging to a thin hope, young man?" he asked benignly. "Lydia's death has come as such a tragic blow to—"

Thomas managed a tight smile. "Of course I cannot be sure that I am not clutching at straws," he replied, casting around him at the laid table and the fine glasses, as if he might find something tangible to back up his latest hypothesis. "But 'tis better than having no hope at all," he said finally.

Sir Theodisius lifted the bottle of claret and angled the neck over Thomas's glass, but the doctor laid his hand over the rim. Rebuffed, the coroner poured himself another glass, slurped a mouthful, and thoughtfully licked his lips. "So you think the coffin at Boughton may contain someone else?"

"Mayhap." Thomas's heart was beating as fast as a bird's in flight, but he was trying to remain outwardly calm. He could not be sure that he was not deluding himself, but the more he dwelt on it, the more his hope bloomed. In the gloomy fug of the dining room, the men's eyes met. There was another avenue of inquiry Thomas wished to explore, but for the moment, he would play his cards close to his chest.

"Shall I make discreet inquiries?" asked Sir Theodisius. "The vicar perhaps?"

"That would be most helpful," replied Thomas. "I, on the other hand, will make my way back to London."

The coroner's head jerked back in surprise. "London?"

"There is a line of investigation I need to pursue there, as well," Thomas told him. He needed to follow his instinct. He needed to return to Bedlam. The seed of doubt over Lydia's death had taken root. He rose quickly from the table. "It is not yet dark. I can be on the road shortly to make the most of the light."

Sir Theodisius seemed taken aback. "But what about Turgoose's murder?" he barked. "I heard they have a man in custody at Oxford and another is on the run."

This was the first Thomas had heard of an arrest.

"Who are they?"

"An old coppicer and his son, apparently."

Thomas thought immediately of the Diggotts, the elderly man as fragile as a stick; his son, furtive and suspicious of authority; and the young boy, cruelly whipped for arson. "There is evidence?"

The coroner nodded. "Apparently so, although I know not what."

"A trial has been set?"

Sir Theodisius shook his head. "Next week, sometime, so I am told. You will be required to deliver your postmortem findings."

Thomas, his hand now on the door handle, took a deep breath. "Have no fear," he said reassuringly. "I shall return in good time, and if the old man is innocent, then he shall be saved the noose." And with these words he opened the door and was gone, leaving the coroner alone with his claret and his quiet contemplation of the day's events.

Chapter 25

The sound of patients screaming and hollering in the distance did nothing to unsettle the comparative calm of the reception desk at Bethlem Hospital. Such echoing agonies were politely ignored by those who came and went through the great portico and into the grand hallway. Thomas was one such visitor. When he presented himself on his return from Brandwick, he was surprised, and relieved, to find that the usual clerk with the bulging eyes was absent.

"May I help you, sir?" asked the new clerk, a younger man with, it seemed, a more helpful disposition, who was seated behind the desk.

Thomas gave a tight smile. "You are new here."

The man smiled back politely. His teeth were as large as tombstones and bucked out at the front like a rabbit's. "I am, sir. How may I help, sir?"

The absence of the obstreperous clerk with his disconcerting eyes could, thought Thomas, prove to be to his advantage. "I am Dr. Thomas Silkstone and I am come to see one of my patients." On the long return journey from Oxford, he had concocted a vague story to cloak his deceit.

The clerk slid the large leather ledger in front of him. "Name, sir?"

Thomas recalled the flash of her large brown eyes and the melancholy air that shaped her delicate features.

"Miss Kent," he said, peering over the register. "Miss Anna Kent."

"Miss Kent," repeated the clerk. He licked his lips and ran his pen down a column of names. "Miss Annalise Kent, sir," he said, emphasizing the last syllable in "Annalise," as his nib stopped suddenly. He frowned. Tapping the entry with his forefinger, he looked up.

"Oh, Doctor," he said.

"What is it?" queried Thomas, his unease growing by the second.

"Were you not informed?"

The doctor leaned forward nervously. "Informed of what?"

The clerk slid the ledger back toward him and turned it so that Thomas could see the name *Annalise Mary Kent (spinster of the parish of Southwark)* written quite plainly. There was her last known address and her age, and beside her sketchy details was written the word *deceased.*

The words swam before Thomas's eyes. "Dead. But when?"

The clerk retrieved the register. "On Thursday, April 26, sir, it says."

"Last week." Reeling from the news, Thomas tried to collect himself quickly. "I should have been informed," he said sharply.

The clerk's cheeks reddened as he became flustered. "I can only apologize, Dr. Silkstone," he replied.

Thomas could see that indignation was his best method of attack. "I shall, of course, need to know more."

"Of course." The clerk nodded. "May I direct you to the mortuary?"

A few minutes later Thomas found himself outside a door in the basement area, away from the main building. He did not need to read the sign to know he was in the right place. The reek of death and of vinegar seeped over the threshold. He walked in and gave his name to a male attendant.

"I am inquiring of a patient of mine who died last Thursday," he told him.

"The name of the deceased, sir?"

"Miss Annalise Kent."

The attendant checked the register. "Yes, sir."

"There has been a postmortem?" Thomas came straight to the point.

The attendant's eyes hovered over the notes and delivered his answer as if he were delivering the laundry. "Yes, sir."

"And the conclusion?"

Without bothering to embellish his reply, the attendant said neutrally, "Suicide."

Thomas tensed. He leaned over and scanned the text of the relevant page. Under *Cause of death* were written the words: *Self-murder. Method: wrists cut with a sharpened spoon.*

So Annalise Kent had killed herself just the day after he last saw her and less than a week after Lydia's removal from the hospital. For a few seconds Thomas was lost in his thoughts.

"Sir?" The attendant saw the doctor's face fall. "Will that be all?"

The ledger closed with a dull thud. The sound made Thomas start.

"Wait!" he said, raising a hand. "Has the body been released?"

The attendant, surprised by this sudden volte-face, reopened the volume and viewed the relevant page. "Yes, to an undertaker, sir, a Mr. Wilkins in Chiswell Street, the day after the postmortem," came the reply.

Armed with this information, Thomas knew exactly where to go next. He strode purposefully back toward the great gates. Just beyond them lay normality, a world where logic was not a foreign word and where order was maintained by the courts, not like this topsy-turvy place where nothing was what it seemed. He welcomed the cries of the hawkers, the muffin men and peascod sellers, as the music of the everyday that drifted through the great iron grille. He could not wait to return to the refuge of Hollen Street, but just before he reached the exit, he heard someone call his name in a hoarse whisper.

"Dr. Silkstone!"

He turned to see a woman behind him in silhouette. She was leaning by a wall, seemingly to avoid detection. He watched her hook her finger and beckon to him. When he leveled with her he recognized her as the plump warder who had taken him to visit Lydia. She backed against a nearby pillar as he approached, and for the first time he could see an anxious look on her face. She leaned toward him so that she came close enough for him to catch her scent. She smelled of lemons.

"Sir, I believe you have been making inquiries about Miss Kent." Her eyes darted around her, as if she was fearful that she might be seen. Away from the madness of the asylum she looked much younger, thought Thomas. The authority she had commanded inside had ebbed away, leaving a more vulnerable woman in its wake.

"I am," he replied, aware that she seemed acutely nervous.

"A most distressing affair, if I might say so," she replied, as if seeking permission to hold her own opinion.

"I know she is dead," said Thomas, trying to ease her path.

The warder shook her head mournfully. "I see many patients come and go in this hospital, sir, but the manner of Miss Kent's death—" She broke off.

"I can see you are distressed." Thomas allowed the warder to take her time. She tried to snort back her tears.

"As you know, she and Lady Lydia had formed an . . . an attachment during her stay." Her speech was deliberate, hesitant almost. "And when her ladyship . . . when she left, well, Miss Kent became distraught. We knew she'd done herself mischief before, so we put her in a cell for her own safety."

Thomas was aware that this was standard procedure in such cases. "But then what happened?" he pressed.

"She was searched, sir, but somehow she had secreted a blade about her person." She shook her head as if reliving the moment. "And when we next checked on her . . . Oh, the blood!" She clamped her hand over her mouth.

Thomas tried to ease her obvious concern. "A terrible sight, I am sure," he sympathized. He himself had been called to such a scene when a young man had taken his own life by the same ghastly method. It was never easy dealing with the aftermath of such an experience. Despite his sympathy, however, Thomas's senses were not dulled to his task. What the young woman had just told him triggered alarm.

"You say a blade?" he queried. "But the register cited a sharpened spoon."

"A spoon?" The warder regarded him with surprise. "Oh no, sir, it was definitely a knife, a sharp kitchen knife."

"But how did a patient manage to secure such a knife?" Sounds of clanking locks and screeching gates echoed in Thomas's head. Bethlem, he knew, was as secure as the Tower of London.

The warder shook her head and let out a shallow mouthful of air. "That's the mystery of it, sir. None of us knows."

Thomas's mind flashed back to the face of the young woman, frightened and helpless. He knew little of her story, save that her heart had been broken when her fiancé had died and that her distress had brought on her madness. He only hoped that now she was dead she would gain the peace she deserved.

"Thank you," he said finally. "You have been most helpful." He doffed his tricorn.

The woman raised her hand as if forbidding him to go. "But you have word of Lady Lydia?"

He was ill prepared for such a question. "She is well," he said, although as the words left his lips he questioned why he had invented such a lie. The warder seemed satisfied with his reply. He thanked her and bid her farewell. As he walked away from Bethlem, he asked himself why he had not told the warder that Lydia was also dead. Perhaps it was because somewhere deep within him, he refused to believe it himself.

Chapter 26

The last rays of sunlight reached through the gaps in the London roofline like translucent fingers. Thomas knew this was not a good time of day to be hunting for the undertaker's premises, but he could not suppress his anxieties. His unexpected encounter with the concerned warder and his knowledge that Annalise Kent had somehow managed to procure a kitchen knife had planted a seed of consternation in him that was growing by the hour. The fact that the warder's version of events was at odds with the official report into the death suggested to him at best some form of collusion, and at worst a conspiracy. He could not wait until the morning to follow up the fragile lead he had been thrown at the mortuary.

The undertaker's business was but a short walk away in Chiswell Street. Thomas noted that it was conveniently situated close to both the Artillery Ground and the City Burying Ground. The shop sign, an iron coffin, had fallen off one of its hinges and creaked forlornly in the intermittent gusts that assaulted the corner of the lane. He walked in, his arrival heralded by the tinkling of a bell over the door.

The shop was a shabby, dismal affair, displaying several accoutrements of death. On one shelf was a folded pile of plain shrouds and on another a selection of mourning gloves and other funereal accessories. The sound of hammering and sawing could be heard from a back room. Thomas assumed it came from a workshop where coffins were fashioned.

An elderly bespectacled gentleman, sporting a jet-black wig with a frock coat to match, shuffled out from the back, his face as solemn as his attire.

"May I help you, sir?" he inquired in a gruff voice that clearly lent itself to hawking rather than dispensing platitudes.

"Mr. Wilkins?" asked the doctor.

On his way to the premises Thomas had decided to further embellish his story in the hope that it would allow him to gain access to information that might be sensitive and not shared with anyone apart from close relatives and involved professionals.

"I am he," replied the man, seemingly flattered to be addressed by name.

"I am a physician and I am inquiring about my recently deceased patient," Thomas began. "Miss Annalise Kent."

Wilkins eyed Thomas oddly and sniffed. "Yes," he drawled.

"I have been away and was only told of her death by Bethlem Hospital today," said Thomas.

The undertaker cocked his head in a well-rehearsed gesture of sympathy. "Very remiss of them, if I might say so, sir."

"Indeed." Thomas fingered his hat nervously. "I wish to know when her funeral might take place, if you please?"

The undertaker frowned, peered over the rim of his spectacles, and looked at Thomas questioningly.

"I remember the order very well, as it happens, sir," he replied with a sniff.

"You do?" Thomas could not hide his surprise.

"Indeed."

"How so?"

"I had the impression that Miss Kent's father was a man of considerable means, yet his agent said he was not interested in our ruffled crepe linings or our superfine sheet and shroud." The undertaker obviously took this flagrant disinterest in his wares as a personal slight. "He opted instead for the most meager of cloths and the cheapest of woods for the casket."

Such penny-pinching was not, agreed Thomas, the customary behavior of a grieving father. He needed to know more.

"Perhaps grief clouded his judgment?" he suggested.

The undertaker shrugged.

"You mentioned his agent?" pressed Thomas.

"Why, yes. A man most brusque in his manner, with strange eyes, as I recall." Thomas thought of the original clerk at Bethlem. "He seemed only interested in dispatching poor Miss Kent with the greatest possible haste," added the undertaker.

Thomas knew he should have guessed the officious clerk was in Sir Montagu's pay.

"So what happened next?" he urged.

Wilkins shook his bewigged head. "I was told in no uncertain terms that the plainest coffin was to be dispatched the following day up north." He pointed heavenward with his thin finger.

"Do you have the address?" asked Thomas. He hardly needed to ask. With each passing exchange he grew more convinced that his inclination was right.

"Yes. Now, where is it? Let me see." The undertaker squinted over his order book, leafing through its pages until finally he pronounced, "Here we are. Boughton Hall, Brandwick, Oxfordshire." He looked up at Thomas over the rim of his spectacles. "Miss Kent's remains were dispatched five days ago."

Back at Hollen Street, Thomas found Dr. Carruthers dozing in his chair after supper, some of which was spilled down the front of his waistcoat. He had eaten something accompanied by gravy by the looks of it. Not wishing to startle his mentor, he gently laid a hand on his.

"Sir, 'tis Thomas. I am back."

The old anatomist stirred, mumbled something inaudible, then came to his senses. "Thomas, dear boy!"

Pulling up a chair, the young doctor proceeded to bring his mentor up to date with developments in Boughton and his recent visit to Bethlem.

"When I heard that Miss Kent had stabbed herself with a knife from the kitchens, I suspected it must have been supplied to her by someone who might profit from her death," explained Thomas.

"You're not telling me Malthus was behind it?" the old anatomist asked incredulously.

"Yes, sir. I should've known. By befriending Lydia, Miss Kent inadvertently put herself in danger. A clerk at the hospital must have been employed by Sir Montagu."

"And when Miss Kent reacted badly to Lydia's departure, he saw his chance?"

"Exactly. The clerk facilitated the poor young woman's death. He may as well have slit her wrists himself."

"And afterward?"

"He replaced the knife with a sharpened spoon and the post-mortem was straightforward. He made all the subsequent arrangements and saw to it that the body was dispatched."

Carruthers paused for a moment, as if trying to digest all that he had just heard. "And you say the remains were delivered to Boughton?"

"Aye, sir." Thomas nodded.

"So this could mean . . ." He dared not say what he was thinking, so Thomas, even though he, too, was filled with trepidation, said it for him.

"It means that the body buried in the vault at Boughton may not be Lydia's."

Carruthers paused for a second, then clapped his hands together and clenched them into gleeful fists. "Oh, dear boy! Could it be that she yet lives?"

Thomas felt his heart barreling in his chest. Hearing his mentor say these words brought home to him the prospect of a hope he had thought dashed and lost forever. "Perhaps," he replied softly. He must not allow himself to dwell on such an overwhelming possibility. He could not dare to dream. For now, his immediate concern was how he might obtain access to the Crick vault at Boughton. He cast his mind back to the dark, damp, airless space that was home to the last three generations of the family. The latest casket to join the ranks of the dead might well contain an innocent impostor. Only when he could see inside the coffin and gaze upon the face of the woman who lay there could he be sure that his beloved Lydia was still alive.

Chapter 27

Armed with a hastily written autopsy report on Jeffrey Turgoose that merely threw up more questions than it answered, Thomas rode through the gates of Boughton Hall once more. Sir Theodisius had managed to pave the way, insisting that Thomas be allowed to deliver his postmortem document in person, and Lupton had fallen for the ruse.

Will Lovelock, the groom, hurried out to take his horse, but the boy's efficient manner soon dissolved into a melancholy look.

"Oh, sir . . . ," he began.

Thomas touched him on the shoulder. "I know," he replied, as he handed him the reins. "We must all be brave. Her ladyship would not wish to see tears," he said, forcing a smile.

Delving into his pocket, Thomas pulled out a penny and placed it in Will's palm. The boy looked up, bemused. "I have an errand for you. Tell your father I must meet him at the chapel. He is to be there at noon with the cart and a shovel and pickax. You understand?"

"Very well, sir," came the puzzled reply.

By this time Howard had emerged from the hall and stood on the front steps. He did little to disguise his sorrow in front of Thomas.

"Dr. Silkstone, on behalf of the staff, please accept our condolences."

"Thank you, Howard," Thomas told him.

The butler nodded and led the doctor into Lupton's study. No signs of mourning were on show and the steward's manner seemed bullish rather than subdued.

"Silkstone!" he greeted him churlishly. "I am sure you know you are here under sufferance after your appalling behavior at the meeting. Perhaps now we can get to the bottom of this Turgoose murder. You have completed your famous report?"

Thomas knew Lydia had meant something to the steward. He had seen Lupton's manner with her and supposed he had designs on her. Yet today he appeared oddly bombastic. The doctor felt his stomach knot. He had gained access to the hall under false pretenses. His report was by no means complete until he had heard from Professor Hascher about the caliber of the pistol that he believed to be the murder weapon.

"I have made a preliminary one," he said, lifting up the leather folder he carried. He was just about to lay it on Lupton's desk when the steward's hand flew up.

"I fear you have wasted your time, Silkstone," he said, eyeing Thomas smugly.

The doctor's brow creased. "How so, sir?"

Lupton seemed even more confident than usual. He picked up a pencil and began twirling it between his fingers. "I'm sure you know we have one of Turgoose's murderers in custody and the other will be captured soon."

Thomas thought of sickly Abe Diggott languishing in Oxford Jail and of his son, a fugitive, no doubt somewhere in Raven's Wood.

"I am aware there has been an arrest, but you will need proof to secure a conviction and—"

Again the steward broke him off. He shook his head, still smiling.

"You see, Silkstone, I already have proof."

A look of puzzlement etched itself on Thomas's face. "Oh?"

Lupton nodded. "A flintlock pistol, along with the chainman's pocket watch, was found in Diggott's cottage."

The news came as a shock to Thomas. The shot that killed Jeffrey Turgoose most definitely came from such a weapon—

most probably Sir Theodisius's—although Lupton and his men could not have known it. He tried to recover himself with a well-aimed jibe. "How very convenient," came the response.

Such a reaction wiped the smile from the steward's face.

"You are right, Silkstone." He nodded. "It should be very easy to see the culprits' necks broken." At that moment he snapped the pencil he had been toying with in two and threw the halves down on the desk. His complacent smile switched to a stare, bald and unflinching, and he reached for the servants' bell.

Thomas realized any further discourse was futile. He knew he should leave, but he wanted the last word.

"You have made your position very clear, sir," he told Lupton. "In the absence of proof, supposition suffices," he said, placing his report carefully and deliberately on the desk.

The steward opened his mouth to reply, but before any words came forth, Howard replied to his summons.

"Dr. Silkstone is ready to leave now, Howard," announced Lupton.

Thomas threw the steward a sour look, then walked toward the door. He thanked the butler as he handed him his hat and left by the front entrance.

Descending the steps, Thomas glanced around for his horse. Will must have taken it for water, he supposed. As he searched about, however, he saw another horse being ridden toward the stables nearby. At a distance the rider seemed familiar, a young man with lank hair, but it was his leg that led Thomas to place him. It was the stable lad from the Three Tuns. The youth did not notice Thomas but rode straight into the yard. His presence was puzzling and the doctor was just contemplating it when, as arranged, Will Lovelock brought his mare to him.

"You've told your father?" asked Thomas in a low voice as the boy steadied his mount.

Will looked around shiftily. "He'll be waiting for you, sir," he replied.

The youth handed him the reins and Thomas eased himself into the saddle.

"One more thing," he said, looking down on Will. "There was a young man, just rode into the yard. Did you see him?"

Will nodded. "Aaron Coutt from the Three Tuns, you mean? He comes here quite regular." He shrugged. "I don't know his business."

Thomas looked toward the stableyard. "I believe I may," he said in a low voice, to himself rather than anyone else. He thanked the boy and urged his horse back down the tree-lined drive once more.

A few minutes later he was approaching the estate chapel, its spire as sharp as a needle against the pale blue of the spring sky. He looked about, making sure there were no prying eyes upon him, and rode to the side of the building. He found Jacob Lovelock to be true to his word. Will's father, the head groom, had parked his cart behind the chapel and out of view from the main drive. Thomas tethered his horse and joined him at the front door.

"I need to know if it is her ladyship who is buried in the vault," Thomas told the groom, who came armed with his tools.

"There is doubt, sir?" Jacob asked, his pock-marked face registering shock.

"We can only hope," came the doctor's reply.

Together the two men entered the holy gloom of the chapel. The familiar smell of damp assailed their nostrils. The wooden rood screen and the fine hatchments were there, just as Thomas remembered them. He felt his stomach lurch as he remembered, too, his last encounter in this dark and melancholy place, when he performed an autopsy on the decomposing corpse of Lydia's brother. Now he prayed that it would not be Lydia herself who was lying in the family vault beside Lord Edward.

Thomas led the way to the flight of shallow stairs that descended to the door of the vault. Lovelock followed close behind, carrying the shovel and pickax he always kept on the cart. The doctor had lit a lantern, and holding it aloft, he quietly lifted the latch. The door creaked open on stiff hinges. The sound jangled both men's nerves before they ducked below the lintel and entered the eerie space.

It was all coming back to Thomas with disquieting clarity: the sudden drop in temperature and the familiar sickly sweet note of decomposing flesh that wafted vaguely on the stagnant air. Lovelock lit the wall sconce at the foot of the stairs, illuminating the eight coffins that lined the facing wall, and awaited instructions.

Thomas paused for a moment, mesmerized by the shadows that wavered in a macabre dance against the plaster walls. He had to clear his mind of all extraneous thought and focus on the task in hand. He lifted his gaze to the large stone shelf. The elaborate coffins of the fifth and sixth earls had been joined by another, much plainer, casket. It was smaller, too. Without a word, he glanced at Lovelock. The head groom knew what was required of him. Retrieving the coffin from the shelf was out of the question on this occasion, so Lovelock dragged a wooden box that contained candles and positioned it to enable him to climb up. From his vantage point he could get a good purchase on the coffin lid. With no elaborate locks or fastenings to fool would-be grave robbers, the lid was loosened without much difficulty, but Lovelock did not remove it. He left that dubious honor to Thomas.

Jumping down from the shelf, Lovelock handed Thomas the lantern with an apologetic look. He did not envy the task the doctor was about to undertake. Thomas took the lamp with a trembling hand, knowing that this would be the hardest thing he had ever done in his life. He had never felt more alone than he did at that moment. How he wished that Dr. Carruthers or Sir Theodisius or Professor Hascher could be there at his side. The nausea rose in his stomach as he mounted the crate and set down the lantern. No longer secure, the lid was now at a slight angle to the coffin and already the stench of decay was escaping into the vault. There was no time for sentimentality. No time for the self-indulgence of mourning. Thomas closed his eyes for a second and willed himself to be strong; then, opening them, he seized the lid and slid it down toward the narrow end so he could have a better view of the cadaver's face. A noxious gas rose into the air, a deathly perfume so familiar yet so abhorrent to him. He knew he would have to force himself to look. He collected his wits. His focus would be crucial. He had no desire to linger. Mentally he counted down. Three, two, one.

"Oh my God!" he muttered, clamping his kerchief to his mouth.

"Sir!" exclaimed Lovelock anxiously.

Thomas turned, retching as he did so.

"Sir!" cried Lovelock once more, rushing to Thomas's aid, but he waved him away.

Gulping for breath, his shoulders heaving up and down, Thomas shook his head. "'Tis worse than I feared," he gasped.

"But is it her ladyship, sir?" asked Lovelock, raking his fingers frantically through his hair.

Thomas looked at him with wild eyes, his expression one of anguish. He had lost count of the number of corpses he had examined during his career. Despite their various states of decomposition, he had always remained calm and collected and professional. These bodies were mere vessels that had housed a being, a soul, a spirit, call it what you would. But this cadaver was altogether different. It lay in a plain white shroud that had lifted slightly as the torso filled with gas. But it was the corpse's face, purplish blue and blistered, like a squashed plum, that he found so very disturbing. The dull hair, short and cropped, gave no clue as to the cadaver's identity or even its sex. He tried to blink away the vision of the eyes that bulged out of their sockets and the tongue so swollen that it had protruded from the mouth. The blowflies had already begun feasting and appeared at every orifice. He shook his head, but still the sight remained of a ghastly apparition that was not of this world.

"I cannot be sure," he cried. "I cannot be sure."

"What shall we do, sir?" By now Lovelock was also suffering from the effects of the poisonous air and held his neckerchief to his mouth.

Thomas, all color drained from his face, looked at him with glazed eyes. "I will have to examine it more thoroughly," he replied.

He turned to face the coffin once more, but as he did so, the sound of a latch dropping reverberated in the chapel above.

"What was that?" Lovelock asked in a hoarse whisper.

"Someone is up there," said Thomas. He suddenly remembered he had left the door to the vault steps open to allow the light from above to penetrate the depths. He pressed his finger to his lips.

Footsteps fell on the flagstones overhead. They seemed to be coming nearer. Thomas's ears were filled with the sound of his own heartbeat, so that he could no longer hear clearly. He and Lovelock had no choice but to simply wait in the reeking vault, their breaths becoming shorter and shallower with every passing moment, until finally the groom could bear it no more.

"I need air, sir," he whispered, staggering against a stone pillar.

Thomas nodded. Whoever had entered the chapel must have left it by now, he guessed. Several minutes had passed. He watched as Lovelock zigzagged toward the half-open door and put his head 'round it, gulping like a fish in the fresher air. So relieved was he to emerge into the stairwell that it took him a few seconds to blink away the gloom of the crypt. When he did he noticed a deep shadow on the steps. Looking up he saw a large figure glowering down at him from the threshold of the chapel door.

"Well, well. A sack-'em-up man, eh?" It was one of the new guards Lupton had hired. "Thought you could steal the newest resident, did ya?"

Lovelock leapt upright. "No! No! I—"

"Save your breath for Mr. Lupton," he barked. "Now, shut the door on that stink and come with me!" In his hand he carried a cudgel and he raised it threateningly as he spoke. Lovelock turned and retreated back down the steps to the door, which had remained ajar. He glimpsed inside and saw Thomas, who gave him a silent nod and closed the door from the inside. Lovelock did not hear the latch fall. At least he was safe in the knowledge that Dr. Silkstone could escape from the suffocating chamber, as he began to climb the stairs toward the waiting guard.

Meanwhile Thomas opened the door very slightly so that a chink of light from the stairwell illuminated the reeking space of the vault. He reached for his pipe and lit it with one of the candle flames. The smoke masked the putrid stench but made it no easier to breathe. He waited for what seemed an age before opening the door more fully. It creaked in protest. Emerging into the half-light of the stairwell, he breathed deeply, then inclined his head, listening for any sounds. He knew it would be only a few minutes before more men came to inspect what they thought Lovelock had been about. His opening was small and he realized he must take the chance or risk apprehension. Any proper examination of the corpse would have to wait, though he was relieved at being unable to delve once more into the coffin. It was not that he was repulsed by the rotting flesh or the bloated features. He had, after all, seen worse in the form of Lord Crick, who had been dead almost a sennight when he took his knife to him. No, it was more that if the body was Lydia's, God forbid, this was not how he wished to remember her. He feared that if he were to prove that this putrefying corpse was once his beloved, then he would find it hard to think of her without picturing her eyes straining in their sockets or the maggots emerging from her nostrils. He would be the first to acknowledge that he of all people should not be so afflicted by such an irrational dread, yet he worried that he might be unable to shake off an image that had been seared onto his brain. He dispelled the thought, leaving it in the blackness of the vault as he headed out, abandoning the corpse to nature once more.

Creeping softly up the stairs, he reached the door. He put his ear to the keyhole. As far as he could tell, the chapel was deserted. The door opened slightly with a squeak of dissent, giving him a narrow field of vision. He glanced about him. He was alone. Lovelock had been marched off to face Lupton's wrath. Thomas feared for the outcome of his interrogation. It was not a crime to steal a body, but the groom could still face any number of trumped-up charges, including trying to pilfer from the cadaver. Such a felony could carry the death sentence, and he would not expect Lovelock to sacrifice his life for his own sake. Thomas would not blame the groom if he cracked under questioning, but he knew he must flee the estate as soon as possible, before Lupton's men returned to apprehend him.

Making his way down the side aisle, keeping close to the wall and pressing himself into the shadows, he reached the heavy oak door. Twisting the round handle, he saw the latch lift, but as he heaved the door open, instead of a clear path through the porch, he was greeted by Lovelock, the guard, and another man.

The groom's pock-marked forehead puckered into a frown. His arm was being held behind his back by the guard.

"Oh, sir. They saw your horse," he blurted. "I am so sorry."

The other man stepped forward and grabbed Thomas roughly by the shoulder.

"To the hall with them," said the guard. "You can explain everything to Mr. Lupton yourselves."

Chapter 28

Lupton's men hustled Thomas and Lovelock into the very cart that had originally brought the groom to the chapel and drove them the short distance to Boughton Hall. Thomas knew there was no point in resisting. On arrival he was taken straight to face Lupton. He watched Lovelock being dispatched below-stairs to await his fate.

The steward eyed Thomas for a moment from his desk, elbows planted, fingers tented. He did not invite him to sit, but suddenly rose and circled him in silence, his arms folded.

"So, Dr. Silkstone," he said finally. "I thought better of you than to act like a common thief."

Thomas clenched his jaw. "And I thought better of you and your master than to act like jailers and then murderers, sir."

"Serious allegations, Dr. Silkstone," came a voice behind him. Thomas wheeled 'round to see that Sir Montagu Malthus himself had suddenly swooped into the room. "I trust you have proof."

Thomas narrowed his eyes and took a deep breath, but he found he could no longer control his fury. Jabbing a finger at the lawyer, he felt himself spitting out his words as if they were poisoned darts. "I will find it, so help me God, Malthus, even if 'tis the last thing I do."

Sir Montagu, who had stood impassively by the door, now sallied further into the room, a henchman Thomas recognized from the meeting at his heels. He allowed the butler to take his cloak, then handed him his kid gloves.

"You are distressed, Dr. Silkstone, at the loss of her ladyship." He tilted his head mockingly. "But you really must try to curb your morbid fascination with the dead. You need not have gone to the trouble of opening the coffin to say your farewell."

Thomas shot a puzzled look at the lawyer, whose lips twitched into a smile.

"I spoke with Lovelock, you see," he explained. "He told me the corpse was already unidentifiable."

Thomas tensed. He knew he was beaten on that score. "Lovelock was right," he replied. "There was no way of telling if the corpse was Lydia . . ." He paused for effect. "Or whether it was Annalise Kent."

At the mention of the young spinster's name Sir Montagu's brow arched. He seemed uncharacteristically disconcerted. It was clear Thomas had riled him. He steadied his mood by walking to the window and staring out. After a moment he said, "It appears I underestimated you, Doctor."

"Where is she, Malthus?" cried Thomas, marching up behind him. "What have you done with her?"

Turning to face the young doctor, Sir Montagu let out a strange, muted laugh. He was the puppet master, pulling the strings, and he wanted to make Thomas dance to his tune.

"Don't you see, Silkstone," he began, "it really is of no consequence whose cadaver lies in the vault? What you must understand is that Lady Lydia is dead to the world and"—he poked Thomas's chest as he delivered his verbal blow—"in particular, to you."

Unable to hold himself in check, Thomas responded by lurching forward toward the lawyer, but the henchman grabbed him by his coat sleeve and pulled him back.

"Your conduct does not become a gentleman, sir," butted in Lupton.

Thomas turned on the steward. "And what would you know about being one?" he cried, tugging his disheveled frock coat back into place. "Lady Lydia put her trust in you and you betrayed her."

Sir Montagu shook his head. "We acted in her ladyship's best interests," he corrected.

Thomas stared at him incredulously. He wondered how a man could be so contemptuous and cruel toward his own flesh and blood. Still, he realized that if Sir Montagu ever found out that he knew the truth—that the lawyer was Lydia's real father—he would be placing himself in grave jeopardy. Being privy to Sir Montagu's secret was his trump card and he would play it when he felt the time was right. Now was not the moment. Instead he took a different tack.

"In her best interests?" he echoed. "And what of her son? What of Richard? Where is he? Or have you disposed of him to suit your purposes, too?"

Lupton took particular offense at this last remark. "Curb your tongue, sir!" he roared indignantly, but Sir Montagu lifted his hand to silence the steward.

"My purposes, Dr. Silkstone?" queried the lawyer. "And what, pray, does your razor-sharp intellect tell you they are?"

Thomas shook his head. "I know you wish to control the Boughton Estate. That is why you want to enclose it with your fences and hedges."

Lupton intervened. "Enclosure is the only way forward, Dr. Silkstone."

Thomas nodded. "I'll admit 'tis a convenient way of controlling the landless and the poor and washing your hands of your responsibilities to your tenants."

Sir Montagu slid an odd look toward the steward and gave a wry smile. "My responsibilities?" he huffed. "You have been swayed by the Frenchman Rousseau and his social contract, have you not, Dr. Silkstone? With rights come responsibilities, yes? Such notions do not hold weight with we *English* landowners." He put particular emphasis on the word "English" to try to alienate the young doctor even further.

Thomas could see it was futile arguing with a man so Machiavellian in his outlook. He suspected he had an even deeper purpose than the control of Boughton and its many hundreds of acres. Men like Sir Montagu, ruthless yet enterprising, always kept their eye on the wider scheme of things. Something was brewing. He gleaned it from the looks that were exchanged between the lawyer and his steward and from the new guards employed on the estate. They were plotting and Lydia was an inconvenience in their scheme, an obstacle that needed to be swept aside before their plans could come to fruition. Boughton's old order was changing, yielding place to a new, less benevolent structure, so at odds with her ladyship's own vision for the estate. Thomas knew he had to do everything in his power to mitigate it in Lydia's name.

The young doctor shot back, "You do the people of Brandwick a disservice if you think they will lose their common land and woods without a fight, sir."

Sir Montagu arched a formidable brow. "A threat, Dr. Silkstone? Surely not?"

Thomas's mind flashed to Mr. Turgoose's corpse and to the cottagers and tenants who had gathered to protest on the common. He knew the villagers would not go quietly into the long, dark night of dispossession that surely lay before them and their families.

"There will be trouble, sir, unless you compensate people fairly for their losses," Thomas warned.

"Oh, what a very noble sentiment," sneered Sir Montagu. "But I am afraid the people of Brandwick have proved themselves little more than savages in their treatment of those I engaged to survey the estate."

Swooping upon the desk, Sir Montagu retrieved some bound sheets of foolscap. Thomas recognized them instantly. "Your enlightening postmortem report did not make comfortable reading, Silkstone," said the lawyer, waving the document in the air. "And one of the barbarians who killed my surveyor is still at large and may well strike again." His great shoulders rose in a sigh. He threw the postmortem report back at Thomas in disgust, as if the parchment on which it was written were bloodied. "So," he continued, "I know exactly where my responsibilities lie, Silkstone. I will avenge the death of the man who has died in my service."

Chapter 29

By the light of a single tallow candle, Thomas tried to marshal his thoughts. He was still reeling from his encounter with Sir Montagu, and for more than an hour since his return to the Three Tuns, he had been unable to do anything but pace up and down across his bedroom floor, considering the options open to him in his search for Lydia. There was now no possibility that Sir Montagu would allow him to ascertain once and for all the identity of the body in the vault. Every time he closed his eyes he was reminded of the woman's face: the bruising around her mouth and the swollen tongue. The uncertainty was eating away at him, just as surely as the maggots were feasting on the cadaver's flesh. But he must not allow his own vexation to cloud his judgment. There would be another way. There had to be. If Lydia was still alive, and he had to believe that she was, then his search for her would have to resume at the Bethlem Hospital. He had reached a dead end at Boughton. There was nothing left for him here. He would return to London the following day. He dipped the nib of his quill into the inkpot. He would write to Sir Theodisius and inform him of his inconclusive trip to the Crick family vaults and of his decision to revisit Bethlem.

As his pen hovered above the paper, however, he heard a noise, like rain on the pane. He lifted his gaze to the window, but the glass was dry. Rising from his chair, he looked out onto the street. All was deserted; everyone had heeded the curfew; everyone, that is, except a figure who stood in the half shadows below. Thomas watched him as he aimed a handful of dirt at the pane again. Opening the window, he peered down to see the familiar face of Adam Diggott looking back up at him. Without a word, he motioned to his visitor, then slipped out of his room and down the stairs to lift the latch of the inn's side entrance. The coppicer scurried in through the door like a frightened mouse. His face was hazed with stubble and he stank of stale sweat, reminding Thomas that he had been hiding in the woods for several days.

"You should not be here," Thomas told him bluntly. "If Lupton's men find you—"

Adam Diggott grunted but had to catch his breath before he spoke. It was clear he had run a long way. Doubling over, he planted his hands on his thighs and sniffed, before standing upright.

"You know my pa is charged with the murder and they're after me, too?"

Thomas knew, of course, and suddenly felt guilty that he had not paid more attention to the men's plight. He pictured the old drunkard lazing by the hearth, babbling and confused, barely able to lift his head, let alone a pistol. "And you say you are innocent?"

Lifting his shoulders, Adam let his breath escape from his chest in a loud sigh. "I swear we never hurt the mapmaker, sir."

Thomas did not respond for a moment, then said, "What makes them think you did?"

Adam shook his head. "They see'd my pa wandering after curfew and found a pistol and a pocket watch in the cottage, sir," he replied. "But they put it there. I know they did." His fists were balled and raised to shoulder height, as if pleading for help.

The doctor nodded. He could easily believe that Sir Montagu was capable of such a feat. He wanted revenge at any price, even if it meant victimizing an old man and his innocent son. He must have given orders to arrest and charge any man breaking the curfew, no matter their innocence, no matter the unlikeliness of their guilt. That Abe Diggott just happened to be grandfather to a boy whipped for arson made a conviction even more likely. As far as Sir Montagu was concerned, the whole family bore the stain of guilt.

"Please help us, Doctor. I've heard you've ways to prove a man's innocence or guilt. Save my pa, will ye? I beg." The coppicer clasped his hands together in supplication.

"There is no need to beg," replied Thomas. "Of course I will try and help your father, because I believe he played no part in the murder."

A sigh escaped Adam's lips. "Thank you, sir. Thank you," he said.

"Save your thanks until I see your father pardoned," he replied.

At that moment a latch clicked nearby and a shadow appeared in a candle's glow against the far wall. "Who's there?" called a voice. It was Peter Geech.

"Go," whispered Thomas, bundling Adam Diggott out of the door.

"Who's there?" The landlord drew nearer, his silhouette looming larger. Thomas managed to draw the bar across just before he turned the corner.

"Dr. Silkstone!" came the startled greeting.

"Mr. Geech."

"Everything all right?" The landlord squinted into the darkness, holding his candle aloft.

"My horse," replied Thomas.

"Your horse?"

Thomas nodded. "Your stable lad . . ."

"Coutt?"

"Yes. He saw a cut on her forelock. I was checking on her."

Geech let out an odd chuckle. "Doctoring animals now as well, eh?" He shook his head as if he found the very notion amusing.

Thomas smiled flatly. "All's well."

"I'll bid you good night, then, sir," said the landlord. He turned and chuntered to himself as he walked back down the corridor.

Thomas's breath quivered in his chest as he exhaled. On the morrow he would leave for Oxford.

"I must settle my account," Thomas told Geech early the following morning.

"You are leaving us so soon?" The landlord was wiping spilled ale off the bar counter with a dirty rag.

"Urgent business in Oxford, I'm afraid," said Thomas, not wishing to enlighten the landlord further. But from the look on his face, he already knew.

"Old Abe Diggott's in trouble, I hear." There was a cruel glee in Geech's voice.

Thomas indulged him. Leaning across the bar he said, "And one of your best customers, too."

The landlord nodded in agreement. "He likes a tipple."

"Gin, I've heard. I'll take some, if I may."

Geech narrowed his eyes. His gin was supposed to be a secret, known only to the regulars and to his business associates.

"Gin?" he repeated softly. "Are you sure, Dr. Silkstone? 'Tis not a beverage normally consumed by gentlemen such as yourself."

"A flagon, if you please." Thomas laid a shilling on the counter.

The landlord looked puzzled.

"'Tis not for me, Mr. Geech. 'Tis for Abe Diggott," he replied, adding: "'Twill help him take his mind off the noose."

Chapter 30

Sir Montagu Malthus glanced up from examining the estate's accounts to see his clerk approaching. Gilbert Fothergill entered the study at Draycott House laden down with a pile of scrolls, his face masked by his burden. Finding the sight vaguely amusing, the lawyer arched a heavy brow.

"Is that you, Fothergill?" he asked with a smirk.

The little man's reply sounded muffled. "Aye, sir."

"So what have we here?" he queried, just as the clerk's burden fell and scattered across the desk.

"Petitions, I fear, sir," came the reply. It was not only the cottagers and commoners who were angered by the plans to enclose the Boughton Estate. Despite their acquiescence at the public meeting, it seemed several yeoman farmers had changed their minds on seeing the plans. After digging deeper, they felt they were being cheated by their new lord, too. Their many petitions bore testament to the fact. Some asked to increase the size of their allotment, while others simply opposed the move altogether. All were dissatisfied.

The deposited scrolls covered most of the desk, and Sir Montagu leaned back to survey them. "Well, well. The plebeians have been busy," he commented. He waved a large hand above the sea of white tubes secured with lengths of ribbon or sealing wax.

"Indeed, sir. There is general disquiet, I fear," Fothergill informed his master. He pushed back his spectacles, which had slipped down his glistening nose.

The lawyer looked up at his clerk and sketched an odd smile.

"General disquiet, eh?" he asked. He leaned forward. "We shall see about that," he said, and in one fell swoop, he extended his arm and brushed all the scrolls from the desk. They toppled to the floor and scattered like leaves. Fothergill watched wide-eyed as the papers tumbled over one another and rolled across the boards.

"That is what I think of these petitions, Fothergill," said Sir Montagu as soon as the last scroll had settled. "There is no question of any amendments to the act, so I see no point in prevarication."

A flustered Fothergill stood stunned for a moment before bending down to pick up the wayward petitions.

"No, sir. Quite, sir," he replied, his spectacles slipping along the bridge of his nose every time he bobbed down to pick up a scroll.

Sir Montagu walked over to him, his shadow looming over the clerk, blocking out the natural light and darkening his vision.

"Do not waste my time again, you hear?" he barked. He kicked a nearby scroll hard and sent it flying into the air before seating himself behind his desk once more. Indeed, Boughton's new lord had been extremely swift to act when it came to implementing his program of enclosure. Felling was in full swing, and within the next few days enough spars and posts would be produced to start fencing off the common.

Fothergill, the petitions now bundled under his arms, stood once more before his master. The latter had resumed the work that had engaged him prior to being so rudely interrupted. The clerk cleared his throat.

"I beg your pardon, sir," he began nervously. "But there is one more matter that craves your attention at Boughton."

Sir Montagu slapped the desk and clicked his tongue. "Do I not engage Mr. Lupton for such trivialities?"

Fothergill nodded. "Indeed, sir, but this request comes from Mr. Lupton himself."

"Well?" he snapped.

"He wishes to know if you will sanction the beating of the bounds, sir?"

Sir Montagu leaned back in his chair and looked thoughtful. Next week it would be Rogationtide, the three days over which this infernal tradition was usually enacted. It had completely slipped his mind. Having little care for such a custom, he intended to instruct Lupton to begin fencing the common that same week. The beating attracted hundreds of people from the surrounding parishes, too. Implementation of his plans would undoubtedly mean that a tradition as old as the Domesday Book itself would be consigned to the soil heap of history. The idea of quashing such an ancient custom rather appealed to him. If he were to instigate his plans, the observance could no longer go ahead.

The lawyer drummed the desk. "Tell Lupton to begin fencing," he said finally. "Allow the peasants to exercise their ridiculous ceremonies and in no time at all they'll be sacrificing virgins! Make sure the work gets under way as soon as possible so that they know who is in command."

Fothergill, who had anticipated such a reply, exhaled slowly. He did not relish the thought of being the bearer of more bad news. "Yes, sir," he said, bowing. He was about to beat a hasty retreat when Sir Montagu raised his large hand.

"Oh, and, Fothergill," he called, his features suddenly softening.

"Sir?"

A smile reappeared on the lawyer's lips, as if he had found a certain pleasure in his own generosity. "Send word upstairs to Lady Lydia, will you? Tell her she is invited to join me for tea this afternoon."

Fothergill, slightly bemused by his master's change of mood, found his own lips twitching into a smile. "Yes, sir," he replied.

Later that afternoon Lady Lydia Farrell glided into the drawing room. Her back straight and her eyes bright and alert, she seemed to have regained the health that had deserted her in Bedlam. Her cheekbones, though remaining prominent, sat above the pale blush of a fair complexion, and she filled her new gown well. Indeed, the lace cap that she wore to disguise the fact that her hair was above shoulder length was the only outward sign of the terrible torment she had suffered.

"My dear, how well you look," said Sir Montagu, walking toward her with his arms outstretched.

They exchanged a well-meaning, if stiff, embrace.

"I feel much restored, sir," she replied with a nod.

Sir Montagu gestured to the sofa and rang the bell.

"And young Richard?" he inquired.

Lydia smiled. "He is enjoying the warmer weather and has been playing in the gardens."

"That is good news, indeed," said Sir Montagu, seating himself opposite her. "I shall pay him a visit in the nursery shortly, although I find that my time is most precious at the moment."

Lydia nodded. "Running two estates cannot be an easy task, but you know you can rely on Mr. Lupton."

At that moment, Sir Montagu's butler and two maids entered carrying the tea service on trays.

"Would you do the honors, my dear?" asked the lawyer.

"Of course," replied Lydia, and the maids set down their trays on a table at her side.

Waiting until they were alone once more, Lydia took the lid off the tea canister and spooned some leaves into the pot. She was acutely aware that Sir Montagu's hawklike eyes were following her as she lifted the jug. Adding a little milk to the bowl, she poured in the tea and handed it to him as he sat on the opposite side of the small table.

"Thank you," he said with a nod.

An air of polite civility pervaded the room. There was an unspoken acceptance between them; a scene of domestic quietude, if not bliss, that seemed to defy the events of the past few weeks. Yet, as Lydia sipped her tea, it was obvious that beneath her calm exterior, she remained troubled.

"You have heard nothing, sir?"

Sir Montagu shook his head. "I fear not, my dear. Your last letter was sent five days ago. If a reply was to be forthcoming, I am sure it would have reached you by now."

Lydia's shoulders sloped suddenly. This was the fourth letter she had written to Thomas and the fourth that had gone unanswered. Ever since Sir Montagu had rescued her from Bedlam, she had taken refuge in Draycott House, where she had been reunited with her son. The nightmare of her stay in the hospital remained with her, but it was receding. Her strength had grown daily and her confidence returned. What she could not forget, nor forgive, however, was Thomas's role in her incarceration. She did not understand how someone she had loved so fiercely and so passionately could have abandoned her.

"I know you are right, but it has hit me hard, sir."

Sir Montagu nodded. "Of course it has, my dear, but I did warn you."

It was true, she acknowledged, but it still galled her. Night after night she had cried herself to sleep, longing for Thomas to come and take her away from the living hell that enveloped her, and when, eventually, after weeks of waiting, he had come, he had conspired with Dr. Cameron to let her remain. Oh, he had appeared full of righteous indignation at the time. He had championed her, railed against the restraints used on her, pretended to be appalled by her mistreatment, when in fact he had sanctioned it all. Of course he did not reply to her letters. His plans had misfired. Sir Montagu had heard of her travails and sent a carriage to take her away. She had been sorely mistaken before, thinking that her son's legal guardian and the man who had revealed himself as her real father was responsible for her terrible misfortune. Yet she had been cruelly misled. Sir Montagu had explained everything to her. All along it had been Thomas, the man with whom she had intended to spend the rest of her life, who had seen that she was taken to Bedlam. It was he who had left the instructions for her confinement. Sir Montagu was insistent that he and Dr. Fairweather had simply been acting on his orders. Had she not seen Thomas's signature for herself she would never have believed such calumny. The script, so familiar, yet so shocking, sat next to Dr. Fairweather's on the paper that certified her insane. She had not credited it at first. How could he have betrayed her trust in such a cruel and heartless way? It had taken her many weeks to come to terms with the loss. She had written to him so many times asking him to explain himself, yet he had steadfastly ignored her. She had been jilted in the cruelest of fashions, and slowly but surely she was reconciling herself to the fact that she would never see him again.

"Yes, you did warn me," she acknowledged. Yet again her own judgment had proved flawed. The three men she had loved in her life had all been unworthy. First there was her cousin Francis when she had been little more than a child, then her late husband, Michael, who had been such a wastrel, and now Thomas. His betrayal had been the worst because he had appeared so unswerving in his love, and it was very much reciprocated. Despite being a colonist he had seemed nobler than any highborn aristocrat she had ever encountered. Perhaps now she should lay her future at the feet of her own father, the man who had shown her such infinite wisdom. Lifting her gaze, she looked directly at Sir Montagu. "And I am so very grateful to you, Papa," she said.

Chapter 31

Taking the main road to Oxford via Milton Common, Thomas paid his dues where two turnpike roads intersected. A corpse had been strung up at the gibbet. The body, blackened by tar to preserve it, dangled in an iron cage. A raven sat perched on the gallows frame, eyeing up the banquet that swayed before it in the stiff breeze. It was a sight intended to reassure travelers that highwaymen would be dealt with in the most severe way. It was also a warning to would-be offenders. Thomas only hoped that Abe Diggott would not be treated in the same manner. He urged his horse on even faster.

It was late afternoon by the time the anatomist rode into the city. Going straight to Christ Church, he soon found himself outside the familiar brass-studded door of Professor Hascher's study. He knocked and waited. No reply. Putting his ear to the keyhole, he listened. There was movement within. He knocked again, only louder. Still no reply was forthcoming, and yet it was evident someone was inside. Fearing a mishap had befallen his friend, Thomas seized the handle and pushed the door hard, the momentum carrying him into the room. No sooner had he entered than he was blinded by a bright flash. Simultaneously a loud report filled his ears. It tore through the air, filling it with the smell of saltpeter. Instinctively he dived to the floor as a missile flew past his head, narrowly missing him.

"*Mein Gott!*" came the cry, and the next thing the doctor knew was that Professor Hascher was standing over him, patting his back and encouraging him to stand. Thomas could barely hear his words at first, so great was the ringing in his ears, but seeing the professor safe, he staggered to his feet.

"Sir!" he cried with a mixture of surprise and relief.

"Vhat?" cried the Saxon; then, suddenly realizing his ears were stuffed with gauze, he removed the wadding. "I could've killed you!" he huffed, waving a walnut-handled pistol.

Thomas had to acknowledge that the professor was right.

"I not hear you," wailed the older man, pointing to his ears, which protruded from beneath clouds of white hair. "I vas doing experiment."

Thomas took a deep breath and managed a smile. Of course the professor had been oblivious to his knocking. His mind, let alone his hearing, had been fixed on greater things. Nor had he been expecting a visitor. He had rigged up a makeshift target from a tea chest on the other side of the room and had been aiming at it when Thomas interrupted. In his hand he held Sir Theodisius's pistol.

"So what conclusions can you draw, Professor?" asked the doctor, steadying himself against a chair.

"Ah!" came the response. "I shall show you."

Walking over to his workbench, the professor beckoned. "Look here," he said. "I procure several shots of differing caliber from local gunmaker."

Thomas followed him. "And?"

"And ze only one zat fired correctly vas zis one." The professor held up the small ball between his finger and thumb. It was no bigger than a pea. "I am told it belongs in a tventy-five-bore pistol."

"The same size as the missile that I extracted from our surveyor."

"Exactly."

"If I'm not mistaken, that means twenty-five lead balls of the right size to fit into the barrel of the pistol would weigh a little over half an ounce each and the caliber would be just over half an inch," said Thomas, thinking aloud.

"Correct again," said the professor with a clap of his hands.

Thomas arched a brow. "So it is safe to say that the shot that killed the surveyor was fired from Sir Theodisius's pistol."

"*Ja.*" The professor jerked his head. "Find ze pistol and you find ze killer."

Thomas frowned. "If only it were that simple, Professor." Events had moved on apace since their last meeting, and Thomas knew he needed to ensure that Hascher was informed. "I fear the pistol has been found, but in the possession of a man I believe wholly innocent of the crime," he told him, picking up the duplicate from its box on the workbench. "I am convinced Sir Montagu's men planted it in his home. I am going to have to find some other means of proving he did not commit murder."

"Vhat vill you do?"

"I need to gain access to the accused in Oxford Jail," replied Thomas. "But first I must visit Sir Theodisius."

Before he left, however, Thomas remembered the small flagon of Geech's gin in his case. Handing it to Hascher, he asked, "May I prevail upon you to analyze the contents of this vessel, Professor?"

Taking the flagon, the Saxon unstoppered it and sniffed. His head jerked back as if electricity had just shot through his body. "*Mein Gott!*" he cried, his eyes clearly smarting from the escaped vapor. "Not schnapps?"

Thomas smiled. "No, not schnapps, but the English equivalent. Gin."

Hascher nodded knowingly. "Mozer's ruin, as zey say!"

"Indeed. And anyone else's who is fool enough to drink it," quipped Thomas.

The professor held the flagon at arm's length to avoid breathing in the fumes. "You vant me to find vhat is zerein?"

Thomas went a step further. "I would be most obliged if you could test for lead," he answered.

Hascher's eyes widened. "Lead?" he repeated.

On the ride from Brandwick to Oxford, Thomas had been musing on the seemingly nonspecific symptoms of some of Brandwick's residents. Abe Diggott appeared to suffer from the most striking debilitations—confusion and lethargy, to name but two.

Yet there were others whom he had encountered who might be construed as affecting the signs of some ailment. He'd noted unexplained hair loss in younger men like Josh Thornley and bluish gums and discolored teeth, as in Abel Smith. He recalled that Mr. Peabody, the apothecary, had also commented on the growing band of both men and women who were suffering from bellyaches and gripes. These seemingly disparate symptoms might well be manifestations of a substance that was contained in a source that was tainting all those who partook of it. That source, mused Thomas, could well be the illegal gin distilled by Peter Geech at the Three Tuns. That he did so to avoid duty was neither here nor there to Thomas. What worried him was that somehow a noxious miasma or substance had entered into the liquor. Such a possibility had led him to cast his mind back to a paper he had read by a fellow Philadelphian, Thomas Cadwalader, about the similarities of the dry gripes suffered in the West Indies to an outbreak of colic in France. It was this treatise that had prompted Sir George Baker, the highly respected physician, whom he had met several times in London, to investigate the possible cause of an outbreak of colic in his native Devon. Sir George had conducted a series of tests on cider, that drink so beloved of Devonians, and found that much of it was contaminated with lead.

"I know from my father's correspondence with Benjamin Franklin that lead has long been recognized as injurious to health," explained Thomas. He recalled having been shown a letter from the great man about an episode from his boyhood in Boston when several residents complained of the dry bellyache and the loss of use of their limbs after consuming New England rum. "A subsequent examination of the distilleries led physicians to believe that the mischief was occasioned by the use of lead in the still heads and worms," he concluded.

"So zat is vhy you believe lead could be present in zis gin?" The professor held up the flagon.

"It is a distinct possibility, so we will need to devise ways to test for it," replied Thomas.

At his words, the professor's eyes suddenly brightened, as if he relished the prospect of such a challenge. "Zen allow me to get to vork straightavay," he declared, rubbing his hands together excitedly.

The coroner's office was Thomas's next destination. Not only did he wish to convey the news that Sir Theodisius's pistol had definitely fired the shot that killed Mr. Turgoose—news that would hardly be welcome—but he also needed permission to visit Abe Diggott in jail.

"So they have charged the brigand!" boomed Sir Theodisius as soon as Thomas set foot inside his office. There was a triumphant tone in his voice and he banged his clenched fist onto the desk as if it were a gavel in court and the case had been closed. Yet Thomas had a sneaking suspicion that such bravado and such faith in the judicial system were but a wafer-thin veneer. What information the doctor had to impart was therefore most undesirable. His solemn expression warned the coroner of the bad news to come.

Sir Theodisius raised a brow. His bravado was already crumbling. "You do not share my satisfaction, Silkstone? You are going to tell me they have the wrong man, are you not?"

The doctor gave him a mildly disapproving look, like a child who has been caught telling tall tales. "In your heart of hearts you know it to be true, sir."

The coroner tilted his head upward and rolled his eyes. "Another of your theories?" He did not attempt to hide his frustration.

Thomas strode up to the desk. "Conveniently they found your pistol in the coppicer's cottage."

"My pistol?" he barked.

There was no easy way to break the news. "I fear it has been proved beyond doubt that 'twas your pistol that fired the fatal shot, sir," said Thomas.

Sir Theodisius's forehead furrowed instantly, and he raised his fist to his mouth. "Dear God, no," he mumbled.

"Tests have been conducted, sir—" began Thomas.

"You and your tests, Silkstone!" blurted the coroner. His fist stamped the desk and he took a deep breath to calm himself. "So this man, this coppicer, is the victim of a conspiracy? Is that what you are saying?"

Thomas nodded. "That is my belief, sir, and I would ask you to give me access to him in jail so that I can prove his innocence."

Sir Theodisius sighed deeply once more, sending his jowls quivering. "Very well," he said, taking up his quill. "I will grant you a meeting with this man, but on one condition."

"Sir?"

The coroner leaned his bulky frame forward. "If you prove him innocent, you will not stop searching for Turgoose's murderer." There was a thinly veiled plea in his voice.

Thomas eyed him squarely. "You have my word, sir," he said.

Chapter 32

Armed as he was with Sir Theodisius's letter of authorization, it did not take long for Thomas to gain entry into the jail. Not that he welcomed having to return. Even after all this time, the memories were still raw. The sounds, the smells, the sights, all conspired to remind him of his visits to see Lydia's late husband as he, too, wallowed in a stinking cell in Oxford Jail awaiting trial for murder.

Captain Michael Farrell had been kept in relative luxury. At least he had not been forced to share his cell with other criminals; at least he had his own pot to piss in and had not been shackled to the wall, the irons chafing his flesh. Abe Diggott had been accorded no such niceties. Three other men and a boy were crowded in with him, not to mention the cockroaches that scurried and scrambled across the floor.

The door groaned open and the turnkey allowed the doctor entry. One of the prisoners rushed up to him and tugged at his topcoat. The jailer fended him off with a quick clip of his cosh and the man retreated, whimpering.

"Anyone else?" growled the jailer. He flexed his muscles and slapped his palm with his cosh. "There he is," he said to Thomas, using his weapon as a pointer. "There's your man."

Abe Diggott was lying in a crumpled heap on the slippery cobbles, manacled at the ankles.

"'Tis Dr. Silkstone, Abe," he said softly, kneeling down beside the woodsman. Diggott lifted his head slowly, as if waking from a dream. Thomas noticed that his eyes were swimming in their sockets as he tried to focus. His cheeks caved inward and his shirt draped itself as loose as a shroud over his torso.

"Here," Thomas said, holding up a cup of a draft he had prepared to give the old man energy.

Diggott lifted his hands slowly upward, but as he tried to hold the cup, his fingers seemed to freeze.

Thomas frowned when he saw that he seemed unable to grasp the vessel. "What is it?" he asked.

The coppicer fixed him with a blurry gaze. " 'Tis my fingers, sir. I can't move 'em," he moaned, studying his hand like a curious child might look at a strange, alien object.

Thomas reached out. The digits were icy cold. Holding them between his own palms, he began to rub the fingers, trying to encourage the blood to circulate, but with little success. "How long have you suffered like this?" he inquired.

The old man shrugged. " 'Tis hard to say. A few days now," he replied with little conviction. "I ain't been able to hold an ax or a knife for a few weeks—I know that much," he added.

"Enough now," shouted the turnkey. "Your time is up," he told the doctor.

Thomas protested. "I have had no chance to examine the prisoner properly."

"He'll be dead soon enough, anyways," came the crushing reply.

Abe Diggott shook his head resignedly. "He's not wrong," he groaned.

"But you are innocent, are you not, Abe?" asked Thomas.

The accused man shrugged. "Makes no difference, Doctor," he replied. "If Sir Montagu wants me dead, then I may as well put the noose 'round me own neck."

Thomas gave no reply. He could not counter the man's words because he knew them to be true. It was left up to him to prove otherwise.

"I will not abandon you, Abe," he assured the woodsman. But Diggott simply rolled himself into a ball once more, his head in his hands, seemingly accepting his fate.

* * *

Returning immediately to the anatomy school, Thomas found Professor Hascher hard at work in his laboratory. In fact, such was the Saxon's enthusiasm that he had even donated the last of his bottles of finest-quality schnapps to act as the controlled element in the experiment he was conducting.

"I have forfeited it to ze greater cause," he announced dramatically, brandishing an empty bottle. Thomas cast an eager eye over the various paraphernalia that had been assembled for the test. "It is to your satisfaction, yes?" asked the Saxon.

"Most definitely."

"Zen ve begin?"

Thomas nodded and, slipping off his coat, he rolled up his sleeves and set to work. First he soaked a clean piece of paper in fifty drachms of Professor Hascher's schnapps, then another in the suspect gin. Next he took a flask containing a volatile tincture of sulfur, produced by dissolving crystals in a measure of warmed aniseed oil, and exposed the papers, one at a time, to the fumes. The results were rapid, if not instantaneous. The paper soaked in schnapps remained unchanged. However, the sheet soaked in the gin turned much darker in color before their eyes.

Thomas turned to Hascher. "An encouraging start," he said.

"Ve certainly follow ze right path, Dr. Silkstone." The professor nodded. "Vhat next?"

"Hepar sulfuris?" suggested Thomas. When added to lead, it was known to discolor.

"A good choice," agreed Hascher, and he scanned his shelves for a bottle. "I prepared zis myself," he said, recalling with great pride how he had saved discarded oyster shells after a particularly good college dinner and burned them before adding pure flowers of sulfur. "Let us see if zey—how do you say?—do ze trick."

A few drops of the substance were added first to the paper impregnated with schnapps, then to the gin-soaked piece. The men stood back to watch. They did not have to wait long. Within four minutes the gin sample had turned a murky gray.

The professor clapped his hands. "I believe ve have our proof, Dr. Silkstone. Zere is lead in ze gin."

Thomas, however, did not share his colleague's enthusiasm. "This sample does indeed contain lead, Professor, and it would certainly explain some of the chronic symptoms that seem to afflict the residents of Brandwick." Thomas thought of the discolored teeth, the strange hair loss, and the gripes that, according to Mr. Peabody, regularly troubled the village imbibers. He went on: "I am afraid, however, it is in an insufficient quantity to cause the kind of symptoms I have seen in the accused man: the paralysis; the befuddlement. It would take a much more concentrated amount of poison to result in his severe reaction."

Hascher suddenly looked crestfallen. "So ve have vasted our time?"

Thomas did not wish to dishearten the professor. The discovery of lead in the liquor was only the first step in what he knew would be a long and no doubt hard-fought battle to prove Abe Diggott's innocence.

"Let us just say, we must continue our mission." He gave a reassuring smile. The problem was, he knew the trial would be held within the next few days and he was rapidly running out of time.

Chapter 33

The men met under cover of darkness at Maggie Cuthbert's cottage in Raven's Wood. Despite Abe Diggott's arrest, Lupton's lackeys still patrolled the streets of the village to enforce the curfew. More important, however, they were on the lookout for Adam Diggott, also wanted for the brutal murder of Jeffrey Turgoose. Will Ketch and Josh Thornley had made good their escapes from their cottages unnoticed. Zeb Godson, living in the forest as he did, had not needed an alibi.

"You seen him?" Ketch asked Godson.

The charcoal burner's eyes seemed to glow white from out of his grimy face. "He'll be here."

They were sitting on the floor in front of a blazing fire that threw long shadows across the room. Nevertheless, the light was sufficient to allow them to see the fear on one another's faces well enough. In the forest silence they heard an owl hoot. A few seconds later its call was answered by another. It seemed that even the night birds were mocking them, this party of fools, this band of Davids who would take on the might of Sir Montagu Malthus and his ilk.

Suddenly Thornley straightened his back. "Footsteps," he whispered. The men froze, held their breaths. Maggie Cuthbert went to the window and lifted a ragged drape.

"'Tis him," she said, and the men exhaled as one.

Adam Diggott stood in the doorway and was ushered in quickly. The other men rose to greet him, like a long-lost friend or a hero returning from war. He strode to the hearth and held his hands to the fire.

Maggie Cuthbert joined him, a red-hot poker in her hand. She laid it in the embers for a few seconds, then thrust it inside a tankard of gin. The liquid inside fizzed and hissed, and she handed it to Diggott. He downed it in one.

"What news from Oxford?" asked Will Ketch.

Adam Diggott wiped his mouth with his sleeve and scowled. "They've charged him," he grunted.

Josh Thornley shook his balding head. "Then 'e's as good as dead," he muttered unthinkingly.

Barely had his words left his mouth when Adam dived at him, grabbing him by his jerkin, his fist primed to land a punch. Widow Cuthbert came between them.

"Stop that!" she cried. "Save your fighting for Lupton and Malthus or I'll box your ears myself!"

The two men pulled away from each other, knowing what the old woman said to be true. She may have been as wizened as a willow trunk, but she was wise with it.

Thornley looked to her for guidance. "What's to be done, then?"

The widow eyed the circle. She set down the poker and planted herself in her customary chair at the hearth, cradling a tankard.

"First we need to know where we're at," she told them plainly. "You can't start a journey, not knowing where you're coming from."

The men nodded at the logic of this statement. Adam Diggott was the first to proffer information.

"The American doctor has gone to Oxford to see my pa," he said.

"The knife man?" Thornley mocked. "And what good can he do?"

Maggie Cuthbert held up an admonishing hand. "Dr. Silkstone's a good man. He's helped young Jake, and he'll help Abe, too, in whatever way he can."

Thoughts turned to the young boy who'd been so cruelly

whipped along the High Street and whose wounds still oozed pus two weeks on. No one knew when or if he would be able to work again.

"Damn them at the hall!" cried Adam, suddenly leaping up and hurling his tankard across the room so that it hit the wall. "I say we get our revenge. I say we march up to Boughton and burn the house to the ground!" His eyes were aflame as the anger inside him bubbled over.

Will Ketch tugged at his arm and pulled him down into the circle again. "We know you're angry, Adam. But 'twould do no good."

"'Twould do me good," he growled, giving the hearthstone a hard kick.

Zeb Godson had remained silent throughout the exchanges, save for the odd phlegmy cough. With a long stick he had been making patterns on the earth floor. He addressed his fellows for the first time. "Them up at the hall are still going to rob us of our land. Even if Abe is spared the noose, all of us will go on suffering."

His words hung on the air for a moment before the silence was filled by the hoot of another owl.

"He's not wrong," said Will Ketch, slapping his thigh. "We must further our cause. We can't let them take our ancient dues. I say we carry on fighting!"

Widow Cuthbert snorted. "Like ya did before? Let your boys set fire to fence posts or black your faces and make noises in the woods? Look where that's got ye." She fired her words so quickly that her spittle hit Adam Diggott in the face. But they knew she was right.

"You got a better idea, old woman?" sneered Josh, leaning forward.

The widow chewed her gums as she eyed each man in the circle at her feet. She knew she had more balls than all of them put together. But it did not need brute force to overcome the powers at the hall. What was needed was cunning and guile.

"As a matter of fact, I have," she told them.

"You'll put a curse on 'em, yes?" jeered Josh Thornley.

The other men laughed, but Maggie Cuthbert tut-tutted at them as if they were small boys.

"No curses. No witchcraft," she said, lifting her gnarled finger up to her temple. "Just my head."

Will Ketch leaned forward. "And how might that be?"

"You heard what they did at West Haddon?"

The village lay only a few miles away over the county border, but news of what the residents did had traveled the length and breadth of England. It was the talk at markets, fairs, and water pumps up and down the land. It was talk of how the calling of a football match had gathered together a great mob that trampled down fences and set light to them in defiance of the landlord who wanted to enclose the commons.

The men slid each other sideways glances. They had heard all right.

"But we don't need no football match," said the old woman, shaking her head.

"No?" pressed Josh Thornley.

Maggie Cuthbert smirked and let out an odd chuckle. "No," she said, shaking her wiry old head. "We got the beating of the bounds."

"But Sir Montagu has banned it," protested Zeb Godson.

The old woman shook her head and fixed him with a wry smile. "If every man, woman, and child of this parish comes together, there ain't nothing we can't do," she said.

Chapter 34

The thought had come to Thomas just as he was about to retire to his bed at the Jolly Trooper in Oxford that night. The room was stuffy and he had poured himself some small beer from a jug on the nearby nightstand. As he looked out the window onto a starless night, his mind returned to Abe Diggott. He thought of the whites of the man's eyes, fretted with red veins, of the strange bluish hue of his skin, and of his hands unable to grasp a cup, let alone fire a gun. He knew there had to be some reason why this malevolent gin was affecting him so badly, why his symptoms were so much worse than anyone else's in the village. True, he drank as much, if not more, than any other man, but for the spirit to have such a dramatic effect there had to be something more, by Thomas's reckoning. He drained his cup, and that's when it hit him. He suddenly remembered the earthenware flagon that he had seen at the old man's side in the Diggotts' cottage. The gin was stored in the vessel for days on end. What was more, it was glazed inside. It occurred to him that perhaps the spirit might have reacted with an ingredient in the coating. He remembered, too, Adam's words about his father's reliance on gin: "Drinks the stuff like mother's milk, he does."

If he could prove that this poisoned liquid had rendered Abe Diggott incapable of the most straightforward of actions, let alone firing a pistol, then a court might be persuaded of his innocence. To test his theory, however, he needed to obtain the flagon itself. He would have to return to Brandwick straightaway.

Zeb Godson could not be sure what woke him that morning in his makeshift shelter in Raven's Wood. Was it the sound of wood cracking and spitting above the usual dawn chorus of birds, or perhaps the strange smell like roasted meat that wafted up his nostrils? Either way, as soon as his eyes had steadied themselves after his deep sleep and as soon as he had planted his feet on the rush mat by his leaf-stuffed mattress, he decided something was amiss. His head ached so badly from the gin the night before, it felt as if it had been cleaved by an ax. The act of rising caused him to grab his temples and press them hard with his knuckles to ease the pain. But it was not until he had stamped on his boots and pulled on his hat before venturing out of his hovel that he knew exactly what was wrong.

The charcoal burner had spent the previous day stacking wood in the nearby kiln. He'd laid the first layer of seasoned timbers in an open cartwheel shape to allow the air to enter at the base. That way there'd be a good first burn. Next he'd begun placing cut logs around the circumference of the kiln, before spiraling them inward, leaving a hole in the middle for a stack where the smoke could escape. It was then that he gathered together the tinder and stuffed it down the central hole. This was the secret to a good, strong fire, a dry charge that would burst into flame as soon as it was lit, as if with one smoldering look from a wanton woman. By the time he'd stuffed the stack, the light was fading, so he'd decided to finish laying down the rest of the logs on the morrow. He'd killed a pheasant for the pot, roasted it on a spit, then spent the rest of the evening downing Geech's gin in Mad Maggie's cottage before somehow managing to return to his shelter for the night.

Now, as he stood stretching his aching limbs at the entrance of his humble abode, the rays of the rising sun lanced through the leafless trees onto the forest floor, forcing him to blink. He blinked again, only this time not to fend off the piercing light, but to satisfy himself that his eyes were not deceiving him. From out of the half-made kiln in the clearing, smoke was dancing like feathers in the gentle breeze. Black smoke.

"No!" he shouted out loud. His lone cry sent roosting crows to flight.

His first thought was that the sun's rays must have been so powerful that they'd set the tinder alight. He rushed over to the kiln. Flames! The logs were well alight. How could this be? He'd lose the whole batch; all his hard work was going up in smoke, literally. He reached for his beater and, leaning over the rim of the kiln, started flaying the flames as if they were hissing serpents rising and trying to bite him. But it was no use. The smoke filled his lungs and the flames leapt at him, forcing him to retreat. He grabbed a flagon of small beer he'd left by the kiln and downed it quickly, as if to douse the burning of his own lungs.

The fire had a good hold, hungrily feeding off the energy the logs gave it. He guessed it must have been burning at least an hour. But there was something else, too, a trunk toward the center of the kiln, near the stack. He had not put it there. It was too large. It would not burn well, and yet the flames seemed to relish it, caressing it with long tongues. The familiar cracks of the wood were punctuated by an odd sound, like the spitting of a hog roasting. He watched transfixed as now and again the fire flared around this large log, as if fat had been poured into the blaze. Soon, however, his puzzlement and fascination turned to anger. Someone must have started the fire deliberately. Hal Thornley sprang to mind. Perhaps he'd acquired a taste for making fire and not learned his lesson in the pillory. Or mayhap it was someone with a grudge. He wondered who might wish him ill. The new master at Boughton. Yes, that was it. He wanted to enclose the woods, and this was his way of telling Zeb that he and his sort were no longer welcome. Next his men would come to tear down his home. But if this firing of his kiln was meant to frighten him, well, the new lord would have to think again. He'd stay rooted to this woodland like the very trees that he lived among. No Act of Parliament could rob him of a way of life that had been his father's and his father's before him.

A small explosion suddenly jolted him back to the moment. In reality it was more a loud pop, but it made him curious. He shielded his eyes and braved the smoke. It seemed the end of the trunk had detonated itself and exploded into hundreds of pieces. But what was that? Strange. He peered closer. Something burned red hot. Metal? Surely not? He could wait no longer. He took a pail and headed for the nearby stream. Filling his bucket, he returned and splashed its contents over the trunk. He repeated it a second and a third time as the wood hissed in protest at the water and finally acquiesced.

For a moment the smoke defeated him once more, but it soon dissipated, and taking a long-handled rake, he reached across the rim of the kiln. Leaning over at full stretch he prodded the trunk with the end of his rake. It did not feel like wood; it was soft. He prodded again, bringing the rake down on something hard that gave out a hollow clank. It was metal. Then it struck him. His eyes ran down the length of the trunk to the tip of a bar that glowed red in the heat, returning thrice more, out of a compulsion, a need to be sure, and with each sweep of his eyes, his body tensed more. A sense of panic rose from inside his chest and struggled out of his throat in a strange half cry.

The flames had all but gone now, but the heat remained intense. Still he could not venture nearer to investigate, but in truth he did not need to. The horror had already dawned on him. He was not looking at a charred, oversized hunk of wood that had somehow strayed into his charcoal kiln, and whoever had set the blaze had done so not to intimidate him, or to spite him. No, the person or persons who had torched his half-laid batch of wood had done so with the sole intention of incinerating a human corpse.

Chapter 35

That same day at the Jolly Trooper, shortly after noon, Thomas was making ready to leave for Brandwick. He needed to retrieve the earthenware flagon from the Diggotts' cottage in order to prove his theory, which would, if all went to plan, save the old man's life. He was therefore not prepared for an urgent message he received from the coroner's office. A breathless courier handed it to him as he was about to leave the inn. He recognized Sir Theodisius's hand immediately. The note read:

My Dear Silkstone,
I regret to inform you there has been another murder in Raven's Wood. I ordered the immediate recovery of the body and it will be at the anatomy school later today. I would ask that you conduct a postmortem on it with all haste.
Very sincerely,
Theodisius Pettigrew

Once again Thomas found himself in the company of Professor Hascher in the small mortuary, and once again the tang of death was in the air. Only this time there was another element added to the stench.

Thomas sniffed the fetid air. "Burn?"

Professor Hascher, leading him toward the dissecting table, nodded. *"Ja."*

"Where was the body found?"

"In—how you say?—a kiln. A charcoal burner found it."

Thomas thought immediately of Zeb Godson and his hovel in Raven's Wood.

Hascher nodded. "Ze body vas half-incinerated," he said, pulling back the sheet to reveal the ghastly, blackened corpse.

It was a sight that even Thomas found shocking. The victim had been reduced to little more than a blackened shell on the left side of his body, while his skull had been shattered in the blaze, ridding the brain of what little protection it had from the flames. The face was charred beyond all recognition. A greasy residue covered what remained of the flesh, while both arms were oddly contorted, the hands clawed and the thighs raised. The cadaver was bent in a posture of agony that told of tormenting flames.

"The pugilistic stance," muttered Thomas, holding his lantern aloft and casting its meager light over the corpse. It appeared as if in a defensive position, with its elbows and knees flexed and its hands clenched in fists. "The muscles stiffen and shorten in high temperatures."

Hascher shot him a horrified look, and the younger anatomist read his expression. "It can occur even if the person is dead before the fire," he explained, adding: "Let us hope that this is such an instance."

Hanging his coat on a nearby peg, Thomas opened his medical case and took out his apron.

"Has the body been identified?" he asked.

The professor looked blankly. "I do not know."

"No matter," said Thomas as he set to work.

Starting with a cursory examination, he could be sure the corpse was male, even though the hair had been scorched and what was left of the skin was blackened. It was while he was looking more closely at the lower torso, however, that his heart missed a beat. From his case he retrieved a small hammer and with it tapped what at first glance appeared to be a shinbone. On closer inspection, however, Thomas knew he was mistaken.

"Vhat is it?" asked Hascher, as Thomas tapped again.

"'Tis metal," answered the anatomist, staring at a twisted and buckled iron leg. He straightened his back. "I know this man," he said, his voice flat with shock. He thought of lank-haired Aaron Coutt leaping around like a hare on his makeshift limb. "He was the stable lad at the inn at Brandwick."

"So vhat vas he doing in ze voods?"

Thomas had a good idea but said nothing.

"And zis . . ." The professor remained transfixed by the corpse. "An accident?"

Thomas refused to commit himself until he had probed further, although a theory was beginning to take shape. The old ruins and the secret stash of smuggled goods he had uncovered came to mind. Now that he knew the hapless youth's identity, there was little doubt in his mind that he was dealing with a murder rather than an accident. Recalling the isolated woodland glade where illicit goods were traded, he thought it was very likely that the stable lad had met his untimely end at another's hand. However, as Dr. Carruthers frequently reminded him, as an anatomist, his was to discover not the why, but the how. Thomas narrowed his eyes in thought and focused on the task in hand. "The corpse is only partly incinerated," he observed. "If it had been completely burned, then only fragments of bone and the metal would remain." He bent down low, his magnifying glass in hand. "A human body burns rather like a tree trunk, you see, Professor. First the outer layers of the skin fry, then peel off, until, shortly afterward, the thicker underlayer of skin shrinks and splits. It is then that the yellow, subcutaneous fat starts to ooze out."

"And zis fat makes good fuel, *ja?*" asked Hascher.

"Only if it has sufficient material nearby to act as a wick," replied Thomas, plunging a scalpel into the blackened tissue.

"Like a candle?"

"Indeed. The youth's clothes absorbed the fat and drew the flames toward it."

The professor watched Thomas examine the corpse in silence for a moment before he asked: "So you are saying ze burning process vas interrupted?"

Thomas looked up. "I'm saying it was never properly begun. This was a halfhearted botched affair to dispose of a corpse. It takes approximately seven hours for a body to sustain its own fire. This was only alight for half—" Suddenly he broke off. His attention had been diverted by something on the dead man's chest.

"The gorget, if you please," Thomas said, holding out his hand.

Professor Hascher quickly obliged, selecting the probe from the array of instruments on an adjoining table.

"You have found somezing more?"

Thomas was holding his breath, concentrating on an area of chest near the heart. As he pierced the charred skin, there was a sound like rustling leaves. "Tweezers!" he called, and within a few seconds of probing he had retrieved the object of his curiosity from within the thoracic cavity. He held up a small spherical ball to the lantern's light.

"A shot!" cried the professor, his eyes opening wide in surprise.

"That is what killed Aaron Coutt," said Thomas emphatically. "He was, most definitely, murdered."

Hascher's finger suddenly flew into the air. "Could it be . . ."

The thought occurred to both men at the same time.

". . . the same pistol that killed Turgoose?" Thomas finished his colleague's sentence. "As far as I know it remained at Boughton Hall after it was found in Abe Diggott's cottage."

"So . . . ," began Hascher. "Another weapon is surely responsible?"

"Or," said Thomas thoughtfully, "the same weapon in the hands of Lupton's men."

There was a pause as both anatomists contemplated the implications of the discovery, until suddenly the professor's finger darted in the air again as if he had just remembered something.

"What is it, professor?" asked Thomas.

"Abe Diggott, ze man charged viz ze surveyor's murder?"

"Yes. What of him?"

Hascher lifted his clenched fist up to his forehead as if reprimanding himself. "It slipped my mind," he said apologetically.

"What, Professor? You have forgotten something?"

Hascher nodded. "Ze old man's date of trial is set."

"Yes?"

The Saxon eyed Thomas apologetically. "It is ze day after tomorrow."

Chapter 36

As he rode out of the quadrangle at Christ Church on his way to Brandwick, Thomas knew his mission was twofold: First he needed to collect Abe Diggott's earthenware flagon, which might prove the old man's innocence, and second he wished to visit the kiln where Aaron Coutt's badly burned body was found. During an investigation he had made it a principle to always see for himself where crimes of such a serious nature were committed. He felt it imperative that he familiarize himself with the terrain and conditions and, of course, that he conduct a thorough examination of the surrounding area. He was becoming more convinced with every investigation he undertook that everything, be it human or animal, animate or inanimate, left a trace.

Accordingly, late that afternoon, he found himself outside the Diggotts' cottage. He knocked and was answered by the coppicer's wife, Rachel. She was clearly relieved to see her caller was Thomas, but fearful of what he might say.

"Dr. Silkstone! You bring news?" she said, quickly ushering him inside.

The room was gloomy but warm, and Thomas glanced over to the bed where he could see the young boy still lay.

"How does he fare?" he asked, walking over to him. He saw that he was now on his side, although asleep.

His mother, wringing her hands, pulled her features into a smile.

"The fever is gone," she said. "And the pain lessens."

She showed Thomas to a chair by the fire, and he settled himself down as she poured a tankard of small beer and set it by his side. It was clear she was anxious to hear news.

"I have seen your father-in-law in jail," he reported. She sat opposite him and leaned forward. "He is frail. Very frail," he said.

"And . . . ," she urged impatiently.

"And it is clear to me that he was physically incapable of firing a pistol, and has been for some time."

"But . . . ?" Thomas felt the woman's eyes tugging at his.

"But the court will not take my word for it, Mistress Diggott. I need proof."

"Oh?" Rachel frowned, then followed Thomas's eyes to the earthenware pot, now standing on the mantelshelf.

"The flagon," Thomas said bluntly. "It has gin in it?"

She bit her lip and nodded. "'Tis full. It's not been touched since they took him."

"May I?"

Thomas rose and, leaning toward the hearth, picked up the vessel, the liquid sloshing inside it. He peered into it. It was as he suspected. The glaze of the pot was pitted inside.

"May I take this with me back to Oxford?" he asked.

Rachel gave him a quizzical look. "You think 'twill help?" She was putting all her trust in Thomas.

"I do," he replied with a shallow nod.

"Then you must do anything you can to bring Abe back safe, doctor," she replied.

With the earthenware flagon and its contents stored safely in a saddlebag, Thomas rode up to Raven's Wood in search of Zeb Godson. The climb was steep, and now and again his horse stumbled on the jagged shards of flint that peppered the bridle path. Before long, however, he reached a plateau and the going became easier.

The weather seemed to have turned; the wind had changed direction and there was a sense that spring, so long absent, was beginning to show its welcome face. Thomas noted that the woodland floor was bursting into life, too. Clusters of cowslips and celandine peeped yellow heads above the leaf carpet, and the green spears of bluebell shoots pushed through the beech mast underfoot. Now and again a breeze made the fallen leaves rustle and dance. The slightest sound caused him to look about him. He now knew that Raven's Wood belonged not only to sawyers and coppicers and charcoal burners, but to smugglers as well as highwaymen.

He ventured farther into the forest, all the while following the main track that he had taken before, and after a while he came to a clearing. A familiar structure in the shape of a dome, half turfed, like some prehistoric burial mound, loomed up ahead. Zeb Godson, wearing his strange hat, was at work near it, shoveling turf.

At the sound of approaching hooves, the charcoal burner looked up. When he saw Thomas, he stopped what he was doing. Leaning on his shovel, he pushed back his bonnet with a thumb and wiped his forehead.

"Mr. Godson," greeted Thomas as he drew near.

"Dr. Silkstone," said Zeb Godson, returning a wary look.

"I am come about the body. I am here with the coroner's authority." Thomas knew Sir Theodisius would have sanctioned his visit.

Zeb Godson grunted and gave a shallow nod.

"I need to see where you found it."

The charcoal burner's grimy finger pointed to the disheveled pile of turf and wood only a few feet away. It seemed unkempt and unfinished. "There," he said.

Thomas dismounted and walked forward to inspect the kiln. Half of the logs were laid neatly, but the rest of the timbers seemed already charred and blackened. He turned to Godson.

"The body was in here?"

The charcoal burner nodded. "Aye." He coughed suddenly and spat phlegm on the ground.

Thomas could see that this interview would be like drawing blood from a stone.

"Where, precisely, if you please?"

Godson pointed to the blackened circle that measured around six feet in diameter at the nearest edge of the kiln.

"And how do you suppose it got there?" He was purposely evasive, not wishing to disclose the victim's identity.

The charcoal burner shifted uneasily, as if affronted by the question. "I didn't kill 'im, if that's what you mean," he snapped. His blackened hands tensed around the handle of his shovel. His eyes gleamed from out of their sooty sockets.

Thomas smiled. "I am not suggesting you did, Mr. Godson, but I am trying to ascertain—" Thomas stopped himself and began again in more colloquial language. "I am trying to gather information as to what circumstances may have led to this death. I would be most obliged if you could tell me when and how you found the body."

At this assurance, Godson seemed to relax a little. "I woke early and smelled smoke," he began. "So I came out and I saw the kiln was alight."

"How could that be?" interrupted Thomas. "Someone had to set it alight, I assume."

The charcoal burner could not hide his low opinion of a city dweller, ignorant of country ways. "'Course they did. I'd laid most of the logs for the burn, but I'd not finished. They'd put 'im over the side and put a light to 'im to get 'im started. Only 'e didn't take proper. Too much air, you see."

Thomas was aware that a human body could be as slow to burn as it could be quick. The combustion depended on so many various factors.

"And you have worked on the kiln since?" Despite evidence to the contrary, Thomas very much hoped that the kiln had remained as it was when Godson discovered Coutt's body. He was sorely disappointed.

The charcoal burner snorted. "I needs earn a crust, Doctor. I can't waste a whole burn."

"So you are stacking new logs on top of the charred ones?"

Godson shook his head. "Them that's charred are wasted. I'm taking 'em out." He lifted his shovel slightly from the ground.

"And have you found anything among the burned wood? Anything you think strange?"

Again Godson remained taciturn. He shrugged. "No," came the reply.

Thomas leaned over the shallow ridge of the kiln and peered into the blackened remains of Aaron Coutt's funeral pyre. There was nothing obvious to be seen, save for the charred logs that carried blooms of white ash upon them.

"There is one more thing, Mr. Godson," said Thomas, walking toward his horse. "Did you hear a shot at any time last night?"

The charcoal burner thought for a moment. "I got pissed last night, fit for nothing," he replied. "No, I didn't 'ear nothing."

Thomas would wager it was Geech's gin that put him in such straits. He thanked Godson for his cooperation.

He grunted once more. "So you going after 'em?" he asked, just as Thomas was about to mount.

"After whom?"

"Them that killed Coutt, o' course."

Thomas turned. "You knew Coutt?" Thomas thought of the lad's metal leg, which would have made him easily identifiable to the villagers.

"I knowed 'im all right," said Godson, adding: "'E played a dangerous game."

"What do you mean?"

"'E were a spy for them at the hall," came the blunt reply. "For that new steward."

The unexpected sight of the stable lad at Boughton suddenly flashed before Thomas. He knew there had to be some connection with the stash of smuggled goods at the old ruins.

From his saddle he looked along the track, now framed by

verdant leaves. "How far is it from the old ruins to where Mr. Turgoose was murdered, Mr. Godson?" he asked.

The charcoal burner cupped his sooty hand and rubbed his neck in thought. "A mile, I'd say."

Thomas wondered it was so far. The distance cast doubt on his theory that the surveyor and his party had come across the smugglers' stash at the ruins.

"Thank you, Mr. Godson," said Thomas. He was just about to turn his horse when the charcoal burner raised an arm.

"There is something you wish to tell me?" asked the doctor.

The charcoal burner squinted against the sunlight that now lanced its way into the clearing.

"Abe Diggott," he said.

"Yes?"

"He didn't kill the mapmaker. Nor did Adam."

Thomas steadied his horse, which was growing restless. "What makes you so sure?"

Godson shifted awkwardly and paused before delivering his words. "Because we was near the place where the mapmaker was killed, sir."

Thomas whipped 'round. "Oh? Why was that?"

"We wanted to fright 'em," he mumbled. "They wasn't welcome, so we gave 'em a scare."

Thomas thought of the soot he had scraped off the foliage near the scene of the murder. "You blacked your faces, yes?" It suddenly made perfect sense. He'd heard of gangs in Surrey sooting themselves so they could continue hunting free of charge on common land. From the charcoal burner's expression, however, there was more. "You saw something, didn't you?" pressed Thomas. "You saw who killed Mr. Turgoose?"

The charcoal burner shook his head vigorously. "I swear we never. We 'eard the 'orse whinny when it fell into the pit and we 'eard the shot. Then we ran as quick as lightning."

"We?"

"There was a few of us."

"Who?" As soon as he had asked the question, Thomas knew

it would be futile to ask the man to betray his friends. "What were you doing in the woods?"

The charcoal burner lifted his smoke-smudged face and looked Thomas squarely in the eye. With a rueful expression that betrayed his deep regret, he confessed: " 'Twas us that dug the pit."

Chapter 37

"So vhat have we here?" asked Professor Hascher, watching Thomas set down the earthenware flagon on his workbench back in Oxford.

"I very much hope it is the proof that will save a man's life," he replied.

For a moment, the professor looked puzzled until he realized: "Ah, it contains ze gin?"

Thomas nodded. "This is Abe Diggott's flagon. The glaze inside is deeply pitted."

"And you zink zere is lead in ze glaze zat is reacting viz ze gin, *ja?*"

"I am convinced of it," he replied.

The pair of them set to work. Professor Hascher took charge of the controlled experiment once more, impregnating a piece of paper with schnapps, while Thomas worked with the gin. To each sample *Hepar sulfuris* was added. Both of them tensed. Hascher's sample remained unaltered, but within a minute the gin sample had turned a murky gray; within four it was completely black.

"You vere right." The professor beamed. "Ze lead concentration must be at least double zat of ze ozer gin."

Thomas nodded. The relief was obvious in his expression, although he knew it was only one step in proving Abe Diggott's innocence. He took a deep breath and shrugged. "Now all I need do is convince a judge and jury of the effect this poison can have on a man," he said.

The trial of Abraham Diggott, coppicer of Brandwick, was held on the tenth day of May. The old man was due to be arraigned with four other defendants, who were charged with lesser offenses such as theft and poaching, but in all cases the specter of the gallows loomed large.

Such a prospect drew a sizable crowd, and the courtroom was full to bursting a good half hour before proceedings began. The fashionable ladies and gentlemen of Oxford had ensured they took the seats with the best view, whereas the rest of the rabble had to make do with standing like cattle in market pens. The room itself had been sprinkled with herbs and scented flowers in order to prevent the spread of disease. However, the gesture did little to mask the smell of the spectators, let alone the unwashed prisoners who stood accused. The stench caught in the back of more genteel throats, sending those of a delicate disposition reaching for their kerchiefs and nosegays.

Thomas was accompanied by Sir Theodisius that morning. The coroner had insisted he be present for the trial of the man accused of murdering his friend, even though he doubted his guilt. The previous evening, over dinner, Thomas had presented a very good case for acquittal and had swayed his friend's opinion on the matter. The coroner had, however, been wary of the prosecution counsel. He had already warned his dining companion.

"Watch out for Martin Bradshaw," he had said through a mouthful of mutton. "He's a slippery one, and a personal friend of Malthus's to boot, I fear." His warning only served to make Thomas even more determined to fight in the accused coppicer's corner.

Consequently, in court the following morning, the coroner introduced Thomas to an official as a medical man wishing to offer his expertise in Abe Diggott's defense. The clerk made a note of his name and assured him he would be called in due course.

It was then that Thomas spotted Nicholas Lupton, seated on a chair by Martin Bradshaw. The two men were engaged in conversation, and Sir Theodisius's words echoed in the anatomist's head. Seeing these adversaries crouched in collusion was a reminder that the odds were stacked most firmly against poor old Abe Diggott.

Thomas did not fancy his chances of squeezing his way along rows of rowdy spectators to a seat and so was relieved when another official offered him a chair near the front of the courtroom, between the witness stand and the huddle of black-clad lawyers. As he sat down, Lupton caught his eye and acknowledged him with a leer before turning to converse with his neighbor. Sir Theodisius saw the rebuff and clamped a friendly hand on Thomas's arm. He then nodded to him to signify that they must part, and he eased himself onto a bench a few feet away.

On the stroke of nine o'clock Judge Anton Dubarry entered the court. He was a large man, and his enormous wig made him seem even larger. His scarlet robes lent a sense of religiosity to the occasion. A reverent hush descended on the proceedings, imbuing upon them an instant solemnity that previously had been so absent. The preliminaries were observed in a well-rehearsed manner—the selection of a jury and the swearing of oaths. As was the custom, the lesser cases were heard first, with startling efficiency. Only one man pleaded guilty, and he was dealt with in less than a minute. Three others protested their innocence, but even they were dispatched in less than ten. It seemed that, come the end of the day, when it was time to sentence all the miscreants, Judge Dubarry would have recourse to don the black cap more than once.

Any hope of leniency that Thomas might have held for Abe Diggott was fast ebbing away. As they brought the old man from the prison, the anatomist tried to catch his eye. The coppicer staggered up the steps of the dock and looked with an unseeing gaze at the masses who jeered and shouted at his arrival. Word had been put about that they were to see a dashing rake who had held up the surveyor's party in the woods. At first, it was said, there had been playful banter. He had knocked off the chief mapmaker's hat and taunted him and his man a little but had no intention of harming either. Shortly after, however, he had been joined by others not yet apprehended and the mood turned ugly. Coshes were wielded, a pistol was drawn, and a single shot fired. The chief surveyor fell mortally wounded and the rest of the cowardly gang fled, leaving the surveyor's assistant and their guard in a most terrible state and remaining in fear of their lives.

What they saw in court, however, could not seem further from the truth. Could this decrepit old fool be one and the same? A highwayman of renown? It was hard to envisage high-society ladies clamoring for an audience in his cell as they did with dashing James MacLaine. Nor could they see this dolt chatting to the topsman before launching himself off the ladder like the famous Dick Turpin. A murmur of undisguised disappointment rippled around the courtroom.

The charge against Diggott was that on the afternoon of April 20, on the Boughton Estate, he "did lie in wait in Raven's Wood for Mr. Jeffrey Turgoose and his chainman Mr. James Charlton and did willfully and without regard rob them of their possessions." He then assaulted Charlton, causing him injury to his head, before firing a single shot that killed said Mr. Turgoose.

"How do you plead to the charge?" asked the clerk of the court.

Diggott, who seemed not to have registered his predicament, let alone indictment, remained silent. Shaking violently, he appeared overwhelmed by the entire proceedings. What was more, he began to sway. Within less than a second he had disappeared below the stand.

Many in the court leapt to their feet. Ladies gasped; fans fluttered. "He's saved you a job, Judge!" called one cove from the gallery.

"Let's gibbet him and be done!" shouted another.

The two guards who flanked Diggott tried to right the defendant, and one of the officials actually slapped the old man's face. Seeing the situation, Thomas presented himself. He was acutely aware that if the accused did not enter a plea, then standing mute would be deemed the same as admitting guilt. He spoke to the clerk amid the surrounding uproar.

"Sir, as you know, I am the surgeon here to speak on this man's behalf. I would testify as to the nature of his illness and its bearing on his ability to commit the crime," he told him. "Would I be allowed a moment with him?"

The official raised a brow. "You would speak for the man's character?"

"I am an expert in my field, acting for the defense, sir," Thomas told him.

The clerk considered the request for a moment before marching straight to Judge Dubarry. Pointing at the anatomist, he relayed his message, and the judge lifted his gaze toward him. A second later he brought down his gavel.

"This court is adjourned for twenty minutes," he barked. It was more than Thomas could have hoped for.

The jailers dragged Abe Diggott into a small anteroom where Thomas could attend to him. They sat him down and a cup of water was offered. The old man put his face to the rim and lapped like a dog. Thomas knelt down at his side and took from his pocket a phial of smelling salts. He uncorked it and wafted the pungent vapors under Diggott's nose.

"Abe, 'tis I, Dr. Silkstone."

Diggott's head suddenly shook from side to side as he gasped for breath, and his lids blinked as he tried to focus.

"Do you remember I came to see you in jail?"

There was a flicker of recognition between coughs. Thomas looked at the man's hands. They remained bound by cord, pinioned in front of him. He held them in his and touched his fingers.

"Do you remember you had lost the power of movement in your hands?" he said softly.

Diggott frowned, then nodded. "I can't move 'em, Doctor," he hissed through his gappy teeth.

"They trouble you still?"

"Aye. Aye," he mumbled. "That and the gripes."

These were classic symptoms, thought Thomas. "And your bowels?" he asked.

The old man shook his head. "'Tis a long, long time since I shat, sir," came the reply.

Thomas knew his case was growing stronger by the minute. The guards stood on either side of the door, allowing them a little privacy. He put his hand on the accused man's shoulder.

"You do realize that you are being tried for murder, Abe?" the anatomist said calmly.

At his words, however, the old man suddenly became agitated. He tried to haul himself up but was not strong enough. "Murder? Whose murder?" he protested.

The guards suddenly became more alert, their hands on their coshes, at the ready. Again Thomas tried to soothe the accused. Such confusion was a well-known symptom of lead poisoning.

"When we return to the courtroom, the judge will ask you how you plead." Thomas glanced over his shoulder at the guards and lowered his voice. "You must say, 'Not guilty.'"

"Not guilty," repeated the old man, parrot-fashion.

"Do you understand?" asked Thomas.

"Yes, sir. I didn't kill no one."

"I know you did not," Thomas assured him, rising to his feet once more. Turning to the guards he said, "The prisoner is ready."

Chapter 38

Once again, Abe Diggott was forced to run the gamut of raucous shouts and taunts, even though he did not seem to realize fully the seriousness of his predicament. He dragged himself up the steps and into the dock. He seemed more alert, but that also meant he became more nervous. When he was asked a second time how he pleaded, his shriveled frame juddered in reply.

"Not guilty, sir. I'm not. I swear on my life."

Judge Dubarry brought down his gavel as the court erupted in laughter at the accused's protestation of innocence. The clerk called the counsel for the prosecution. Thomas exchanged a nervous glance with Sir Theodisius. He knew they were about to listen to a tissue of lies, fabricated, no doubt, to suit Sir Montagu Malthus's plans.

For the prosecution, Martin Bradshaw delivered his opening speech. He was a thin, short man with an intense stare that could seemingly slice through a man's mind. With great clarity and precision, he outlined the case against Abe Diggott.

"Gentlemen of the jury," Bradshaw began. "What you are about to hear is a tale of a bungled robbery carried out in the most perfidious way that ended in the brutal murder of a man who gave his life while carrying out his duty. Mr. Jeffrey Turgoose was a gentleman and a commissioner, esteemed by those skilled in his profession and held in most high regard by all who knew him."

Thomas had expected this concerned tone, designed as it was to engage the audience and arouse sympathy among the jury. Indeed, he found himself being curiously drawn into the prosecution's version of how Turgoose and Charlton, led by Talland, had ventured out on that fateful afternoon. The court was told how Raven's Wood was a notorious hideout for thieves and cutpurses and how, alas, the party had been forced to abandon their vehicle because of the boggy ground and to continue on foot. Suddenly, their single horse, which was being led by Talland, fell into a terrible pit that had been dug by the scoundrels as they lay in wait for any passing travelers. It was then that Abe Diggott and his men pounced. They demanded that Messrs. Turgoose and Charlton hand over their personal possessions, while more ruffians plundered the laden horse for their valuable equipment. When the surveyors refused to cooperate, there was an altercation. Mr. Charlton was beaten, while Talland was held fast. Mr. Turgoose protested and rushed forward to assist the young surveyor, so Diggott shot him at near point-blank range. Turgoose fell, mortally wounded, and seeing what he had done, Diggott immediately fled, followed by the rest of his murderous crew. Mr. Charlton and Talland were left wounded and afeared, while the surveyor lay in a pool of his own blood.

The courtroom listened in hushed silence as through his words, Mr. Bradshaw painted a most vivid picture of events. Such a delivery deeply troubled Thomas. The account seemed to him almost plausible, save for a crucial omission. Bradshaw had distinctly said that it was Abe Diggott who had pulled a gun. Yet if, as Thomas planned to prove, the pistol was in Mr. Turgoose's possession prior to his murder, then he was sure someone must have wrested it from the surveyor before firing it. It was a missing piece of the puzzle that Thomas would pursue later.

Next a bellow went up. "Call Mr. James Charlton."

The young chainman entered the courtroom with his head swathed in a bandage that covered his right eye. There were loud exclamations from the gallery as he walked in and expressions of sympathy from some of the more genteel ladies. Thomas recalled seeing Charlton thus bandaged at Boughton Hall shortly after the incident and again at the public meeting at the Three Tuns. He wondered if the injury was real, or simply another ruse employed by Malthus and Lupton to enlist the jury's sympathies.

It was clear that Charlton was even more nervous than usual as soon as he took the stand. His hand was evidently shaking as he laid it on the Bible to take the oath, but it was his speech affliction that caused much mirth in the gallery. Bradshaw tried to assist by skillfully leading him into scenarios.

"Please tell us what happened when you heard the horse neigh, Mr. Charlton."

"I . . . I . . . I . . ." The young man was sweating profusely, his freckled face glistening for all to see. "I s-saw m-men c-come out of the w-woods, s-sir."

"How many?"

"I . . . I . . . I cannot b-be sure."

"Was the accused one of them?"

Charlton glanced over at Abe Diggott, then looked away again. His reply was mumbled. "I cannot be s-sure."

The prosecutor's patience seemed to be wearing a little thin. "Speak up, if you will, sir."

Charlton straightened his back. "I cannot be s-sure, sir," he repeated.

Bradshaw seemed a little put out by this revelation, as if he had previously believed the witness could make a positive identification. Thomas watched for a reaction among the jurors. He saw some swap looks and arch their brows.

"Tell us what happened next, Mr. Charlton. Did the men demand you hand over your belongings?"

"Y-yes, s-sir. I gave them my p-pocket watch."

"This watch?" Bradshaw held the article aloft and angled it toward the jury.

"Y-yes, sir."

"And were they threatening toward you?"

"Y-yes, s-sir."

"You were beaten about the head, were you not, as your guide was pinioned by two other scoundrels?"

"Y-yes, s-sir."

"And was it not the case that when Mr. Turgoose refused to hand over his compass, one of the men produced a gun?"

"Y-yes, s-sir."

At that moment Bradshaw walked over to a table in front of the judge and picked up a small firearm. "This pistol?" he asked, brandishing it in front of the jury.

The gallery gasped and hollered as if they had never seen such a weapon before.

"I think s-so," Charlton replied.

"And that man was holding it?" Bradshaw pointed to Diggott in the dock. He was shaking his head violently.

The young man looked at the accused, paused for a moment, then replied, "I-I-I cannot b-b sure."

At this admission, the gallery erupted once more. Charlton scanned the crowd, and as he did so his one visible eye welled up and a tear ran down his cheek. Judge Dubarry called for order, but it was too late. Seeing that his witness was about to dissolve into tears, and to avoid his further humiliation, Bradshaw dismissed the young chainman. He was escorted away from the courtroom, and Seth Talland was called next.

Thomas directed his gaze toward Sir Theodisius, who nodded to him from across the floor. Both men knew that Charlton's vague evidence would not be enough to convict Diggott. Everything now hinged on Talland's testimony.

The burly prizefighter made his way to the stand and gave his name and took the oath in a voice that was low and coarse. Thomas noted a fresh cut on his right cheek that ran from his nose to his ear. He wondered if it was self-inflicted, a badge of victimhood to strengthen his credibility. Coming to the end of the oath, with his right hand remaining on the Bible, Talland suddenly lifted his left hand to his ear and tugged at his lobe. It was an odd gesture, but one that Thomas knew he had seen somewhere before. He secreted it in his memory and remained listening intently as the prizefighter embarked upon his evidence.

Despite his uncouth manners, Talland made a much more convincing witness than Charlton. He seemed confident and sure of his facts. Yes, he had been pinioned by two ruffians and had watched as Mr. Charlton was cruelly beaten. Yes, they had stolen some of the surveyors' tools. Yes, he had seen the accused man draw the pistol and fire it. Yes, he had seen the gang, about four men in all, run off into the woods, knowing Mr. Turgoose to be dead. He and Charlton had lifted the body onto the horse and somehow managed to make it back to Boughton Hall.

The courtroom was enthralled by the exchange between the counsel and his witness. This crude man had given them what the young surveyor could not—seemingly reliable testimony—delivered with a clarity and purpose. And there was more.

"But that is not the end of the story, is it, Mr. Talland?" asked Bradshaw, turning his piercing eyes onto the jury.

"No, sir. Next evening—"

Bradshaw broke in: "The day after the murder?"

Talland nodded. "Aye, sir. Afterward, I rode into Brandwick with another sideman."

"Why was that?"

"I wanted to find the men who murdered Mr. Turgoose, sir."

"A noble sentiment." Bradshaw jerked his head toward the witness. "And what did you find?"

Talland swallowed hard. "It were curfew, sir."

Bradshaw stopped him short. "Curfew, Mr. Talland?"

"Sir Montagu called a curfew after the killing, Your Honor. No one was allowed out after dusk, sir."

"And you went to the home of the accused?" Again Bradshaw pointed at Diggott. "Why was that?"

Talland scowled at the old man. "Because I knew it was 'im that shot Mr. Turgoose."

"You saw him with your own eyes?"

Thomas felt his muscles tighten. "That I did, sir."

"And you knew where he lived?"

"Abe Diggott is well-known in the village."

"And why is that?"

"Because 'is grandson is a ne'er-do-well. He was whipped for firing some fence posts last month."

The rabble, clearly taking Talland's side, cheered at this last remark. The judge called for order once more. "So you went to his dwelling. Why?"

"I wanted to look for the dag and the booty."

Bradshaw smiled in a smug manner. "By 'dag,' you mean 'gun'?"

"I do, sir."

"Go on."

"We was near the cottage when we see'd Diggott. Fighting with the constable, 'e were, sir."

"Fighting?"

"'E were in 'is cups, sir," Talland replied. "So we took 'im back to 'is dwelling."

"And what did you find, pray tell?" he asked.

Talland lifted his gaze to the gallery. "We found the pistol and Mr. Charlton's pocket watch hidden in the old man's cottage."

Amid gasps and cheers, Bradshaw pointed to the table. The noise was slow to die down, but when it did, it left the prosecution counsel with a self-satisfied look on his face. He had not only the corroboration of a witness and evidence, but a motive, too. The fact that his grandson had been whipped to within an inch of his life for arson was the last nail in Abe Diggott's coffin for the masses and, in all probability, the jurors. Thomas knew it was now solely up to him to change their minds. The fact that he could prove the murder weapon had previously been in Mr. Turgoose's possession could be his trump card.

Chapter 39

At the sound of his name being called, Thomas rose. All eyes turned on him. He could hear hostile barbs fly through the air as he walked to the witness stand. He was already known in Oxford from his previous exploits. They called him "the colonist" or "the American," and their voices were always tinged with suspicion or derision or both when they spoke his name.

Judge Dubarry addressed him directly after he had sworn the oath. "You intend to give the accused a character witness, Dr. Silkstone?" he inquired, looking slightly perplexed as to how a gentleman, albeit a foreigner, might want to testify on behalf of a man of such low breeding, especially as he was not in his service.

Thomas nodded. "I would speak as an expert witness, Your Honor," he said. "I appear in my capacity as a man of medicine and as physician to the accused."

The judge shrugged. "If you can throw light on the case, then please proceed, Dr. Silkstone."

Thomas took a deep breath and looked directly at Abe Diggott. He came straight to the point. "You have seen for yourself, sir, that the accused is in ill health. I can prove that this is due to his consumption of gin that is contaminated with a high concentration of lead."

The judge raised a brow. "Go on."

"Lead poisoning presents a variety of symptoms, the most acute of which are rapid weight loss, severe abdominal pain, and paralysis. The accused suffers from all three." Thomas lifted his gaze toward Abe Diggott.

Judge Dubarry, however, seemed unimpressed. "This is all very well, but what bearing does this have on the case, Dr. Silkstone?"

"By your leave, sir, I would suggest that this man is far too weak to have traveled into Raven's Wood as both witnesses have suggested, let alone discharge a weapon," said Thomas.

With the judge's agreement, Thomas left the stand and strode over to the table where the pistol lay and picked it up. There was another murmur from the gallery. Walking over to Abe Diggott, Thomas stopped in front of him.

"I would ask that the prisoner be untied for the moment, sir."

The judge looked askance. "For what purpose?"

"In order to prove this man's innocence, sir," came the reply.

Judge Dubarry appeared exasperated. "This is most unusual, Dr. Silkstone!" he cried.

"I would crave your indulgence, sir," said Thomas with a bow. "A man's life depends on it."

The judge flapped a hand in submission. "Very well," he snapped, and a guard untied the cord around the prisoner's wrists.

Facing the accused, Thomas addressed him directly. "Mr. Diggott, would you please take this pistol and show the gentlemen of the jury how, if you had killed Mr. Turgoose, you would have aimed it and pulled the trigger."

Abe Diggott looked even more confused. "But, Dr. Silkstone—"

Thomas was firm. "Here, show them," he insisted, handing the man the pistol.

Diggott looked at the weapon, his eyes wide with fright.

"Take it," urged Thomas.

The court watched in silence as Abe Diggott began to move his unfettered arms toward the gun. But the expression on his face changed from fear to pain as he extended his grasp.

"Take it," repeated Thomas.

Diggott flinched. He tried to move his fingers, but he could not. He let his gaze fall to his hands, as if willing them to move, but he could not.

"My fingers, sir. I can't . . . ," he wailed.

A wave of amazement rippled through the gallery. More caterwauling ensued, until the judge brought down his gavel.

"Your point being, Dr. Silkstone?" he barked.

"You see, Your Honor, this man's fingers are paralyzed through lead poisoning. It is a slow poison that takes many weeks to elicit such an effect. I understand he has been incapacitated for more than a month now. It is proof that he could not possibly have been responsible for the murder of Mr. Turgoose."

Judge Dubarry sniffed. "I take your point, Dr. Silkstone. But just because the man is incapable of pulling the trigger of a pistol does not mean he was not an accomplice."

"Of course, Your Honor," Thomas deferred politely. "But what if that pistol was in the possession of the victim himself, sir?"

The judge looked puzzled. "Explain yourself, sir!" he barked.

Thomas cleared his throat. "I conducted a postmortem on Mr. Turgoose, sir, and can prove, beyond doubt, that the pistol that fired the fatal shot was on his person prior to his death."

"Are you saying there must have been some sort of struggle?" The judge, a frown planted on his forehead, was thinking out loud.

Thomas nodded. "I believe so, sir. Yet Mr. Talland's testimony made no mention of an altercation." Now was his chance. He could reveal his findings and postulate that the gun was planted by Lupton's men. As it was, however, he was robbed of the opportunity.

"Enough, Dr. Silkstone!" The judge brought down his gavel. It was obvious he had heard all that he cared to. He fixed Thomas with a glare. "Sir, you are a surgeon and an anatomist, but you are most certainly not a barrister, and you would do well not to meddle in affairs about which you know very little," he said crossly. "I will not have my courtroom turned into a tavern for every Tom, Dick, or Harry to have his say. It is clear you believe this man is innocent and have made your point well. Now it is up to him to speak for himself."

Duly chastened, Thomas returned to his seat, his heart pounding in his chest. He was not sure if he had made or marred Diggott's chances of acquittal. He cursed himself for his brashness. He had let his unwavering belief in the old coppicer and his hatred of injustice make him act with a passion that was unseemly. He had not endeared himself to the judge, and for that he felt quite wretched. Had he done enough to persuade the gentlemen of the jury to find the accused not guilty? He did not know. All he could hope was that he had sown a seed of doubt in their minds that was enough to acquit the old man.

Told to make his own case, Abe Diggott remained confused. He appeared befuddled and agitated. Over and over again he merely repeated: "I didn't kill no one. No one."

On the fifth identical protestation, the judge brought down his gavel with an abruptness that betrayed his irritation. "Enough," he boomed. He looked at the clutch of jurymen nearby and began his summing up. It did not take him long, but what he said most certainly gave them much to consider. The case, said Judge Dubarry, was by no means cut-and-dried in one direction or the other. No doubt a gruesome murder had been committed and no doubt the surviving members of the party had been sorely abused and deeply affected by their experiences. Yet there was an ambivalence in the evidence they had heard; some of it was at odds with testimonies. Did they feel, Judge Dubarry asked, that Abe Diggott had murdered Mr. Turgoose beyond reasonable doubt? As God-fearing Christians, the jurors knew much was at stake. If they found the accused guilty, they would be liable to the vengeance of the Lord, so it was said, upon family and trade, body and soul, in this world and that to come, if he was innocent. It was likely that they would err on the side of caution rather than risk eternal damnation. Thomas saw a chink of light as finally the judge asked the gentlemen of the jury to consider their verdict.

The next few minutes could as easily have been hours to Thomas, so slowly did they drag, until, shortly before midday, the jury's foreman rose.

"Do you find the prisoner guilty or not guilty?" asked the clerk.

Thomas's mouth went dry, and his palms became clammy. For a moment all he could hear was the sound of his own heart pounding.

"Not guilty," came the reply.

"And is that the verdict of you all?"

"It is."

Thomas, unaware that he had been holding his breath while this exchange had been taking place, now exhaled deeply. As he did so, a huge weight seemed to lift from his shoulders. He looked at Abe Diggott, still dazed and addlepated. The old woodsman had not yet registered that he was a free man and regarded the guards who unfastened his wrists with a childlike incomprehension.

As members of the public rose and began to file out, chattering like querulous hens, Thomas walked over to the dock.

"You are free to go," he told Diggott, touching him gently on the arm. "You shall journey with me back to Brandwick?"

Behind him, Thomas heard Sir Theodisius call his name. He turned to see the portly coroner standing at his side.

"You did a good job, there, Silkstone," he said, but, reminding Thomas that Turgoose's killer was still at large, he added: "But there is still more to do."

Thomas took his meaning and nodded. As he did so, he noticed Nicholas Lupton from out of the corner of his eye. He was marching out of the courtroom, his face like thunder. He and Sir Montagu did not take defeat lightly. Thomas knew it would not be the last of the affair. Adam Diggott was still at large. Proving he had no hand in the killing of Jeffrey Turgoose would present even more of a challenge.

Chapter 40

News of the acquittal was carried back immediately to Brandwick by Abe Diggott's supporters. By the time Thomas arrived in the village with the newly freed coppicer by his side, crowds lined the street to greet them. Some of the women even threw flower petals at the carriage as it drew up outside the old man's cottage.

To cheers and shouts of encouragement, Thomas helped his charge down from the vehicle and lent him his arm as he turned to scan the sea of smiling faces. Rachel Diggott was at the fore. She scrambled forward and hugged her father-in-law, who seemed reluctant to be the center of attention, dipping his head bashfully.

Latching her arm through the old man's, she smiled broadly at Thomas. "Thank you, Dr. Silkstone," she said, her voice taut with emotion.

"Justice has prevailed," he replied. He looked about him. "Your husband—he is still in hiding?"

At the mention of Adam, Rachel's features hardened. "'Tis not safe. They'll come for him no matter, Dr. Silkstone."

Thomas knew what she said was true. Until the real killer of Jeffrey Turgoose was unmasked, Adam would be forced to live in the woods like a common outlaw. The doctor had decided he would head back to the Three Tuns when, in among the throng, a tall man suddenly appeared, his face half-hidden under a large-brimmed hat. Thomas watched him make his way up to Abe Diggott and hug him. It was Adam.

The doctor sidled up to him. "Take great care, Adam," Thomas told him.

"I will, sir," said the coppicer with a nod, and tugging the brim of his hat to pull it down even further, he disappeared once more.

The pushing and shoving continued around them, and Thomas feared for Abe Diggott's safety. "Your father-in-law needs to rest," he told Rachel above the din.

"I'll see to it, sir," she replied.

Thomas nodded. "And remember, no more gin!" he said firmly. He turned to find a path away from the melee and began to walk down the High Street, away from the crowd. The carriage had taken his luggage on to the inn. He felt quite drained. The past few days had taken their toll on his own well-being. Above all he needed a good night's sleep. Then and only then could he hope to apply himself to his next challenge—finding out who really did kill not just Jeffrey Turgoose, but Aaron Coutt, too.

"How was this allowed to happen?" Sir Montagu Malthus banged a clenched fist on his desk.

In front of him Nicholas Lupton was floundering. His usual bluffness had deserted him and his forehead was furrowed by a frown.

"It was Silkstone."

Sir Montagu scowled. "I should've known he had a hand in the acquittal." He clenched the edge of the desk until his knuckles went white. "So now these troublemakers are at liberty once more. A fine state of affairs!" He rose and began pacing the floor. "And Charlton?"

Lupton recalled the young surveyor's unconvincing performance as a witness for the prosecution. He had returned with him to Boughton Hall and seen for himself his mental anguish. "He still suffers in the aftermath," he said, not daring to catch Sir Montagu's eye.

"Where is the lily-livered fool now?"

"He is resting, sir." Lupton had watched Charlton sob and

wail all the way back from Oxford. He wondered he had any tears, or energy, left.

The lawyer had not been in court to witness what he considered to be a mere formality; the accused would be found guilty of murder, hanged, and gibbeted for all to see at Milton Common, and the people of Brandwick would have learned a valuable lesson—that he, Sir Montagu Malthus, was not to be crossed. Their protests and petitions counted for naught; they were merely pawns in his game. Now, however, he had arrived at Boughton to be greeted with news of this preposterous acquittal. Such incompetence could not be tolerated.

Standing at the French windows, he looked out onto the lawns, his balled fist tapping on his chin. Finally he said, "We need to get rid of Charlton."

"Sir?" Lupton's startled gaze shot up.

"He needs to be gone. Just get him out of here." The lawyer took a deep breath and fixed his hooded eyes on his steward. "Do you understand?"

Relieved that he had misinterpreted his master's original instruction, Lupton nodded. "Yes, sir. I shall see to it right away." He knew, however, that such a dismissal would not be well received.

The steward decided to deliver the message in person. In the hallway he saw Howard and instructed him that Mr. Charlton would be leaving. He was to be packed and ready to go by the end of the afternoon. He then proceeded to Charlton's bedroom. The chainman had been staying in a room in the servants' quarters since the murder. He seemed in no fit state to resume his normal duties.

Lupton knocked. There was no reply. He knocked again. Still no reply. He tried the door. It was locked. He called for a key. He unlocked the door and entered. The room was darkened, the shutters half-closed. The steward made his way toward the bed and stood stock-still. There, slumped across the counterpane, his left arm outstretched, lay James Charlton. And in the semi-gloom, the blood from a slash on his wrist dripped relentlessly onto the rug below.

Chapter 41

In the Three Tuns, dozens of villagers had crammed into the pump room to toast the release of the old woodsman. The threat of rain had brought them all inside to enjoy the tavern's hospitality and Peter Geech's cheap gin. Thomas had no wish to join them. While he felt a great relief at the acquittal, he was in no mood for celebration.

On his return journey from the Diggotts' cottage, he had been forced to stop and press himself against a wall in the High Street to allow a heavily laden cart, accompanied by two outriders, to go ahead. Other riders and pedestrians had also been obliged to stand aside to let the wagon pass. Its cargo was wooden poles, each cut to the same length. Fencing for the common, he thought. Malthus and Lupton were intent on making a show of their power. The wagon did not have to travel through the main thoroughfare to reach its destination, but here it was, with escorts, as if in some sort of a religious procession for all to see. The message to the people of Brandwick was clear. The Boughton Estate would countenance no opposition. Enclosure of the common land would proceed, with or without the consent of Parliament.

Above the muted din from below, there came a knock at Thomas's door.

"Enter," said the doctor, shutting the open casement.

In walked Peter Geech carrying the supper tray that Thomas had ordered. The noise of laughter and singing from downstairs suddenly invaded the room through the open door. He had not seen the landlord since he had conducted the postmortem on the stableboy. There were several questions that needed answering. He seized his chance.

"You are busy," commented Thomas.

"Aye, sir. There's some carousing to be done tonight." He smiled as he set down the tray. "Thanks to you, I believe, sir."

Thomas thought of the revelers celebrating the release of Abe Diggott. Pints of poisonous gin would be sold to punters that evening along with the plugs of untaxed tobacco that Geech dealt in. He suspected the relatively low levels of lead he had detected in the gin could be attributed to the still heads and worms of the landlord's apparatus. What concerned him more, however, had wider implications.

"You'll turn a pretty profit tonight, no doubt," he commented as he sat himself at his table.

"That I will," replied the landlord with a chuckle.

Thomas tucked his napkin into his stock. "And the excise man won't see a penny."

Peter Geech suddenly seemed keen to focus all his attention on placing a fork on the tray. "Sir?" he queried with a shrug.

Thomas smiled. "Come, come, Mr. Geech. There's no need to play the innocent. You ply a lucrative trade in smuggled goods on the sly."

Geech proceeded to set down a plate of cold meats in front of Thomas. "I'm sure I don't know what you mean, Dr. Silkstone." His eyes slid everywhere but on his guest.

"So your late-night excursions into Raven's Wood are for pleasure?"

The landlord's head whipped 'round and his eyes fixed on his accuser. "How do you know . . . ?"

"I saw you and Coutt go up to the woods. Meeting with your business associates, were you?"

The color suddenly drained from Geech's face. It went as pale as the pastry on the mutton pie he had just served. From somewhere, however, he managed to draw on a little courage.

"You can't prove it, Dr. Silkstone."

"What about the note: *Beware of Raven's Wood*?" Thomas reached for a bill, written in Geech's scrawl. "'Tis your hand and no mistake. I found it in Mr. Turgoose's pocket."

"It don't prove I killed the mapmaker, nor young Coutt."

Thomas fixed him with a glower. "Ah, yes. Coutt. Shocking business. You should've seen the poor lad's body, all twisted and burned. It—"

Panic now registered on the landlord's reddening face. "I didn't kill him!"

Thomas could tell he had touched a raw nerve. "I'm not saying you did, but I do know you are involved in a smuggling ring in the woods."

The accusation riled Geech. He paused for a moment, like a cornered rat, then hissed his reply through thin lips. "'Tis your word against mine, and you are . . ."

The innkeeper could not bring himself to say the word "American," but Thomas took his meaning and was able to trump him.

"I am afraid I can prove it, Mr. Geech. You see, I have samples from your secret stash of smuggled goods at the ruins. Tobacco and your famous gin," he told him. "But I shall not go to the law if you answer me this. Were you with Coutt on the night he was murdered?"

Geech bit his lip. His customary swagger suddenly deserted him. He stood back from the tray and his gaze dropped.

"'Tis to my regret I was not, Doctor," he said.

Thomas sensed that the landlord might wish to unburden himself. "Will you sit?" he said, gesturing to a second chair by the grate.

Geech accepted the invitation, sighing deeply as he sat. He looked at his hands and fingered his knuckles.

"It was my wife, see. She had the gripes again. We was busy here, and besides, she didn't want me to leave her."

Thomas thought of the businessman he had seen in the bar. "But you had an order to deliver and so you sent Coutt on his own?"

Geech swallowed hard and nodded.

"So you helped the boy load the gin, then saw him off. But

something went wrong, didn't it?" Thomas rose and walked to the mantelshelf.

Geech began twisting his fingers. His face was reddening and he was becoming increasingly agitated, shifting in his seat. "Piece of piss, I said it would be. Just deliver the gin and get the money." For a second he looked up, but then let his gaze drop once more.

Thomas pictured the rendezvous in the woods. This so-called businessman, dapper and sophisticated, was no fool. He called himself the Raven. Sir Theodisius had told Thomas all about his exploits. He was a notorious highwayman turned smuggler in the area. He paid a good tailor and drank fine French wine. He would drive a hard bargain and he would not stand for being duped. He would have checked his goods before taking delivery.

"Only you didn't keep your part of the bargain, did you?" pressed Thomas. "Did you?" he repeated, looking down at the miserable innkeeper. "When he tasted your gin, he knew you'd deceived him. Water, was it, or did you fill the barrels with the piss the night-soil men couldn't collect?"

It was as if the doctor had plunged a knife into the landlord's guts and twisted it. Geech's head jerked up and his face was contorted.

"We couldn't make enough. We were that busy that week." He began to crumble.

Thomas had come to the nub of the matter. He bore down on the landlord. "So you let the boy draw the smuggler's fire. He pleaded with him. Told him he had no idea that there was water in the barrels, because he didn't know, did he? You deceived him in the hope you would get away with deceiving the Raven. Only he was too smart for you, wasn't he? He took out his pistol and he shot young Coutt as he pleaded for his life."

The landlord's shoulders slumped. He closed his beady eyes for a moment, then, through his shame, Peter Geech mouthed an affirmation. With his thin lips quivering, he mumbled, "I knew if I didn't deliver the goods, he'd make me pay in other ways."

Thomas frowned. "What did you say? Who would make you pay?"

Geech looked up and retreated in his chair, as if regretting his aberration.

Thomas eyed him warily. "Does Sir Montagu Malthus have a hand in this, Geech?" he asked him.

The landlord shook his head vigorously. "No, Doctor," he replied. "He knows nothing of this, I swear."

"Then who—?" Thomas broke off and in the silence the realization dawned. "It's Lupton, isn't it? You are paying him money to run this smuggling ring under his protection."

It had troubled Thomas seeing Geech and Coutt break the curfew the other night. The pair had driven the cart, laden with contraband gin, virtually under the noses of the Boughton thugs who were there to impose the emergency law, and yet they were allowed to pass unimpeded.

"Has Lupton sanctioned this operation?" he pressed.

Geech gulped hard, as if he wanted to swallow the words that were already halfway up his throat.

"I can't say, sir."

"Can't, or won't, Mr. Geech? I am sure you would be able to tell the excise men were I to inform them of your little racket."

Such a threat seemed to loosen the landlord's tongue, and he could force down his words no longer. He nodded. "Aye, sir. He lets us do it in return for a cut."

Thomas remained stony faced. "How much?"

"Half, sir."

He had guessed as much. Lupton had a vested interest in the continued terrorizing of the village by this so-called Raven and his ruthless gang. He suspected, too, that it was these brigands who had attacked Turgoose and Charlton. It was a bungled attempt at robbery that had gone seriously awry. It would make sense that Lupton would not wish them to be caught and tried for murder, thus depriving himself of a lucrative source of income. He and Malthus were trying to pin the blame on innocent villagers, indeed, the very villagers who were so vociferous in their opposition to enclosure. By making an example of them, Lupton was hoping his problems would be dealt with in one fell swoop.

"Thank you, Mr. Geech," Thomas said to the landlord. "You have been most helpful." He picked up his knife and fork and began to eat. For the first time in many days, he found himself feeling very hungry.

Chapter 42

Under cover of darkness that night, Thomas rode to Boughton Hall. Tethering his horse by a wall that had fallen into disrepair, he climbed over it and skirted the lawns, arriving undetected at the drawing room window. Through the pane he could see Nicholas Lupton, sitting by the roaring fire, surrounded by the elegant splendor to which he had no right. Seeing him thus, a brandy in his hand, enjoying the accompaniments that his usurpation brought, stirred Thomas into action. Grasping the handles of the French doors, he flung them open.

Hearing the intrusion, Lupton leapt to his feet. Craning his neck into the gloom he called out, "Who goes there?"

Seeing Thomas stepping out of the shadows, Lupton lunged for the bell by the fireplace.

"I would advise you to hear me out, sir, if you value your own position," Thomas told him, hastening toward him.

Lupton arched a brow and regarded Thomas with a sentient look, as if he feared what he would say next. "What is your meaning, Silkstone?"

"My meaning, sir, is very plain," said Thomas. "Unless you want me to inform Sir Montagu that you are in league with local smugglers and are taking a cut of their profits to line your own pockets, I suggest you tell me the truth about Lady Lydia."

The color rose in Lupton's cheeks and he opened his mouth to let out another laugh, only this time it was tinged with nervousness, not the customary derision. "You have been digging in the dirt again, I fear. 'Tis your word against mine, and Sir Montagu would never believe you over me." He spat out his words so that spittle flecked his lips.

Thomas refused to be fazed. "You forget Sir Montagu is a lawyer used to dealing in evidence."

"And where is yours?" Lupton jabbed an aggressive finger in the air.

"It is lodged with a third party, as it happens, which is under instruction to hand it over to the relevant authorities if I have not returned by midnight," replied Thomas. On his way to Boughton, he had stopped off at Mr. Peabody's apothecary shop in the High Street and delivered a sealed parcel into his hands for safekeeping. In it were the samples of the tea and tobacco Thomas had collected from the woods, which could be used in evidence against the smugglers and connect them to the surveyor's murder and to Coutt's.

Lupton's shoulders rose in anger. "You are lying, Silkstone!" he boomed.

Thomas knew he was taking a dangerous gamble, but he managed to keep his nerve. "You are the one who will be clapped in chains if Sir Montagu ever finds out that his trusted steward is playing him for a fool."

Lupton flashed a look of horror at Thomas. "What are you saying, man?" he protested indignantly.

The doctor laid bare his thoughts. "It is my supposition that Turgoose and Charlton inadvertently stumbled across, or came close to, the old ruins, the place where the smugglers store their loot—the very smugglers who give you a cut of their ill-gotten gains." His eyes flared as he accused Lupton. He was about to turn the tables and play the steward at his own game. "The Raven, Lupton. I am sure the name means something to you."

"I know of him," replied Lupton after a moment. "He is a highwayman and a common thief."

"Who also goes by the name of Seth Talland, does he not?"

Lupton's neck suddenly jerked back into his shoulders. "I

have no idea what you're talking about, Silkstone!" he remonstrated loudly—a little too loudly, as far as Thomas was concerned.

"The Raven and Seth Talland are one and the same, are they not?" the doctor persisted. It had come to him as he was interrogating Geech earlier that evening. He recalled the well-dressed man at the bar, talking to the innkeeper a few days back, and the gesture he had made, stroking his earlobe. Talland had made the exact same movement on the witness stand. "You were double-dealing, were you not? Not content with protection money from Geech, you were turning a profit from smuggled goods yourself. The prizefighter disguised himself so he could act as your go-between, and when Geech tried to shortchange your man, the stable lad paid with his life."

"You cannot prove it!" blurted Lupton.

Thomas nodded. "I'll admit it would've been hard had I not been able to trace the murder weapon."

"What?" The steward's brows dipped.

Thomas nodded. "You see, the pistol that killed Jeffrey Turgoose also killed Aaron Coutt." Professor Hascher had been able to measure the caliber of the shot that killed the stable lad. It was exactly the same as the one that felled the surveyor.

Lupton snorted. "But this is ludicrous."

Thomas felt relieved to be stepping on solid ground. "It is fact, sir, and can be proven. The pistol belongs to Sir Theodisius Pettigrew and is the same one that was planted in the Diggotts' dwelling. I cannot prove that Talland killed Mr. Turgoose yet, but I am working on it."

"Then you are wasting your time," the steward mocked. He reached for the glass of brandy he had discarded earlier and took a gulp.

"You know I can make life very awkward for you, Lupton." Thomas was determined not to leave empty-handed.

"So what do you propose?" Lupton took another gulp.

"A deal," replied the doctor. "If I drop my investigations into Aaron Coutt's murder, you will tell me the truth about Lady

Lydia." He paused, his eyes boring into Lupton's. "She is alive, is she not?"

In the firelight glow, Thomas could see the steward's neck shrink back into his shoulders. His nerve had been rattled and his ensuing silence condemned him. Thomas knew he had him, just as surely as if he were a worm wriggling on a hook. He stared at him for a moment, watching him writhe, before offering a way out.

"So," he said, his voice tinged with victory. "You will tell me where Lady Lydia is being held." This time his words came in the form of an order rather than a question.

Lupton, whose gaze had fallen to the floor, now lifted his head and shook it as if in a daze. "I cannot tell you," he replied, his head lolling from side to side.

Thomas set his jaw. "So you are prepared to be exposed to Sir Montagu?"

Again Lupton's head swayed. "I cannot tell you because I do not know," he snapped. "Sir Montagu refused to tell me. He said the secret would be safer that way." He looked at Thomas in the same manner that a deeply religious man might react if asked to recant his long-held convictions. The anatomist found himself believing him.

"But she is alive?" asked Thomas, trying to coax Lupton with a softer tone. At first the steward remained sullen, but the doctor persisted. "The body in the crypt is that of Miss Annalise Kent, is it not?" He craned his neck to try to latch onto Lupton's eyes. "She became so distraught after Lady Lydia's departure from Bedlam that she was given the means to take her own life by a clerk in the pay of Sir Montagu, who then seized the opportunity to announce her ladyship's death."

The steward threw a grudging look at Thomas, but remained silent.

"But Lady Lydia is not dead, is she?" The anatomist's patience was wearing thin. "Is she?" He raised his voice.

"If I tell you, will you stop meddling in affairs that do not concern you, Silkstone?"

Thomas regarded Lupton for a moment. He had the upper hand and, although he did not relish it, he knew only a fool would throw it away.

"I shall tell Sir Montagu nothing of your little ruse, as long as you tell me if Lydia is really dead."

Lupton drew breath; then slowly, as if realizing his defeat, he began to shake his head. "No, she is not," he mumbled.

"What did you say?" pressed Thomas.

Lupton bit his lip, as if trying to stop his mouth from forming the words, but their power overcame him. "Lady Lydia is not dead," he repeated reluctantly.

It was all that Thomas needed to hear for the moment. He inhaled deeply, then exhaled slowly, like a man filling his lungs with fresh air for the first time in days. It was the confirmation he had so craved, the news that he had been so desperately seeking.

"Thank you," he said softly, his stifled breath fleeing from his lungs as he spoke. "I am most grateful."

Chapter 43

The sound of his horse's hooves thundered in his ears as Thomas rode directly to Draycott House the following morning. He felt the blood course through his veins and a surge of energy, or anger—he was not sure which—wash over him. Not only was Lydia alive; he knew where she was. Draycott House. Of course. Franklin, his white rat, had sown the seed in his brain when he had rushed back to his cage after he'd been disturbed, but events in Brandwick had sidetracked Thomas's time and energies. How stupid, how blind he had been. Convinced she had been shut away in some private institution, he had ignored the most obvious location for her incarceration. At least he could be thankful that she was no longer in that hellhole they called a hospital. A memory of her emaciated frame draped in that terrible restraining garment flashed into his mind. He saw her tear-stained face, her shorn head, and heard her pleas to be rescued. He had felt so impotent at the time. He had been totally powerless, but it was clear from the look of anguish on Lydia's face that she no longer trusted him. Her view of him had been skewed by Sir Montagu's lies. She was convinced that Thomas was responsible for her awful fate, and her faith in him had not merely waned; it had completely disappeared. Somehow he needed to rebuild her trust in him, but first he had to find her.

Riding across country, he made good time. The ground was

still damp after heavy rain, but the roads were passable. The journey by coach from Boughton to Draycott would normally take two hours in such conditions. Thomas had done it in under an hour. He had ridden his horse hard and arrived at the steps of the house spattered with mud and damp with sweat. Inside he was still seething. He had been played for a fool by Sir Montagu Malthus yet again. Striding up to the door, he did not even bother to pull the cord, but walked straight into the hallway.

A flustered butler appeared. "Sir, can I help you?"

Ignoring the man, Thomas stormed in and looked about the entrance hall. There was a door on either side of the staircase. He stormed up to the first and opened it. The room was empty. He slammed the door shut. He tried the second.

"Sir!" pleaded the butler.

"Where is she? Where is Lady Lydia?" Thomas shouted angrily, flinging open the second door. "Lydia! Lydia!" he called.

Suddenly a voice boomed from the half landing. "Really, Dr. Silkstone, have your manners deserted you?"

Thomas looked up to see Sir Montagu glowering down at him, his broad black shoulders hunched over the banisters.

"I'd heard colonists were unsophisticated, but this sort of behavior will not be countenanced."

Thomas marched to the foot of the stairs. "I know she is here, Malthus. Let me see her!" he demanded.

The lawyer seemed unconcerned. He floated down the stairs without a sign that he had undergone surgery barely three months previously. Following closely behind was Gilbert Fothergill. "And what if her ladyship does not wish to see you?" Sir Montagu asked. His voice was tinged with a smugness that infuriated Thomas.

"Of course she wishes to see me. I have come to release her from this . . . this prison." Thomas lifted his arms in a wide sweep.

Now standing on the bottom step, so that he remained gazing down on Thomas, Sir Montagu shot him a disingenuous look. "A prison? Such harsh words, Silkstone. On the contrary, it is I who saved her ladyship from Bethlem and brought her here. You were happy to leave her there, were you not?"

Thomas scowled. "What do you mean? You were the one who committed her there in the first place."

At his words, Sir Montagu suddenly snapped his fingers and Fothergill emerged from his shadow to give him a piece of parchment. He raised one of his thick brows. "I think you'll find your signature is on the committal papers, Silkstone," he said, flapping the document in front of Thomas's face. "I have a copy here."

Unable to contain himself any longer, the anatomist snatched at the paper and tore it first lengthways, then across, before flinging the pieces to the ground. Up until now he had nurtured a vague hope that Lydia had not been shown his signature; that she might still have harbored a doubt as to his complicity. Now he feared otherwise. "You know this is a lie!"

Sir Montagu merely smiled. "Her ladyship has seen it and knows it to be yours."

"You planned this all along, didn't you?" His voice trailed off wanly as he realized he had been well and truly entrapped.

Sir Montagu shook his head. "And all those letters she sent you, but they were returned unopened. How could you be so heartless?"

"She wrote to me?" Such a revelation was the final straw.

Enraged, Thomas flew at the lawyer, but his clerk stepped in the way, and the butler, sensing the possibility of trouble, had already called two lackeys.

"If I were you, I would return to London, Silkstone," said Sir Montagu between clenched teeth. "Her ladyship has seen you for what you truly are. You were only ever interested in her fortune, and now that it is no longer within your reach, you can find yourself another rich heiress."

Thomas balled his fists and felt his pulse race even faster. He was used to hearing slurs on his character from Malthus, but this latest barrage was beyond the pale. That the lawyer should have turned Lydia against him with his false accusations and elaborate hoaxes went further than he had ever envisaged. He wanted to barge past Malthus and search through the upstairs rooms, where he was convinced she was imprisoned.

"Lydia! Lydia!" he shouted, lunging forward.

It was no use. The two lackeys appeared from nowhere and hooked their arms under his, pulling him away. However, just as they released him from their grasp, the main door opened, and into the hallway ran the young earl, followed by an anxious Nurse Pring.

"No, Master!" she shouted after her charge, but it was too late.

"Richard!" cried Thomas, his voice a mix of surprise and exultation.

Seeing the anatomist, the child stopped in his tracks. His face was flushed pink and his curls were disheveled. The light blue satin of his breeches was caked in mud at the knees. The boy wiped his streaming nose with the back of his sleeve and looked at Thomas. There was a flicker of recognition.

The doctor, forced to compose himself, managed a gentle smile. "You remember me, do you not, sir? 'Tis Dr. Silkstone. I am a friend of your mamma's."

The boy frowned, then nodded thoughtfully. "You made my arm better," he said.

Relieved, Thomas rushed forward. "Yes. You remember! I am here to see your mamma again." Bending low, he held out his hand, but the child looked at it suspiciously and then at his nursemaid, before ignoring the gesture.

"You have made my mamma very sad, sir," he said, fixing Thomas with an intense glare. "You must leave this house."

Thomas felt the pain of the young earl's wounding words tighten his chest. "What? No. I am your mamma's friend!" He forced his features into a broad smile to appear less threatening. But the child turned and hid his face in his nursemaid's skirts.

The boy's performance delighted Sir Montagu. He had witnessed the scene from the study doorway and was smirking. "Out of the mouths of babes, Silkstone," he said, unable to disguise the glee in his voice.

Thomas was silent for a moment as he felt the weight of humiliation and defeat press down on him. All he could hear was the blood pumping through his ears as his heart beat faster and faster.

Finally he said, "I will not give up, Malthus. 'Tis not in my nature." He turned and headed for the door. The butler held it open for him, but before he crossed the threshold he rounded on his heel and shouted at the top of his voice: "Lydia, I will not give up!" He did not know if she heard him, but in light of his crushing defeat, it eased his burden a little to think that maybe, just maybe, she had heard his voice and knew that all was not lost.

As he left the hallway, however, he became aware of Sir Montagu's voice behind him. "Save your breath and your strength for Brandwick, Silkstone," he called. "The villagers will almost certainly have need of your services."

Meanwhile, in her bedchamber upstairs, Lady Lydia Farrell had flown to her door and was pulling at the handle. It was locked. She banged on it, but no one came in answer to her calls. She had been seated looking out of her window onto the drive when, to her shock, she had seen a horse gallop up to the front entrance. It took only a second for her to realize the identity of the rider. Her heart had fluttered just as it always used to at the sight, when Thomas paid a visit to Boughton Hall. Now, however, everything had changed. The sight of him set her mind in a flurry. His betrayal had been total and utter. The one man whom she believed she could trust in the world had turned out to be a Judas. By his own hand he had committed her to Bedlam. Sir Montagu had only been following his advice, and when he had seen for himself the terrible conditions in which she had been held, he had ordered her immediate release.

Thomas, on the other hand, had allowed her to wallow in the depravity of the asylum. She saw to her astonishment how he conversed with Cameron, how he distanced himself as if she were a stranger. He had abandoned her to her terrible fate, and for that she could never forgive him. Although her head told her that it would be best to cut him out of her life and not to waste another tear on him, at the sight of him she suddenly felt compelled to confront him. She had wheeled 'round and made for the door. She wanted to tell him in person how he may as well have taken his scalpel to her chest and cut out her heart while it still beat. Had he ever truly loved her, or was his insinuation into her life and her affections simply his way of reaching her fortune? Now that Sir Montagu, or rather her father, had explained everything to her, it was as if the scales had been lifted from her eyes. It all made perfect sense. How could she have been so naïve and foolish as to think that a lowly anatomist, and a foreigner to wit, could have declared his undying love for her with his lips and not had his heart set on her fortune? Had she learned nothing from her experience? Captain Michael Farrell had been cut from the same cloth: sophisticated, debonair, and yet always with an eye to the main chance. How had she not seen past Thomas's caring, gentlemanly façade? A wolf in sheep's clothing—that was how her father had described him. How grateful she was that after all these years, Sir Montagu had finally revealed himself to her. He had, he told her, always had her best interests at heart. At last here was a man she could trust. A man whose word was his bond. Here was her own flesh and blood.

Now was her chance to confront her tormentor. Now was the chance to hear the truth from his own lips. She could ask him, in person, why he had betrayed her.

"Let me out," she called. Again, only louder: "Let me out." She twisted the handle once more. She pulled at it. She pushed it. No one came. She put her ear to the door. She could hear voices; then, suddenly, she heard Thomas call her name. She rattled the door handle again in vain.

Hurrying back to the window, she saw his horse tethered and a groom in attendance. Downstairs raised voices drifted upstairs, and a moment later she saw Thomas remount his mare. Something compelled her to knock at her window to attract his attention. She rapped loudly on the pane.

"Thomas!" she called. But he did not look up. Instead, she watched him retrieve something from his pocket—she could not make out what—and cradle it in his palm. After a moment's reflection, he returned the object and set off back down the drive once more at a gallop.

Chapter 44

Despite Sir Montagu's order to ban the beating of the bounds, a small cohort of villagers had decided to defy him. Knowing they ran the risk of arrest, they had approached the Reverend Unsworth for his blessing. Traditionally it was the vicar who led the procession, guiding it to various landmarks or bounds on the edges of the parish and stopping by each one to say prayers or give a short sermon. The younger ones loved to beat the markers with sticks or cut crosses in nearby tree trunks. Some of the parents would even bump their youngsters' heads against the boundary stones so they wouldn't forget where they came from. Sometimes coins were flung into brooks or fords and there would be a scramble among the boys. Yet, fearing Sir Montagu's wrath, the reverend had declined to lead the procession and advised the villagers to change their plans. A few had taken his advice. Several, however, had ignored it.

In Brandwick, housewives were sweeping their floors and several had even seen to it that their menfolk had given their houses a lick of whitewash. The baking ovens had been fired up nonstop for the past two days, producing bread and pies, and shopkeepers polished their windows to make sure their wares looked their best. But as for the ceremony itself, most would have none of it for fear of recriminations.

The Three Tuns was doing a brisk trade ahead of the curfew. In the saloon bar, men stood cheek by jowl, downing ale or gin and even cider. The floor was sticky and the air thick with smoke.

But the fug did not stop the lively conversation, even though tongues were necessarily constrained.

Into this maelstrom slipped Adam Diggott, unseen by most, but recognized by those who mattered. The little cluster of militants sat themselves in a corner nursing their pints of ale and speaking in low voices. Will Ketch, the cowman, was there with his dog, together with Abel Smith. They sat alongside Black Zeb and Josh Thornley and his son, Hal. The coppicer, still wearing his hat pulled down below his brows, elbowed his way between them.

" 'Tis set for tomorrow," Zeb Godson told him. The charcoal burner had spent time in the spring, washing off the soot that clung to his skin, but the whites of his eyes still shone brighter than anyone else's from out of his grimy face.

"Here's the plan," began Josh Thornley. "There's fifteen of us, and maybe more, and we start at the edge of Raven's Wood and work our way along the ditch till we reach the edge of Arthur's Hollow."

Adam Diggott put up his hand and shook his head. "Fifteen? There's nigh on two mile of fencing. We'll want at least fifty." His face was pinched and anxious. "And we need to be more cunning."

Suddenly a familiar voice sounded behind them.

"All well, gents?" Peter Geech appeared from nowhere, carrying a fistful of empty tankards.

Adam Diggott turned his head away and sank into the corner. The landlord nodded to his patrons, then looked about him before drawing closer.

"You best look out," he warned them. "A military man came in late this afternoon. Ordered enough ale and bread for eighty men, 'e did, for the morrow."

"How's that, then?" queried Ketch.

Geech scooped up their empty tankards. "Malthus must've got wind. They say it were the vicar that told him. There's a platoon on its way. Make sure you're careful."

It did not take long for word to spread among the parishioners that a company from the Fifty-second Regiment of Foot had been requested by the local magistrate, Sir Arthur Warbeck, and was to be stationed at Boughton Hall. They knew its men could be called upon if, as rumor had it, the beating ceremony went ahead. The raucous merriment in the Three Tuns was suddenly dulled as the news seeped out, and in its place, a feeling of distinct unease emerged. It was clear that Sir Montagu had anticipated that the villagers would seize their chance and defy his orders. It was the excuse he had sought, and now, as well as the law, he had the militia on his side.

Thomas wasted no time in returning to Brandwick from Draycott House. Fury still coursed through every fiber of his body. He urged his horse to gallop faster and faster, cutting across country, breasting hedges and ditches instead of following the roads. Taking the track up to the top of one of the hills, he surveyed the landscape. The vale lay stretched out before him; to the south, Milton Common, and farther beyond, London. To the west sat Oxford. The road was a winding ribbon that cut through a gently sloping valley. One side was heavily wooded, with the trees meeting the floor. He strained his eyes. There was movement. He looked away, blinked, and looked back. At first he had thought himself imagining it, but no. When he fixed his gaze on the road, he saw it color red. Urging his horse nearer for a better view, he squinted against the pale spring sunlight once more. His eyes were not deceiving him. The roadway had turned bright crimson, like a trickle of blood looping its way along the valley floor, and he suddenly realized why. Marching along, four abreast, on the road from Oxford to Brandwick was a platoon of foot soldiers. Sir Montagu's enigmatic warning to Thomas that his services would be needed suddenly made perfect sense. Now he understood why. The redcoats were coming to the village. There would be trouble. There could be blood.

Galloping back to Brandwick, Thomas rode into the courtyard at the Three Tuns and let the new stable lad, Rogers, take his mount. He was about to go straight up to his room when the landlord called out to him.

"Dr. Silkstone!"

Thomas turned on his heel. Geech was the last man on earth he wanted to deal with. After yesterday's revelations, he had even less respect for the rogue, but he seemed impatient to talk once more.

Leaning on the bar, he dipped his head and said, "Sir Montagu expects trouble at tomorrow's ceremony, sir."

Thomas suddenly remembered. "Of course, the beating of the bounds." It would explain the advance of the troops.

Geech, busying himself with wiping a tankard, lowered his voice still further. "Under its cover Adam Diggott and his men plan to destroy the fencing 'round the common, but Sir Montagu got word and has called in the militia."

Thomas eyed the landlord suspiciously. He knew the soldiers were on their way—he had seen them not five miles hence. A shiver suddenly ran down his spine. "Why are you telling me this, Geech?" he asked.

The landlord looked indignant. "I may be a smuggler, but I'm a Brandwick man, too," he protested. "I can't have the redcoats killing all my customers, now, can I, Doctor?" he said, setting down the tankard. He shook his head and dipped low to whisper into Thomas's ear. "There'll be trouble," he said before he drew back, allowing the doctor to ponder the gravity of the situation. Molly, as timid as a mouse, but a good worker, happened to be passing at the same time. "A tankard of ale for the doctor, on the house," Geech directed, as if nothing were amiss.

Thomas, meanwhile, decided to head upstairs to his room. Tired and anxious, he needed time to consider his next move. Standing by the window, he lifted his gaze over the High Street to the wooded ridge above. Through the opened casement he could hear noises coming from the common, of more fence posts being hammered in, more horses pulling carts, more Brandwick men shouting. He could hear, too, the dull thud of mallets as the wood stakes were driven into the damp ground, like so many nails into the villagers' coffin.

So the soldiers had been summoned to cast their shadow over the illicit festivities. Dissent was rising, like a winter bourne that suddenly bubbles up from belowground and spills across the landscape, flooding fields as it goes. The redcoats were there to stem its flow. Thomas had no idea of their orders, but it was clear they had not been called in simply to keep the peace. Malthus had got wind of some planned disruption that was afoot, some insurrection, whether large or small, that threatened his vision of an enclosed estate. Thomas feared what the morrow would bring for the people of Brandwick, just as he feared for Lydia.

Chapter 45

The day dawned calm enough. There was a nip in the air, customary for early May, but the clear sky told Thomas that the spring sun would soon warm the soil. As soon as he was able to rouse Rogers, he mounted his horse and rode out to Boughton Hall. He did not know whether Lupton would receive him, but he hoped the sway he now held over the steward with regards to his smuggling exploits might carry some weight. He was right. He was shown into the morning room.

Lupton was seated at the dining table, a plate of half-eaten eggs and ham in front of him. He did not rise when Thomas entered, but merely nodded in his direction while continuing to eat. The doctor, about to open his mouth to berate the steward, was pre-empted.

"I thought you might be paying me a visit this morning, Silkstone." Lupton wiped his mouth with the corner of his napkin. "Would you care to join me?" He gestured to a chair opposite.

Thomas fixed him squarely in the eye. "I find my appetite deserts me in the circumstances," he replied.

Lupton gave a little shrug. "Ah, you have heard that the Oxfordshire Regiment is on its way. Sir Montagu had word that his ban may be flouted." There was a flippancy in his tone that riled Thomas. The men in question, the doctor had learned, were drawn from the same regiment that had fought at Lexington and Bunker Hill. They were battle hardened and would as soon turn their muskets on their own kind as on a native Indian.

"Calling out the infantry to police a village custom? That is surely a most draconian measure?" asked Thomas. From the way Lupton's gaze slid away, he could tell he had more intelligence than he was admitting to. "This is not simply about the defiance of the ban, is it?"

Lupton toyed with the knife on his breakfast plate. "I know that there are killers on the loose in Brandwick. I know that a surveyor in this estate's employ has been murdered by a gang of barbarous woodsmen who may strike at any time. The men of the Fifty-second are here for the villagers' protection."

Thomas leaned forward and planted both hands firmly on the table. "You do realize that the common is like a powder keg? One spark from these soldiers is all that is needed and it will ignite." He stormed across the room and pointed through the window toward the village. "If men and women are injured today, their blood will be on your hands."

Lupton shook his head. "The villagers' fate is in their own hands," he countered. "Either they follow Adam Diggott and his cronies and face the consequences, or obey Sir Montagu. The choice is a simple one."

Thomas shot the steward an uneasy look. "You know something, don't you?"

Lupton shrugged. "As you are aware, Sir Montagu's spies are everywhere, Silkstone. Of course we know that Diggott and his miscreants are planning mayhem."

Thomas suddenly felt his chest tighten. "So that is why you called in the army."

"A company cannot be called out on a whim," came the glib reply.

Thomas wheeled 'round in desperation and walked back to the window. "But the troops have muskets. You know there could be a massacre."

Lupton snorted. "Just be thankful Sir Montagu did not call in the cavalry!" His unbridled arrogance had never been more evident to Thomas.

Thomas turned back, exasperated. "And what of the villagers' ancient rights? The rights they have enjoyed for hundreds of years. Do they count as naught?"

Lupton suddenly let out a derisory laugh. "Ancient rights? An American lectures an Englishman on ancient rights?" He slapped the table. "Sir Montagu looks forward, not backward, Silkstone. Surely you don't think he intends to stop at enclosure?"

Thomas frowned. "What do you mean?"

The steward shrugged. "Enclosure is merely the first step."

"The first step before what?"

Lupton rose from the table. "Come, I will show you something," he said, leading the way out of the morning room, across the hall, and into the study.

Under the window had been placed a long table, and on it, secured at all four corners by paperweights, was a large piece of vellum. It measured at least a man's height in length. Thomas peered over it.

"A map of Oxfordshire?" he queried.

Lupton shook his head. "Not just Oxfordshire, but Northamptonshire, too."

Thomas looked again, focusing at the top of the map. There were names that were vaguely familiar to him, Banbury and Bicester. He saw Draycott House was clearly marked, too. He let his eyes wander west to Oxford, and then it dawned on him. He suddenly realized what he was seeing. A thick blue line ran from the River Cherwell in the north to join with the River Thames in the east.

"But these are plans for a . . . for a canal."

"Bravo, Silkstone! A canal that would link Banbury to Oxford. Such a route will open up huge commercial possibilities and—"

Thomas interrupted. "Hold, sir! You speak as if this is a fait accompli."

Lupton smiled. "That's because it is. There are several financial backers on board, and the act will go through Parliament in the next few weeks."

Thomas balked for a moment as he digested the information.

"So Malthus intends to not only enclose Boughton, but build a canal through Brandwick, too?" he asked incredulously.

Lupton patted the map. "Precisely. Wharves will be erected and factories built."

"And what of the people of Brandwick? This is their future."

Lupton tilted his head and looked at Thomas oddly. "They will work in the factories, of course. They will leave the land and man the machines, just as they are doing in the north and the Midlands."

Thomas knew Lupton was referring to the new mills that were being built in Lancashire. The fulling mill would soon be replaced, if Malthus had his way, with one of Richard Arkwright's power mills, which were springing up all the way from Manchester to Scotland. Arsonists had set fire to one of his ventures at Chorley not five years before, and Thomas could imagine exactly the same resentment simmering in Brandwick. Children as young as six would be forced to work in the mills with long hours and low pay. The canal would cut a great swathe through the heart of the Boughton Estate, changing the landscape forever. Trees would be felled in their thousands to be replaced by factory chimneys, the sides of the meandering river would be straightened to make a canal, hillsides would be tunneled out, the tenter lines would give way to steam looms.

"And you expect them to accept this, this transformation, without any consultation?"

Lupton shook his head. "Consultation can only lead to compromise," he replied. "And that is not a word in Sir Montagu's vocabulary."

Thomas felt indignant on behalf of the villagers. "You are pushing good people too far," he warned, shaking his finger in the air.

Lupton simply smirked. "It is merely progress, Silkstone. Just as you and your ilk make advances in medicine, so must landowners make advances in the countryside."

Thomas arched a brow. "The difference is we do it for the benefit of mankind and you do it for your own," he replied.

At that moment there was a knock on the door and Howard appeared to address Lupton.

"There is a Captain Ponsonby to see you, sir," he announced.

"Ah yes, do show him in. Dr. Silkstone was just about to leave," said the steward with a leer.

A fresh-faced young soldier stood by the threshold. Thomas looked at the officer, then at Lupton, and nodded. "Indeed, I must warn the people of Brandwick they are walking into a trap," he muttered. Only Lupton heard.

Chapter 46

Thomas knew that he had to act fast if bloodshed was to be avoided. As he rode away from Boughton he glanced back and saw smoke from the campfires rising over the ridge. He caught sight of the company of men being put through their paces in a field not far from the hall. He spurred on his horse and shortly arrived back in the village. There were few people about; it seemed that most had obeyed the order and retreated to their homes. Thomas was puzzled, however, to see that Walter Harker's window was opened wide onto the street. Thinking that the constable would be on duty at such a time, he decided to call on him. Knocking at the front door, he was answered with a long, low mumble and entered to find Harker seated by his hearth, downing a quart pot of gin.

"Mr. Harker, you have heard some villagers plan to beat the bounds?" Thomas thought it odd that the village constable should not be policing his patch.

Hearing the anatomist's words, Harker lifted his blurry gaze. "They need to do what they need to do," he mumbled.

Thomas smelled the strong liquor on the constable's breath and looked into his bloodshot eyes. He realized he was too far in his cups to be of any use. Walter Harker was washing away his duty in gin. Thomas bent low and pawed at his sleeve.

"Where is Adam Diggott?"

The constable grunted and supped more gin.

"You know he is planning something and that Sir Montagu has laid a trap."

"I can't change nothing," Harker groaned, shaking his head. The drink had reduced him to a quivering mass, robbing him of his pride and dignity. There was a time, not so long ago, when Thomas knew he could rely on Walter Harker in a difficult situation. Now, however, he realized he would have to act alone.

Riding to the edge of the village, to the Diggott cottage, Thomas found Abe asleep in a chair. He was alone. Gently he put his hand on his shoulder to wake him.

The old man's eyes flew open, swimming in their sockets. A moment later they were focusing on Thomas. "Dr. Silkstone?" he croaked.

"Yes, Abe. Do you know where Adam is?"

Diggott gave a qualified nod, but no more.

"Is he at the beating?"

"I'm not to tell no one," came the reply.

Thomas took a deep breath and explained. "I believe Adam and his friends are in grave danger. Sir Montagu knows they want to tear down the fences, and the troops will be under orders to fire." Kneeling beside him, he touched the old man's arm. "Do you understand?"

Abe grunted. Despite the faraway look in his tired eyes, he seemed a little more lucid. "The redcoats would shoot them?"

"I fear so. I must speak with them and warn them," replied Thomas, his voice becoming more urgent.

The old man nodded. "He went to the common, him and Zeb Godson and the others. You're right, they'll have them fences down, but I don't know how they plan to do it."

Thomas rocked back on his heels and rose. "I shall find them," he said. "But if you see them before I do, tell them their lives are in danger."

Adam Diggott was among friends. He knew that, but he also knew that in these straitened times, even those he counted as good friends might betray him to the authorities for a shilling or two. It was a risk he had to take, but so as not to make himself obvious, he took to wearing a disguise as he went about spreading word. Dressed as a peddler, his large-brimmed hat still pulled low, he was hawking his wares among the few souls who had gathered by the common and revealing himself to those he knew he could trust.

Zeb Godson, Josh Thornley, and Will Ketch did not have to adopt such drastic measures. There was no price on their heads, but still they had to be guarded. Hands were cupped over mouths, voices were low, gazes direct. The plan was simple. That afternoon those villagers and commoners brave enough to defy the law and practice their ancient custom would gather on the main road to Oxford near Arthur's Hollow. The natural amphitheater on the common was the only ground that was still accessible. The rest had been fenced off over the previous few days. There they would sing a song and begin to process up the slope toward the line of stark wooden posts that barred their way to the top of the hill. As the villagers' chants came to a crescendo, the dissenters would quickly make their way to the fencing and begin tearing it down with axes and mallets that had been set aside. Posts and gates would be flattened before the troops got wind of the destruction, and the perpetrators would melt away just as surely as they had appeared. That was the scheme that had been conceived, and Adam Diggott and his cohorts had been gathering surreptitious support for it all day. Mingling among their neighbors, men and women of like minds, cottagers and woodsmen, country folk with the Brandwick soil in their bones and the water of the bournes of the Chilterns in their veins, it had not been hard to persuade them of their cause. They'd been born to their rights to common land, and by God, they'd die for them.

Just before St. Swithin's clock struck one, a crowd began to gather. What had begun as a handful of stalwart dissenters was swelling all the time. Emboldened by the gathering of a few, more and more villagers took to the common, so that by the time the clock struck two, upward of one hundred people had massed. With not a redcoat in sight, there was a carnival atmosphere. Girls wore flowers in their hair or carried posies. Others fixed ribbons to sticks and waved them like wands.

Thomas snaked his way through the crowd, looking for Adam Diggott. It was his broad frame and tall stature that gave him away.

"Thank God I have found you," said the doctor, unable to hide his relief.

"Dr. Silkstone." The coppicer's expression remained serious and aloof.

Thomas frowned. "I am come to beg you, and anyone else for that matter who is rash enough to pull a prank, think again." The doctor laid his hand on Adam's arm and spoke with a fearful intensity, but he was quickly rebuffed.

"I know the redcoats are at Boughton, if that's what you mean, sir," came Diggott's reply. It was as if the soldiers posed no more of a threat to the procession than troublesome flies. He turned away.

Thomas tried to reason with him and tugged at his jacket, so that he turned to face him once more. "Eighty men, many armed with muskets," he cried. "Are these people's lives worth the price of a few fence posts?"

Adam narrowed his eyes and, without warning, pulled away from Thomas. Climbing onto a stile nearby, he addressed the crowd.

"Good people of Brandwick," he shouted above the din. "Good people of Brandwick," he cried, louder this time. The chatter fell silent. All eyes turned to him. "Are we ready to make a stand?"

"Aye!" came the universal shout. They were united against enclosure, but the mood was excitable rather than angry.

"Then let us sing!" cried Adam Diggott. He cast a triumphant look at Thomas before signaling to the drummers and fiddlers to strike up their rendition of "Hey Down, Derry Down."

Meanwhile from his vantage point on a hill near Boughton Hall, Captain Samuel Ponsonby of the Oxfordshire Regiment was surveying the scene with his telescope. At his order his men began falling in. The crowd had gathered near the new boundary. They had riotous intentions. The law of the land had been broken. It was up to him and his men to enforce it. Within a few minutes a second order was given to move out. The troops were on the march, their mission to protect the lines of newly erected fencing, whatever it took. Just as the first song came to an end, the crowd started moving up the slope.

Hal Thornley, who'd been given the job of watching for the soldiers, brought word. "They're on their way!" he panted.

"Let's see where they station themselves," replied Adam, leading the crowd. "They'll expect us to go for the fencing on the ridge." He jerked his head toward the line that lay in front of them.

"Yes." Zeb nodded.

"But we won't," countered Adam.

"We won't?" queried Will, Bess trotting by his side.

Adam shook his head. "We'll surprise 'em by taking down the fencing that skirts Raven's Wood. 'Tis where they'll least expect it. There's a good half mile we can get our teeth into there. We'll have it all down afore they know it."

Zeb and Will nodded in unison. "'Tis a good plan," said Josh Thornley. "Let's spread the word."

And so it was that, while most of the villagers made their way up to the fencing on the ridge, another three dozen or so broke off from the main group. The majority of the dissenters clapped in time to music as they ascended the slope, causing a distraction for the others, who broke off, willy-nilly, heading west toward Raven's Wood.

Meanwhile Thomas had stationed himself on a ridge to the east of the action so he could see any troops approaching before the villagers below. It was not long before he, too, saw them, and he watched their arrival with trepidation. They spread out and stationed themselves around the perimeter of the common, as if corralling the villagers like sheep that could be penned in and shepherded at their will. But these man-made barriers, these soldiers, were well spaced out, with at least twenty yards between sentries.

Keeping himself distant from the main body of the crowd, Thomas walked up the slope toward the long line of fencing that marked the newly claimed Boughton land. Stopping by a broad oak, he looked back down toward the hollow. Taking out his spyglass he could see that a group of maids, all wearing their long white May robes, had formed themselves into a ring. A fiddler struck up, and in time to the music, the circle began to configure itself. Threading through one another and forming into circles and shapes, the girls moved in unison, bobbing and skipping like young puppies at play. They were obviously meant to distract the soldiers, and turning his glass on the redcoats on the ridge, Thomas could see that they were doing an excellent job. Perhaps, he thought, the protest—for that was what it was, a protest dressed up as an ancient tradition—would pass off without incident. Perhaps a shot would not be fired. Perhaps he had worried unnecessarily.

Suddenly a voice came from behind. "A fine sight, eh, Dr. Silkstone?"

Thomas turned to see old Maggie Cuthbert standing beside him, looking down at the dancers. "The Uffington Horse," she said.

Thomas looked at her quizzically.

"The dance," she explained. " 'Tis named after the great white horse on the downs."

"Ah," replied Thomas with a nod. He thought of the enigmatic creature cut into the chalk hillside a few miles away.

The old crone smiled. " 'Tis said that when King Arthur awakes, the horse will rise up and dance on nearby Dragon Hill," she chuckled.

Thomas tilted his head. "And what will wake King Arthur?" he asked.

Maggie Cuthbert pursed her lips as she surveyed the dancers, then turned to him and said with the utmost conviction: "If England is in peril."

Chapter 47

Lydia studied her father across the dining table. She watched his jaw move slowly up and down as he chewed each mouthful of food assiduously. His long fingers, like talons, grasped the stem of his wineglass before he washed down his dinner with a good vintage. She had seen him eat before, of course. He had been a regular guest at the Crick family table during her childhood, conversing easily, holding sway and charming with his wit and repartee. She had respected him then, before she had known the secret that he kept with her mother. Those little asides she had seen them share; those trifling moments when one had brushed up against the other, thinking no one else had seen. They had all seemed so innocent to her and quite beguiling at the time. And now she knew the truth. The late afternoon sun that filtered weakly through the casement began to throw her newfound father's face into sharp relief, and the shadows started to play tricks on her eyes—elongating his nose, highlighting his cheekbones, turning the unremarkable into the striking. His whole countenance changed as the light altered, and it troubled her that the same man could appear so very different; that the person she had known, and feared, could take on the mantle of her protector and yet still cause an unsettling doubt in her mind.

"You seem most pensive," he remarked finally, placing his knife and fork side by side on his empty plate.

She had not realized that he, too, had been studying her,

watching her slyly as she pecked at her food like a bird in summer. She managed a wan smile. As a young child taking its first steps, she felt herself toddling toward him, arms outstretched, and yet . . .

"I have much to think about, sir," she replied. She did not mean to sound impertinent, but she saw him arch a brow as he dabbed his mouth with his napkin.

"Silkstone's visit has disturbed you." His perception, like his gaze, was always razor-sharp, thought Lydia. That was why he was at the top of his professional game, she told herself. Yet still she found his acuity unnerving. She could not hide her unease.

"Yes, sir," she replied. "I had wished to confront him, and yet I found myself locked in my room." Her voice was tinged with reproach, but he countered her obvious disaffection with a disarming reply.

"But, my dear, that was purely for your own protection. Did you not hear him shout your name? He tore in like a madman, intent on harming you."

It was true. She had heard Thomas call her name, more than once. He sounded furious, but what if he was desperate? What if those cries were not angry but anguished? What if her father was lying to her? After all, his whole relationship with her mother had been based on a lie. If he had lived under a pretense for all those years, then surely there was nothing to stop him from adding to his litany of deceptions and manifest untruths. And yet she had seen Thomas's signature with her own eyes, been present when he had spoken with Dr. Cameron. Her mind kept traveling in circles, whirling 'round and 'round, unable to find its own path through the tangle of intrigue and deceit that engulfed her. For now she would keep her own counsel. After all, Richard was with her, and she would do nothing to jeopardize his presence again.

"Yes. I am most grateful to you," she replied.

Thomas stayed on the hillside for a few moments longer after Maggie Cuthbert went on her way. It was a good vantage point. He counted upward of forty soldiers strung out along the fencing and could watch the dancers below, too. He guessed the rest of the company would be patrolling the estate's perimeter. The band kept on churning out lively tunes and the revelers continued to stomp and clap in time. But of Adam Diggott and his men, there was no sign. He glanced to his left. The soldiers he could see were still being kept occupied watching the village girls below. The dissenters had sloped off to cause mayhem elsewhere on the estate, and he'd wager he knew where. Down the bank he slipped, leaving the common, unseen by revelers and soldiers alike. Mounting his horse, he headed for Raven's Wood.

In ten minutes he was approaching the shaded edge of the trees. Up ahead he could see others, too. Squinting into the shadows, he made out several people. He heard noises, too; dull thuds and sharp cracks broke into the spring air. He hurried forward to see what was going on, and there, in the gloom, he could make out dozens of men and women uprooting fence posts or hacking at them with axes. The main gate into Raven's Wood lay chopped to pieces, and some of the women were gathering the shards into their aprons to use, Thomas presumed, for kindling. He strained his eyes to look down the line of fencing. As far as he could see along the boundary of the wood, people were vandalizing the stakes. The stronger men ripped posts from the ground as easily as rotten teeth from gums; others simply trampled on spars when they were flung to the ground, cracking them under foot. Some took obvious glee in the destruction, grunting and growling as they did so. Others were more workmanlike and methodical, settling into a rhythm of tugging, breaking, and throwing to the ground. All travailed with an intensity of purpose that came from knowing that their livelihoods were in peril.

Thomas surveyed the scene with a quiet horror. He could not help but admire the villagers' tenacity and ingenuity, yet his overwhelming immediate feeling was fear for these brave but, he felt, misguided souls, and the consequences of their actions. The infantrymen were stationed not half a mile away; one whiff of such insubordination and they would rally and train their muskets on the rebels. It would be just as he dreaded. The soldiers would fire. Blood would be shed, and Sir Montagu would be vindicated. The tyrant would enjoy nothing more than to see the village troublemakers dance on the end of a rope, and it seemed that soon his wish might be fulfilled. Thomas knew Adam Diggott would be somewhere at the center of this mass insurrection. He hurried along the lines searching for him. He dared not call out for fear of alerting the soldiers, so he zigzagged from man to man in his search. It did not take him long to find the coppicer himself, directing operations at the farthest gate.

"Diggott!" Thomas panted in a hoarse whisper.

The rebel's head, still covered by his large-brimmed hat, shot up.

"What in God's name do you think you are doing?" hissed Thomas, keeping his voice low.

Diggott snorted and pushed back his hat with his thumb.

"I be doin' what is right, Dr. Silkstone. These fences don't belong 'ere, so we're taking 'em down."

Thomas flung an arm in the direction of the soldiers by the common. "If they find out, they will shoot. There are women here. There will be no quarter!"

Diggott, his ax in his hand, straightened his back and looked down on Thomas. There was strong liquor on his breath.

"If we lose our rights, then we lose our way of life, Doctor. We got nothing more to live for." He turned 'round and, shaking his fist in the air, he raised his voice. "Let the soldiers fire. We're ready to be martyrs for our cause!"

At the rally cry, the villagers all looked up. Some shouted "Aye!" in reply, and Will Ketch's dog began to bark, but there were others who, fearing the infantry might be alerted by the outburst, slipped off silently, melting into the woods or sloping off down the hillside.

"Do you want to rouse the redcoats?" Thomas asked incredulously.

The coppicer turned and raised his ax above his head. "I'm past caring," he chuntered, and he brought down his blade on the fencing rail, splitting it in two.

Seeing it was fruitless arguing with Diggott, Thomas made his way back along the line. At each woman who remained, he stopped to ask if he could accompany her back to the common and out of harm's way. He could see that some of them were frightened, but most refused his offer. They would stand by their menfolk, they told him. One woman, however, her skirt a buttercup yellow, insisted that her young daughter return with Thomas to the village.

"You be goin' now, Daisy. I'll follow later," she told her.

Thomas took the girl's hand. She was no more than ten years of age. He smiled at her, but she returned a frightened grimace. Together they began their descent toward the common as the destruction of the woodland fencing gathered momentum. Now more than ever, it was vital that the soldiers remained distracted, thought Thomas. He would do what he could to divert their attention. Lost in his thoughts, he was trying to formulate a plan when, halfway down the slope, a loud cry went up from below.

"Turn out! Turn out!"

The shrill notes of a bugle suddenly sounded and Thomas stopped in his tracks. He looked down at the little girl, her eyes wide in fear. The secret was out. The soldiers had been alerted. Soon they would be marching toward them. Thomas pulled the girl to him and together they rushed off the track and ducked behind a hawthorn bush.

"Stay there. Don't move," he told her. He prayed the rebels would have heard the troops' rallying cry. The sound would surely have carried across the hill, but he wanted to make certain they all had the chance to get away. Keeping off the main path, he began to climb up the slope once more toward the wood. The sound of his heart drummed in his ears as he went, but the pounding was soon joined by a louder, deeper beat. Wheeling 'round, he saw the infantry, marching two abreast up the footpath, carrying their muskets. At their head on horseback was the young officer. Summoning all his strength, Thomas renewed his efforts, scurrying between the gorse bushes, until he reached the plateau at the edge of the wood. In the shadows, he could make out the few remaining commoners who still wielded their axes and mallets.

Cupping his hands around his mouth, he called to them. "The redcoats are coming!" he cried. "Get away!" He flailed his arms wildly in the hope that those who saw him would heed his warning. One or two did, but the rest either did not, or would not. They remained hacking and breaking right up to the moment that the officer ordered his men to fan out, at the top of the plateau with the forest edge in full view. They did so, forming two lines, the first on one knee, the second standing close behind.

The order was given. "Fix bayonets."

From out of the edge of the woods, Thomas watched horrified as figures suddenly emerged. First he made out Adam Diggott, but he was swiftly pursued by another dozen men. A clutch of women followed in their wake, so that the two sides were now lined up against each other, fewer than twenty yards separating them.

"Come no farther!" shouted Adam Diggott. His cohorts raised their axes threateningly. "No farther," he repeated.

Captain Ponsonby, remaining on his horse, shouted back. "You have willfully destroyed property belonging to the Boughton Estate. Desist immediately in the name of King George."

Adam Diggott stood firm. "We will not move from what is rightfully ours. These woods belong to us!"

There was a chorus of approval from the men at his side. Tensions were heightened. Ponsonby hesitated. He had not anticipated such willful disobedience. "Take aim," he ordered.

Thomas knew if he was to act, now was the moment. Revealing himself from behind his cover, he walked out between the two rows, his hands held aloft. The muskets suddenly trained on him, but he knew he must hold his nerve.

"Captain Ponsonby!" he called.

The young officer shot back, "Make yourself known, sir."

"I am Dr. Thomas Silkstone," he replied. "I was at Boughton Hall this morning."

Ponsonby, nonplussed for a second, nodded an acknowledgment. For an instant tension slackened. "You may approach, sir."

Thomas began to walk toward the officer. His pace was measured. One sudden move and he knew a nervous soldier might fire his half-cocked musket. He had barely gone five steps, however, when he heard something whistle past his right ear. He ducked instinctively as a broken fence post came hurtling through the air toward the officer. It hit his horse's flank, causing it to rear and let out a loud whinny. Will Ketch's bitch began to bark, too, and more missiles suddenly began flying about through the air, pieces of flint and shards of wood. They rained down on the front row of the soldiers. One was hit on the head and he fell. Another caught Thomas on the shoulder and he dived for cover.

Under attack, the young officer panicked. He had lost control of the situation. As the villagers approached, armed with their makeshift weapons, he gave the order.

"Above their heads, fire!"

The first volley cracked through the air and sprayed the trees, sending twigs showering to the ground, but the warning shots did nothing to dampen the villagers' ire. For a moment they froze amid the musket smoke, the gunshots ringing in their ears, but Adam Diggott would not be deterred. Lifting his ax above his head, he gave his own battle cry.

"Forward!" he shouted. There was no time for anyone to make their escape. He surged forward, together with half a dozen stalwarts, forcing the officer's hand.

"Fire!" cried Ponsonby. This time there was no mercy. The second line of musketeers aimed their shot right into the band of villagers that rushed toward them, their makeshift weapons held aloft. Some of the women began to scream and held back, calling to their men. Three fell instantly, but their fall did not make the others flinch. Three more men came hurtling toward the soldiers, brandishing axes as the troops reloaded. Another order, another volley, and they, too, fell. Keeping low to the ground, Thomas wiped his forehead with his palm and looked at it. It was covered in blood. It was not his own.

The tang of gunpowder filled the air and the smoke quickly cleared to reveal the carnage. Thomas hurried to where the wounded villagers lay. Below the sobs and wails from the women, he heard low groans. He rushed toward a wounded man, lying facedown, a hole blown through his left arm. He turned him over. It was Zeb Godson. Nearby lay scrag-headed Josh Thornley, sprawled out, his eyes open and blood trickling from his mouth. Thomas could see that he had taken a ball in his chest and died instantly. Abel Smith, the fowler, lay nearby, a shot in his head. The bury man, Joseph Makepeace, had fared better. He was on his knees, clutching his side, but at first glance Thomas believed the wound was a graze.

"Press against it," he told him. "Stay still and help will come."

Next he checked the pulse of another man, whom he did not know. He was dead, too, his guts gaping, coiled like bloodied snakes on the ground below. By him, a red-spattered boy whom he presumed was his son sat rocking to and fro. He was in shock but, as far as Thomas could see, remained unhurt.

Another casualty sat clutching his thigh, screaming in agony. As Thomas approached, he could see it was Will Ketch. It seemed he'd taken a ball above his knee, and the wound was bleeding profusely. His dog had not been so fortunate. It lay at his side, a shot in its head. A woman hurried over.

"Your apron. Give me your apron!" ordered Thomas.

The woman quickly obeyed, and Thomas began tearing the linen into strips. Securing a makeshift bandage around Ketch's thigh, he instructed the woman to keep it tight until help arrived.

A few yards away a burst of yellow caught Thomas's eye. As twilight approached, the wind had got up and was catching the hem of a woman's skirt. Hurrying to her, he turned her over to see that the color of her laced bodice was deep crimson. She had taken the full force of a shot to her chest. Suddenly, from somewhere behind him, he heard a plaintive cry.

"Mamma! Mamma!"

He turned to see the little girl he had left behind the hawthorn bush, running toward him. Seeing her mother covered in blood, she cried out and threw herself on top of her. Another woman bent low to comfort her. As Thomas rose, he was aware of someone at his shoulder. He turned to see Adam Diggott, blood trickling from a wound above his left brow. He had joined Thomas to lean over the dead woman. Both men eyed each other; Diggott's lips trembled. Thomas returned his look with a mixture of pity and reproach. It was not his place to judge. He must put his emotions to one side. It was up to him to salvage as many shattered lives as he could.

Suddenly he heard Ponsonby shouting another order.

"Round up the rest!" the officer called from his mount. Even in the gloom, Thomas could see that the captain's pristine white breeches were spattered with blood. He saw several of the soldiers run at full pelt toward the woods in pursuit of the few villagers who remained. Adam Diggott went easily enough when confronted. He and two other men knew it was futile to resist arrest and offered themselves up without a struggle.

The sound of the musket fire had caused panic among the revelers on the common below. Many of the men began to surge up the slope. The soldiers who did not pursue the stray rebels remained to confront the villagers who now converged at the top of the hill. When some of the women saw the bodies on the ground, they began to scream hysterically.

A sergeant tried to restore order. "Go back to your homes now," he shouted above the din. "Go home."

The soldiers re-formed and stood firm, their bayonets fixed and their glare on the crowd. The atmosphere was as taut as catgut until, one by one, the men started to turn and descend toward the common.

"Go home!" barked Captain Ponsonby. "And no charges will be pressed against you."

The crowd, shocked and dazed by what they had seen, poured slowly down the path. One or two jostled against the soldiers, but they were rebuffed and were reluctantly driven back.

Thomas remained, checking on the wounded. An earlier plea for help from the soldiers had gone unanswered. He felt overwhelmed, but he knew he must fight his own battle to stay calm.

Ever since he arrived in England, he had needed to harden his heart to patients' screams as they underwent surgery, but even he had not heard the like of the unearthly wails of the battlefield before.

"I need help over here," he called to Ponsonby. This time the captain rode over to him in person. "We need to move the injured. We should get them to the inn," said Thomas, pressing hard on Zeb Godson's arm to stem the flow of blood, as the woodsman groaned in agony.

Even though it was growing dark, Thomas saw the young captain's revulsion at the sight of so much blood. He turned his head, then nodded.

"Very well." He called to one of his men. "Sergeant, assign six men to help Dr. Silkstone care for the wounded," he said, adding: "But make sure they don't escape. They are all under arrest."

"Very good, sir." The sergeant saluted, and soon those who were able to walk were being escorted down the hill, muskets at their backs, while a cart arrived to take the seriously wounded and the dead back down to the village.

Thomas supervised the operation. Using the shirts of the injured and women's aprons, he had managed to rig up tourniquets to stem the flow of blood, but it was clear to him that at least three wounded men would draw upon his chirurgical skills. He was about to climb up into the cart himself, when one of the soldiers who was ferrying the dead to the wagon called him over.

"Doctor!"

Thomas rushed over. Abel Smith, whom he at first had believed dead, was groaning; a low noise was issuing from his bristly beard. Grabbing a bandage from his case, Thomas was applying pressure to the head, when he heard a woman's voice behind him. Turning, he saw Maggie Cuthbert.

"You'll be needing my help," she called down to Thomas.

He was glad of her offer. He had watched his father work in a field hospital in the Indian wars, and he knew that the more assistance that was given, the more lives could be saved. Swift action was the key to such traumatic injuries. He allowed himself to smile with relief.

"Indeed I will, Widow Cuthbert," he said. "Here." He rose, still pressing on Smith's head wound, and the old woman knelt and took his stead. Just as she did so, the air was split by a raucous cry. Simultaneously Thomas and the widow looked up to see a raven circling overhead. They both knew it was waiting to taste dead flesh.

Chapter 48

The cart trundled down the hill, bouncing and lurching without regard to its passengers, who clung to life by a thread. By the time they reached the Three Tuns, word of the rout had already set the wheels in motion. Mr. Peabody, the apothecary, had been summoned and had brought with him an array of medicaments. He had even overcome his usual reticence to instruct Peter Geech and his staff to line up tables to receive the wounded.

Outside the inn an anxious crowd had gathered, so that by the time Thomas arrived, the soldiers had to clear the way to allow the injured to be transported inside. The taproom had been turned into a makeshift hospital. Mr. Peabody had already ordered pails of water, and a large kettle was steaming on the blazing fire.

There were more injured than Thomas had at first feared. A long straggle of villagers with ferocious splinters in their hands or faces now presented itself. Thomas guessed they had been holding fencing stakes when the soldiers fired on them, sending shards of wood piercing like spears through their flesh.

"Dr. Silkstone! Dr. Silkstone!" Peter Geech approached Thomas wearing the expression of a man on whom the sky was about to fall. "What is to be done?"

Thomas knew that above all he had to remain calm. "I would ask that you provide me with plenty of your finest spirits, Mr. Geech," he replied.

"Spirits, Doctor?" repeated the puzzled landlord.

"Yes," Thomas replied firmly. "They will both dull the patients' pain and clean out the wounds, so none of your gin, Mr. Geech."

"Very good, sir. But who will pay for my best brandy?"

Thomas took a deep breath. Even in times of crisis, it seemed that Mr. Geech had an eye to the main chance. "I will see you are compensated," he said.

The doctor knew he had to prioritize treatment. Now that the battle had been fought, there were new enemies to confront. Lurking unseen among the blood and guts of his patients would be the seeds of certain diseases, the rigors and wound fever that needed to be destroyed before they held sway. He set Widow Cuthbert to work cleaning and dressing minor wounds, which he would check on later. For the moment he knew that lives could still be saved if he acted quickly. With Mr. Peabody at his side, he began his taste.

First he tended to Will Ketch's leg. Laying him flat, he let the apothecary administer a liberal dose of laudanum before he inserted a gag between the man's teeth to silence his agonized cries. Cutting away his breeches, Thomas could tell immediately that the shot had missed the femur. Molly had paled at the sight of so much blood, but after a moment to compose herself she had rallied and fetched the doctor his medical case from his room upstairs, before attending to the kettle. Using his forceps, Thomas managed to remove several large pieces of splintered wood from Ketch's wound. There was little hope of the flesh knitting together again naturally. It would need suturing, but at least if he could prevent blood rot, the cowman stood a chance of survival. The ball had embedded itself deep within the thigh muscle. Incising the wound at such a depth not only would be exceedingly painful but, Thomas feared, might also cause even more trauma to the patient, possibly leading to wound fever. There were many surgeons who would, he knew, question his judgment, but he'd seen more men die of subsequent infections than of gunshot wounds themselves. Most of his fellows would advise he take the saw to the leg and have done with it, too. Taking neither action was debatable, but it was a risk he was prepared to run. Satisfied that the wound was as clean as he could make it, Thomas sutured the thigh, leaving Mr. Peabody to bandage it. He moved on to the next casualty.

Zeb Godson's weathered face had turned as pale as a corpse. The tourniquet had saved his life, of that Thomas was sure, but staunching the blood flow once and for all grew more imperative by the minute. The brachial artery in the arm had been severed, causing a torrent of blood to gush from it. The makeshift tourniquet he had applied was now dripping with blood, so Thomas quickly replaced it with a screw tourniquet from his case. It was his goal to dam the great flood for good. His senses dulled by gin and laudanum, Zeb Godson offered little resistance as Thomas probed his wound. Taking a ligature from his case, he got to work, managing to bind the blood vessel securely with catgut. Widow Cuthbert had moved in to dress the wound when suddenly an urgent plea went up from Mr. Peabody.

"Dr. Silkstone," he cried. The apothecary was standing over Abel Smith. He had lapsed into unconsciousness and his breathing was very shallow. Thomas felt for his pulse. It barely registered. Head injuries always presented their own problems. On inspection it seemed as though Abel had been hit by a musket ball just above the left temple. It should have killed him outright, but by some remarkable chance, it had lodged in his skull.

Thomas sighed deeply. "I fear trepanning is the only course," he replied warily. The procedure was precarious, but he was aware that another respected surgeon, Percival Pott, had employed the method in field hospitals on several occasions. He had reduced the risk of infection in head wounds by extracting blood from extradural and subdural spaces by cranial draining. Thomas realized that if he were to save the fowler's life, he would have to do the same.

"I will need your assistance, Mr. Peabody," he told the apothecary.

The little man looked askance. "But I am no surgeon, sir."

"You have a brain in your head and a pair of hands, haven't

you?" said Thomas curtly, without waiting for a reply. "Smith's life hangs in the balance."

Next Thomas called to the landlord, who was busying himself with supplying kettles of hot water. "Mr. Geech, we need to get this man into another room. I need absolute quiet for the procedure I am about to perform."

Geech nodded. "This way, sir," he told Thomas, leading him into the private dining room. It was small, but the table was large and serviceable and Smith was laid on it flat with his head resting on a folded sack. Candles were quickly lit and Thomas tilted the skull away from him so that he could see the wound more clearly. It was evident that he had been hit at fairly close range. The swelling and contusions around his left eye were such that Thomas feared for Smith's sight, but it was the cranium that needed his most urgent attention. The flint had cracked it as if it were an eggshell, and a slice of bone the size of a walnut had been forced downward to press on the brain.

Although Thomas had performed the procedure twice before with success, he had seen many other surgeons' patients die shortly afterward. Sometimes death came swiftly, on the operating table; for others the surgery triggered delirium, agonizing headaches, or terrible seizures. He knew, however, that without treatment, Abel Smith's death was assured.

Reaching into a case, the surgeon brought out his trepanation implements. Mr. Peabody's eyes widened at the sight of them, as if they were instruments of torture rather than healing. Thomas, however, remained focused.

"Hot water, if you please," he directed, craning his head over to the kettle in the hearth, where a good fire flickered.

After cleaning the head wound, Thomas carefully shaved the area of the fowler's head around the entry point of the ball. And there it was: a fragment of lead embedded in the bone. Peabody watched, transfixed, as Thomas fixed the top of the trepan handle with his left hand and turned it cautiously with his right. Lowering his own chin onto the turning instrument to stabilize it, he reinforced the pressure on the crown and rotated the handle slowly in a workmanlike fashion.

Tension seeped through Thomas's pores and appeared as dots of perspiration on his brow. No one dared speak. No one dared move. For a few moments it seemed that even the horses' hooves that clattered on the cobbles outside were stilled. The only noise was the whirring of the instrument as it tunneled through the bone. Each rotation of the trepan handle took the metal tip a little closer to this man's brain. Slowly but surely, the skull gave way to the trepan's bore and a small disc of bone was extracted, bringing with it the embedded lead shot.

Thomas straightened his aching back and gave a self-satisfied nod. "'Tis done," he said quietly. "Now all we can do is wait and hope the swelling of the brain goes down."

Mercifully, the patient had remained completely motionless during the procedure. It would be several hours before Thomas could ascertain whether or not his gamble had paid off. "Call one of the women to sit with him," he said, wiping his bloodied hands on a towel.

For the first time in six hours, Thomas looked out of the inn's window, as the sky was lightened by the rising sun. It had been the longest night of his life, but he feared this new day just as keenly. Peabody had left the door ajar, and suddenly shouts from the taproom confirmed the doctor's worries.

Looking 'round the door, he could see a commotion in the hallway. Men and women were jostling with redcoats. Peabody returned with Molly and an anxious look on his face.

"They're arresting some of the wounded men," he said breathlessly.

"Takin' them to Oxford, they are!" blurted Molly, her face crumpled with concern.

Thomas strode out of the dining room to see a clutch of villagers being herded through the main doorway. Rushing back to the window, he watched as the men, some with their hands tied behind their backs, were bundled into waiting wagons. Those who were injured were not spared. He saw Joseph Makepeace, his torso swathed in a bandage, and Zeb Godson, his arm in a sling, being prodded and poked like cattle. It seemed that most of the male population of the village was being rounded up and sent off for trial to the Oxford assizes.

The thud of heavy footsteps was suddenly heard coming down the passage, and the door burst open. Two soldiers thundered in but stopped short when they saw Abel Smith lying on the table, the fluid still draining from his head. A look of disgust swept over their faces when they realized what they were seeing. One of them turned and retched. The other eyed Thomas.

"Sir, this man is under arrest. We are to take him to Oxford to await trial." His delivery was garbled and lacked conviction, and he turned his head away from the table so that he did not have to linger on the fluid draining from Smith's brain.

Had it not been made in earnest, the request would have been comical. Thomas snorted. "This man is going nowhere. If he is moved he will die." He pointed to Smith's head.

The soldier who had spoken gulped hard. "'Tis Captain Ponsonby's orders, sir," he replied, almost apologetically.

"Then I would speak with the captain," countered Thomas. "Tell him Dr. Silkstone would see him."

Moments later the young captain was standing in the dining room. Thomas could see that his eyes were being drawn involuntarily toward Smith's fractured skull, which was now being drained of fluid through a cannula.

"This man is close to death as it is, Captain Ponsonby. Any movement and you may as well tighten a noose around his neck," he told the officer in no uncertain terms.

Ponsonby nodded. "You make yourself plain, sir, but I will need to station a man to guard him, so that if he revives, he will stand trial."

Thomas nodded. He knew that even if Smith lived and was transported to Oxford Jail to await trial, he would probably contract a terrible fever and die before the hangman could get to him. He was doomed just like the rest of the dissenting villagers. Yet again, Sir Montagu appeared to have scored a victory over the people of Brandwick.

Chapter 49

Now, it just so happened that Oxford was making ready for St. Giles Fair, a highlight of the city's calendar. Scores of carts and caravans had planted themselves on the ground, and an encampment of striped tents and sideshows had been erected during the day. Fiddlers and jugglers meandered among wooden horses and whirligigs. Gaming tables appeared to entice the men, and fortune-tellers wooed the women. All around there was a gaiety and sense of anticipation that had not been seen since before the Great Fogg of the previous year. Into this feverishly excited atmosphere trundled the four wagons carrying forty-one villagers from Brandwick and its surrounds.

Thomas had decided to accompany the prisoners, riding behind them. He had maintained that at least four of them were too badly injured to stand trial, but he had lost the argument and Captain Ponsonsby, backed up of course by Nicholas Lupton, had won the day. They had been bundled into the carts on crutches or on makeshift stretchers and forced to brave the buffets and blows of the journey, regardless of whether they arrived at their destination alive or dead.

As he saw the throng ahead of him, Thomas sensed there would be trouble. He had seen Oxford crowds turn ugly before. The city was not known for its restraint, and despite the fact that it was still early in the day, strong liquor flowed like water among the revelers. Four horsemen of the Oxfordshire Militia had ridden ahead, announcing the arrival of a platoon with their prisoners. It had been their task to prepare the way, but instead of causing the crowd to stand to one side in respectful reverence for the law, the prisoners' arrival only seemed to fuel the event's incendiary mood.

Thomas knew their entry into the city would be risky and that the officers had underestimated the strength of support for the villagers. Interestingly, he could see no musketeers in the ranks. Could it be they wished to avoid further bloodshed? he wondered. Overnight, word had spread from Brandwick about the destruction of the common fences and the arrest of those who had dared defy the new laws. Rather than condemn them, the citizens of Oxford and visiting country folk decided to show their support. As the militia approached, the men in the wagons raised the cry "Brandwick forever," the crowd took it to their hearts, and a chant struck up.

"Brandwick forever! Brandwick forever!"

The cry could be heard on hundreds of lips. Thomas surveyed the mob. Fists were raised against the guards and lips curled. He dropped back from the main procession. He did not wish to be associated with the platoon of about twenty militiamen.

"Brandwick forever! Brandwick forever!"

From the mouths of men and women, youths and children, the cry welled up and rose into the air. Everywhere he looked, Thomas could see the people pressing 'round the wagons, slowing their progress. The drivers and mounted soldiers were whipping away those who gathered around them with their riding crops, but they were no match for the sheer numbers that surged forward.

By now the procession had drawn level with St. John's College. Thomas remained by the Eagle and Child inn, but had a good vantage point. Just a few more yards and the procession would arrive at Beaumont Street and the way toward the jail would be clearer. Then suddenly, someone in the crowd hurled a brickbat at one of the guards. Others followed suit, and sticks and stones rained down on the militia from every side. With each missile that hit its target, the crowd seemed bolder, and Thomas watched amazed as the guards were overpowered and the back boards of the carts were let down, allowing the prisoners to escape. They came streaming down from the wagons and melted into the melee. The crowd swallowed up the men and resumed the business of reveling and feasting, leaving the outnumbered militiamen to re-form and march away, their pride as tattered as their uniforms after the fray.

Over dinner at the Jolly Trooper that evening, Thomas related the whole extraordinary episode to Sir Theodisius.

"This is a terrible state of affairs," bemoaned the coroner, chomping through tough venison.

Thomas had to agree. "I can see no good outcome, sir," he replied. "The men will return to the village, but they will be rearrested for sure."

Sir Theodisius nodded. "Malthus will see to that. His authority has been challenged and he will not stand for it."

"And I fear, sir, there will be more trouble to come," said Thomas.

"Oh?"

"When I was last at Boughton Hall, Lupton showed me a map detailing new plans for the estate and beyond."

"Beyond Boughton? Speak plain, if you please!" Sir Theodisius's jowls wobbled with indignation.

Thomas took a deep breath. "There are plans to connect the canal at Banbury to Oxford, sir. There is a consortium of landowners, led by Sir Montagu, which is raising funds as we speak."

Sir Theodisius hit the table with the butt of his knife. "Of course," he drawled. "Why did I not see this?" His forehead was scoured with deep furrows. "I remember an Act of Parliament authorized the canal about fifteen years ago. The intention was to link the industrial lands around the Midlands to London via the River Thames. It reached Napton a few years back, but the money ran out. If I recall correctly, a second act allowed the company to raise more funds and the canal reached Banbury about six years ago."

"Sir Montagu's home turf," interrupted Thomas.

The coroner nodded. "I might've known he would want to put his finger in that particular pie," he said, unthinkingly dipping his own finger in a jug of gravy at his side. "But there were money problems again."

Thomas arched a brow and nodded. "Hence the need to raise more income from the land by enclosing it."

Sir Theodisius licked the gravy from his finger. "So Malthus is a man of business now, as well as a lawyer and a landowner."

"And an unscrupulous villain," added Thomas bitterly. He leaned closer to the coroner. "My first concern is not for Sir Montagu's plans, sir, but for the escaped men. They will surely face the gallows on their return to Brandwick."

Sir Theodisius nodded slowly. "Indeed they will," he agreed. "And they will need to be taken to Oxford again." As he spoke, Thomas could see that a kernel of an idea was taking root in the older man's brain. His eyes widened as the thought blossomed. "There was a great show of support for them today, you say?"

Thomas had to agree. "It seemed that most of the city was behind them. What do you have in mind?"

The coroner's eyes betrayed a sudden excitement. "I believe the court of public opinion might be convened to help us in our quest for justice," he told Thomas enigmatically. And with that, he emptied the jug of gravy onto the rest of his venison and resumed his meal.

Thomas returned to Brandwick early the next day. If all the arrested villagers had gone home, the injured ones would surely be in need of his care. His route took him 'round the edge of the common, and for the first time he could see the full extent of the havoc that the rebels had wrought. The neat rows of fencing that had crisscrossed the undulating grasslands had been uprooted. Staves and posts still lay where they had once stood, and some were even charred and blackened where fires had been set. What was most extraordinary, however, was that where the land had been cleared by Lupton's men, cattle had now returned to graze. A dozen or so chewed the cud peacefully, while turkeys and chickens pecked at the ground on the fringes. It was a sight that brought a smile to Thomas's lips. The people of Brandwick had spoken with one voice and, almost overnight, had restored their ancient rights.

As he rode into the village, he was surprised to see some of the men who only the day before had been shackled in the back of a wagon on their way to jail. Two of those he had seen corralled were walking up the High Street like free men. The question, he asked himself, was for how much longer? Riding into the yard at the Three Tuns, he soon learned from young Rogers that all of the escapees had returned to a hero's welcome late yesterday afternoon.

"It were a sight to gladden the heart," the stable lad told the doctor as he took his horse.

"I am sure it was," agreed Thomas, dismounting. "And the injured men?"

Rogers shrugged. "I don't know about them, sir."

Heading straight inside, Thomas sought out the landlord.

"Mr. Geech," he called as soon as he spotted him in the hallway.

"Ah, Dr. Silkstone! Welcome back, sir," he replied. "You'll be wanting some refreshment."

Drawing closer, Thomas managed a smile and waved a hand as the landlord thrust a tankard he was carrying in front of his face.

"I must first see to the injured," he replied.

Geech nodded. "They're all together, sir. 'Tis not our best room, but . . ." He tilted his head awkwardly.

"I will see that you are reimbursed any expenses," replied Thomas sharply.

Geech led him along the dark passageway to a room at the back of the inn that, judging by the number of crates and barrels, was usually used for storage.

"Here we are," said the landlord cheerfully. "All still alive."

Thomas arched a brow and Geech took his leave. Abel Smith and two others lay on the floor on thick straw. Although he would have preferred beds inside the inn for his patients, Thomas was satisfied that the conditions were as clean as could be expected and that the blankets provided were adequate. Mr. Peabody, who had kept vigil during his absence, looked up from Smith's side. Mistress Geech had doled out bowls of pease pottage for the men, and Maggie Cuthbert was coaxing some down Hal Thornley, who had suffered a stake through his abdomen, although it had missed his vital organs.

"How fares he?" asked Thomas, bending low by the youth's side.

The widow nodded. "He grows stronger," she said.

Thomas checked his wound. He had sutured it, and a yellow crust was beginning to form. "We must keep the dressing clean and dry," he told her.

Moving on to Abel Smith, he inspected the head wound. As far as he could see, the swelling of the brain had lessened considerably. The patient had even returned to consciousness for a brief period that morning, according to Mr. Peabody.

Thomas felt as satisfied as he could that the remaining men were all in a stable condition. He was just about to leave the room when the landlord's wife entered.

"Doin' all right, are they?" asked Mistress Geech, craning her neck to watch Thomas at work. "I don't like the sight of blood myself. Turns my guts up, it does. Still, there'll be some good news when the others have their meetin'."

Thomas looked up. "Meeting?"

Mistress Geech gave a nervous giggle. "You've not heard, Doctor? Adam Diggott has called a commoners' meetin' this evenin' in this very inn." She smiled broadly at the thought of even more customers.

Thomas considered the news. Adam Diggott was making a bold move, flaunting the mass escape in Sir Montagu's face. He had to be confident of support to call such a public meeting.

"We'll be rushed off our feet again, I can tell you."

"I am sure you will," he replied. His only fear was that the militia might call in as well.

Chapter 50

Sir Montagu Malthus stood brooding by the study window, his black-garbed frame silhouetted by the pale evening light. He was awaiting Captain Ponsonby. Close by sat James Charlton. The chainman's shoulders were hunched, and he kept twisting his kerchief between his fingers like a nervous schoolboy awaiting a caning. His right eye remained bandaged, and now and again he would press it as if to ease the pain it was causing him. His left wrist was also tightly bound. Dr. Fairweather had tended to him after his attempt to take his own life.

Now Howard made the announcement and the captain entered the room with the trepidation of a soldier who fears he is about to be tried in a military court. Malthus remained looking out of the window in a show of studied indifference. Charlton did not rise. With his sound eye he regarded the soldier only briefly before his head fell into his hands.

"Sir Montagu," said the captain, saluting the lawyer in the hope that he would turn to acknowledge his presence. Seeing, after a moment or two, that his gesture had carried no sway, he let his arm fall limply to his side.

Another awkward moment passed; then the lawyer finally turned to face the officer. Fixing him with a piercing gaze, he dispensed with the usual courtesies and came straight to the point.

"You have let me down, Captain Ponsonby," he said flatly.

"Sir, I—" the young officer began nervously.

Sir Montagu's hand swatted away any anticipated excuses as if they were irksome gnats. "Do not try and defend your men, or yourself. What happened in Oxford yesterday has made your troops a laughingstock."

"I apologize on behalf—"

The lawyer repeated the earlier gesture. "Save your excuses for your commanding officer, Captain Ponsonby," he said laconically, adding viciously, "and your father." He walked over to his desk and seated himself. "My good friend the general will be most disappointed when he finds out about your shoddy handling of the situation." He fixed the young soldier with a glare that made him squirm like a fish on a hook, then inclined his head. "I will give you one last chance to redeem yourself and your men," he said.

"Sir?" The young officer shifted where he stood.

Picking up a piece of parchment that lay on the desk, Sir Montagu handed it to the captain.

"The wanted men will all be attending a meeting tonight at the Three Tuns. Here is the reissued warrant for their arrests, and an additional one."

Taking both warrants, the officer scanned the second document and looked up, puzzled. "But this is a warrant for murder, sir."

Sir Montagu gave a shallow nod. "I am fully aware of that, Ponsonby. New evidence has come to light." He turned his head toward Charlton. The soldier's eyes followed his and settled on the young surveyor, whose head remained bowed. "Adam Diggott will be at tonight's meeting, and you are to charge him there." His large hands suddenly opened a desk drawer. "And make sure this is found about his person," he said, his lips twitching in a smile.

The young officer's eyes bulged from their sockets as he regarded a compass as it lay flat on the lawyer's palm. He turned it over to inspect it. The initials "J. T." were engraved on the back.

"Make sure you do not fail me this time, Captain," Malthus said. "After all, you have your family's reputation to uphold."

The threat was as barbed as a spear. The young man's back went ramrod straight. "You can be assured I will not fail you, sir," he barked in reply.

In the distance the thunder rolled and rumbled. A storm was approaching and the air was thick and heavy. At the appointed hour, the villagers began to assemble in the stuffy lower room at the Three Tuns. The smell of unwashed bodies pressed together mixed with stale smoke and spilled beer.

From his upstairs vantage point, Thomas watched the villagers arrive in their droves. In the sultry atmosphere the stench wafted up and in through the window. It was soon evident that there was not enough room for everyone, so the doors were opened and people began to spill out into the courtyard, pressing against one another and jostling for space. Yet the mood was good-humored. A great victory had been scored, albeit a temporary one. It seemed the commoners' voices had been heard and the good denizens of Oxford had been swayed by their cause, for the moment at least. The power was in the people's hands, but they knew it could escape from them as easily as grains of corn between their fingers.

Moving to a reception room at the back of the inn that overlooked the courtyard, Thomas leaned out of the window to view the proceedings. Adam Diggott was the first to address the crowd. Clambering up onto an upturned barrel, his head still swathed in a bandage, he seemed to have grown even more in stature, as if his recent encounters with authority had only strengthened his resolve.

"Fellow commoners," he began. "I speak to you now as a free man!" A great cheer rose from those assembled. "But I know I will not be for much longer." He lowered his voice accordingly, and people shook their heads and cried, "Shame!"

Diggott continued: "Some of those who fought with me the other night have gone. Josh Thornley, Josh Price, and Martha Winslett, all good people. They must not have died in vain. Their blood nourishes our land." More voices were raised in support. "That is why I am asking you to spare what money you can to pay to defend our rights through the courts."

Such a notion was news to Thomas and, judging by the reaction, to the rest of the crowd as well.

"You saying we need to pay some fancy lawyers?" asked Joseph Makepeace.

Adam Diggott nodded. "I say we need a charter with our rights set down to restore Brandwick Common to its ancient state; how it was after the lady rode 'round the common with her burning brand and gave the land to our ancestors."

"And then we'll be left alone?" A woman's voice rose above the rest.

"Aye. That be the plan. Remember, we have the law on our side," replied Diggott. "Our forefathers had tended this earth for generations until him at Boughton took over." He scowled at the very thought of Sir Montagu. "But this way our rights'll be set down for all to see and we'll no longer be living under this shadow that threatens us all."

Thomas scanned the faces below. They seemed thoughtful but not entirely convinced.

"And where will we find such a lawyer?" asked Will Ketch from the crowd.

"That be a good question," replied Diggott, but before he could answer it, a shout suddenly went up.

"Militia!" cried a voice through the archway, and the news was answered with panic. The crowd divided: Some took refuge inside the inn; others scampered out of a side gate. But Adam Diggott remained standing on his barrel as the troops approached four abreast through the archway, Ponsonby at their head.

"Adam Diggott, I arrest you in the name of King George."

Thomas looked on. He knew it would be futile to challenge the officer. The coppicer seemed resigned. He even held out his hands for the shackles as the soldiers came for him.

Only a few of the villagers stayed to watch. Many had fled, for fear of being apprehended themselves. Of the handful that remained, however, one man, who was not familiar to Thomas, dared to question the troops' actions.

"On what charge do you take him?" he cried.

Ponsonby looked distinctly uneasy, anxious that the remaining stragglers might turn on his men. "For the murder of Jeffrey Turgoose," he announced.

Hearing the charge, Thomas shot up. "Captain!" he shouted through the window, but Ponsonby made no reply.

Although he had expected the charge, it was clear Diggott would not go quietly. Instead he started to struggle. "I ain't murdered no one!" he yelled.

"You can tell that to the judge," snapped Ponsonby. "Search him!" he ordered.

One of the militiamen clamped his hands up and down Diggott's torso, then delved into his coat pocket.

"Here, sir!" he cried triumphantly, brandishing a brass compass.

Diggott's jaw dropped open. "What? No!" He stared wide-eyed at the compass. "I ain't never seen it before. I never!" His protests, however, carried little weight with the soldiers who advanced on him. Just as they were about to loop their arms through his to lead him away, however, he lunged at the nearest redcoat, sending him off balance. He raced toward the street, outrunning the handful of soldiers who pursued him. Ponsonby ordered his men to fire, but they were slow to load and by the time the first volley of shots rang out, Adam Diggott's figure was but a blur amid the shadows of the houses.

"After him!" the captain ordered, as a dozen soldiers fanned out across the slope at the village's edge. Their quarry had disappeared into Raven's Wood, but they would track him down.

Adam Diggott may have been the most wanted villager, but he was by no means the only one. Other men were being rounded up, too. Thomas rushed back to his room and looked out over the High Street. Soldiers were going from house to house, rooting out the rebels who had escaped their clutches once before.

Running downstairs, he called after the officer as he rode out of the courtyard. "Captain! Captain Ponsonby," he shouted. The young officer turned at the sound of his name and looked down to see Thomas tugging at his bridle.

"You are making a grave mistake, Captain."

Ponsonby struggled to control his horse in all the chaos. It shuffled and nodded in protest. "I have my orders," he replied above the melee, adding firmly: "And I have evidence. You can have your say in court, Dr. Silkstone." And with that he gave the call to his men to move out the wagon. Adam Diggott might be temporarily at large, but at least this time there would be no escape for his fellow dissenters.

A large crowd of mainly women and children was gathering around the waiting wagons as more and more men were bundled into them. Thomas strained to watch above the chaos. Bodies now pressed against him as mothers and wives frantically tried to reach their sons and husbands. In among all the chaos, however, Thomas recognized one man. Wearing a black frock coat, he was tall and lanky, with flame-red hair, and he wore a patch over his right eye. It was James Charlton. He was in conversation with Molly from the Three Tuns. Thomas knew that now was his chance. Here was the man who certainly held the key to Jeffrey Turgoose's death and would surely testify as to Adam Diggott's innocence. He badly needed to speak with him alone, away from Malthus and Lupton.

"Mr. Charlton! Mr. Charlton!" he called, trying to make himself heard above the cacophony of sobs and wails.

Charlton heard his name shouted. His head shot 'round, and for a split second, Thomas thought he might oblige, but then he wavered. He clearly thought better of it and started off in the direction of Raven's Wood. The first of the wagons jerked forward as it moved off, blocking Thomas's path, and in another second James Charlton had disappeared altogether from view.

Chapter 51

From the refuge of his upper room at the Three Tuns that evening, Thomas watched the rain drive hard along the High Street. Rivulets had begun to form, coursing down from the woods and depositing stones and broken twigs on the roadway. For a while, hailstones as large as balls of shot hammered down on the roof, and the gusting wind sent an empty barrel rolling across the street. The thunder Thomas had heard rumble an hour or so before now vented its full rage over Brandwick, rattling windows and setting dogs barking. Every few seconds, sheet lightning would illuminate the sky, making it as bright as day.

The storm raged on into the hours of darkness, preventing Thomas from sleeping. Not that he would have been capable of rest even if it had been a calm summer's evening. "Lydia is alive. Lydia is alive." He kept repeating the phrase as he lay on his bed to remind himself that he should be the happiest man on earth. He had been functioning as if on opiates smoked by Chinese men. His brain had been in a dark place until that thought had flooded it with light. And yet he still carried with him a terrible burden, as if a millstone were 'round his neck. Yes, his beloved was alive, but where was she and, more important, in what state? The memory of her held captive in Bedlam flashed before him once more; her shaved head, her gaunt features, her eyes, reproachful. She blamed him for her misfortune. Sir Montagu had managed to turn her mind against him. Had it not been for his own persistence, perhaps she would never have allowed herself to accept his proposal of marriage. As a foreigner and an American, moreover, he had had no right to venture into the hallowed echelons of the English aristocracy. In a society that valued birth over merit and wealth over intellect, he should have known he was trespassing on alien territory.

During the small hours, the wind seemed to abate and the thunder was reduced to a distant rumble. The withdrawal of the storm meant that its clamor was replaced by the steady dripping of water as it trickled through the ill-fitting window frame and fell onto the floor below. The unremitting flow was every bit as distracting as the roar of the wind and the clapping of the thunder. Sighing deeply, Thomas rose and placed a ewer underneath the window to catch the water. Such practicalities seemed to pull him back into the moment. He had battles to fight on two fronts. At first light he would ride to Oxford and visit the Brandwick men who once more found themselves behind bars.

Bart Bailey, the fuller, was a solid, practical man and as reliable as the cuckoo's call in April, yet even he found it difficult to rise the following morning after a broken night's rest. Along with most of the other residents of Brandwick, he had been kept awake by the buffeting wind and driving rain, not to mention the rolls of thunder. That was why the villagers were not in the least fazed when the stocks at the fulling mill had not begun pounding when the bell of St. Swithin's tolled six. Yet it was not Bailey's tardiness that was the reason for the silence of the valley. The heavy rain meant that he had opened the sluice gates during the night, and not even a mere three hours' sleep could keep him from starting up the stocks. On this particular morning he had risen as soon as the day dawned and walked the few yards from his cottage to the millhouse. He did so eagerly. The storm had been so fierce that he knew the surge of water from upstream would be great. The river would be in full flood, no doubt, and the mill wheel would be turning at a fierce speed. The heavy overnight rain that had drenched the valley meant the water flow should have been particularly good that morning. He would open the sluice gates fully to allow the river to thunder through and power the paddles. But once inside the millhouse he saw that for some reason the flow was down to little more than a trickle.

"Jack," he told his boy, "go walk upstream to see if there's a tree down."

"Aye, sir," replied the gangling youngster, and he bounded off, up the course of the river, to investigate. It would not be the first time an oak or a beech had come crashing down into the river and swept downstream. In the meantime, Bailey checked the frame and the shanks of the stocks to make sure that the fault was not mechanical. He suspected the rack and pinion might have been damaged. On inspection, however, he could see they were not.

By this time the workers, mainly women, were arriving for their daily shifts. They filed into the millhouse expecting to see the stocks pounding away at the cloth, but the great wooden boots were motionless.

Bart Bailey, standing on a low wall, addressed them. "There's trouble with the waterwheel," he told them. "Young Jack has gone to look upstream. He'll be back soon, but we may need some sturdy hands to move a trunk or suchlike."

The fullers nodded. They'd seen debris clog up the wheel workings before. Two men stepped forward for the job should they be needed to clear the water channel.

Seconds later, Jack, red-faced and out of breath, delivered his verdict to his master. "River's clear, sir, save for a few branches, and there's nowt to stop the flow."

The head fuller grimaced. "Very well. We'd best look at the sluices. You two come with me." He beckoned to the two men, who followed him out onto the footbridge to check the shutters. The river was rushing at full pelt toward the wheel, but something was damming its flow so that the water was building up behind it, threatening to burst over the banks and flood the racking close. Bailey's son, Charles, volunteered to see what, if anything, was jamming up against the gate. He was young and fit and as strong as an ox, but as he tied a rope around his waist, his father felt even more apprehensive.

"Take good care, now," said the fuller, watching his son wade into the turbulent river. The two men kept a firm hold of the rope, slacking it off only a little to allow Charles to ease himself closer to the sluice. In his hand the youth held a long staff, using it to prod under the water.

"I feel it," he shouted after only a moment. His voice was drowned out by the sound of the gathering waters behind him, but the fuller could see by his son's reaction that he had found the obstruction. He continued to watch as Charles prodded further with his stick, then looked up once more at his father. This time the bravado and the determination had been replaced by another expression: one of terror. He began wading back toward the bridge as fast as he could.

"What is it? What have you seen?" questioned Bailey.

Wet through and barely able to catch his breath, the young man bent double for a moment, before straightening himself. Fixing his father in the eye, he pulled his features into a grimace. "There's a blockage down there right enough," he cried above the water's roar. " 'Tis the body of a man."

Thomas had packed his belongings and was making ready to leave the Three Tuns for his homeward journey when he heard a shout go up in the High Street. Soon there were more calls. Although he could not make out what was being said, there was an urgency in their tone that spoke of something serious. He rushed to his window to see a crowd gathering around a young man. He recognized him as the fuller's son from the mill. He was trying to reach the door of the inn. It was then, as he approached a little nearer, that Thomas could hear what he was saying.

"Dr. Silkstone. I am to fetch Dr. Silkstone!" he cried out above the furor that engulfed him.

Making haste down the stairs and out into the street, his bag in his hand, Thomas presented himself.

"What is it, Charles? What's happened?"

Breathless and distracted, the young man suddenly seemed relieved to have found the doctor. "Oh, sir," he cried. "My father says you're to come straightaway. There's a body, sir. Stuck in the sluice, it is."

The crowd suddenly parted, allowing Thomas to follow the youth up the High Street, past the racking close, and into the mill. Several women were clustered at the entrance; one was in tears. When they saw the doctor approach, they drew to one side to allow him access.

Inside Thomas saw the fuller and another, much younger man with wet hair and clothes, crouched over something on the flagstone floor.

"I believe I am needed, Mr. Bailey," called Thomas as he approached.

The fuller wheeled 'round. "Thank the Lord you are here, sir," he blurted, taking Thomas by the arm and guiding him closer. "You'll need a strong stomach."

What Thomas saw, lying on the cold flags, was indeed a most unsettling sight. He had witnessed many a man mangled under cartwheels or crushed by a millstone, but this was a particularly vicious incident, where the paddles of the mill wheel had repeatedly struck the young man's torso and the back of his head. Half the body remained only as a fleshy, bloodied pulp. The face, too, was grazed and bruised, and an open eye bulged reproachfully at any onlooker. Thomas took a deep breath but regretted it immediately. His lungs were now filled with a noxious reek that made his stomach lurch for a moment. He had been caught off guard, and as he knelt down to inspect the corpse he breathed through his mouth. As soon as he did, he felt a terrible charge surge through his entire body. It was the tattered black frock coat that confirmed to Thomas that he was dealing with no ordinary mill accident.

"What happened?" he asked, his eyes playing on the flayed face of the victim.

"We found him stuck in the undershot of the wheel, sir," explained Bailey. "It seems he'd been washed downstream in last night's storm."

Thomas nodded and swallowed hard. "I believe I know him," he said finally.

Bailey slid his men a sideways glance and leaned closer to Thomas. "It looks like the young chainman, sir."

The doctor rose to his feet. For a moment he felt light-headed for want of fresh air, but he forced himself to give orders. "You have a room? Somewhere I can examine the body, Mr. Bailey?"

The fuller, who had deliberately turned his back on the corpse so that he did not have to look upon it, nodded and directed his horrified men to move the body, which they reluctantly did.

"To the storeroom, lads," he said, a look of apology etched on his face.

"You'll need to notify the Oxford coroner, Sir Theodisius Pettigrew, too. Get word to him as soon as you can and tell him I am examining the corpse," Thomas instructed, as he followed the men and their stinking and bloodied cargo into a storeroom at the far end of the millhouse.

On one side of the wall were stacked bales of woolen cloth that were awaiting scouring. There were barrels of urine, too, collected daily from the villagers by the piss cart, that gave off the sharp tang of ammonia. The stinks combined to produce an overpowering reek, while the resultant vapors brought tears to Thomas's eyes, but it was still infinitely preferable to the stench that rose from poor Mr. Charlton.

On the other side of the room lay a long plank supported at either end by trestles. It was here that the men deposited the corpse with indecent, yet understandable, haste, then retreated to the door. Thomas dismissed them with a nod before beginning the task in hand.

A shaft of bright morning sunlight pierced through the narrow window and shone directly onto the body, making inspection slightly easier, although no less traumatic. Here lay the tall, thin, young man, so neat and formal, a model assistant surveyor, no doubt, yet so timid and reticent. His experience in the woods had taken a terrible toll on his mental faculties, as was patently clear by his performance in court. What had become of poor Mr. Charlton that he had ended up in such a vile state? His corpse bore the marks of countless glancing blows and buffets as it made its way downriver over the rocky bed, only to be pinioned by the waterwheel and crushed. Had someone wanted him dead? If so, why? These were pressing matters, the anatomist told himself, that would need to be addressed later. For the moment, the cause of death must be his focus.

It was immediately clear to Thomas that some of Charlton's injuries had been sustained at the millhouse as his body was struck by the paddles of the waterwheel before it had finally stopped turning. Yet how had he been washed downstream in the first place? Moreover, had he been alive when he entered the water? Was James Charlton's death an unfortunate accident, a tumble in the woods, perhaps, or had he fallen prey to the same villains who had killed Mr. Turgoose? Could it be that the Raven and his gang had added a third murder to their tally? Those were the questions that Sir Theodisius would put to Thomas as soon as he heard of the corpse's discovery, and it was to these pressing issues that the anatomist now turned his undivided attention.

Looking at the corpse, Thomas let out a faint sigh. In life Mr. Charlton had struck him as quite tall, yet now his remains seemed so very slight and fragile as they lay on the table. The smart black coat was left a bundle of shredded rags. The breeches, too, were all tattered and torn, and the stockings muddied and bloodied. He would strip the body of its clothes to give himself the entire picture before going any further.

Before he did so, however, there was an obvious clue to the manner of the surveyor's death, one that Thomas noted immediately. From his mouth there exuded a fine white foam. It was a sign that Mr. Charlton had been alive when he hit the water.

He began divesting the corpse. A few seconds into his task, however, he heard the mill wheel crank into action and the pent-up water start to gush and roar once more. A little later and the fulling stocks began to pound, slowly at first, then gathering pace. Thomas found the sound almost unbearable. He had previously conducted postmortems in the most undesirable circumstances, but he felt this noise all but intolerable. He would request that Mr. Charlton's corpse be removed to the Three Tuns for further examination. He was about to give orders to that effect when the sound of men's voices outside rose above the roar of the water.

"Sir, I beg you. No!" Mr. Bailey was pleading with someone.

Seconds later Nicholas Lupton came barging through the door and stormed toward Thomas.

"You have Charlton?" he barked, before pulling himself up suddenly within a few feet of the cadaver, driven back by the stench.

Thomas, momentarily caught off guard by the intrusion, composed himself. "I believe so, although no formal identification has been made," he replied, his voice raised over the rhythmic thud of the stocks.

Lupton, struggling for breath in the foul-aired room, reached for a kerchief from his pocket and clamped it over his mouth. "I feared this would happen," he cried. "Now all hell will break loose. He'll hang for this and not before time!" Incandescent with rage, he strode back toward the storeroom door.

Perplexed, Thomas called out to him. "Who, Lupton? Who will hang?" he asked.

The steward turned. "Diggott, of course. Who else could have killed Charlton?"

The anatomist frowned. "Adam Diggott? But I thought he escaped." Thomas recalled yesterday's commotion and seeing the coppicer fleeing into the forest.

The steward clenched his jaw. "My men found him cowering in Raven's Wood in the early hours," he replied. "He's as guilty as sin." His voice was tinged with a victor's disdain.

Thomas felt suddenly roiled. He did not believe for a moment Adam Diggott could be capable of murder, and yet, admittedly, he was the most obvious suspect, and his capture fitted Lupton's plans so perfectly. Too perfectly.

Just as the steward began to make his way out once more, Thomas called to him.

"One more thing, Lupton."

"Yes?"

"When did you last see Mr. Charlton?"

Lupton frowned. "After I returned from Oxford. Midafternoon, I suppose."

"And what sort of state was he in?"

"The man was a wreck, as usual," came the barked reply.

"Thank you," said Thomas. Such information might not have been specific, but it might prove helpful in pinpointing the time frame of death. It might also prove invaluable in solving this particularly unsavory death.

Chapter 52

Word had been sent ahead to prepare a room at the Three Tuns to receive Charlton's body. Geech had offered the game larder, a cold room with a flagstone floor that could easily be sluiced. The lack of a good source of daylight was a concern to Thomas, but a plentiful supply of tallow candles had compensated. By now Walter Harker had been informed of the death, and he joined Thomas for the postmortem examination. In his capacity as village constable, he had seen some grisly sights over the years, but still, he was shocked at the severity of Charlton's injuries.

The back of the young man's skull had been smashed to a pulp by the mill wheel, and his left leg, what remained of it, was mangled and broken. Normally in such cases, Thomas would look for signs of a struggle: bruising to the face or skin under the fingernails. As he examined the arms, however, the doctor's attention was immediately drawn to the left wrist. Taking his magnifying glass, he peered at a deep laceration. It was recent, but not so recent. The wound had been sutured and was possibly no more than a week old. Yet while the outward appearance of the corpse was most shocking, Thomas knew it was its inner workings that held the key to the chainman's death. That was why he wasted little time in incising the chest cavity. He retrieved a small saw from his medical case. Beginning at the clavicle, he made a Y-shaped incision and opened the rib cage so that he could examine the lungs. They appeared heavy and overinflated, a sure sign of death by drowning. Slicing through the trachea, he found what he suspected: more of the fine foam he had seen oozing from the young man's mouth.

"It seems that Mr. Charlton was alive when he hit the water," he told Harker, who was peering over his shoulder.

As Thomas pried further into the lungs, there was more evidence to back up this theory. A quantity of silt and some splinters of twigs were also present. The river was a raging torrent after last night's storm, full of mud and debris. If Charlton had been in the woods during that storm, he may have stumbled and lost his footing, sending him plunging into the water.

Thomas knew three options now presented themselves: firstly that the chainman had slipped and fallen into the water, in which case his death was an accident; secondly that he had jumped into the water with the intention of killing himself; or thirdly that he had been pushed into the water, in other words, that he had been murdered, whether by Adam Diggott, or by a person or persons as yet unknown. Yet there was one more avenue Thomas wished to explore.

"The candle, if you please, Constable," he said, directing Harker to position the taper so that its light was directed toward Charlton's left ear, the one least damaged. Bending low, his magnifying glass in hand, Thomas inspected the auditory canal. It was bloody. He motioned to Harker to raise the candle over the nose. The nasal cavities were filled with blood, too.

He stared once more at the dead man's face and tried to remember it in life. He recalled seeing Charlton less than twenty-four hours before, at the inn, as he witnessed Adam Diggott being arrested. The thundery air had been still and close, and his freckled face had been moist with sweat. He had mopped his brow with a kerchief. It was then that Thomas remembered the patch that had covered his right eye. There was no trace of it. The force of the water must have swept it away.

"More light, if you please, Mr. Harker," he called.

The constable held the taper just above Charlton's head so that the light fell directly onto his forehead.

"Interesting," muttered Thomas, scrutinizing the area. The tissue surrounding the socket was bruised, yet it was clear to the doctor that the injury was not postmortem. He lifted the lid. The white of the eye was bright red, and there was yellow discharge exuding from the tear duct.

"I need to remove the eyeball," Thomas announced. "Will you hold the candle steady for me, Mr. Harker?"

The constable nodded. He seemed unfazed by the request.

Selecting forceps, Thomas eased the gelatinous ball out of its socket and snipped the stalk of the optic nerve before dropping the eye into a dish. It was as he suspected. A small piece of metal had pierced the cornea. Using tweezers, he teased out the offending shard, no wider than a fingernail. Nevertheless, it was big enough to cause serious damage.

Thomas held the foreign body up to Harker's candle. "Mr. Charlton had been blinded," he said.

The constable frowned. "By the attackers in the woods, sir?"

It was a reasonable supposition, but Thomas could not be so sure. He peered at the shard again with his magnifying lens, then handed it to Harker.

"What do you make of that?" he asked the constable.

Taking the glass, Harker deliberated for a moment before giving his verdict. "'Tis a flake of flint, or steel, Dr. Silkstone," he concluded.

Thomas nodded.

"Precisely," he agreed before returning once more to the eyeball, which sat forlornly in the dish. The eye, he knew, purported to be the window into a man's soul, but this specimen, thought Thomas, went even further. It was a window onto Charlton's recent past, for embedded within its gelatinous layers it contained not only what appeared to be a particle of steel, but a fiber of felt, too.

"And this, Mr. Harker, if I'm not much mistaken, is wadding."

The constable shook his head. "What are you saying, Dr. Silkstone?"

Suddenly Thomas realized that he had said too much already. He had been thinking out loud, something that was not judicious in the circumstances.

"An anatomist's indulgence." He shrugged. "I fear I digress," he said, returning to Charlton's corpse.

Next he examined to the dead man's left wrist, which had been bandaged. Thomas recalled that in court the chainman had claimed he had been attacked. He wondered if the injury had been sustained when he resisted giving the brigands his pocket watch, although he had not noticed the dressing at the time. But no, the scarring was too precise, too deliberate. There was no doubt in Thomas's mind; the wrist had been deliberately slit to sever the radial artery.

Suddenly it all made sense. The young man's agitated mental state, the lungs full of water and debris, the blood coming from the inner auditory canal and nose, indicating hemorrhaging, and finally the cut artery. All these were indications that while in an unstable mental condition, James Charlton deliberately took his own life by jumping from a height into the river. He could even envisage the place above the gorge in Raven's Wood that was most likely his launching ground.

Thomas thanked Harker and dismissed him. He needed time alone to think. Charlton's body had spoken to him, although what it had told him was of such a momentous nature that he wanted to be entirely sure of the facts before he confided in anyone. It seemed that in death this corpse had revealed what the chainman himself refused to acknowledge in life. Corroboration of this theory would, of course, be needed, but he knew it would be possible to obtain.

Chapter 53

Once again Thomas rode up Boughton's drive. He was anxious to inform Lupton of Charlton's autopsy findings as soon as possible. Howard came out to greet him on the steps as Will Lovelock appeared to see to his horse. The doctor dismounted and acknowledged the apologetic bow from Howard.

"Mr. Lupton has instructed me to tell you he has no wish to receive your report, Dr. Silkstone," the butler told him with a look of embarrassment.

It was just as Thomas had feared. The steward wished to deprive him of the chance to face his adversaries once more. He took a deep breath and shook his head.

"Then he is in luck," replied Thomas.

"Sir?" replied a puzzled Howard.

"I have not committed my findings to paper yet, so I am able to deliver them to your master verbally," he said.

The butler opened his mouth in a halfhearted attempt to protest, but Thomas barged past him and headed straight for the study door. Bursting in, he found Lupton seated at the desk. Looking up, the steward smiled wryly, as if he had anticipated the intrusion. He leaned back in his chair.

"Silkstone." His eyes latched on to Thomas. "You really are too trying. If you come with one of your reports, I am not interested. Adam Diggott is in my custody."

Thomas glowered at the man, so at ease in Lydia's seat, like a cuckoo in another's nest. "How can you be so sure that the coppicer is your man?"

Lupton let out a laugh. "Come. Come," he chided. "Any fool can see he has the motive. Charlton witnessed Diggott shoot Turgoose."

Thomas shrugged. "I'll admit it is very convenient, but 'tis not what happened."

Suddenly the smile was wiped from the steward's face. "Oh?"

The anatomist nodded. "I believe I know how Mr. Charlton died."

Lupton snorted through flared nostrils. "So do I! By Diggott's hand."

"Not so," countered Thomas.

The steward narrowed his eyes. "Do you expect a jury to believe your science over the hard evidence?"

Thomas was quick to correct him. "Evidence that is circumstantial. The fact that both men were in the woods last night proves nothing."

Without standing on the usual courtesies, the doctor made his way to the window and looked out over the lawns.

Lupton watched him with a frown. "Well, man?"

Thomas remained facing the window. "Yes, I do know how he died, but, more importantly, I believe I know why."

He heard the scrape of Lupton's chair on the polished wooden floor as he rose and walked toward him. Thomas wheeled 'round.

"You must think me most foolish," he challenged.

Again there was a wry smile from Lupton, only this time it was followed by a mocking laugh. "I'm sure I don't know what you mean, Silkstone," he replied, standing by the mantelpiece.

"You see, in life Charlton may have been able to keep his secret, but in death, it has been divulged."

Thomas's words caused the steward to furrow his brow.

"I do not follow you."

The doctor fixed Lupton in the eye. "There was no ambush in the woods, was there? No attack by highwaymen."

The steward held his nerve and adopted a look of puzzlement. "What are you talking about, man? Of course there was. Adam Diggott and his gang killed Turgoose and now he has killed Charlton, too."

"And that would suit your purpose, would it not?" inquired Thomas, but he did not wait for an answer. Instead he called Lupton's bluff.

"I now know what you and Sir Montagu have known all along."

The steward swallowed hard and leaned an elbow on the mantelshelf, assuming an air of self-confidence. "And that is?"

"It was James Charlton who fired the pistol. He killed his master."

"Hah!" Lupton's response was a cross between a snort and a laugh. For a moment he remained silently smirking, until his composure cracked. He stood upright and tugged at his waistcoat. "You cannot prove it," he snapped.

Thomas was happy to volunteer the proof. On a nearby table, he opened his medical case and retrieved a glass phial containing his evidence.

"I removed fragments of metal and linen from Charlton's eye. They only need to match the remnants I found in Turgoose's wounds." He felt quietly triumphant, but there was little joy in his victory. "That was why Charlton killed himself, was it not? He shot his master, but a public confession would not suit your purpose. You needed to pin the blame on the villagers so the law would deal with them, teach them a lesson. Boughton will not tolerate any opposition to enclosure. That was why you kept the chainman here, a virtual prisoner. You did not want him to tell the truth, to take the blame, so you concocted a story about footpads stealing his pocket watch and planted it, together with the pistol, in the Diggotts' cottage."

"Such fantasy!" snorted Lupton.

Thomas persisted. "Charlton couldn't live with the guilt, could he? He'd tried to slit his wrists after Abe Diggott's trial. But it was the massacre of the villagers that was the final straw. He felt responsible for the deaths of three innocent people and so he threw himself into the river." He replaced the phial in his case and turned again to face the steward. "What I don't understand is why he murdered Turgoose."

"And you never shall," muttered Lupton, his attention drawn by sudden movement outside the window.

Thomas frowned. "What did you just say?"

Lupton rose, went to the door, and opened it. "I said you never shall understand," he repeated, the familiar disdain tempering his voice.

As he held open the door, a messenger entered. "You have the charge?" asked the steward.

The courier gave a shallow bow and held up a piece of parchment. "I do, sir," he replied.

Lupton allowed himself a moment of self-congratulation. "Excellent. Then we can proceed. See that it is delivered to the governor of Oxford Jail, along with the prisoner."

The messenger bowed and within a second was gone.

Thomas shook his head in disbelief. "Have you not heard a word of what I have been saying? There was no murder. The coppicer is innocent." There was a note of exasperation in his tone. "Charlton killed himself."

Lupton shook his head and clicked his tongue. "I doubt the judge will agree when he sees Adam Diggott stand before him and hears how he tried to evade arrest."

Thomas's eyes widened. "So, he is to be charged with Charlton's murder as well as Turgoose's."

"There is a pleasing symmetry to it, is there not?" said the steward, walking over to the fireplace.

"But you know he is innocent," Thomas protested. "Not only can I prove that Charlton killed himself; I can prove he killed Turgoose, too, and you know it!"

Yet Lupton refused to be drawn in. He threw Thomas a scornful look. "Save your theories for the courtroom, Silkstone. Adam Diggott and his co-conspirators are as good as dead already," he said, reaching for the bell cord. Howard appeared almost instantaneously. "Show Dr. Silkstone out, will you?"

For an instant Thomas considered refusing to leave until he had been heard, but he was forced to silently acknowledge any defiance would be futile. Instead, he simply nodded. He would have to rely on his scientific findings to reveal the truth. "I shall see you in court in Oxford, Lupton," he said.

Chapter 54

News of the gruesome discovery at the fulling mill had spread quickly. It was soon added by village gossips to the canon that included the trial of so many Brandwick men and Adam Diggott's murder charge.

"Working hard again tonight, Dr. Silkstone?" Mistress Geech inquired with a glint in her eye.

Thomas had just agreed with the landlady to pay extra for the privilege of a spermaceti candle instead of the usual tallow. Yet her flirtatiousness did nothing to lighten the prospect of the coming hours spent writing James Charlton's postmortem report. The standard inn candles, which smoked and guttered, were an added irritation that he could well do without.

"I fear so," he replied. He thought she held on to the shaft of the wax candle as she handed it to him over the counter a little longer than was strictly necessary.

"Would you like your meal in your room?" she asked, cocking her head. "Cook's made a lovely mutton stew."

"I would like that very much," Thomas replied with a smile. He knew she meant well.

He found his room quite stuffy. The warmer weather left the upper-story rooms often much warmer than downstairs, and he immediately flung open the windows to take in a good lungful of air. Holding his arms out wide, he stretched and breathed deeply. It had been a day of tragedy and of revelation, but it was not yet over. His inkstand remained on his desk, and he was just summoning up the energy to embark upon his postmortem report when he heard a tap at the door.

Opening it wide, he saw Molly, holding a tray of victuals. He smiled at her and bade her enter, although he noticed she seemed even more reticent than usual. She did not return his greeting, and her eyes planted themselves on the floor. She walked purposefully toward Thomas's table and set down her cargo carefully and deliberately, lingering longer over the laying of the cutlery than was usual or necessary.

Noting her behavior, Thomas attracted her eye. Lowering his face to hers, he asked, "Is something troubling you, Molly?"

He saw the girl's small bosom heave as she took a deep breath and turned her gaze on him.

"There *is* something, Doctor," she acknowledged. "I think 'tis you I must tell."

"Tell me what?"

Her eyes now met Thomas's, and she delved into her apron pocket to produce what looked like a sealed letter.

"I think you best have this, sir," she said, handing it over.

Thomas reached for the knife on the nearby table and broke the seal.

Molly watched him, twisting her apron. "The mapmaker's man gave it to me, see. I told him I wasn't good at letters, but he said if anything happened to him, I was to ask someone I trusted to read it. And now he's gone . . ." She bit her lip. "I know I can trust you, Doctor, can't I?"

Thomas lifted the letter to the window to catch the last of the light and read the few lines of script quickly.

"You can trust me, Molly," he replied, looking up from the letter. His body was suddenly stiff with shock. "You have done the right thing. You have saved a man's life."

The trial of Adam Diggott for the murders of Jeffrey Turgoose, master surveyor, and, in a separate incident, James Charlton, his assistant, was to be held the next day at Oxford assizes.

Thomas set off for the city from the Three Tuns at first light, armed with Charlton's letter. His horse, however, had fallen lame and he had been forced to stop in Headington, just on the outskirts of Oxford, to have the mare reshod. He therefore arrived a few minutes after the proceedings had started and walked in just in time to see Seth Talland, the guard, take the witness stand.

Once again, the courtroom was packed with the flotsam and jetsam of the city, together with members of the legal fraternity. The same judge, His Honor Judge Dubarry, was presiding. Thomas was not sure if that was to Diggott's advantage. He saw Lupton, too, who returned a thunderous scowl as soon as he clapped eyes on Thomas.

An uneasy silence settled on the assembled crowd as Seth Talland began his testimony. Looking bullish, his shovel hands clasping the stand as confidently as a vicar in his pulpit, he repeated the same fabrication he had concocted for Abe Diggott's trial. Once more Thomas found himself forced to listen to his well-rehearsed litany of lies. Talland related how he and the surveyors had been separated when their packhorse fell, whinnying, into a pit, and how Turgoose had checked to see what the tumult was and then returned to the clearing. Seconds later Talland had joined him, only to find himself witnessing a vicious attack. He saw four men demand Charlton hand over any valuables. Initially he refused, but when they hit him in the face, injuring his eye, he handed over his pocket watch. When, however, they asked the same of Charlton's master, he refused. Instead Turgoose pulled out a pistol and pointed it at the varlets. There was a struggle. In this version of events, it was Abe Diggott who wrested the weapon from the surveyor, while Adam snatched it from him and shot the surveyor point-blank.

The prizefighter's delivery had been fluent. The same prosecutor, the ruthless Martin Bradshaw, had not interrupted him once, and by the looks on the jurors' faces, his account of the incident seemed wholly plausible. Thomas, however, had every faith that he would soon put paid to any credibility the guard had with the jury.

As soon as Talland had stepped down from the witness stand,

Thomas approached the clerk and handed him Charlton's letter. In a low voice he told him it was vital evidence and must be presented to the court immediately. The clerk, scanning the paper, concurred, and a moment later the missive was set before the judge himself.

"The court will adjourn," said Dubarry, reaching for his gavel.

In the judge's chamber, Thomas explained how he had come across the letter and how Molly Trott, the serving girl at the Three Tuns, was waiting in the courtroom. She was, he said, prepared to testify as to how the missive came to be in her possession and Charlton's parting words to her before he walked up to Raven's Wood on that fateful day.

Once again the judge called the court to order, and the meek and diffident girl from the tavern reluctantly took the witness stand. Once the formalities were over, Judge Dubarry announced that new evidence had come to light. He fluttered Charlton's letter in the air.

"Tell us how you came by this, pray tell, Miss er . . ." The judge squinted at his notes. "Miss Trott."

As she looked about at her hushed audience, Thomas feared the maid would buckle under the glare of their hostile stares. She licked her cracked lips and shifted nervously, but he managed to catch her eye and gave her a smile, which seemed to reassure her and confirm her purpose.

"It were when they was taking the men away, sir," she began.

The judge frowned. "You must be more specific, Miss Trott," he told her.

She returned a quizzical look.

"Which men?" he asked.

She gave a little nod to signify that she had understood the question.

"It were after the village men that were accused of riot came back from Oxford," she said. There was no emotion in her voice. "Everyone were outside to greet 'em, and Mr. Geech—"

The judge stopped her. "Mr. Geech is . . . ?"

"My master, sir, the landlord at the Three Tuns. He tells me to go outside and take some gin to the men, on the 'ouse, like. So I goes, and then I see the soldiers come again to take them away. And there was panic and while I'm watching 'em, Mr. Charlton comes up to me."

Again Judge Dubarry interrupted. "How did you know it was Mr. Charlton?"

Molly, turning her head to face the judge, replied, "Mr. Charlton and his master were staying with us, sir, while they made their maps. Mr. Charlton always showed me great kindness."

"I see. Carry on," instructed Dubarry.

"So Mr. Charlton, he seems distracted and upset when he sees the redcoats back, and he comes up to me and hands me the letter."

"And what did he say to you?"

"He says, 'Molly, if anything should happen to me, then you're to give this to someone you trust.' I says, 'Sir? Is something wrong?' And he looks at me real strange and says, 'I'm going to put it right.' "

Her recollection hung on the stale courtroom air for a moment, until Judge Dubarry asked, "And what happened next?"

"Next, sir, I heard Dr. Silkstone's voice. He were calling out to Mr. Charlton, but he just ignored him and turned and started walking away quick." Her delivery was deadpan and melancholy, and she held the courtroom enthralled. "That was the last I see'd of him until I heard he were gone."

Judge Dubarry arched a brow. "And when you heard he was 'gone,' Miss Trott, what was your reaction?"

The girl shrugged. "I was sorry, sir, and shocked, and then . . ."

"Yes."

"Then I remembered the letter he gave me."

"So you read it?"

A ripple of laughter went 'round the courtroom, and the girl, bowing her head briefly, replied, "I don't know my letters, sir. That is why I took it to someone who I could trust to read it and do the right thing."

"And that person was Dr. Silkstone?"

Molly nodded and shot a look across the floor to where Thomas sat.

"I knew him to be a good man, sir. He'd helped all them that was shot at by the redcoats," she said.

The judge nodded. "Thank you, Miss Trott. You may step down," he told her.

Next it was Thomas's turn to take the witness stand. He had not expected to be called and felt ill prepared for any cross-examination. Nevertheless, he had taken the liberty of comparing the letter purportedly from Charlton with bills the chainman had signed at the Three Tuns and had shown them to the clerk for verification.

Initial formalities over, Judge Dubarry addressed Thomas. "I would ask that you read this letter from Mr. Charlton to the court, Dr. Silkstone," he said. The missive was passed across from the bench to Thomas, and in a clear voice he began:

> *To Whom It May Concern*
> *I write this letter in the sure knowledge that when it is next read it will be after my death. My own folly and cowardice have drawn me to the conclusion that I have no honorable course but to take my own life. I cannot expect forgiveness from those who have been compelled to deal with my self-inflicted misfortune, but I do crave their understanding.*

At this point Thomas looked up and saw that the courtroom was hanging on his every word. Somewhere a fly buzzed. He resumed:

> *On the afternoon of April 20th I found myself extremely nervous. The local villagers had been trailing us and tormenting us. We were in fear of our lives when we entered the woods, and when I heard the horse whinnying, I was convinced we were being ambushed. Mr. Turgoose, seeing my*

distress, put me in charge of his pistol, little knowing that I was not fit to have it. He left me alone to see what had happened, and when he returned I mistook him for a brigand. God help me, it was me who fired the shot that killed Mr. Turgoose. I do not recall much that followed immediately afterward, only that I was in shock and great pain when fragments flew into my eye when the pistol discharged. Our guide, Mr. Talland, helped me back to Boughton Hall. It was all my fault and I alone should be judged for my actions. I was forced to perjure myself in court in the case of Abe Diggott but I cannot stand by and watch as another innocent man is charged with the murder of Mr. Turgoose. I therefore own up to my reckless crime and hope that my confession will ensure the dismissal of any case brought against any other man and a subsequent pardon.

Thomas looked up to address the captivated court directly.

I go to my Maker in the hope that he will grant me forgiveness for my most grievous sins.
James Charlton

For a moment it seemed that time in the courtroom stood still as everyone reflected on what they had just heard. Finally Judge Dubarry spoke.

"Thank you, Dr. Silkstone. That was most enlightening," he said before addressing the defendant. "I have no choice but to say: Adam Diggott . . ." The coppicer straightened himself in the dock. "I hereby dismiss all charges against you. You are free to go."

Thomas felt his whole body suddenly lighten. A heavy burden had been lifted from his shoulders. Jeffrey Turgoose's death had been a tragic accident. As if Charlton's torment at his own mistake was not enough, Sir Montagu and Lupton had forced him to comply with their elaborate charade to cover up the truth. It suited Sir Montagu's purpose to mark the villagers as lawless murderers, so that his own brand of justice could prevail. And now he and his allies had been revealed in court as nothing but liars and tyrants. He allowed himself a smile, but it was only a flicker before it snagged on Lupton's gaze. The steward was standing, talking with Prosecutor Bradshaw. He wore the dazed look of a man not used to defeat. The brief encounter reminded Thomas that despite this immediate victory, his battle with the Boughton Estate, and Sir Montagu in particular, was far from over.

Chapter 55

The journey from Draycott House to Boughton Hall was almost at an end. It had passed smoothly enough. Richard had slept for much of the way, while Lydia had contented herself with looking out of the carriage window at the familiar countryside, or conversing now and again with Nurse Pring. The rolling hills were clothed in bright spring green, and the sun was coaxing the leaves in the beechwoods to unfurl. She was taking simple delight from the vista. She was going home. Suddenly, however, she heard a great rattle up ahead, and her pleasure was rudely curtailed as the carriage lurched, plunging her forward. The coachman cussed loudly and was forced to pull up the horses to allow another carriage to pass at speed on the right-hand side. Lydia's head whipped 'round to see a passenger inside, railing at his driver to go faster. For a moment she thought she recognized the man, but then decided she must have been mistaken.

"All well, your ladyship?" the footman called down from his perch.

Richard had taken a tumble but thought it rather amusing. Nurse Pring was fussing over his clothes, which had gone askew.

"All well," Lydia assured him, smoothing her skirts.

Yet she could not pretend that she did not feel apprehensive. It was not that this small, yet sudden, incident had unsettled her, but that she was uncertain as to the reason for her journey. The message had come from Sir Montagu only the previous day. He was away on business, but they were to rendezvous at Boughton Hall. He did not say for what purpose, but she hoped very much that it heralded a permanent return to the place she loved and missed so much.

They drove on for another mile or so, until the carriage swung through the huge wrought-iron gates. Lydia felt her heart lurch in her chest as she caught sight of the hall for the first time in almost three months.

"Look, my darling!" She reached out her arms across the carriage and drew Richard close to her. Together they stared out the window onto the hall's ornate façade, with its barley-sugar chimneys and its elegant pediments. "We are home!" she cried.

Her son, although not sharing his mother's obvious delight, seemed happy enough to be returning. "Is Mr. Lupton here?" he asked.

Lydia smiled and pushed a wayward curl away from her son's eye.

"Yes, I think he is," she replied, remembering the enthusiasm that Richard had shown for the steward's company.

As the carriage progressed up the driveway, Lydia's excitement grew as she saw the staff gathering on the front steps to greet her. There were Howard and Mistress Firebrace, the housekeeper, Mistress Claddingbowl, the cook, and a dozen more familiar faces, all smiling and ready to welcome their mistress.

The moment the horses pulled up, Sir Montagu stepped out, too. His expression was somber but not foreboding, and he managed a polite smile as she alighted from the carriage, helped by the footman.

"Welcome back, your ladyship," he greeted her.

Lydia slipped him a strange look—Sir Montagu welcoming her into her own home; the irony was not lost on her. At first she had believed it was he who had deprived her of her beloved Boughton. Then, as the story unfolded, she had come to realize that her father was in fact her ally and that all along she was being betrayed by the man whom she had come to trust above all others. The wound was still raw, and even to think of Dr. Thomas Silkstone pained her, but as she glanced at Richard as he made his way down the carriage steps, she knew she could endure anything as long as her son was with her.

"After you have settled yourself, we shall take tea," Sir Montagu told her, holding out his long arm in a sweeping gesture up the steps.

Mistress Firebrace, her face wreathed in uncustomary smiles, showed Lydia to her bedchamber. It was just as she had left it: the bed draped in silk, the escritoire by the window, and a huge arrangement of peonies on the table that fragranced the air. Walking over to the window, she looked out onto the lawns, to the rose garden, still tended but wanting Amos Kidd's touch. She ran her fingers over her chest of drawers, her washstand, the embroidered shawl her late husband had brought back from India, draped over her favorite chair. They were so familiar, so comforting, and yet strangely different. Perhaps it was that so much had changed since she had last opened those drawers, or brushed her hair in this room. Perhaps it was because her own life had taken a different direction that she perceived these objects differently. Each one held a memory, a thought, or a moment frozen in time. Making for the bed, she let her fingers hover over the pillow where Thomas's head had once lain. She dared not touch it for fear it was still warm. She knew it was a ridiculous notion, but every time she recalled his caress, his scent, his breath, a terrible sense of loss washed over her. Trust was the bridge that had joined them, the thread that had bound them, and now that it had gone, there was nothing, except a deep and irrepressible yearning for something no longer there.

"Tea is ready, your ladyship," Mistress Firebrace announced a little later. "I shall see that your luggage is unpacked in the meantime."

"Yes," replied Lydia flatly. Being back at Boughton after all that she had endured still seemed like a dream to her. She was afraid she might wake at any moment. "Thank you," she said, and she made her way downstairs to the drawing room, where Sir Montagu was waiting. This was where it had happened; where she had been restrained, where order had descended into chaos before she was taken to the madhouse. And now gentility ruled. Decorum had been restored. Her nightmare seemed no more than that, a terrifying dream to be forgotten and never spoken of again. She took a seat opposite her father.

The tea tray lay on a cabinet by the sofa. "You will do the honors, my dear?" Sir Montagu asked.

Lydia, who sat smoothing her skirts self-consciously, declined. "I would rather not," she said with a polite smile.

"Of course," he replied. "You must be fatigued after your journey, my dear," he said, and he nodded to the maid to serve the tea.

For a few moments they sat in silence, the clink of the china cups the only noise in the room, as Lydia's eyes lingered on familiar objects and on the view over the lawns. She was aware that her newfound father, with his hawkish gaze, was watching her every move. She willed herself to pretend that her joy at her return outweighed all her other emotions, but she had never been adept at hiding her feelings. Returning to Boughton brought back so many memories of Thomas that her happiness and relief were tempered.

She steeled herself to make conversation. "Mr. Lupton," she began.

Sir Montagu, in the midst of a sip of tea, made an odd slurping noise.

"Lupton, my dear?" He could not hide his surprise that his steward should be paramount in her thoughts.

"I trust he is well?" Lydia did her best to ignore her father's thinly disguised astonishment. "Richard is looking forward to seeing him."

Sir Montagu arched a brow. "That will not be possible, I fear," he replied.

"Oh?"

"I fear Mr. Lupton and I have parted company."

The memory of the carriage speeding its way down the country lane flashed in front of her eyes. So it was Lupton she had seen, his face darkened by fury.

"A disagreement?" She knew she was being bold.

Sir Montagu twitched his lips, but his eyes remained cold.

"Of sorts. I maintained he was incompetent and he disagreed, so I dismissed him."

Lydia looked away with a little sigh. "Richard will be disappointed."

"Not as disappointed as I was in the man's capabilities, I can assure you, my dear."

Another awkward silence ensued. The clock on the mantelpiece ticked away the seconds as if they were minutes.

"You are still pained," her father told her, after a few uneasy moments had passed. It was an observation, not a question. "But it will ease," he added unsympathetically. He took another sip of tea. "And we have plans to make."

"Plans?" Lydia blinked and looked up from her cup. Plans were for those who could see into the future, a place she had not dared go for many weeks.

"For the estate," riposted her father. "Changes are afoot, and we must discuss them. Boughton needs you."

She inclined her head thoughtfully, then said, "And what can I give that you and Mr. Lupton could not?" Her time away had exposed her as weak and ineffectual. Boughton could be run just as efficiently, if not more so, without her. She was an irrelevance.

"I am sure you have ideas, my dear."

She knew his words were calculated to make her feel at ease, but in truth she felt overwhelmed. She managed a weak smile, but for now she was content to live in the moment. Thoughts of Bedlam, betrayal, and Thomas still whirled around in her brain, sapping her of her strength and any confidence she had previously acquired. Yet, as if her father had read her mind, the past reared its head once more.

"I know Silkstone has left you bruised, but surely you must now see how he tried to use you? He abused your wealth and status to further his own career, and—"

Suddenly something inside her snapped. He was trying to boost her confidence while vilifying Thomas. The nerve was still raw, and he had touched it directly. "He saved your life," she interrupted.

Taken aback, her father's bushy brows lifted. "He did, indeed, save my life, and for that I am most grateful, but he did it for his own gain. By saving me, he made both of us indebted to him." He took another sip of tea. "A cold and callous calculation," he added, returning his dish to the tray.

Lydia knew that everything he said made perfect sense. After all, his lawyer's cunning ensured that all his arguments were neatly taken care of, all objections swiftly overruled with the finality of a judge's gavel. She knew, too, that she needed time to herself. What was it the Reverend Lightfoot had told her after her brother Edward's death so long ago? Time is a great healer. At this moment her wounds were still exposed. Time would, no doubt, heal them, but she also needed the balm of space. She rose.

"Forgive me, but I need to go to my room," she said with a nod. To hear her father go through a catalog of Thomas's faults and failings was too much for her to bear.

Sir Montagu got to his feet, too. "Of course, my dear," he replied.

In Lydia's absence, Mistress Firebrace had supervised the unpacking of her luggage. Her scent bottles had been returned to her dressing table, along with her hairbrush and mirror. Her favorite novels had been arranged on her bookstand and the painted dressing screen positioned in its rightful place. Yet rather than ease her anxiety, such familiarity only reminded her of Thomas more. Her room had returned to its former self, and Thomas had been a part of it.

Moving over to the escritoire, she recalled the times she had sat there, composing letters to him, her words pouring like summer rain on the page. She had laid her feelings bare, exposed herself to him, and he had cut her with all the precision his surgeon's scalpel could muster. Her fingers played on the top drawer, smaller than the rest. In one swift move she opened it, and there, lying bound by a blue ribbon, were his letters. She had kept them all, testaments to a love she had believed so real and true. Seizing them, she untied the ribbon as she walked over to the fireplace; then, one by one, she began feeding them to the flames and watched through glassy eyes as they crackled and spluttered and disappeared.

So lost in her own grief was she that she did not hear footsteps and the opening of the door. In fact, the first she knew that someone was behind her was when she heard a voice.

"Welcome back, your ladyship!"

She turned to see Eliza, her eyes welling with tears, standing in the middle of the room. Instinctively Lydia hurried forward and took her by both hands.

"Oh, Eliza! How I have missed you!" she cried.

"And I, you, your ladyship. We thought you was dead!"

Lydia took a step back and let her maid's hands fall. "Dead?" The word bounced off her tongue.

"Why, yes, your ladyship. We was told you died. Sir Montagu put a notice in the newssheet and—"

"Dead?" repeated Lydia. She slumped down on the nearest chair, her face suddenly pale.

Eliza crouched down beside her. "We didn't know what to think, your ladyship. There was a funeral and—"

Lydia shook her head. "I have been unwell," she acknowledged. "But why would Sir Montagu say I was dead?"

In her joy, Eliza could not think to question. She shrugged. "I do not know, my lady, but you are here now."

Lydia, however, could not put her questioning to one side so easily. Her happiness at seeing her maid once more had been blunted, dealt an inadvertently cruel blow. If she was still dead to all intents and purposes, then did Sir Montagu plan to keep her dead, unable to reveal herself once more to the outside world? Could it be that he intended to bury her alive at Boughton? She tried to shrug off the ridiculous notion. "But of course you will let everyone know in the village that I am still alive!" A nervous laugh escaped from her lips.

Walking over to the grate, Eliza had taken hold of the poker. At Lydia's words, she turned and looked grave.

"We are sworn to secrecy, your ladyship. Sir Montagu says we must tell no one that you are here."

Lydia looked wide-eyed at the girl, as if she had suddenly

hammered another nail in her coffin. She watched Eliza mend the fire in silence, with a rising feeling of fear.

A moment later the maid had straightened herself and was moving away from the hearth when she noticed the remaining letters on the mantelshelf. She switched 'round and fixed her mistress with a questioning frown.

"You are burning Dr. Silkstone's letters?" she asked. Lydia realized her maid had seen her read them on countless occasions. The script was so familiar to her, and the girl had even bought the ribbon that bound them from Brandwick market herself.

Lydia's gaze fell, as if she suddenly felt ashamed. She did not address her maid directly. "I am," she replied, the confession clearly paining her.

Eliza shook her head. "But why, your ladyship?"

Lydia felt a wave of despair surge over her. "Because I fear he has betrayed me, Eliza."

"Betrayed?" repeated her maid, frowning.

Lydia sighed deeply, and her eyes moistened. "He was the one behind my admission to Bedlam."

Eliza's face registered the shock.

"He was the one who signed the certificate that committed me. I have seen the papers myself."

Again Eliza shook her head. "No. No, my lady. 'Tis not so!" she protested, rushing toward her mistress.

Lydia rose suddenly and moved over to the window. Eliza followed her.

"Sir Montagu has revealed Dr. Silkstone to be a liar and a fraud," she said. Her slight shoulders heaved in a deep sigh. "He was using me to gain social status and wealth. I suited his ambitions."

Now drawn alongside her mistress, Eliza looked her in the eye. "Please, your ladyship. Whatever Sir Montagu has told you is false. Dr. Silkstone came here looking for you, just after they took you away. Frantic, he were. And when he thought you was dead—"

Lydia interjected. "He came looking for me?"

Eliza's words raced in front of her. "Yes. Yes, my lady. He

even went into the vault when he thought they'd buried you. He's been here since, too, pleading with Mr. Lupton to let him know where you were. Moved heaven and earth, he has."

Suddenly Lydia's hands flew up to her ears, and she pressed her palms against them. "No more," she cried. "I cannot take any more."

Eliza held her breath. She had overstepped the mark between mistress and maid, but she knew that Lydia's happiness was at stake. Slowly she stepped away, putting a little distance between them.

"Forgive me, your ladyship, but 'tis the truth. Dr. Silkstone's heart belongs to you, and that's for sure," she said. Walking over to the mantelshelf, she reached for the remaining letters that had not yet been consigned to the flames, then returned. Thrusting them under Lydia's nose, she said, "If you still doubt me, just read one of his letters, and I am sure his own words will convince you." And with that she bobbed a curtsy and ran from the room, leaving Lydia cradling the sheaves of paper in her trembling hands.

Chapter 56

The good news from Oxford had come earlier in the day. Thomas had just returned to his room at the Three Tuns after changing Zeb Godson's dressing. All the seriously injured men were now out of danger. He was about to pack for his return journey to London when he heard the clatter of hooves on the cobbled High Street and the sound of cheers. Moving over to the window, he looked down to see the villagers gathering 'round a horseman. Moments later Molly delivered the news he had been awaiting. Without bothering to knock, she flung open the door, set down the tray she was carrying, and with uncharacteristic exuberance declared, "They're free!"

"A great relief, Molly. I am most grateful to you for telling me," said Thomas, smiling broadly.

"They'll be back before nightfall," she added. "There'll be some rejoicing tonight!"

Thomas had dearly wished to return to London as soon as Adam Diggott's trial ended but had remained in Brandwick to see to the welfare of the injured and to hear the outcome of the trial of the rest of the accused men before he headed home. The jury at the assizes, he was soon to learn, had returned a verdict that showed not only the strength of public opinion, but Sir Theodisius Pettigrew's valiant efforts to lobby on their behalf, too. While they found the defendants guilty of having been present at an unlawful assembly on May twenty-first in Brandwick, it was their unanimous wish to recommend all the parties to what they termed "the merciful consideration of the Court." The judges, Mr. Justice Boswell and Sir John Clearhugh, responded favorably to this appeal, and the longest sentence inflicted was for two months' imprisonment.

Such satisfactory outcomes meant that Thomas could now concentrate his efforts on tracking down Lydia's whereabouts. He would return to London to marshal his thoughts and enlist the help of the Westminster coroner, Sir Stephen Gandy, to engage a trustworthy solicitor. He had arrived at the notion that he would have to play Sir Montagu at his own game and force the issue of Lydia's well-being through the courts. Threatening to go public with the revelation that her ladyship was, in fact, the lawyer's illegitimate daughter would throw the future of the Boughton Estate into the air. The Crick bloodline had been broken. The consequences could be dire.

No sooner had he closed the door on Molly and begun to resume his packing, however, when he heard more footsteps thundering along the corridor outside. A second later his door was flung open, and there, his face crumpled into a scowl, was Nicholas Lupton. Seth Talland stood, arms crossed, behind his master.

"Silkstone!" boomed the steward. From his flaming cheeks and the smell that wafted into the room, Thomas could tell he was emboldened by strong liquor.

"Lupton." Not wishing to inflame his passions any further, Thomas remained calm. "To what do I owe the honor?"

The steward snorted. "Honor? What would you know about honor? An honorable man has guts." He swayed slightly as he spoke.

Thomas surmised that the outcome in the courtroom and the leniency of the verdicts had frustrated Sir Montagu. He had clearly vented his spleen on Lupton, who had turned to the bottle for solace.

"You need to rest, sir. I shall call the landlord, who will find you a bed," said Thomas, walking toward the steward. His suggestion, however, was swiftly rebuffed.

"How dare you tell me what I need?" thundered Lupton, slamming the doorjamb with his gloved hand. "You are the cause of all this. Had you not set your sights on a woman not of your class, none of this would have happened."

Thomas could see that Lupton's fury would not be easily assuaged.

"Please, Lupton." He moved closer, an arm outstretched, but the steward batted it away.

"You can have her now. You're welcome to her." He lowered his voice as if he was resigned to his loss. Thomas knew that he had nurtured his own designs on Lydia. He knew, too, that he must surely be privy to her whereabouts. He seized his chance.

"Where is she, Lupton? Why don't you tell me? You have nothing to lose now." It was all he could do to stop himself from grabbing the steward by the coat and shaking him into submission, but he restrained himself.

Lupton looked deep into Thomas's eyes, and his face suddenly broke into a broad smile. "You really care for her, don't you? You want to know where she is more than anything," he jibed. Thomas was so close to him he felt his liquor breath hot against his skin.

Thomas bit his lip, but Lupton continued to twist the knife.

"Admit it, why don't you?" he taunted. "Or is it that you are a coward? A cowardly colonist! Yes, that's it." As he spoke he pulled at the fingers of the glove on his right hand. "You, sir, are a coward, and if you want to know the whereabouts of Lady Lydia, you will have to fight like a man!"

Suddenly he drew back his glove and slapped Thomas hard across the cheek. "I challenge you to a duel, Silkstone!" he cried.

Shocked, Thomas staggered slightly, his hand nursing his stinging cheek. "A duel?" he repeated.

"And Talland is my witness," replied Lupton, glancing at his henchman.

Emboldened by his challenge, the steward strode into the room, his eyes scanning its contents. Suddenly he turned. "I shall commit her ladyship's location to paper and put it in a sealed envelope. In the event of my death, you will open it." He slapped his palm with his gloves.

Thomas felt his throat constrict. "And in the event of mine?" he asked.

Lupton sniffed and fixed him with a glare. "England will be rid of an American coward and my honor will be restored."

"And what if I refuse to accept your challenge?"

"Then you will lose all hope of ever seeing Lady Lydia again."

With the consequences of his refusal put so starkly, Thomas had no choice. Lupton had him backed into a corner. He cast a glance at Talland, who stared at him with the menace of a vicious guard dog. He had to fight. "Then I accept your challenge," he replied.

For a moment Lupton was silent, as the realization of the summons he had just laid down sank in; then suddenly his eyes lit up with excitement. Finally he barked, "Good. Pistols at dawn on the common!" He threw a look over to the table. "Enjoy the rest of your meal. It may well be your last."

Lydia had made her excuses. She had spent the early part of the evening in the nursery with Richard and Nurse Pring, although she had not joined in his play. She had mired herself too deep in her own thoughts. Dinner, the little that she could eat of it, had also been taken in her room. And now, by the light of her lamp she read the remainder of Thomas's letters, the ones that had escaped the flames. His words raised a smile, but they also triggered tears. She studied his signature at the bottom of the sheet of paper she held in her hand from an early missive. His tone had been more formal, as befitting their relationship at the time. He had signed himself *Dr. Thomas Silkstone, anatomist & surgeon*. His signature was there for all to see and for her father to plunder. She knew now that Eliza's words were true.

In the early hours of the following morning, before the sun had risen above the hills, Lydia was woken from a light sleep.

She had stayed awake for most of the night, reading Thomas's letters, her eyes straining in the candlelight's weak glow, and she had wondered. In her head she kept hearing him call out her name in the hallway at Draycott. And the more she wondered, the more she doubted. She recalled how, just before he had mounted his horse outside her window, she had seen him take something from his pocket. The thought had struck her like a bolt of lightning. Could it have been the locket she had given him all those years ago as a keepsake?

Suddenly she felt her bed shaken and someone press hard on her shoulder. Opening her eyes and blinking away the darkness, she saw Eliza standing over her, looking anxious. She raised her head from the pillow.

"What is it?" she asked through the fog of sleep.

"'Tis Dr. Silkstone," came the maid's breathless reply. "He's to fight a duel!"

"What?" The news jolted Lydia into the moment. She threw off her bedcovers.

"Mr. Lupton challenged him last night."

"Lupton?" Lydia leapt from the disordered blankets that signified a restless night's sleep. "Why?"

Eliza rushed to fetch her mistress's chemise. "Molly heard 'em last night."

"Molly?" asked Lydia, stepping into her petticoat.

"She works at the Three Tuns. She heard 'em arguing and then Mr. Lupton, he says if the doctor ever wants to see you again, he'll have to kill him first."

Lydia's hands flew up to her mouth. She could barely register Eliza's words. So Thomas had remained true to her. Everything that Sir Montagu had told her was a tissue of lies.

"How could I have doubted him?" she asked as the maid laced her stays. "Oh, Eliza. I should've known better than to believe . . ." Her voice trailed off wanly.

"'Tis no time to fret, my lady," Eliza told her firmly. "Lovelock's waiting with the carriage. If we hurry we'll make it before a shot is fired."

Rushing downstairs, mistress and maid bundled into the conveyance and Lovelock set the horses off at a gallop. They thundered along the drive, then veered left to take the road that led to the common. Lovelock knew the spot. Arthur's Hollow had long been a popular place for duels. Lydia's late brother had killed a man there over a gambling debt and injured another.

They arrived as the mist covered the ground like gossamer. Light was beginning to penetrate the gloom of a chilly May morning. Looking out of the carriage window, Lydia could see two clusters of dark figures standing huddled on the grass, several yards apart. It would be useless to take the carriage farther. The ground became boggy at this point, so Lovelock was forced to pull the horses up behind the ridge.

Opening the door, he apologized to Lydia.

"I'm sorry, your ladyship. I can't take you yonder. You'll have to go on foot from here," he told her.

Sweeping down from the carriage, Lydia lifted her skirts and hurried as fast as she could over the heavy-dewed grass. Her feet kept sinking into the moss as she went. Following behind, Eliza struggled to match her pace. Soon they had climbed the ridge to get a better view. From the vantage point she strained her eyes to focus through the mist. They were not too late. There were five men: two standing back to back, with another close by, and one at either end of the hollow, separated by a distance of fifty yards or more. She could make out Thomas, standing taller than Lupton, but slightly stooped. She veered in his direction, but as she did so, the men began to walk away from each other in straight lines. Five paces, ten. She started to run.

"No!" she cried, but her words were lost on the chill air.

Fifteen, twenty.

"No!" she cried again.

"Fire!" came the call.

Thomas's pistol fired first, but it seemed that he had aimed deliberately too high. Lupton remained standing, steadfast. He took aim.

"No!" screamed Lydia once more. This time her voice carried down the hollow, and Thomas, for a split second, turned his head. It was enough. A loud crack shattered the air, but he did not see the ball as it left the barrel, nor the smoke in its wake. All he could see in that moment was Lydia rushing toward him, her arms outstretched. All he could hear was her voice, calling his name. All he could feel was the sharp jab of a lead ball as it pierced his chest.

Postscript

In 1787 the first act to enclose an area of wetland and grassland, known as Otmoor, just northeast of Oxford, was lodged. Legend had it that "Our Lady of Otmoor" rode a circuit 'round the moor while an oat sheaf was burning and gave the area within it to the people of Otmoor in perpetuity. Consequently, any moves by local landlords to enclose the land met with strong opposition from the villagers. Matters finally came to a climax on September 6, 1830, when around one thousand people walked the seven-mile circumference of Otmoor in broad daylight, destroying every fence in their way.

The Riot Act was read to them, and the Oxfordshire Yeomanry was summoned. The rioters, however, refused to disperse. Several were arrested, and forty-one were transported to Oxford Jail. The prisoners' arrival in the city happened to coincide with the famous St. Giles Fair, and the crowd turned into an angry mob and helped those charged to escape. At a later trial the judges showed mercy to the recaptured Otmoor men. The longest sentence handed down was two months' imprisonment.

Though the villagers held out for their rights for many years, the land was finally enclosed from 1835. More recent threats to the natural area included a government proposal in 1980 to route a motorway across Otmoor. A major campaign resulted in the adoption of an alternative route.

Since 1997 much of Otmoor has been made a Royal Society for the Protection of Birds nature reserve, with many acres being returned to marshland. It is also home to a large population of rare insects and plants.

Glossary

Chapter 1

chainman: Still known in modern surveying by the same name, this is the surveyor's assistant, who originally took charge of the measuring chains.

circumferentor: Toward the end of the eighteenth century the formerly popular circumferentor was being replaced by the theodolite as the surveyor's instrument of choice.

measuring chains: These were the surveyor's basic tools of measurement. Made of thick steel wire, they usually came in a two- or four-pole (thirty-three feet or sixty-six feet, respectively) format. This would then be subdivided into fifty links for the two-pole or one hundred links for the four. In a four-pole chain, each link would therefore be equal to 66/100 feet, or 7.92 inches in length.

The Lady of Brandwick: Many people of the seven Oxfordshire towns, around an area of wetland known as Otmoor, fueled the story that the Virgin Mary had ridden the circuit of the moor and given the land to the villagers, possibly before the Norman Conquest in 1066.

Bastard William: William the Conqueror, who invaded England and established Norman rule from 1066, was often called William the Bastard.

Chiltern: An area formed from a chalk escarpment, covering the counties of Buckinghamshire and Oxfordshire.

turners: Craftsmen skilled at turning wood on a lathe. The first reference to a turner making chairs in the Chilterns dates to before 1700 and is found in the parish register of High Wycombe in the 1680s. They were later known as bodgers.

pit sawyers: In order to cut tree trunks lengthwise, they were placed over pits known as sawpits. Balanced on smaller logs, the trunks were attached to them with iron hooks called dogs. Cutting was done with a two-man saw. The man on top was known as the "top dog," while the "under dog" stood in the pit and would be unfortunately covered with all the falling sawdust.

gin traps: Used mainly by gamekeepers, these cruel devices were banned in the United Kingdom only in 1958.

seventeen thousand acres in just over a sennight in Virginia: In 1750, John Buchanan, the deputy surveyor of Augusta County, reported that his party had surveyed eight tracts totaling seventeen thousand acres in just fifteen working days.

enclosure: Between the fifteenth and early twentieth centuries, landowners began fencing off land previously available for common use. During the eighteenth century, enclosures were regulated by Parliament; a separate Act of Enclosure was required for each village.

Euclid: Euclid of Alexandria was a Greek mathematician who is often referred to as the Father of Geometry. He lived around 300 BC.

mariner's black spot: Although now in popular culture thanks to Robert Louis Stevenson's *Treasure Island,* published in 1883, the black spot might owe its origin to the historical tradition of Caribbean pirates showing an ace of spades to a person condemned as traitor or informer.

sawpit: Several depressions can still be found in Chiltern woodlands, indicating disused pits.

a murder of crows: According to an old folktale, crows will gather to judge the capital fate of another. Their appearance was also thought to be an omen of death by some.

Chapter 2

Bethlem Hospital: Bethlem Royal Hospital, to give it its full name, was originally founded in 1247 but did not begin to treat the insane until the fourteenth century. In 1676, the hospital moved from the site of what is now Liverpool Street station, London, to a magnificent baroque building designed by Robert Hooke, at Moorfields. The hospital moved to its third site in 1815 and now forms part of the Imperial War Museum.

elaborate carvings: A detailed description of Bethlem in 1786 is given by Sophie von La Roche, a European lady who kept a diary of her travels.

Newgate Prison: The prison had to be completely rebuilt following the Gordon Riots of 1780. It reopened in 1782.

Primum non nocerum: Translated as "first do no harm," the phrase does not appear in the Hippocratic Oath but in the Hippocratic Corpus, a body of work containing around sixty medical treatises.

Chapter 3

hanging: During the eighteenth century there were fifty-six public executions at Oxford Castle, for crimes ranging from sheep stealing and arson to spying.

Amersham: A day's ride northwest of London, the Chiltern town was a natural resting place for men and horses. By the late 1770s there were no fewer than seventeen licenses granted to innkeepers and alehouse keepers.

Tyburn: The site of London's gallows was moved from Tyburn to Newgate in 1783. Executions were carried out outside the prison.

clustered 'round the dead men's feet: The death sweat from a hanged person allegedly had the power to cure scrofula, a form of tuberculosis.

the High: Locally the main street in Oxford is often known as the High.

the Jolly Trooper: Now known as the Bear, the inn is one of Oxford's oldest, but the present building, just opposite Bear Lane, was built in the early seventeenth century as the residence of the coaching inn's ostler. It was converted into a separate tavern, the Jolly Trooper, in 1774.

an Act of Enclosure: Originally, enclosures of land took place through informal agreement; however, during the seventeenth century the practice of enclosing land, that is, fencing it off, required authorization by an Act of Parliament. Most attempts by landlords went unchallenged, although some caused discontent and riots.

compensation: Although commoners were usually compensated for their losses, they were often given smaller holdings or inferior-quality land or allowed to remain only on the condition that they fence their allotment at their own expense.

stint: The fee for pasturing animals on common land to prevent overgrazing.

set fire to a hayrick: There are several reported incidents of arson attacks in protest at enclosures during the late eighteenth and early nineteenth centuries. An anonymous letter sent to an Essex farmer in 1773 warned, "As soon as your corn is in the barn we will have a fire."

Eton: Still arguably the world's most famous school, Eton College, Eton, near Windsor in Berkshire, was founded by King Henry VI in 1440.

Chapter 4

sack: A sweet wine fortified by brandy.

riots: While social unrest was quite widespread at this time, opposition to enclosures, together with a number of other factors such as the rising price of grain, did not come to a head until after the Napoleonic Wars. In 1830 there were widespread riots in England, known as the Captain Swing Riots.

Chapter 5

Great Tom: Housed in Tom Tower at Christ Church, the bell is the loudest in Oxford.

Christ Church Anatomy School: Built between 1766 and 1767, it is now usually known as the Lee Building and used as the Senior Common Room of Christ Church College.

their faces blackened with soot: It was very common for poachers to blacken their faces. The Black Act of 1722, which made poaching a capital offense, took its name from the practice.

scalded with a red-hot iron or oil: Until the sixteenth century, gunshot wounds had been treated this way in the belief that gunpowder was poisonous. A French barber surgeon named Ambroise Paré (c. 1510–1590) put paid to the practice but still recommended extraction, which carried on until the end of the eighteenth century and risked the infection of the wound and therefore death.

blunderbuss: An early form of shotgun. The word comes from the Dutch *donderbus,* which literally means "thunder gun." It was often carried by coach guards for protection against highwaymen.

Chapter 6

coppicing in the coupe: Coppicing is the traditional method of producing firewood or wood for fencing and furniture. The part of a woodland coppiced is called a coupe, but many other terms are used, such as "burrow," "hagg," "fell," "cant," "panel," or "burrow," depending on the locality.

stools: Coppice stools consist of the roots and stumps, which give rise to the coppice shoots, which are cut at regular intervals.

London fires aglow: By the eighteenth century Chiltern trees had become an important source of firewood for London and local towns.

small beer: Water was so often polluted that weak ale was frequently drunk by servants and even children.

messuages: An archaic term for a dwelling house and its surroundings.

Chapter 7

schnapps: A type of distilled spirit made from fermented fruit, this remains a popular drink in Germany.

matching pair: Most pistols were made and sold in pairs.

Chapter 8

London hospitals: Several hospitals were founded in the eighteenth century as a result of the growth of associational charities, such as the Lock Hospital in 1747 and the British Lying-In Hospital, established in 1749.

Chapter 9

bury man: Archaic name for a gravedigger.

bellman: An ancient officer in some English towns, who also doubles as the town crier, as in Hungerford, Berkshire.

as required by law: Before 1801, villagers had to be informed of the intention to enclose by way of a notice posted on the church door.

the bitter winter: Following the Great Fogg (described below, under Chapter 10), temperatures in Europe in the winter of 1783–1784 were about 3.6 degrees Fahrenheit below average for the late 1700s. The Laki eruption has been blamed for this, although new research points to other factors.

Chapter 10

fulling mill: Fulling is the beating and cleaning of cloth in water.

tenter frames: Once the woolen cloth was finished and washed, it was stretched to dry on tenter frames, which were set in what were called racking closes. The phrase "being on tenterhooks," meaning to be held in suspense, is derived from these structures.

stocks: Stocks were like huge wooden mallets that swung in an arc down onto the cloth contained in a wooden trough.

a wooden cross: A cross made of rowan and bound with red thread was used as a protective charm. Examples can be seen in the Pitt Rivers Museum in Oxford.

Great Fogg: A deadly fog, now most widely attributed to the eruption of the Laki fissure in Iceland in 1783, covered the eastern half of England, killing thousands of livestock and contributing to the deaths of several thousand people. (See *The Devil's Breath,* the third book in the Dr. Thomas Silkstone series.)

kiln: Charcoal kilns contained a pile of wood, which was covered in bracken, followed by a layer of clay.

cunning woman: The term was most widely used in southern England and the Midlands to denote a healer or wisewoman or white witch.

shew stones: Polished objects engraved with magical names, symbols, and signs were often used as tools for occult research.

Chapter 11

commoners: In this case the term refers to people who share rights over an area of common land in a particular locality.

an elected council: There were often courts that upheld the rights of villagers to graze their animals on the land, enforcing strict rules about when and how they did so.

glean the grain: One of the many perquisites of a commoner was the right to glean the grain, or gather what remained on the ground after the harvest.

pannage: The right to allow pigs to eat acorns and beech mast in the woods, usually applied during the autumn. Acorns are poisonous to other animals.

bailiff: An administrative officer.

The Riot Act: An Act of the Parliament of 1715, it meant that any group of twelve or more people held to be unlawfully assembled should disperse or face punishment. The act, from which comes the expression "reading the riot act," was properly called "An Act for Preventing Tumults and Riotous Assemblies, and for the More Speedy and Effectual Punishing the Rioters." It was not repealed until 1967.

urine: Known as seg, the urine was used to scour wool cloth at the clothier's premises.

Chapter 12

Drury Lane: A street off London's Covent Garden that by the eighteenth century had become one of the worst slums in London, dominated by prostitution and gin palaces.

public view: Indiscriminate visiting by the public for entertainment at Bethlem was stopped in 1770.

Bath Assembly Rooms: These were elegant public rooms at the heart of fashionable eighteenth-century Bath life and remain open to the public today.

taking in every detail: Much of this description was based on the satirical writer Ned Ward's visit to Bethlem, recorded in the late eighteenth century in a publication called *The London Spy*. His descriptions of some of the inmates are both comical and poignant.

Mr. Hogarth's paintings: William Hogarth's famous series of paintings entitled *A Rake's Progress* features a dissolute young fortune hunter who descends into madness. The original series of eight paintings can be seen at Sir John Soane's Museum, in central London.

St. George's: The hospital, founded by a charitable institution in 1734, was located in Knightsbridge, which was then in the countryside.

walk unfettered: Several "patients" were kept shackled.

madness: This quote is paraphrased from the writings of Dr. John Monro, the physician of Bethlem from the mid-1750s.

Chapter 14

wayward son and heir apparent: When George III's son, also called George, turned twenty-one in 1783, he enjoyed a combined annual income of more than one hundred and ten thousand pounds sterling—more than eight million pounds in today's money. However, even this was too little for his lavish lifestyle.

Jack Robinson: The phrase was used by Fanny Burney in her romantic novel *Evelina*, in 1778. The origin is unsure but might refer to Sir John Robinson, who was the Constable of the Tower of London for several years from 1660.

Chapter 15

village lockup: A few lockups, small buildings where drunks or those accused of minor offenses were kept overnight, still remain. West Wycombe, in Buckinghamshire, and Lacock, in Wiltshire, are two good examples.

pillory: These are often confused with stocks. A victim stands at a pillory and boards are placed around the arms and neck and fixed to a pole. With stocks, boards are placed around the legs and sometimes the wrists.

Chapter 16

Dr. William Battie: A delightfully eccentric character himself, Dr. Battie took an enlightened view on mental health. His 1758 *Treatise on Madness* advocates a humane treatment of the insane.

John Monro: The physician in charge of Bethlem at the time, Monro was swift to react to Battie's criticism by publishing *Remarks on Dr. Battie's Treatise.* He advocated "the evacuation by vomiting" as very efficacious in the treatment of madness.

whipped all along the high street: A vividly shocking firsthand account of a public whipping through the streets of Reading in Berkshire is given by former town mayor William Darter in his *Reminiscences of Reading,* edited by Daphne Phillips.

Chapter 17

the civil war: The English Civil War (1642–1651), fought between those who supported King Charles I and those who supported Parliament, led to the destruction of many Royalist family homes.

aloe vera: Although it was used in Egyptian times, it was not until the eighteenth century that the plant's additional healing properties were discovered for conditions such as skin irritations, burns, and wounds.

willow bark: In 1763 the Reverend Edward Stone wrote a letter to the second Earl of Macclesfield detailing the effectiveness of dried willow bark in the treatment of those suffering from malarial symptoms in what is believed to be the first ever clinical trial. Willow bark is now known to contain salicin, which is a chemical similar to aspirin (acetylsalicylic acid).

smuggling: By the 1780s smuggling was so rife that the anonymous author of a pamphlet on the subject lamented that in the countryside thousands of men had turned away from respectable jobs in order to be employed in the smuggling trade, to the detriment of the whole nation.

Chapter 18

gin: England's "gin epidemic" lasted from 1720 to 1751, when the Gin Act was passed, prohibiting gin distillers from selling to unlicensed merchants. Although the act reduced large-scale drunkenness, cheap, illicit gin was still widely available.

turpentine: Made from pine leaves, this was often used as a flavoring for gin instead of or as well as juniper berries.

mother's ruin: Gin joints in eighteenth-century England allowed women to drink alongside men for the first time. It's thought that this led many of them to child neglect and prostitution. So gin became known as "mother's ruin."

One man's meat is another man's poison: The proverb comes from the first-century BC Roman poet and philosopher Lucretius.

Chapter 20

French William: William the Conqueror (1028–1087).

Treacher and *Widginton:* These surnames belong to the families of early chair makers in the Chilterns.

Bedlam: Bethlem Hospital was also, informally and most notoriously, known as Bedlam.

private madhouses: A 1774 act required all "madhouses" within seven miles of London to be licensed by a committee of the Royal College of Physicians, largely as a result of several cases where perfectly sane women were incarcerated on the wishes of their male relatives.

Chapter 21

proper leaves: The excise tax on tea made it a great target for smugglers. On August 13, the Commutation Act of 1784 reduced the tax on tea from 119 percent to 12.5 percent and the smuggling trade vanished virtually overnight.

even the new vicar: Parson Woodforde, the Norfolk clergyman who famously kept a diary of his rural life, admitted to buying smuggled tea in 1777. He also regularly bought smuggled gin and brandy.

beating the bounds: The custom was once found in almost every English parish but has now died out in many; however, in the Chiltern town of High Wycombe it was revived in 1985 and involved parading around the parish boundary and bumping boys on their heads at special marker points along the route.

parish board: In 1782 a little-known private act, drafted and promoted by Thomas Gilbert, empowered parishes to provide a workhouse exclusively for vulnerable parishioners, that is, children, the sick, and the elderly.

Oxford Journal: The principal newspaper in Oxfordshire was *Jackson's Oxford Journal,* published from 1753 to 1928.

Chapter 22

commissioners: There were usually three commissioners appointed to supervise the enclosure.

Chapter 23

blindman's buff: The children's game dates back to at least the sixteenth century.

hunt the slipper: The game is described as a primeval pastime in Oliver Goldsmith's 1776 novel, *The Vicar of Wakefield.*

Chapter 25

self-murder: Suicide was sometimes referred to as "self-murder" in coroners' reports. It was relatively common in eighteenth-century England, so much so that the Frenchman Montesquieu once commented, "We do not find in history that the Romans ever killed themselves without a cause; but the English are apt to commit suicide most unaccountably; they destroy themselves even in the bosom of happiness."

undertaker: By the middle of the eighteenth century, undertaking was an established profession in London. Not only would they take care of the funeral, but undertakers would even sell the deceased's goods if requested.

Chapter 27

Oxford Jail: In the 1770s the prison reformer John Howard visited the castle jail several times and criticized its size and quality, including the extent to which vermin infested the prison. Partly as a result of this criticism, it was decided by the county authorities to rebuild Oxford Jail.

Chapter 28

that Frenchman Rousseau: Jean-Jacques Rousseau was a French writer and political theorist of the Enlightenment.

social contract: Rousseau's 1762 *Du contrat social,* in which he envisaged a civil society united by a general will, inspired the leaders of the French Revolution, as well as many Enlightenment philosophers.

Chapter 30

Rogationtide: The Monday, Tuesday, and Wednesday preceding Ascension Day were the traditional days for beating the bounds.

The custom fell between the end of April and the beginning of June.

Domesday: The Domesday Book is a manuscript record of the great survey, completed in 1086, on orders from William the Conqueror, of much of England and parts of Wales.

Chapter 31

Milton Common: The village marks the intersection of two turnpike roads that were built in 1770 during a time of rapid expansion in both trade and mobility.

intended to reassure travelers: In 1748 the Hawkhurst gang, a notorious band of smugglers who tortured a man and then buried him alive, were executed, and their corpses were displayed in irons and chains in their own villages as a reminder of the brutality of their dreadful crimes.

fellow Philadelphian: In 1745 Thomas Cadwalader (1708–1779), of Philadelphia, who had been a pupil of the famous English surgeon William Cheselden, drew attention to the similarity of the "dry-gripes" of West India and the disease called the *colica Pictonum,* most frequently found in Poitiers, France.

still heads and worms: In his famous "Letter on Lead Poisoning" to his friend Benjamin Vaughan, written in Philadelphia in 1786, Benjamin Franklin cites the prohibition of leaden parts in condensers by the legislature of Massachusetts because lead was found to cause various symptoms of poisoning.

Sir George Baker: A physician to King George III and a pioneer in the use of chemical analysis to solve epidemical problems, Baker was the chief investigator into a case of widespread poisoning in Devon known as Devonshire colic. After conducting several tests, he discovered that the cause was lead. The experiments cited are loosely based on those he carried out.

Chapter 32

Hepar sulfuris: Used today as a homeopathic remedy, this is calcium sulfide obtained by burning oyster shells with flowers of sulfur.

West Haddon: In 1756 a football game was announced, but it was in fact a means to assemble a mob. During the subsequent riot, fences were torn down and burned in protest against the enclosure laws.

Chapter 34

makeshift shelter: Charcoal burners lived in the woods for much of the year and ate a diet of roasted hedgehog, snails toasted in hot ashes, and pheasant.

Chapter 35

pugilistic stance: This position, also referred to in forensic pathology as the pugilistic pose, is caused by high temperatures in fire, resulting in muscle stiffening and shortening.

Chapter 36

blacked your faces: Gangs of men, such as this one, who sooted their faces, both as a disguise and so as not to be spotted at night, were known as "the Blacks," and so the legislation introduced in 1723 was known as the Black Act. Without doubt the most viciously repressive legislation enacted in Britain in the last four hundred years, this act authorized the death penalty for more than fifty offenses connected with poaching.

gangs in Surrey: In 1721 a masked gang paraded through the town of Farnham with eleven deer they had killed in nearby Bishop's Park.

Chapter 37

don the black cap: Not really a cap, but a black square of fabric that denotes mourning at the passing of a death sentence.

James MacLaine: A notorious highwayman, originally from Scotland, he was known for being courteous to his victims. Before his execution in 1750 he reputedly received nearly three thousand guests during his imprisonment in Newgate Prison, many of whom were high-society ladies.

Dick Turpin: An account of the famous highwayman's execution in *The York Courant* notes his gall even at the end, recording that he "with undaunted courage looked about him, and after speaking a few words to the topsman, he threw himself off the ladder and expired in about five minutes."

standing mute: Up until 1772, a defendant who refused to plead, unless they were mute "by visitation from God," was subjected to the ordeal of peine forte et dure, in which they were forced to lie down and have weights placed on them until they either relented or died. The law was subsequently changed so that standing mute was deemed the same as pleading guilty.

Chapter 39

beyond reasonable doubt: William Paley described the situation in 1785, when jurors experienced "a general dread lest the charge of innocent blood should lie at their doors," and were therefore less likely to convict.

Chapter 44

bump their youngsters' heads: Boys were often turned upside down and "bumped" on boundary stones, and the day might well degenerate into a drunken brawl.

redcoat: This historical term used to refer to soldiers of the British army because of the red uniforms formerly worn by the majority of regiments.

The Fifty-second (Oxfordshire) Regiment of Foot: This was a light infantry regiment of the British army throughout much of the eighteenth and nineteenth centuries.

winter bourne: The permeable nature of Chilterns chalk means that the water table sometimes drops and the head of the stream moves down the valley. As this section flows only after winter rains, it is called a winter bourne, "bourne" meaning "stream" in Anglo-Saxon.

Chapter 45

the same regiment that had fought at Lexington and Bunker Hill: The regiment first saw active service during the American War of Independence.

a canal: In 1769 work began on the Oxford Canal, which was intended to link the industrial Midlands to London via the River Thames. Although work had progressed well, by 1774 the canal company had run into financial difficulties. After more funds were raised, the canal had reached Banbury by 1778, but yet more financial problems meant that work on the final stretch to Oxford did not begin until 1786.

Richard Arkwright's power mills: A large new mill at Birkacre, Lancashire, was destroyed, however, in the anti-machinery riots in 1779.

long hours: The factory gates at Arkwright's Birkacre Mill at Chorley were locked at precisely six o'clock every morning. If a worker did not make it in time, regardless of the reason, they lost a day's wages.

Chapter 46

"Hey Down, Derry Down": An Elizabethan folk song with a first line that runs "Hey down, ho down, derry derry down, among the leaves so green-o!"

Uffington Horse: The famous white horse, carved out of the chalk during the Bronze Age, lies on a hillside on the Oxfordshire/Berkshire border and can be seen for miles around. It is also the name of an English country dance.

King Arthur: The subject of many myths, King Arthur came to symbolize English freedom. According to local legend, if the king is disturbed, the Uffington Horse will also awake to dance on nearby Dragon Hill.

Chapter 48

seeds of certain diseases: The widely held belief until this time was that disease was caused by "miasmas" (odorless gases). In 1546 Girolamo Fracastoro published a book called *On Contagion.* He suggested that infectious diseases were caused by "disease seeds," which were carried by the wind or transmitted by touch. In 1683 Antoni van Leeuwenhoek observed microorganisms but did not realize they caused disease.

the rigors: Now known as lockjaw or tetanus.

wound fever: Now called sepsis.

gunshot wounds: Conventional treatment held that a lead shot or ball be extracted with forceps or a surgeon's fingers, and the debris cleaned away. It was thought that gunpowder was poisonous.

trepanning: The details for this fictional trepanation are based loosely on a report of the operation performed by Lorenz Heister, an eighteenth-century German anatomist, surgeon, and botanist, who left an account of the procedure he carried out on a merchant, Heinrich Bachmann, in 1753.

Chapter 49

St. Giles Fair: In the 1780s it was a "toy" fair, selling miscellaneous cheap and useful wares.

Eagle and Child inn: This still survives as a pub in Oxford's St. Giles.

brickbat: A fragment of a hard material, such as a brick, used as a missile.

pease pottage: Also known as pease pudding, this is a traditional savory dish made from boiled vegetables to which ham or bacon is sometimes added.

Chapter 51

racking close: The lines where woolen cloth was hung out to dry on tenterhooks.

Chapter 52

fine foam: White froth exuding from the mouth is a characteristic of drowning and indicates that the victim was alive at the time of entry into the water.

Chapter 56

engage a trustworthy solicitor: According to *The Oxford Herald,* an Oxford wine merchant who challenged the Otmoor enclosure had his legal expenses paid by more than five thousand supporters.

duel: By about 1770, English duelists had adopted the pistol instead of the sword. The first rule of dueling was that a challenge to duel between two gentlemen could not generally be refused without the loss of face and honor. If a gentleman invited a man to duel and he refused, he might place a notice in the paper denouncing the man as a poltroon for refusing to give satisfaction in the dispute.